The Inquisitor's Wife

The Inquisitor's Wife

A NOVEL OF RENAISSANCE SPAIN

JEANNE KALOGRIDIS

St. Martin's Griffin
New York

THE INQUISITOR'S WIFE. Copyright © 2013 by Jeanne Kalogridis. All rights reserved. Printed in the United States of America. For information, address St. Martin's Press, 175 Fifth Avenue, New York, N.Y. 10010.

www.stmartins.com

ISBN 978-0-312-67546-2 (trade paperback)
ISBN 978-1-250-04092-3 (hardcover)
ISBN 978-1-250-03151-8 (e-book)

St. Martin's Griffin books may be purchased for educational, business, or promotional use. For information on bulk purchases, please contact Macmillan Corporate and Premium Sales Department at 1-800-221-7945, extension 5442, or write specialmarkets@macmillan.com.

First Edition: May 2013

10 9 8 7 6 5 4 3 2 1

FOR RAHIMA

ACKNOWLEDGMENTS

I am deeply grateful to my editor, Charles Spicer, and my agents, Russell Galen and Danny Baror.

I am also indebted to true friends: Helen Knight, Suza Francina, Rahima Schmall, and Liz Harward.

And the captivity of this host of the children of Israel shall possess that of the Canaanites, even unto Zarephath; and the captivity of Jerusalem, which is in Sepharad, shall possess the cities of the south. —OBADIAH 1:20

We are those in whom the end of all the centuries is now come.
—ISABEL OF CASTILE, QUOTING ST. PAUL

The Inquisitor's Wife

PROLOGUE

*By the rivers of Babylon, we sat down and wept when we
remembered Zion. We hung up our lyres upon the willows
there, for those who had taken us captive required of us a song;
and they that tormented us required of us mirth, saying, "Sing
us one of the songs of Zion."* —PSALM 137

Christ-killers, they call us, but we did not crucify their Jesus; we were bitter
exiles in Babylon when he died in Jerusalem. When the King of Persia banished us
from our second home, we found our way to the shores of this sun-kissed, fertile
land—one so like our beloved Palestine—and here we remain.

We have lived in Sepharad for more than a thousand years.

When the Lord God made the world, it is said, the land of Sepharad asked
for five blessings: blue skies, beautiful women, fish-laden waters, bountiful harvests,
and a just king. God gave us all save the last—for had He granted us justice,
Sepharad would be now as Eden was.

Children of King David, we tilled the ripe soil alongside our Iberian neighbors,
while the Romans called our land Hispania and covered it with stone in the form
of aqueducts, amphitheaters, palaces, and pavement. By then we knew how to

coax enough wheat from our fields to feed the entire empire, and where to mine the gold and silver destined to bear the profiles of Caesars. We bred the finest, fleetest horses for the emperor's circus. Gregarious, we mastered the Romans' speech and ways and served as their emissaries to the natives, who knew and trusted us. So respected and peaceful were we that only one legion of troops resided in all Hispania, the Jewel of the Empire.

When the Greeks and Phoenicians docked their huge trading ships here in Seville, where the River Guadalquivir widens, we were first to learn their tongues. We became the ambassadors, translators, and scholars who collected the recorded wisdom of all nations.

For centuries we flourished, and the Romans let us rule ourselves. Among us Sephardim, no family went without bread or shelter, no child without a father, no bride without a dowry, no man without an education in Latin, Hebrew, and Greek. When the emperor Constantine converted from pagan to Christian gods, we became the world's merchants, since the disciples of Jesus dared not venture into Muslim lands, lest they be beheaded. But we Jews knew the language and customs of the Berbers, Moors, and Syrians, and were welcomed.

Then the dark years came. Rome crumbled, and the legions fled Hispania in the face of invaders from the north: the Vandals, the Suevi, the Alani——all nomadic tribes who knew only how to wage war and herd sheep. Last to come were the Visigoths, so fierce they drove the others out. Tall, long-limbed beasts they were, with shocking pale skin and eyes and hair, the last falling in wild tangles past their shoulders; they came unwashed and uncombed, their long, matted beards tucked beneath crude belts over the animal hides and coarse cloth they wore. They had no writing in those early years, no philosophers or poets or artists. They followed no principles save those of Arian Christianity——which worshipped God the stern Father but not the Roman's divine Jesus or Mary or the Holy Spirit——and bore a singular, intense contempt for all who were not their own.

The Visigoths looked upon us in the land of Sepharad——on pagan and Catholic and Jew, Roman, Iberian, Palestinian, and Greek, with our lush orchards and well-tilled fields, our temples, churches, and synagogues, our bustling international marketplaces, our fine comfortable homes, our marble sculpture, and wide paved streets—and hated us all. Hated our freshly bathed bodies, our fine and colorful soft garments, our prosperity, our curiosity toward the new and the foreign, our friendliness toward strangers, and especially our passion for learning. We were prepared to welcome them as we had our Roman masters, but the Visigoths wanted only to destroy.

And so they slaughtered thousands of us without mercy. They razed our homes and synagogues, burned our orchards, and smashed the Romans' fine marble statuary. They destroyed the public baths, believing that cleanliness led to womanly weakness; worst of all, they burned our priceless libraries, believing the same of intellectual pursuit. When one of the chieftains proclaimed himself king, they began to fight among themselves, and Hispania dissolved into chaos. Many of us sailed south across the narrow strait to dwell among the Moors, or fled north to hide among the Franks. Those of us who remained watched as the Visigoths stole our fields and let them lie fallow; they took our gold and silver mines and let them collapse into disrepair. The aqueducts ran dry, the amphitheaters crumbled, the roads and city walls cracked and sprouted weeds.

For centuries we suffered, until dark-eyed saviors came galloping on swift horses from a southern land of deserts, palm trees, and poetry. They brandished great crescent swords that sent most of the now-Christian Visigoths fleeing. We Sephardim did not run. We opened the gates to our conquerors, greeting them in their own tongue, Arabic, for our merchants had done business with them for centuries. And they—now practitioners of a new religion that worshipped one God and revered Abraham—trusted us. We broke bread with them, and when they moved on to liberate nearby Córdoba, we guarded the empty streets of Seville until their return.

Under the Moors, Sepharad reached her full glory. The Muslims brought with them a love of art and architecture, literature and poetry, medicine and science. They valued eloquence and language above all. They repaved the streets and *illuminated them with great lamps; they repaired the aqueducts and taught us how to bring water into our homes using hidden pipes. They made the nearby city of Córdoba their capital, and there established no fewer than seven hundred mosques and three thousand public baths. In nearby Seville, we replanted our wheat fields and rebuilt our homes, while the Moors planted citrus, bananas, figs, almonds, cotton, flax, and cinnamon and constructed towering minarets and delicate, ethereal palaces with stone fretwork so intricate it looked like lace. They showed us how to make silk using caterpillars, and how to make crystal using lead; they brought us paper from China, toothpaste, cutlery, tablecloths, and perfumes, as well as astronomy, geometry, optics, and calligraphy. They erected schools, libraries, and public hospitals. Their dwellings centered around courtyards, each with its own fountain or reflecting pool covered in colored tiles and by mounds of flowers and carefully spaced palms; in these pleasure gardens, poets and scholars gathered to read their works aloud, and we sat among them as friends and listened.*

Under the Moors' tolerant rule, international trade again flourished. For half a millennium, we were at peace and prospered. In those days, we strummed our lutes and sang Hebrew songs aloud in Seville's streets, unafraid of who might hear.

But in the year 1248, as in Babylon, we put down our instruments and closed our mouths when a Visigoth king recaptured Seville. Those Moors who did not flee before the pale hordes were slaughtered. Those of us who remained told ourselves that our former persecutors had surely grown more tolerant after the passage of five centuries.

At first, this seemed to be true. Since the Catholic Church forbade moneylending— and we Sephardim had grown very wealthy—King Fernando and his nobles made us their financiers. As with the Muslim caliph, we became the king's courtiers, physicians, and emissaries and grew powerful; but the Visigoths never let us forget, with their insults and laws designed to humiliate us publicly, that we Jews were lesser, wicked beings, deserving of God's wrath because we had rejected Jesus as our Messiah. Nor had they forgotten that our ancestors had assisted our Muslim liberators.

A century after the return of Visigoth rule, the Black Death struck, bringing with it terror. A strange madness swept over the continent when so many died so suddenly; surely, they said, this is the work of sorcerers. Since our religion was not understood, it was deemed magic, born of the Christian Devil. The priests claimed that we stole Christian infants and sacrificed them in blood rituals.

Our greatest detractor was Ferrán Martínez, a poorly educated cleric from the lower classes, who preached violence and hatred toward us Jews. Destroy the twenty-three synagogues in Seville, he urged, for it was God's will that we be punished and humiliated for the "crime" supposedly committed more than a millennium ago by our distant relatives in Palestine. Anyone who killed a Jew, Martínez said, would win God's favor. As we feared, his disciples obeyed and began to attack us. We were forced to live in communities separate from the Christians, and we encircled our neighborhood, the judería, with high wooden walls and had our own watchmen patrol our streets.

In the end, the wooden walls were not enough to fend off those who despised us. As the sun dawned upon Seville on a warm June morning, Martínez's followers stormed our gates and forced their way inside. They brought swords, clubs, and pitchforks, and they skewered and hacked to pieces every man who did not drop to his knees and beg to be baptized. Our streets filled with blood; our homes were looted and burned to their foundations. In the inferno's glow, sobbing widows and children were seized to be sold as slaves. Twenty thousand died, and another twenty thousand fled Seville, never to return; as many saved themselves by converting to Christianity. Out of tens of thousands of Jews, only a few hundred managed to survive. The judería was reduced to ash. The rabbis and scholars wept the hardest, at the irreplaceable loss of thousands of sacred and secular libraries.

Seville's Jewry was decimated, but the few hundred surviving Jews were allowed to remain and rebuild; after all, church law still forbade moneylending, and the Crown had need of its bankers. But the survivors were forced to wear red disks upon their clothing and forbidden to cut their hair.

Tragically, the hatred fanned by Martínez's delusional preaching did not stay in Seville. It swept southward to the port of Cádiz and eastward along the river to Córdoba, then northward to Toledo and Madrid. There are no records to say how many of us died and how many escaped to Portugal and Morocco or elsewhere. But many of us loved Sepharad so dearly that we could not bear to lose her again—and so we converted, or pretended to convert, to Christianity. No matter that church law prohibited forced conversions.

In the wake of the bloody pogroms, the ranks of Spain's church swelled with new converts—conversos, they called us, to distinguish us from the "Old Christians." For a year or two, the hatred fueled by Martínez's preaching died down. But soon, even the most ignorant among the Jew-haters began to realize that they had just traded one "problem" for another: How could they ever be sure that we believed in Christ with all our hearts? How could they be sure we conversos did not covertly continue to practice Judaism?

It was a valid question for the generation that survived the pogrom. But Spanish society had become such a dangerous environment for practicing Jews that most of us reared our children as honest Christians, hoping they would never suffer the horrors that their fathers had. Sadly, many Jewish families were separated, father from son and cousin from cousin, by the baptismal font.

But a few of us revered the God of Abraham so deeply that we remained in clandestine fellowship with our Jewish loved ones. We continued to obey the Law of Moses in our homes—secretly, as our detractors suspected, and allowed our children to marry only fellow crypto-Jews. We hung pork sausages from our windows and replaced the mezuzahs at our front doors with Roman crosses, but our women stole to hidden synagogues for the ritual bath after their monthly blood had stopped, and scrubbed the vestiges of baptismal water and anointing oil from the heads of their infants upon returning from their christenings. On Fridays, we cleaned our homes, cooked food, brought out fresh linens, and then bathed and dressed in our finest clothes to await the Sabbath. Our women lit candles in front of images of Christian saints and gathered with our families at the table to light the Sabbath lamp, which we hid under the table or in back rooms, the windows covered. On Yom Kippur we fasted and begged the Lord God to forgive us our duplicity. We observed Purim—the festival celebrating the brave Esther, who, married to a Persian king, continued to practice Judaism in secret, and who saved her people from slaughter by a jealous noble. Our hearts were not in the holiday feast but rather in Queen Esther's preparatory fast as we echoed her prayer before she risked her life to save her people: "Remember, O Lord; make Yourself known in this time of our affliction and give us courage, O King of the gods. . . ."

We conversos—crypto-Jew and true Christian alike—took advantage of our new status by returning to the very positions that had been stolen from our Jewish forebears. We swiftly ascended the ranks of nobility to become Spain's wealthiest landowners, most powerful clerics, and most favored courtiers; we even married into the Royal House of Aragón. Our rapid rise generated hostility among those Old Christians who hated us and called us not conversos but marranos, swine.

Still, we have hope. When King Enrique died, his half sister Isabel claimed the throne of Castile. She gained it with the help of wealthy, influential conversos and Jews—without our support, a woman could never have gained the Spanish crown—and we conversos arranged for her to take Fernando, then crown prince of Aragón, as her consort. For Isabel is a pale Visigoth, but the dark-eyed Fernando is one of us; although no one in his royal family has practiced Judaism for generations, the blood of David runs in his veins. It is said that the queen doña Isabel so dearly loves her husband that she will issue no command unless he is in agreement.

Can the Lord God move through a woman?

Surely He moved through Queen Esther. And perhaps He can do so with Queen Isabel, who made us weep with joy when she wrote the Jews of Seville, saying: "I take you under my protection and forbid anyone to harm you."

Yet these are dangerous times; our enemies are again stirred to violence by another hate-mongering preacher. We dare not take up our lyres and sing—but we look to our Visigoth queen with hope and pray for her success and the time when we can raise our voices again in the streets of Seville.

One

Seville, 1481

That was the story my mother Magdalena used to whisper in my ear every Friday after sunset when I was still willing to hear it. I was listening to her silent voice as my father led me toward the altar, over the worn black-and-white tile floors laid by the Mudejares, the Christian and Muslim artisans who had erected the cathedral, then a mosque, under Islamic rule. I looked at the building's Moorish features—the arches within arches, the slender columns, the glazed tiles—and contemplated the golden, centuries-distant land of Sepharad. Surely it was all a lie. My mother had died never knowing such a place, and that night, I, Marisol García, was sure that I too would die without ever finding it.

Night muted the ocher and ivory hues of the cavernous Chapel of the Fifth Anguish, but the light from the candles on the altar and two hanging chancel lamps made every gilded surface gleam. There were only four of us, including the priest, so it would have been wasteful to illuminate the entire chapel, now damp and cold from the December rain.

I held a clutch of silk orange blossoms and wore black silk—a tradition among Spanish brides, although I'd worn the same gown to my mother's funeral the previous week. The black veil, though sheer, made my surroundings even darker and more indistinct, adding to the sense of unreality. I kept my gaze lowered as my father, don Diego, and I walked slowly toward those standing at the altar. My father offered me his arm; I ignored it, unable to look at him, afraid that I would cry. Instead, I stared down at my whispering skirts and the fringe of my mother's finest woolen shawl.

As we neared our destination, I glanced up at the aging wraith of a priest. Behind his spare form and the altar, set within a recess beneath a massive golden arch, stood an assembly of painted, life-size statues depicting Christ's Fifth Anguish, his death by crucifixion. Joseph of Arimathea and Nicodemus, on tall ladders balanced precariously against the cross, had fastened a sling of white linen around the dead Savior's shoulders and were frozen in the act of lowering his body toward the grieving Madonna and Saint John. Despite the poverty of this particular parish—my husband-to-be had insisted on going to a distant chapel where we were unknown—the saints' garments were of real cloth, as was the linen sling. The congregation diligently maintained both, and the Holy Virgin's gown was often coordinated with the liturgical season. This night, the color of her gown had faded with the light, but beneath her sunburst halo, her upturned face caught the glow from a hanging lamp, revealing carved wooden tears spilling from her eyes.

My betrothed stood at the bottom of the steps leading up to the altar. Viewed through my filmy veil, his bulk merged with the darkness, leaving his great head to float disembodied.

At the sound of our measured footfalls, Gabriel turned and looked down at us; my father was not a large man, and Gabriel dwarfed him.

At twenty-three, Gabriel had a thick neck, muscular chest, and shoulders twice as broad as most men's. His profile was normal and his nose straight and of reasonable length, if sharply pointed at the tip, with skin that bore a lunar pallor. His limp white-gold hair—so pale that the pink of his scalp showed at the center part—hung a few inches below his surprisingly delicate ears. That evening he wore a black wool tunic with no adornment, in pious Spanish fashion, and a look of terror in his eyes, a light, clear green.

Gabriel moved aside, and my father moved forward into the vacant space, pulling me along by my elbow until I stood beside my anxious groom. At that point, my father reached down for my re-sisting hand—I wouldn't give it to him—and whispered into my ear:

"Marisol . . ." His blue eyes were liquid with sorrow beneath golden brown brows; his hair, mottled with gray at either temple, fell to his collar. *The most handsome man in all Seville,* my mother had generously called him, and he had rightly called her the most beautiful woman. "I know you don't want this, but one day soon you'll understand. . . ."

I turned my veiled face sharply away. When he gathered him-self, he gave my groom a carved wooden box containing thirteen gold coins, representing my dowry as well as the twelve disciples and Jesus. My groom accepted this gift with a timid nod and handed it back to my father for safekeeping. The entire time, neither Gabriel nor I dared meet each other's gaze.

My father accepted the false blossoms I thrust at him, then stepped back. Gabriel folded his huge fingers over my hand—

lightly, tentatively—and together we climbed the few steps leading up to the platform directly beneath the altar.

We stood motionless as the priest, trembling with age, blessed
us with the sign of the cross; we knelt as he turned to the altar
for prayer.

Gabriel bowed his head and let go of my hand. I repressed the
impulse to swipe my palms against my skirts, to rid them of his
sweat. I'd known him all my life—or rather, known *of* him, since
his family, the Hojedas, avoided us, although their family home
stood across the street from ours. Even though my father, Diego
García, was a solid Old Christian who sat on Seville's city council, the Hojedas weren't pleased when he built a palace across
from theirs. My father often entertained his fellow civil servants
and important higher-ups in the local government; he'd once
welcomed the powerful Duke of Medina Sidonia to our home. I
was his only surviving child—I watched my mother suffer seven
ill-fated pregnancies—and grew up overseeing his lavish parties
when my mother was in ill health. Gabriel's family was never
among the guests, despite my father's open invitation.

The Hojedas were a suspicious lot, Old Christians who
owned most of the looms that wove Seville's finest silk. The father, don Jerónimo, was twenty-five years older than my father
and already white-haired when I was born. Stern and scowling,
don Jerónimo was a major donor to the Dominican parish of San
Pablo, many of whose priests taught that *conversos* could never be
trusted because their tainted Jewish blood poisoned their souls.
(Not all Dominicans believed this, however; indeed, there were
many who were themselves *conversos*, and many who were Old
Christians who held fast to church law, which taught that all
Christians, convert or not, were equally beloved by God.) When

don Jerónimo's second son, Alonso, was old enough for school-
ing, the old man sent the boy to the local Dominican cloister
to become a monk. By the time I was born, Jerónimo's first wife
was long dead and his second wife had died six years earlier
giving birth to her first child, his youngest son, Gabriel—my
groom.

Gabriel's half siblings were all much older than he was; he
grew up with an ailing, aged father and was raised by servants.
During his youth, he spent as much time as he could outdoors,
playing with other boys in the narrow neighborhood street that
separated us. His older brother, Fray Hojeda, visited him often.
Tall and heavyset in a white Dominican habit beneath a black
cloak, Hojeda reminded me of a great owl. His head was round
as an orange, with no indentation at the bridge between his eyebrows. His profile continued in one unbroken curve from the top
of his sloping forehead to the tip of his oddly long nose. His eyes
were heavy lidded and large, the opaque murky green of the River
Guadalquivir. The judgment in his gaze never failed to humiliate
me, for I had come to hate myself for what I was—a *conversa*, with
Jewish blood in my veins, a taint that no amount of spiritual
scrubbing could ever wash away. I would often see Gabriel and
his older brother speaking together solemnly at their front door,
usually conferring about their father's health or Gabriel's future.
When Gabriel reached eighteen, don Jerónimo—after much
loud argument with Fray Hojeda on the second-floor balcony
across from ours—sent Gabriel off to the university in faraway
Salamanca, where he studied canon and civil law. Upon his return
to Seville four years later, Gabriel didn't marry as was expected
but worked as a city prosecutor and lived with his father until
don Jerónimo passed away several months ago.

I grew up watching Gabriel play in the street, but because we attended the Franciscan church instead of San Pablo, I encountered him face-to-face only twice. The first time, I was eleven and screaming, and he seventeen, red-faced, and sweating. He'd been kneeling on the dusty cobblestones between our houses, his left arm wound around a struggling fourteen-year-old boy's neck, his right pulling back in order to deliver another blow to the boy's head. I'd cried out Gabriel's name. I remembered how he had looked up, startled, to gape at me, an angry girl, and how, still staring at me, he slowly released his grip on his victim. I remembered too how quickly the rage in his eyes evaporated only to be replaced by a strange light. It was a look I would become accustomed to seeing in men's eyes as I grew older.

The second time I encountered Gabriel, little more than a week ago, I'd been screaming again. This time I was the one pinned by his brute strength; he'd held me back from diving into the deep waters of the River Guadalquivir.

"I'm sorry," he had said. Those were the only two words he said to me before coming to ask my grieving father for my hand.

I fidgeted, fighting to repress memory and tears; by then, the priest had finished his prayer, and we were obliged to stand as he read the obligatory passage from Paul's letter to the Corinthians: "If I speak in the tongues of men and of angels and have not charity, I am become as sounding brass or a tinkling cymbal."

In a strong tenor belied by his feeble appearance, the priest began to sing an abbreviated liturgy. The three men accompanying me sang the compulsory replies, but I couldn't lift my voice. Instead, I stood, face downcast beneath my dark veil, and tried to will myself to another, happier place and time, where the events of the previous week had never happened, where the events of today could never occur.

The priest began his homily, which he rattled off with the same enthusiasm a bored child might a Latin prayer learned by rote. Again, he invoked Paul's words to the church in Corinth: "Charity suffereth long, and is kind; charity envieth not; charity vaunteth not itself, is not puffed up, doth not behave itself unseemly, seeketh not its own, is not easily provoked, thinketh no evil; rejoiceth not in iniquity, but rejoiceth in the truth; beareth all things, believeth all things, hopeth all things, endureth all things."

I remembered my mother, Magdalena, and her constant love, whose perfection would have pleased even Saint Paul; I closed my eyes and saw her smiling beside me. She was more than a decade younger then, stronger of body and mind because she had yet to undergo much suffering. Eager for her company, I returned to her in memory.

Two

My earliest childhood recollection is that of my mother, Magdalena, praying in her bedroom every Friday just as the sun sank beneath the river. I would stand quietly beside her in front of her little wooden prayer bench and altar as she lit two fresh candles, each in precious gold holders brought out only for that occasion. A white shawl draped over her plaited hair, she held one hand reverently in front of her downcast eyes so that she wouldn't see the blessed light too soon; with the other hand, she held a burning kindling-stick to each taper. In the gloom, shadows dappled her fingers, cheeks, and lips as each wick sputtered and caught, making her handsome profile radiant with its glow. To my young eyes, her face seemed as incandescent as the moon, her expression as beatific as that of the Holy Virgin. I would watch her pale gray silhouette loom and recede on the wall as the flames flickered, her shadow melding with that of the Madonna on her altar.

When she was satisfied that the fire had caught, she would cover both of her eyes and whisper. *"Baruch atah Eloheinu, melekh ha'olam, asher kid'shanu b'mitzvotav v'tzivanu l'hadlik ner shel Shabbat. Blessed are You, Lord our God, King of the Universe, Who has made us holy through His commandments and commanded us to kindle the Sabbath light.*"

Then she would pray silently for a moment while I repeated inside my head the prayer she had taught me to secretly preface all others with: *Shema Yisrael, Adonai Eloheinu, Adonai Echad. Hear O Israel, the Lord is our God, the Lord is One.* For good measure, I usually added a few Our Fathers and Hail Marys.

Only then would my mother lower her hands and look joyfully at the light and grace me with her brilliant smile. Often I would reach for her, and she would put an affectionate arm around me, holding me to her as together we faced east and welcomed God into our home for another week.

My mother was more than pretty. She was beauty in its full perfection, with a face and form that sometimes made others gasp. Her shiny black hair glinted indigo in full sun; wavy and thick, it fell two spans below her waist, although she usually wore it in a single fat braid wound at the nape of her neck. Her eyebrows were fine and delicately arched because she plucked them each morning, and her eyes were light, clear brown flecked with gold, the outer edges tilted slightly upward, giving her a faintly exotic look. Her skin was light olive and quick to brown but flawless and smooth to the touch. Although she was short, small, and fine boned, her body could only be described as womanly, with ripe breasts, curving hips, and a honed waist.

I didn't understand then that her black hair gave certain others cause to hate her, or that her olive skin, brown eyes, and prominent nose marked her as an object of derision, not admiration. I was too young to know that my hazel eyes and brown hair, several shades darker than my Old Christian father's, marked me as well. Nor did I understand why, that Easter, the butcher had called her *marrana*—"pig"—and refused to sell her lamb instead of pork, or why she left his shop in tears and never returned, instead buying inferior meat from a less reputable man. I only knew that there was no lovelier sight than my mother leaning forward to light the candles.

No one else was allowed into her bedroom with us, not even her normally ever-present servant Máriam or my father, and my mother instructed me never to speak to them or anyone else about what we did on Fridays, saying that mentioning it would be a mortal sin. My father was a faithful Christian, and to all appearances, so were his wife and his daughter; we attended Mass often during the week and always on Sundays, and went to confession regularly.

My mother was an artist who painted ceramics for a glazer in the working-class neighborhood of Triana, on the opposite side of the river. As a married lady she had no need to work, but her talent was so great and her love of painting so keen that my father permitted her to continue it from home. Her workshop, on the ground floor of our house, was always filled with statues of bland, featureless saints waiting for my mother's fine brush to bring them to life. The potter in Triana sent them to her tin-glazed, the surfaces glossy white. I'd watch in amazement as the Virgin's golden eyebrows were created with two light, deft strokes, and as Mary's eyes came alive with pinprick dabs of blue and black.

From the time I could walk, I watched as my mother crushed pigments in her marble mortar: lapis lazuli or cobalt oxide for blue, copper oxide for green, lead for brown, antimony for yellow, madder root for red. She mixed the powders with water, sometimes adding a pinch of gum arabic to help them stick.

One long worktable held the naked or drying statues, another her tools: stones, powders, thinners, gums, quills, and tufts of marten fur, which made the best brushes. My mother picked out individual hairs, sorting them by width, gathering up swatches, and binding them firmly to the ends of quills of carefully chosen length and width. She then trimmed the ends, leaving either sharp or gently rounded edges. My favorite brushes were for the finest work, made from the thinnest, softest hairs, of which only a dozen or so were fastened to the narrowest, shortest quills. These were for painting the saints' faces.

By the time I was three, I was helping to sort the fur and quills; by four, I was crushing pigments in the mortar. One day when I was five, my mother introduced me to a small, unpainted Madonna set on a low step stool.

"Here," she said, handing me a brush and small wooden palette on which she'd mixed some cobalt oxide to the shade we called "Virgin's blue." *"Paint her mantle."*

Her request left me proud but unnerved; wisely, she showed faith by turning her back to me and busying herself with the application of red to Saint Catherine's lips.

I flushed with anxiety at the start but soon discovered something magical in taking up the brush: the loss of self, and with it, all concerns, fears, and boredom. The focus required was complete, and no idle thought could intrude.

Before I knew it, I had finished. My mother turned to face me and clapped her paint-stained hands in approval.

"Look at you, Marisol! You're an artist!"

I was never more thrilled. Blessed with my mother's eye and dexterity, I had managed to keep the paint within the proper boundaries. Before long, I was applying lead oxide to John the

Baptist's wild tresses. After a year of practicing on pottery shards, I painted my first eyebrow. I soon mastered lips and eyes, but it took years before my painting was indistinguishable from my mother's.

In my early years I saw no contradiction between Old Testament and New, between the Friday lighting of the candles and the countless saints, angels, and crosses awaiting my mother's touch downstairs. I loved my mother fiercely and was thrilled to share a secret that was ours alone.

This sacred secret, she told me, was one that God Himself had commanded us to keep: Women were responsible for welcoming the Sabbath on Friday night, and we were to do it furtively, without telling another soul that it had been done. The priests at church never spoke of it, because, she claimed, they were men and therefore unaware. This duty was the women's alone, and even they never shared it with each other outside the family, because Eve was responsible for the Fall into darkness, and therefore, only a woman could bring the light of Sabbath back into a home.

And then she would repeat the story of the golden land of Sepharad, about the struggle of Jews and *conversos* against Old Christians; when Isabel became Queen of Castile in late 1474, my mother added a message of hope that the queen might become the *conversos'* champion. As I grew a bit older, she began to explain the lighting of the Sabbath candles to me but assured me that we weren't crypto-Jews; while our lighting of the Sabbath candles was never to be mentioned to others, she claimed that she was, herself, as devoted to the church as the Hojedas were, and just as beloved by God—even more so, because we had not forgotten His commandment. I believed her thoroughly; why not, when her downstairs studio was always cluttered with Virgins and Christ childs, penitents and saints?

I didn't know much about my mother's background then; she never spoke of her parents. I assumed that she'd never known them, since she'd lived in an orphanage, where the nuns taught her to paint ceramics. Nor did I ever question the lullaby she sang softly to me only when she and I were alone—a song I was never to sing aloud, or even hum, until I was alone with my own child. The melody was high, haunting, and Moorishly tremulous. The words sounded similar to the Castilian Spanish we spoke, but they had been altered to sound vaguely foreign:

> *"Durme, durme, querido hijico*
> *Durme sin ansia y dolor*
> *Cerra tus chicos ojicos*
> *Durme, durme, con savor.*
> Sleep, sleep, beloved child
> Sleep without fretting
> Close your little eyes
> And sleep peacefully."

Those were sweet, innocent days for us, when it was safe for any person of mixed heritage to walk Seville's streets and for an Old Christian man like my father to give his heart to a New Christian woman. *Conversos* had a powerful voice in the city government and held prestigious positions; we were confident and feared no attacker. I was unaware of the simmering hatred that threatened us—my mother's stories about violence against those of Jewish descent seemed far away, in the distant past—and I loved and believed my mother without restraint.

But on a day not long after my eleventh birthday, I finally learned the ugly truth.

My mother smiled at me on the first pleasant afternoon in April after an unusually wet March. Although the sun was strong and the sky the clear, intense blue I have come to associate with my native city, the faint breeze was cool and dry. Magdalena and I were sitting out on the tiny balcony off her third-floor bedroom, which overlooked the street. Our house—like the others on the narrow street named for the Hojedas—was situated in a small, wealthier neighborhood that straddled the city barrios of El Arenal, the shipbuilding district on the river's east bank, and the crowded inland government district of Santa Cruz. The Hojedas were first to clear a street, a short cul-de-sac, in the center of what had been an ancient olive grove. There they built a mansion in the Islamic-Christian style known as *mudéjar,* of brick three stories tall, with a defensive wall around the ground floor, and an iron gate. The second story was exposed; like ours, it featured large rectangular windows that opened like doors onto tiny balconies with decorative stone railings and small tile awnings overlooking the street. In the center of the Hojeda's second floor was a large patio sheltered beneath a flat orange tile roof trimmed with busy stone fretwork, where those relaxing in the shade peered out from between graceful Moorish columns with arches covered with bright saffron-colored azulejo tiles. Our second-floor patio was similar in style, with the ubiquitous colonnades and the flat roof, but our house was less than half the size of the Hojedas' palace and featured worked stone instead of azulejo tile. Our house faced east, and the front of the Hojedas' palace; fortunately, our street was wider than those in most other neighborhoods where residents on opposite sides of the street could stand on their balconies and easily touch their neighbor's hand. Our house was set far back enough on our property to allow us to build a wall and a gated patio and to plant orange trees flanking the front entrance.

That day my mother, Magdalena, was wrapped in a light silk shawl, with her dark hair loose and combed out to dry; it hung in damp strands over her shoulders, falling half an arm's length past the seat of her chair. The hair at her neck had been lifted so that it fell over the back of her chair, the better to expose it to the sun and air. In her hands—the fingers stained blue from the crushed lapis used to mix paint for the Madonna's mantle—were a needle and an infant's unfinished christening gown. Although she had just lost another baby, she was resolutely determined to finish the gown, which had grown increasingly elaborate after each lost child—as if by making the garment irresistibly pretty, she might lure the next unborn soul into surviving nine months in her womb.

In those days, I thought of my mother as a saint as holy as the Virgin Mary, for I had never seen Magdalena angry nor heard a sharp word come out of her mouth, and she was always taking food and delivering it personally to the poor, even those in the decimated Jewish Quarter. And my mother was more beautiful than any image of Mary I had ever seen. On those evenings my father brought home a new diplomat or municipal official to dine with us, I smiled internally each time the man first set eyes upon doña Magdalena, for he never failed to catch his breath and widen his eyes until his senses returned to him. My mother was gracious enough to pretend she hadn't noticed the man's reaction, and for love of my father, she wore typical Spanish matron's high-necked, dark clothing and no jewelry save her wedding band and a small gold crucifix.

My father had worked as a government official his entire life, and when I was a girl, there were often times that I would go into his office and look at the finely detailed maps of Seville spread across his desk. I'd taught myself to find our house's location and would touch the tip of my finger to the landmarks I knew: the sprawling, rarely visited Royal Palace known as the Real Alcázar, to our southeast, across from the Cathedral of Seville, the largest in all the world; nearby, the Convent of the Incarnation and its orphanage, where my mother was raised; and next to it, the Hospital of Santa Marta, where my parents met and fell in love. Viewed from an eagle's perspective, the winding Guadalquivir River bisected the city; the curves of the more populous east bank looked to me just like the profile of an exceptionally buxom woman from collarbone to narrow waist. Nestled just inland, in the swell of her great breast, stood the huge Dominican cloister with its Church of San Pablo, and east of that, our house, and still farther east, our family Church of San Francisco, whose large plaza served as the city square. On either side of the river stood centuries-old watchtowers, one of them twelve-sided and known as the Torre de Oro, the Tower of Gold. In times of danger, these were connected by a huge chain used to prevent ships from sailing farther upstream. The city itself was flat; one had to ride farther east before the land grew rolling, covered with alfalfa or wheat or endless rows of olive trees with their dusty fruit.

That particular afternoon, my mother and I were both happy and smiling at each other because it was the first time she had risen from her bed in a week after losing another baby and consequently suffering a fever. Although there were still faint depressions of dark purple in the inner corners of her eyes, she'd left her bed at noon, bathed, and washed her hair, then put on her dressing gown and asked her servant, Máriam, to bring food up to her chambers—her first real meal since the miscarriage. I had combed her wet hair out carefully, so that the damp strands fanned out over her back and shoulders like a cloak, and encouraged her to take her shawl so that she wouldn't get chilled. When her hair dried, Máriam would plait it and wrap the long, fat braid in white silk, which she bound with black cord in a crisscross pattern.

She had leaned down then and pressed her hand to my eleven-year-old cheek. *"Sweet Marisol,"* she said. *"My beautiful girl. You're too young to be looking after your mother."* She stroked her palm against my skin. *"You needn't worry about me now. Besides, I have Máriam to take care of me."*

Impulsively, I hugged her. After she gathered up her sewing, we went out onto her balcony so that the breeze would dry her hair faster. It was perfect April weather, not long after Santa Semana, Holy Week—with its endless solemn processions through winding neighborhood streets, led by parish priests bearing flower-adorned statues of the Virgin Mary—but before the spring fair, when each extended family erected a tent for feasting and dancing. The winter rains had stopped, and the unfiltered sun was not yet harsh; even though it was early afternoon, it was still pleasant enough so that we hadn't yet taken up the summertime necessity of the siesta.

Even though my mother's balcony was cramped—she always set the smaller statues out there to dry, leaving barely enough room for our two chairs—I loved it far better than our large,

covered second-floor balcony with the ethereal Moorish colonnade, where my father entertained. I loved it because my mother was
usually with me, and because her geraniums grew joyously there all
year-round, mounding over their pots to creep between the crev-
ices in the railing. That afternoon, the pungent fragrance of their
blatant red blooms mixed with the sweet smell of orange blossoms
on the tree below us, the latter so close I could have touched a
leaf had I leaned far enough over the railing. I would never have
plucked a fruit from it though; the oranges were sour as lemons,
good only for flavoring marmalade or perfuming lotion. I pulled
my chair closer to my mother and sat with my leg pressed against
hers as she pulled the needle through the gossamer lawn of the
christening gown. I eventually wormed my whole body so close
to hers—I'd been terrified of losing her—that she smiled indul-
gently, set her sewing aside, and patted her lap.

I laid my head upon it gingerly. It was firm, not soft, and her
thighbones were prominent. I looked up to see my mother smiling down at me as she stroked my head, her damp hair falling
forward like a veil, lying cool upon my bare arms.

I spent a fleeting moment of joy in my mother's lap, listening
to the sounds of older neighborhood boys as they gathered for
their customary Sunday game of kickball in the street below.
Behind me, from my mother's bedroom, the servant Máriam
called out: *"Doña Magdalena!"*

Máriam's voice was low and resonant in the way that great
orators' and singers' voices are. My mother sighed and turned to
look over her shoulder, reluctant to leave me; I didn't stir but held
my breath, as if by doing so, I could somehow make her stay.

Apparently the look on Máriam's face was urgent enough that
my mother patted my shoulder briskly, asking me to rise. As she

left and stepped into the bedroom, I sat up straight on my little stool and frowned at the players down in the street. Fourteen youths, almost all from the Hojedas' parish of San Pablo, were pulling their Sunday tunics over their heads to reveal white lawn undershirts, sheer enough to show the masculine sweep and sinew of their newly muscular backs and shoulders. They rolled back the long, full sleeves of the white undershirts to reveal gloriously strong young arms. The tunics were folded and set aside, and the players divided into two teams, seven apiece. They faced each other in the street between our house and the Hojedas'; a dozen or so younger boys, too small to play, had gathered along the edges to cheer on their older brothers and cousins.

Seventeen-year-old Gabriel was captain of the Lions—symbol of the kings of Spain—and he stood in the center of his team lineup, his hair white in the sun, the brown ball placed carefully upon the cobblestone in front of his right foot. He was the tallest boy, already barrel-chested, with massive shoulders and long, thick limbs that had sprouted almost overnight, making his head look small by comparison. What he couldn't achieve in speed and accuracy, he made up for with solid brute force. I stared lazily down as Gabriel's booted toe met the ball with a solid, ringing *thunk* and watched it fly over the heads of the Imperial Eagles, the opposite team. Against the sudden cacophony of shouts and scuffling, I heard my mother's voice rise, panicked, in the bedroom behind me.

"He can't stay," she was telling the servant, Máriam. *"Make him go away at once!"*

Máriam murmured an unintelligible reply.

"Then tell him to leave it!" my mother commanded her. *"Hurry . . ."*

There was more, but the players' roars drowned it out. Although the alarm in my mother's voice troubled me, I blotted it out, unwilling to interrupt my happiness. Instead, I focused my attention on the game. One of the Lions—a short, swift, wiry boy—had just succeeded in stealing the ball from the Eagles and was kicking it through enemy territory in the direction of the goal: a pile of crumbling stone at the end of the cul-de-sac, where the cobblestone disappeared and the old olive grove began. Most likely, the stone was the last remnants of a Roman column or caretaker's dwelling, bleached bone from centuries of exposure to the Iberian sun. I leaned forward as the Eagle's captain, tall and spindly, wormed his way past all defenders to retake the ball, to renewed cheering.

Heated tempers and physical violence were the only rules in this particular game. I watched as Gabriel lumbered into the other captain's path and delivered an elbow to his head, which disoriented him enough so that Gabriel could capture the ball with the side of his large foot.

Despite the fresh noise and excitement this generated—and despite my growing curiosity and unease over the fact that my mother had not rejoined me on the balcony but remained waiting in her bedroom for Máriam's return—my gaze wandered away from the players to the spectators, where it caught a gleam of dazzling red-gold. A willowy fourteen-year-old boy was standing near the Hojedas' house, beneath a tree covered with white blossoms and bright ripe oranges. He had reached up to pluck a piece of fruit, and the sun had caught his hair, which was the astonishing color of pale gold mixed with copper. Forgetting my concern, I smiled at him. Somehow he sensed my presence and looked up to return my smile.

The boy was Antonio Vargas, three years my senior. He lived on the property to our immediate north, which abutted the empty lot dotted with gnarled, untended olive trees at the end of the cul-de-sac. Like the Hojedas, the Vargases were Old Christians, but there the comparison ended. Antonio's father, don Pedro, was firm in his belief that all converts were equal before God, and he did his best to make my family feel welcome and at ease; when the weather was inclement or my mother was too frail to walk, the Vargases invited us to ride with them on Sundays or holidays to the Church of San Francisco, our mutual parish. My father socialized with don Pedro, and we were always welcome at each other's table; the wife, doña Elena, was warm and kindly and always brought food and comfort when my mother was sick. Being a girl, I was forbidden to play with their son Antonio without a chaperone—but none of our parents knew about the hole in the stone fence separating the sprawling gardens behind our houses. When I was five and Antonio eight, he grew tired of whispering to me through the gap in the stone and had widened it so that he could wriggle through onto our property. Out of sight of the gardeners, he and I climbed the limbs of the tallest olive tree in Seville, and there we exchanged our secrets.

The smile I shared with Antonio in the street was fleeting; I looked away quickly so that no other boy would notice our affectionate exchange and taunt him.

Fortunately, all other gazes were fixed on the Lions team, as Gabriel and his best friend, a hooligan of a player named Miguel, quickly advanced the ball down the street toward the ancient pile of rubble that marked the goal. My gaze soon followed, and with dozens of boys, I reacted as an intruder moved onto the playing field.

His stooped back was to me, and I assumed that he was an old mendicant monk. He wore an ankle-length black linen cloak with a raised hood, and he leaned upon a great wooden walking stick, heavily favoring one leg. He had been making his way down our side of the street, past our house and then the Vargases' when he darted into the cul-de-sac at the very end of the street, apparently thinking to take a shortcut through the abandoned orchard.

He must have been fairly deaf, since he seemed unaware of the small army of young men hurtling toward him at top speed. Behind him, both Gabriel and Miguel shouted for him to move aside, while the others began to whoop with excitement. He didn't turn to look back at them but limped toward the goalpost of ancient rubble with increasing velocity. Miguel and the closely following Eagle defenders veered off in time to keep from hitting the old man, but the Lions screamed for their captain to kick the goal; this caused noticeable consternation for Gabriel, who couldn't decide between chivalry and winning. At the last instant, he glanced over his shoulder at his teammates, as if trying to gauge the depth of their determination—but he was still running at full tilt, and the act caused him to lose the ball and slam into the old monk's back.

Pushed from the street onto the softer earth of the old orchard, the old man fell facedown, tangled in his black robe; his walking stick flew forward, struck a tree trunk, and rebounded back into the street, clattering against the cobblestones. Gabriel ran to him as Miguel went to fetch the stick, while all the other boys, silent and solemn, hurried to gather around them. Gabriel looked terrified; his older brother Alonso was already abbot of San Pablo by then, and Fray Alonso and don Jerónimo would punish him severely for any harm done to a monk. Gabriel kept glancing over his shoulder at his father's shaded second-floor balcony, as if expecting to hear don Jerónimo's angry voice any instant.

The street had grown so hushed I could hear Gabriel's voice break with nerves as he extended his hand to the fallen man. *"Brother?"* he asked timidly. *"Forgive me. Are you injured?"*

For an instant, the old man lay as still as the dead. But soon he began to move again, slowly, gathering his arms and legs beneath him and pushing himself up. With Gabriel holding his hands, he struggled to his knees, and when he finally stood up and the black hood slipped down to reveal his face, gasps escaped the onlookers. I stood up and strained against the north corner of the balcony railing; the old man's long white beard, streaked with black, hung to his waist, and long white waves of hair fell from his balding crown to well past his shoulders.

In those days, Christian men kept their hair short and their faces shaved so as not to be mistaken for what the old man was.

Miguel, who was in the midst of proffering the old man his wooden stick, drew it back suddenly as the man reached for it; this movement brought the latter's oddly flat profile into my view. Only his large, dark eyes were visible above a dark scarf, which he had tied behind his head to cover his nose, mouth and chin.

"He's a Jew!" Miguel shouted, in a tone that conveyed anger, scorn, and delight. With one hand, he pulled the black cloak from the man's shoulders. Beneath it, his tunic—of the same worn, coarse black cloth—sported a red disc cut from fabric and pinned over the heart.

"A filthy Jew!" Miguel bellowed again. *"One who breaks the law by trying to hide what he is!"* The latter statement was true; the old man should have pinned the badge of shame to his cloak, but I saw forgetfulness, not sinister intent, in the act. *"And worse, covering his face like a bandit!"*

As the old man reached vainly for his walking stick, Miguel taunted him with it, keeping it just out of reach.

The other youths began to hurl insults and accusations. *"Stinking Jew!" "Christ killer!" "Did you come here to poison the wells?" "Look at him, sneaking around our neighborhood in disguise!" "He's looking for a Christian baby to murder!"*

I felt a sickening prickle of heat on my cheeks and neck. By then, I was well aware that Jews were an object of scorn—a fact that ashamed me, since I had overheard others call my mother a *conversa* and had realized that Jewish blood ran in *my* veins, too, and that the fact somehow made me different from the other children in our neighborhood.

Gabriel, who had been supporting the man's elbow in an effort to keep him upright, let go and turned back toward the crowd, his expression reluctant and perplexed. Clearly, he didn't want to do what his teammates expected of him, yet he was obviously swayed by their opinion.

"Get the Jew!" one of the older Lions shouted at his captain. *"He cost us a goal! Uncover his face! What is he doing in this barrio on a Sunday, anyway?"*

"Get the Jew! Get the Jew!" the crowd began to chant. Gabriel squared his shoulders and hardened his expression.

At the same instant, Miguel gripped the base of the walking stick with both hands, swung it back over his right shoulder, then brought it down upon the Jew's stooped back. The old man took a wobbly step forward and sank to his knees as the onlookers roared with approval.

For Gabriel, it was as though a sign had been given; he fell upon the Jew with his huge fists and knocked him to the ground.

I shrieked at him, as if he could somehow hear me over the

roars and cheers and curses in the street below. *"Stop it! Gabriel, stop it! Leave the old man alone!"*

At the same time, the childish part of me wanted to stifle my words and simply turn away. I was humiliated by the Jew's presence; why had he come here to my street, reminding me of my unwanted heritage? Why couldn't he have wandered somewhere else?

But I couldn't bear the sight of his suffering, or the boys' cruelty. I turned and ran into my mother's bedchamber. She and Máriam were sitting on her bed, whispering with their heads together. Between them lay a thick bundle of uncarded wool, bound tightly in dingy cotton, which they were in the process of unwinding. Máriam—tall and lithe, with a dancer's grace—was a Nubian, a slave whose intelligence and kind heart had prompted my father (at my mother's insistence) to free her. Such was Máriam's loyalty that she didn't return to her homeland, which lay south of Egypt, but instead agreed to attend my mother for servants' wages.

I was shocked when Máriam looked up at me—not by her amazing flawless skin, the shade of charred umber with blue undertones, a brown that verged on black and offered little contrast to the black silk scarf wrapped about her head like a turban, one end pulled through and hanging down between her shoulder blades; or by her remarkable features, which looked as though a long-dead Roman sculptor had taken a bust of an alabaster goddess and, with skilled fingers, had pressed the bridge of her nose until it was slightly broader and flatter, then smoothed and rounded the tip and made the lips voluptuously fuller. I was shocked because for once, Máriam didn't smile at the sight of me. If anything, she looked startled and frightened and guilty, just like my mother, who immediately stopped her furious effort to unwrap the bundle.

"*Marisol!*" Máriam snapped; it was not a greeting to me but a warning to my mother.

"*A Jew,*" I wheezed. "*An old man—he can't walk, they took his walking stick, and now they're beating him!*"

My mother glanced in horror at Máriam, who widened her eyes in dismay and pressed long, thin fingers to her rose-brown lips before giving a sharp, anguished nod. Years would pass before I understood what Máriam meant by the gesture.

"*Bastards,*" my mother hissed; it was the first and only time I heard her use such language. She jumped to her feet and dashed through the open door onto the balcony, leaving the bundle in Máriam's care. I followed her as she gripped the railing and peered down and to her left, at the cheering boys gathered at the end of the cul-de-sac.

By then Gabriel had seized the old man's beard and collar and was lifting his frail, bony body off its feet. My mother and I watched as Miguel untied the scarf knotted at the back of the man's head, then stripped it away to reveal his features.

Once again, the crowd stilled; shouts became murmurs. The elderly Jew's chin and mouth were completely hidden by his thick yellow-white beard, but his nose . . .

The bridge of his nose rose from between his eyes and quickly grew very prominent. At its highest point—midway to his beard-covered lips—it abruptly dipped where the knife blade had exited, leaving behind a flat, pinkish white cord of rubbery flesh flanked by elongated, teardrop-shaped reddish holes where his nostrils had been.

My mother let go a faint moan and clutched the railing.

Gabriel turned his face away but didn't loosen his grip on the Jew's collar. For a moment, Miguel too was frozen but recovered himself and lifted the walking stick to deliver another wallop to the old man's backside.

The crowd buzzed with speculation.

"A thief! He must have been a thief!"

"He was punished for something. . . ."

"Maybe we should cut something else of his off for coming into our barrio!"

"Let him go!" my mother called, but she was too agitated to draw sufficient breath to be heard. *"Let him go . . . !"*

I put my arms around her and helped her back into her bedroom. By then, the mysterious bundle had vanished from the bed and Máriam was on her feet, her chin lifted, her stance regal. I delivered my weeping mother into her thin, muscular arms, as Máriam said sternly, *"Marisol! Go to your father at once and tell him an old man is being murdered in the street."*

Her voice was as soft as ever, barely louder than a whisper, yet I heard the ferocity all the same. And while I was puzzled by Máriam's behavior—she could have saved time by running to tell my father herself, instead of waiting in my mother's bedroom—I obeyed her and dashed out her chamber door onto the *mudéjar*-style loggia, the covered, open hallway that connected all rooms on the middle floor. I ran down the half-open hallway, turning a corner where the north wing met the central, and again when the central wing met the southern, where my father's chambers sat.

The door to my father's study was open. He had invited no guests this Sunday but sat alone, surrounded by books and maps of the city as he squinted down at a well-worn tome of municipal code spread open upon his reading desk. Creases had formed above his golden brown brows, and his pale blue eyes held a distant, pensive look, which vanished the instant I ran up to him, gasping and panicked. Still sitting, he turned himself and his full attention toward me and caught my forearms.

"*Marisol, calm down and tell me,*" he said. His grip was soothingly firm, his tone calm.

"*It's a Jew, an old man,*" I blurted. "*Gabriel and the others are beating him out in the street!*" I drew a breath, unable to hold back the most sordid detail. "*He has no nose!*"

At the word *Jew* my father tensed. "*Your mother—where is she?*" His fingers dug deeper into my flesh.

"*In her chamber, with Máriam,*" I said. I didn't understand why he was frightened for her.

My father dropped his hold on me and rose at once; the fear in his eyes had transformed into a deep, smoldering fury. "*Go back to your mother and stay with her,*" he said evenly. "*I'll see to this.*"

But by then I was already halfway out the door, figuring that if I didn't remain long enough to hear his command clearly, I couldn't be held responsible for disobeying it. I ran back the way I had come and took the staircase down to the ground level. There I flew to the front entrance, past the unlocked gate, and out into the street.

The drama in the cul-de-sac had taken a fresh turn. The old man, his maimed face and head uncovered, clung with trembling arms to the trunk of the nearest olive tree. Miguel had gone in search of a knife sturdy enough to slice off a body part; while awaiting the spectacle, the kickball players and their fans had gathered in a semicircle, hurling pebbles at the Jew.

A giant compared to his victim, Gabriel swung the walking stick, clubbing the old man's back and shoulders pitilessly. The man emitted only faint groans; with each fresh strike, his grip loosened and he slipped farther toward the ground.

I ran down the street toward them. Servants had wandered out of the surrounding houses to watch, most of them with honest dismay or faint disapproval, their hands to their mouths, but none of them demanded an end to the violence.

I was halfway down the street when I spied my strawberry-blond friend, Antonio, pushing his way through the crowd. It wasn't until he ran directly up to Gabriel—who was preparing to take another swing with the walking stick—that I noticed Antonio's right hand was clenched in a fist. My jaw dropped: Antonio was nimble and athletic for a fourteen-year-old, but he was no match for seventeen-year-old Gabriel's height and was less than half Gabriel's breadth. I watched in horror as Antonio's fist went flying toward Gabriel. . . .

Three

In the Chapel of the Fifth Anguish, I opened my eyes, startled at the touch of Gabriel's hand upon my elbow; the priest had finished his sermon and had just asked Gabriel and me to face each other. As I turned, I glanced through my filmy veil at the bits of brightness against the backdrop of overwhelming gloom—at the carved white tears of the Madonna, at her gleaming sunburst halo, at the pale, skeletal leer of the priest. Behind us, my father stepped forward and handed something small and shining to my desperate-eyed groom, who took it and turned back to me as if I were his executioner.

I looked reluctantly at Gabriel. Six years had passed since the elderly Jew had wandered into our neighborhood; I was seventeen now, old for a new bride, and Gabriel was twenty-three. He'd returned from university to practice civil law in Seville, reluctantly: He had badly wanted to join his older brother Alonso as a monk at San Pablo Cloister, but don Jerónimo had refused, saying that his offering of one son to the church was sufficient;

it was Gabriel's duty to supply him with grandchildren. Somehow Jerónimo had secured his youngest the post of civil prosecutor, a job many said was ill matched to Gabriel's natural timidity and unimpressive intellect. Gabriel had lived with his father until the old man died, and afterward, continued to live alone in his father's house.

No longer a lad, Gabriel was still taller, broader, and more pious than his peers. Despite his sedentary days indoors either at court or reading law books, he was still powerfully built and strong. He saw the sun twice a day now, when he walked from his house to the government building near the vacant Royal Palace and back; it had bleached his hair stark white and left his fair nose and cheeks tinged with pink. Candlelight glittered off tiny beads of sweat on his upper lip as he reached for my hand.

If I hadn't been trapped within my self-made prison of grief and guilt, I might have pulled away from him and run down the altar steps to disappear into the darkness. But resentment—cold and burning as ice against bare flesh—made me hold my ground and glare into my bridegroom's fear-filled, bovine eyes. I loved my father deeply, yet I was furious because he was sending me away when I needed him most, to live with a man I despised. For that crime, I was willing to be miserable for a lifetime as a reproach to him—and to myself. Fixing that thought in my mind, I listened patiently as Gabriel haltingly repeated the vows fed him by the priest, and when Gabriel reached for me, I lifted my hand to meet his halfway. I pressed my fingertips against his damp left palm and raised my right ring finger, enabling him to slip the thin golden band onto it.

Then it was time for me to make my promise. There would be no ring for Gabriel, just as there would be no fragrant flowers, no happy mother of the bride, and no new wedding dress, only mourning.

"I, Marisol, promise to take you, Gabriel, for my lawful wedded husband. . . ."

My tone was flat; I rattled off the words as quickly as I could. They sickened me, for though I'd often longed to utter them, I was addressing them to the wrong man.

I returned to the tableau frozen in my memory—of the terrified old Jew and his mutilated face, sinking as he clung to the olive tree; of Gabriel, swinging the thick walking stick to the cheering of his teammates; of Antonio, his red-gold hair catching the sunlight as he ran, his right fist raised, up to Gabriel. I called out Antonio's name, fearing he meant to strike the bigger boy, a losing proposition—but at the last instant, as Gabriel turned his quizzical face toward Antonio, the latter's fist opened abruptly to fling sand up into Gabriel's face at the same time that he shouted at the bully and the crowd:

"Cowards! Cowards, all of you, to attack someone weaker than yourselves!"

Gabriel roared and dropped the walking stick; his hands went to his eyes. He lumbered about blindly long enough for Antonio to recover the stick and wallop him behind the knees.

Gabriel fell face forward onto the soft dirt in front of the olive tree, only an arm's length from his shivering victim, who now sat crouched, knees to chest, as he pressed against the knotted trunk.

A palpable beat of silence passed, during which time Antonio draped the cloak over the gasping old man's shoulders and pressed the scarf into his hand; Gabriel's blows had done the poor Jew such harm that he could not stand. By then I was wriggling my way through the crowd; every male was gaping at Antonio, utterly spellbound. Desperate to reach my friend before the tide turned against him, I pushed harder as I forced my way past distracted, motionless boys.

The crowd suddenly caught its collective breath, and one youth giggled, then another; abruptly, the cul-de-sac filled with the Eagles' and Lions' derisive laughter. Beet faced, Gabriel rose to his hands and knees, clearly smarting from the blow, his teeth gritted with hatred and pain. As he rose groaning to his feet, he shot an accusatory glance at his teammates.

But the other boys were fickle; the Jew would provide sufficient entertainment once Miguel returned with the knife. Until then, they found sport in the slightly more even contest between Antonio and Gabriel.

"*Fight!*" one of them shouted, and the rest of them gleefully took up the chant:

"*Fight fight FIGHT!*"

Antonio moved away from the Jew and the olive tree, and, gripping the heavy walking stick at the base with one hand, held it like a swordsman ready to parry. Gabriel squared off against him—a hulking Goliath against a lithe, armed David—and charged, bellowing. By then I had made my way past all but the outer ring of sweating boys and stopped to stare and pray silently for Antonio's sake.

Antonio's free hand moved so quickly to his tunic pocket that Gabriel, focusing on his opponent's weapon, did not notice—not until Antonio flung more sand into his eyes and *thwacked* the side of his head, just above the ear, with the tip of the stick.

The audience roared—some with approval, others with encouragement for Gabriel, who cursed the blue of the Madonna's veil and the Holy Crimson Blood as he rubbed his eyes. The injured Jew had by then retied the scarf to cover his missing nose and his mouth; I fancied that he was smiling beneath it, perhaps because I smiled involuntarily myself.

My grin immediately faded as Gabriel, still half-blinded, grabbed two large handfuls of dirt and pelted Antonio in the face with them. Antonio ducked his head, though not in time. He reached one-handed for his stinging eyes, keeping a firm grip on the walking stick, and swiped randomly at the air.

It wasn't enough. Gabriel recovered faster and caught hold of the stick; all too easily, he wrested it from the smaller boy's grip—then threw it aside and charged Antonio, knocking him to the ground.

Gabriel's bulk collided with Antonio's shorter, slender frame with an ominous *thud*, and Antonio released a sharp, wordless vocalization as his back struck the ground, forcing the air from his lungs. By then, I had screamed and was already pushing my way between the two avid spectators that separated me from the fighters. In less time than it takes to draw in a breath, Gabriel was on his knees, his left arm wrapped tightly around the prone Antonio's neck, his right terminating in a fist that struck the younger boy's head again, again, again. Antonio tried to lift his head, and I caught sight of his face: His features were even and pretty, childlike in proportion, with his straight nose still too short, his eyes still too big for his head. He would grow up to be a handsome man—at least, if the damage Gabriel wrought that day was not too great. At the moment, one of Antonio's eyes was swelling shut and blood trickled from one of his perfect nostrils.

I bolted from the crowd, aware not of Gabriel's massive fists but only of Antonio and his wounds. I ran directly up to his tormentor, who, kneeling, was now at my eye level, lost in an animal fury, unaware of his surroundings. Forgetting all but my rage at his cruelty, I shoved my face in his and screamed:

"Gabriel! Let him go!"

My cry broke the spell. Gabriel looked up at me, startled, as if I were an avenging angel who had spontaneously materialized before him; I suppose it was the first time I'd ever called him by name. My gaze still locked with his, I placed my head between his fist and Antonio's crown and watched in amazement as all anger drained from his homely features and was replaced by an odd, reverent tenderness. Yet beneath the tenderness lurked a guilty sensuality, the look of a penitent who finds himself lustfully beguiled by the Madonna's beauty. His thick arm slowly uncoiled itself from Antonio's neck and dropped.

Antonio immediately rolled into a sitting position. *"Marisol!"* he cried. His bottom lip was cut and bloodied, causing him to lisp, and his red-blond bangs were now dark copper and stuck to his sweat-slicked forehead. His tone held no welcome or gratitude, only disapproval, as if to say, *You might have gotten yourself killed!* But he took the arm I proffered him, and I helped him stand just as the mob went silent.

"Back to your houses!" a man cried sharply. I glanced up to see the kickball players quietly dispersing. The cul-de-sac began to empty quickly, as a commanding voice emanated from the gate of the Hojeda house.

"Gabriel, come inside at once!" Don Jerónimo's voice was thin and reedy yet conveyed such steely authority that every child in the street fell quiet, while Gabriel hung his head. I squinted at don

Jerónimo's figure, stark black, stooped and featureless against the blinding coral of the setting sun. The slightest exertion left the elderly Jerónimo winded, but he was not gasping and breathless, as he would have been had he been notified of the violence and rushed to quell it. Clearly, he had been watching the entire time.

"*Come away, Gabriel,*" he repeated, in a voice that pierced the sudden quiet. "*Come away from that filthy little* marrana!"

Marrana, he called me. A female pig, a sow. Although the term had been directed at my mother, *I* had never been called that name before—the ugliest name you could call a *conversa* in those days—and it cut to the bone.

I stood, stunned and smarting, as Gabriel headed into the dying sun to join his father; as they disappeared behind the gate, Gabriel let go a sharp yelp.

The instant don Jerónimo was gone, the children remaining in the square slowed and turned toward me and began to chant in a scathing singsong:

"*Marrana! Marrana! Marrana!*"

In their eyes was the same hatred I'd seen in the butcher's eyes when he had refused to sell anything but pork to my mother.

Sobbing, I batted away Antonio's protective embrace and ran home, passing my father in the street as he shouted for the children to stop. Later I learned that a family servant saw Antonio home, while one of our drivers took the elderly Jewish man to the hospital. But I went straight to my lonely room and curled up into a ball, weeping. A few moments later, my father entered and tried to comfort me.

"*Those boys did terrible things,*" he said, sitting down on the bed beside me; I wouldn't look at him. "*And what they said to you was horrible.*"

"But why do they say it?" I demanded. *"Why do they hate me and Mamá so much? What did we ever do to them?"*

My father let go a long sigh and, for the first time, began to look old. *"They hate what they don't understand. They're afraid, because your mother's ancestors were apparently . . . Jewish."*

"But why is that so awful?" I demanded.

My father drew in a breath and looked away, toward the door. And then he began to explain to me that some Old Christians were afraid of New Christians because some of the monks— most notably, Gabriel's older brother—preached that New Christians weren't really Christians but were secretly practicing Judaism, and that, of course, was heresy.

I'd heard this story many times from my mother but feigned ignorance. *"What were they doing that was so bad?"* I asked.

My father began to explain to me the actual heretical practices, which involved only meals and holidays, not the slaughtering of Christian babies or Devil worship—and when he came to the lighting of the Sabbath candles on Friday evening, which was done by Jewish women, I looked out the window at the sun's last rays and stopped listening.

Not much later, my father embraced me and left, realizing that there was nothing he could say to soothe me. I immediately went to my mother's room, thinking to confront her angrily, but to my surprise, her door was bolted. When I knocked, Máriam eventually opened the door a crack; her dark face was stern and her attitude dismissive, but I saw pity in her dark eyes. From behind her came the muffled sound of weeping. My mother must have heard the shouts in the street; perhaps she'd even seen from her balcony that they had been directed at me.

"Your mother isn't well right now," Máriam said in her low hand-some voice. *"It will pass, and she'll be happy again soon. But she doesn't want you to see her like this."*

I dropped my gaze and swallowed furious tears; Máriam suddenly stepped out into the loggia and hugged me fiercely. I pulled back in surprise; she was sparing with physical affection.

In the next instant, she was back standing behind the cracked-open door. *"It's a cruel thing this world does to children,"* she said. Her tone lightened. *"Go to Cook and tell her to make you a sweet. Tell her that your mother wants her to do so."*

With that, she closed the door. I didn't turn away until I heard her slide the bolt shut.

The next Friday afternoon, when my recovered mother came to find me, I went with her into her bedroom and waited until all the servants had left and we two were alone. As Magdalena was fetching the key to open the trunk where she hid the golden candlesticks and prayer shawl, I told her coldly that I wouldn't tell anyone about what she did on Friday evenings, but I would no longer join her. I would listen to no more tales of Sepharad, *conversos* or Jews, or utter Hebrew prayers or listen to her songs.

I don't remember the precise words I used; they were forgotten, replaced in my mind by the look of heartbreak on her beautiful face.

I was faithful at keeping my promise; in fact, I kept it too well. Not only did I avoid Magdalena's chamber on Friday evenings, I also took to walking far behind her when she went to market or to church, ashamed to be associated with her, and I shunned her public displays of affection. When I helped her paint ceramics in the studio, I spoke little. I began to identify more with my father and took to avoiding other *converso* children, instead trying to ingratiate myself with Old Christians. I looked forward to the day I would marry Antonio and be free of my mother's heritage.

I was young and stupid enough then to believe the other children would forget the day don Jerónimo had called me *marrana*. I told myself that no one would notice my darker hair, olive skin, or hazel eyes, or judge me by them if I prayed faithfully enough, went to Mass often enough, trusted Jesus and the Madonna hard enough. And I was all too oblivious to the deep pain my rejection caused my mother.

After several months, when Magdalena realized I would never change my mind, she privately explained that she had given up the lighting of the candles, because she hadn't realized the practice was heretical. She had begged God's forgiveness, she told me, and received it, and would behave from then on as a pious Christian for love of me.

I shrugged when she told me this, and left without saying a word, because she'd already proven herself capable of lying. I still loved her dearly but was too busy erecting an invisible wall between us to tell her so.

As the years passed, I grew to love Antonio more and more, and he loved me; I'd never met anyone so fearless, so generous with his affection, so consistently joyful. His parents and mine began to act as if our marriage was inevitable. But the day he turned seventeen, Antonio announced at a gathering of friends and neighbors that he would obey his father's wish by getting a degree in canon and civil law at the University of Salamanca, so very far away. But he said not a word about marrying me.

Even though he'd often spoken about going to the university, I'd secretly hoped he'd stay in town with me. I was fifteen, old enough to marry. That night, I cried myself to sleep thinking of the four years—a lifetime!—we would spend apart.

I hadn't been asleep long when my mother appeared in her nightgown and leaned over my bed.

"Marisol!" she said, shaking my arm. *"Get up! Hurry!"*

I woke with a start. I would have been terrified if she hadn't been laughing. *"What is it, Mamá?"* I couldn't imagine what had been so comical that she'd been moved to disturb me at such a late hour.

"You'll see!" she answered, grinning. *"Put on a shawl; come!"*

I picked up my everyday lightweight shawl—it was spring, cool but not cold.

"No, no!" my mother said. *"Not that one!"* She hurried to the closet and pulled out my best dress shawl, fine black lace shot through with gold.

I couldn't have been more confused. *"Mamá, what is it?"*

But she cheerfully refused to answer. She dragged me out of my room, down the corridor, and into her bedroom. The lamp on the nightstand was lit. In its glow, Máriam stood gazing out onto the balcony, her back to us, her white lawn nightgown revealing the shape of her slender dark torso and legs. Her head was tilted, her hand pressed against the pillar as she listened to the sound wafting through the open door. As we neared, she turned to us smiling and stepped back to make way.

"Go on, go on," my mother hissed at me. She took the lamp from the nightstand and handed it to Máriam.

A man was singing to the music of a lute out on the street below. I stepped out onto the balcony and blinked as Máriam held up the lamp beside me—not so that I could see but so that I could be seen.

Antonio's strong, unabashedly emotional tenor rose on the cool air, along with the perfume of flowers; I blinked again and saw him standing in the street as close as possible to my mother's window, near the bougainvillea covering our outer walls. He was smiling, radiant, happy to embarrass himself for my sake. He wore a blue velvet tunic and cap with a white plume; beside him stood his father's valet, the stoop-shouldered Joaquín, holding a torch at a safe remove from his young master. It cast a wavering arc of amber, painting Antonio's face golden, while the silvery light of the half moon reflected off his hair, off the white jasmine blooms vining on the wall, off the pale orange blossoms on the tree just below the balcony. Sharp shadows obscured his neck and chest; the lacquered surface of his wooden lute flashed.

Delighted, I gripped the cold iron railing and leaned over its edge, laughing softly at the deliciousness of the cloying sweet fragrance of the blossoms mixing with the pungency of my mother's geraniums, at the sound of Antonio's voice, at the clear Sevillian night sky, with the spires of the cathedral and the turrets of the Royal Palace to the southeast.

"Seville mi alma," Antonio was singing. *"Sevilla, corazón."* But at the sight of me, he broke off and gently tossed a bitter orange— it was harvest season and a pile of them littered the street—up onto the balcony, where it landed by my feet.

Grinning, he sang a very old, very traditional tune, one popular with the local troubadours.

"Take this orange, my love
Round and ripe with golden skin

With a knife do not dare part it
For my heart remains within."

I couldn't stop my delighted laughter—not until Antonio grew silent and solemn. He began to strum a tune I'd never heard before, one I soon realized was his own creation. The melody, in a minor key, was faintly Moorish, languid, full of aching desire.

"O fair Marisol
Will you come to your window
Will you come to your window
And grace my yearning eyes tonight?
O fair Marisol
How I've longed for this moment
How I've longed for this moment
Your face glowing like moonlight."

I drew in a breath and realized this was a moment I would long remember, one I would recount to my children, a moment when I was consumed by a happiness so great it swelled to include the entire world, the flowers, the music, the light, Antonio's ardent love.

This is real joy, I thought, and felt no moment in my life could ever be better than this one, but then Antonio began another verse, and impossibly, my joy increased.

"O fair Marisol
Will you come to your window
Will you come to your window
And give your answer tonight?

O fair Marisol
How I've longed for this moment
How I've longed for this moment
Will you be my wife?"

Behind me, my mother let go a soft, girlish squeal; Máriam's lamp swung as she shuddered with laughter.

Antonio played another verse, this one without lyrics. Then he hushed the strings and knelt out in the dusty street beyond the walls of my father's house, the lute resting on one thigh.

"*Marisol García*," he called, in a voice so loud that my impulse was to tell him to be quiet, that he would wake all the neighbors. I couldn't, of course; his extravagant love had touched me too deeply. He was *proud* of me, a *conversa*; he didn't care if he woke the Hojedas, if he woke everyone in Seville.

"*I've spoken with your father*," Antonio called up to me. "*He has given me his permission to ask: Beloved Marisol, will you be my wife? May I call you my betrothed?*"

I steepled my hands, covered my mouth with them, and nodded, giddy. I stood on the balcony, silent, the reverberation of the lute's strings hanging in the air between us.

My mother's elbow nudged me in the back and released a torrent.

"*Yes, Antonio!*" I called out, though not in as loud and confident a tone as he. "*Yes. Yes, yes, yes!*"

Across the street in the Hojeda house, a windowpane on the upper floor glowed with yellow light; I fancied I saw Gabriel's silhouette in the frame.

. . .

We celebrated our betrothal the following week, at Antonio's parents' house. I gave him a fine, gilded statue of Saint Anthony of Padua, his patron saint, the finder of lost things. I'd painted it myself, making sure it was my very best work. He gave me a sapphire ring that made me think of his eyes.

"So even when I'm gone, you'll know I'm watching you," he joked.

His parents, don Pedro and doña Elena, watched the exchange with tears filming their eyes. Antonio embraced don Pedro, who, like his son, was lavish with his emotions and did not hold back his tears. Don Pedro then hugged me, saying, *"You are our daughter now,"* and passed me on to doña Elena for an enthusiastic kiss and welcome. They gave me a necklace with a golden heart, and I put it and the ring on and refused to take either off, even when bathing.

Pedro and Elena embraced my father and mother as well. They admired my statue of Saint Anthony; doña Elena said, *"What talent you have, Marisol. You are just like your mother—accomplished and beautiful."* My mother smiled proudly, but I averted my eyes and mumbled insincere thanks. I did not want to be like my mother; I did not want to look like a Jew, and my flicker of shame must have been obvious, because afterward, Antonio drew me aside.

"How cruel you are to doña Magdalena! If you are to be my wife, I can hold my tongue no longer. You have shamed her. Don't you love your own mother? She is beautiful, she is talented, she is kind! Aren't you proud to be like her?"

It couldn't be said that Antonio had a bad temper; he was rarely angry, but when he was, he didn't hide it. I recoiled, and he put a hand on my elbow, then drew it quickly away, as if afraid he might shake my arm.

"You don't understand," I said stiffly. *"I don't expect you to."*

"But what could possibly make you treat her so? Don't tell me you're ashamed she is a conversa!"

I averted my eyes quickly—an admission of guilt.

He stared at me in candid disgust. *"Still you hate yourself for what you are? Do you realize that this makes you no better than Gabriel, or even Fray Hojeda? Do you really believe the stupid things people say? Your own mother!"*

"It's easy for you," I countered. *"You've never been made to feel ashamed; you've never been taunted for what you are. Your people have never been murdered out of hatred."*

He let go a long sigh, and with it, his anger. But he was still unhappy. *"Marisol, when will you realize that the only way to have victory over such hatred is to love yourself? To love your mother and not turn in shame from her. I've seen you behave this way before. It's unworthy of you. You're a better person than that. Sometimes I think . . ."* He trailed off, unwilling to finish the thought.

"Say it," I said. By this time, my own temper was rising. *"Go ahead and say it. I'm marrying you just because you're an Old Christian."*

He was silent for a long pause and put his hand on my arm tenderly. *"But then I dismiss it. Because no one could possibly feign the love you show me, Marisol. I just want you to be happy with yourself. With your mother."*

My anger withered. *"I don't want to be unhappy. . . ."*

"Then promise me one thing. That you'll look on your mother and yourself with more love. Can you do that?"

"I'll try," I said, and he kissed me.

It was only later that I realized: Antonio loved me more than I did myself.

. . .

Antonio left for Salamanca at dawn, on a day that promised to be brutally hot, as so many were in the late summer—cloudless beneath a blistering sun. Heat rose from the street outside the stucco walls of his father's house, and the dry breeze held the brackish stink of the nearby river. As usual, it hadn't rained a drop since March, the end of the wet season, and the waiting carriage was coated with dust.

Antonio's pale cotton tunic clung to the sweating muscles of his arms and chest; the sparse golden stubble on his cheeks and chin glittered. He'd said his good-byes to his parents, and his trunk was already loaded onto the waiting coach. He held me by my upper arms, studying my face as if afraid he might forget a detail.

"I won't be able to visit often," he said, his eyes filling but his smile determined. *"But I swear I'll write you every day."*

"You won't be able to," I reminded him; I couldn't summon a smile, couldn't keep my sadness from showing. *"Not with your studies."*

"Then once a week, at least," he vowed. *"I mean it. And will you write to me?"*

"Every day," I answered. My small joke failed because I began to cry immediately after saying it.

He tried to stifle my tears by pressing his lips against mine, but my shoulders still shook. I threw my arms around him and held on tightly, but all too soon, he caught my wrists and gently freed himself.

Our faces almost touched as he whispered, *"I'll be back soon enough. And I will marry you, Marisol, and never leave you again."* His voice broke on the last word. As he pulled away, he tried to lighten the mood. *"Don't put me aside for another man,"* he teased, and winked in the direction of the Hojeda house.

I quit weeping long enough to roll my eyes and snort softly at the thought of my ever wanting anything to do with Gabriel Hojeda. *"Don't worry,"* I said.

Antonio kept his word and wrote often; I responded to each letter and waited anxiously for the next. He spoke of a different world—of a village smaller than Seville but crowded with students from all over Europe, eager to study at the three-hundred-year-old university. The winters were colder, sometimes killing the flowers; the summers were milder, but—and this he only hinted at—the atmosphere was far less temperate as far as *conversos* were concerned. Salamanca lay in the northerly province of León, where few Jews had settled, and the population was resoundingly Old Christian.

I paid it little attention; so long as I had Antonio's letters, I was happy enough to believe his heart and mind would never change toward me. And indeed, when he returned to Seville after two years, for his father's funeral, he was just the same and kissed me with just as much passion.

But sometime after he returned to Salamanca, his letters abruptly stopped coming. I wrote him again and again but received no reply. Months passed, and then a year; I finally penned a letter stating that if I did not hear from him within eight weeks, I would consider our engagement broken off.

No reply ever came, although others in Seville had heard from him and knew that he was well and still at the university. Bitterly, I took the sapphire ring from my finger, hid it away, and forbade my parents to speak of Antonio.

· · ·

In the Chapel of the Fifth Anguish, I had finished my vows and stood with my hands steepled—the gold wedding band alien and cold upon my finger—and my head bowed, while the priest asked God to make me fertile in order to give Gabriel many sons. I silently informed God that I wanted no part of it. When the priest began to recite the Lord's Prayer—*"Pater noster, qui es in caelis"*—I repeated it calmly along with the others, but I began to panic at the realization that the service was coming to an end. I was almost Gabriel's wife, and while I'd submitted to the marriage out of pure spite toward my father and myself, my fury had ebbed to the point that I understood I was letting my fate take a stupid, wretched turn, one that couldn't easily be undone. My voice began to shake, and I lowered it to a whisper.

What would my mother have thought, if she'd lived to see me marry Gabriel Hojeda? Had she known that her death would bring about such an unhappy union, surely she would have spared herself. Like me, she despised the Hojedas, especially Gabriel's older brother Alonso, who became head of the Dominican monastery and was renowned across Spain for his preaching against "the filth of Judaism, whose taint is so strong in the blood that no convert, however sincere, can overcome it." We were agents of the Devil, Fray Hojeda said, and used lizards and serpents and the blood of Old Christian babies in magical rituals in order to cover up the stench that normally exuded from Jewish flesh.

When the Queen of Castile, Isabel, came to visit Seville a few years earlier with her husband, Fernando the King of Aragón, Fray Hojeda told Her Majesty that the *conversos* of Seville were all off practicing obscene rituals in their homes. Together with the

Jews, the friar said, *conversos* were plotting to destroy Christianity. Hojeda would have far preferred another violent pogrom, but as Isabel's hold on Castile was still tenuous and she wanted no more civil unrest, he suggested an Inquisition, beginning in Seville.

A few months ago, in September, rumors began that the Inquisitors were already in the city among us, spying on *conversos* and soliciting denunciations. Much to Fray Hojeda's disappointment, he was not chosen to participate in the very process he had instigated, although he had hoped to be appointed its head.

And here I, the dark-haired, dark-eyed child of a *converso* mother, was marrying his youngest brother.

"... *sed libera nos a malo. Amen.*"

The last line of the prayer died on my tongue; I couldn't say *Amen.* Instead, I raised my head for the priest's blessing, and when he pronounced Gabriel and me man and wife, I forced myself to lift my black veil. The world was suddenly too close, too bright; I yearned to cover myself again, but instead I turned toward my husband.

My eyes came to rest at the level of his heart, hidden beneath the matte black of his wool tunic. I tilted back my head to look up at his large, pallid face and his green eyes, as clear as colored glass and full of abject panic. I instinctively recoiled, but he lowered himself from the waist—keeping a respectable distance between us—and abruptly pressed his mouth against mine.

His lips were soft, but their touch reignited my rage and sorrow. I squeezed my eyes shut and fought the violent urge to pull away, to run from all memory of the last week. Yet I remained motionless as Gabriel's chaste, timid kiss lingered. He took a half step closer until I could feel the sudden heat of him on my cheeks; his lips pushed more insistently against mine, and I felt him tremble faintly.

I opened my eyes and pulled away, thinking of the sweating young bully in the street, his expression one of entrancement, his soaked linen undershirt clinging to the muscles of his broad back and the arm wrapped around my beloved Antonio's neck. Blotchy scarlet blooms on his cheeks, my husband straightened with a gasp, then glanced surreptitiously at my father, as if worried his lapse of dignity had been noted.

I couldn't look directly at my father, but from the corner of my eye, I saw candlelight glint off his tears. I hated him so much at that moment that I successfully repressed my own—some of which sprang not from grief over my mother or from leaving my father's house, but from the memory of my friend Antonio, four-teen years old, hanging upside down by his knees from the branch of a great olive tree in my father's sprawling orchard. It was the week after his fight with Gabriel, and his bottom lip was still faintly swollen and bruised.

"Will you stay with me forever, Marisol?" he had asked, grinning, his golden red hair hanging in a thick straight shock below his bright flushing face. *"Will you marry me?"*

At eleven, I was an agile climber. I'd sat straddling the branch beside him, my short skirts tucked about me, my bare legs dangling down.

"You don't want to marry me," I'd answered, rather crossly. *"I'm a* conversa. *All our children would be considered* conversos."

"Nonsense!" he exclaimed, with genuine scorn. *"You're New Christian, I'm Old—and together . . ."* Grinning, he pulled himself up and gave my arm a quick, playful pinch. Antonio always smiled so easily. *"We could make a bunch of little Christians!"*

I shrieked in mock torment and swiped at him. I was laughing when I spoke, even though the words caused real pain. *"Some say my blood is tainted."*

"No more than mine," he said, growing serious. *"After all, wasn't Adam Jewish?"*

I shook my head. *"I don't think so."*

"Yes, he was. He was in the Old Testament. And we're all descended from Adam. Jesus himself was a Jew. So how can anyone's blood be tainted?"

I loved Antonio so.

Now, in the chapel, the priest made a shooing gesture at Gabriel, who gathered some confidence and took my arm firmly, formally. I felt childish panic at the realization that I *had to* take his arm because I was now his wife and required to obey him.

As Gabriel and I stepped down from the altar to rejoin my father, I told myself that I should have run away, just as Magdalena had urged me on that last terrible night.

I pointedly avoided my father's embrace and tried to compose my expression pleasantly as the priest accepted a purse from my father and set to work snuffing out the candles.

"Please take good care of her," my father said softly to Gabriel, who nodded.

As the candles were extinguished one by one, the gloom deepened. I turned my back to the Madonna and her wooden tear and rested my hand lightly in the crook of Gabriel's arm as we set off down the long dark aisle. My father followed us in silence. I struggled against the painful tightening that seized my throat down to my heart, but I couldn't stop my eyes from filling. I fastened my gaze on the faintly glowing archway leading out to the vestibule, where Gabriel and my father had left the lanterns; just to the right of the arched doorway stood the white stone font of Holy Water, gray and indistinct in the dimness.

Beside it, something stirred. I blinked, letting the tear spill to clear my vision, and looked again.

A figure bolted from the back of the chapel to the doorway and passed swiftly beneath the pointed arch. His black cloak caused the edges of his body to melt into the darkness, but his head was uncovered. Not even the weakest light could fall upon such hair and fail to gleam bright, golden red.

Four

At the sight of the man with the red-gold hair disappearing through the archway, I gasped and began to pull away from Gabriel; in the next instant, Antonio—or his twin—had vanished.

"Don't be frightened, doña Marisol," Gabriel said softly, his baritone half whisper echoing off the cavernous ceiling. His use of the word *doña* startled me; I'd never been addressed as a married woman before, and the combination of my name with that word unsettled me and made me think again of my mother. He caught my hand to put it firmly back upon his forearm, just below the crook, and pressed his own atop it, to make sure I didn't break free again. "It was just someone praying."

I glanced up at him, studying his anxiety-bright eyes for any sign that he too had seen Antonio's specter fleeing the chapel, and found none. I looked over my shoulder at my father, whose defeated gaze was downcast.

It took all my patience not to shake free from Gabriel and run through the archway to see where the copper-haired man had

gone, but I calmed myself with the thought that the red hair had
been a coincidence, a trick of the light, or the result of my imagination. Our pace seemed agonizingly slow, but we soon made it
out into the vestibule, whose hanging lamps made it much
brighter than the chapel. It was as empty and silent as when we'd
come. I squinted at the air, as if to read whether its wake had been
disturbed; I stared at the massive wooden portal leading outside,
to see whether it was still swinging shut, but it was motionless. If
anyone had passed through it, he'd done so with great speed, as if
he'd wanted to escape detection.

Gabriel opened the door and held it for us, letting in a gust of
cold air. The three of us stepped outside. The heavy rains had
stopped, leaving behind the elemental smell of wet earth, but
clouds still lingered, half obscuring a radiant moon.

Out on the brick street, a two-horse carriage with lit lanterns
waited; the driver was huddled inside for warmth, but at the sight
of us, he scrambled out with as much dignity as he could muster.
The streets were quiet on this third night after Christmas, some
three hours before midnight, and not an hour ago, it had been
raining solidly; droplets clung glittering to the lanterns' glass
casings. I lifted my face to the sky for an instant, listening. In the
near distance, galloping horse hooves clattered against brick; in the
far, the wooden wheels of the plague cart rumbled, harmonizing
with the undertaker's singsong summons for the bodies of the
dead. The latter sound no longer frightened me, though it added
to my melancholy. The plague came and went with great regular-
ity in Seville and worsened when the weather warmed, but it usually confined itself to the poorest quarters near the riverbanks.

The driver held the door open while Gabriel helped me and
then my father up into the coach. The ride home was mercifully

short, the silence punctuated by Gabriel's few tentative efforts at conversation and my father's and my monosyllabic replies.

When we pulled up to my father's house—mine no longer, now—the torch was burning near the front entrance. In its yellow glare stood the motionless African, Máriam, her dark features impassive, her black gown hanging upon her bony frame, leaner in the days after my mother's death. She'd spoken barely a word to anyone since then, except to gain permission from my father to be the sole person responsible for seeing to my mother's belongings. Máriam didn't smile as our carriage approached; Fray Hojeda had been adamant about not permitting her to attend the ceremony, as she'd been born a Muslim and therefore wasn't welcome at San Pablo. Her rose-full lips, lightening at the seam, had thinned with determination. Sitting on the pavement next to her was a small trunk.

My father leaned out the window and signaled for the driver to stop. The driver reined the horses in, hopped down, and opened the door so that my father could get out, even though our ultimate destination was the Hojeda house across the street, several long strides away.

My father slammed the door shut behind him, leaving Gabriel to look questioningly at him. There was supposed to be a small supper at the Hojeda house, followed by wedding cake, but I saw the agitation and tears in my father's dark eyes and knew he couldn't bear to stay. He had never before set foot beneath his neighbor's roof—he'd never before been welcome to do so—and I knew that, like me, he was thinking of how horrified my mother would have been to have seen me wed to a *converso*-hating Hojeda.

He turned, put his hands upon the edge of the open window of the carriage, and with his troubled gaze fixed firmly on my husband, said to Gabriel, "I wish to give my daughter a wedding present." My father gestured with his chin at Máriam, standing nearby.

"A slave?" Gabriel asked politely enough, although his tone conveyed reluctance at the thought of permitting this exotic creature to dwell under his roof.

My father shook his head. "A servant. I'll pay her wages—and extra for her room and board, if you wish. She cared for my wife and . . ." His voice grew thick and trailed off. When he recovered, he added, "And she helped to raise my daughter. It would be a great comfort to Marisol if . . ."

Embarrassed by my father's proximity to tears, Gabriel's expression grew kindly. "Of course, don Diego," he murmured in a low voice.

As my father turned away abruptly from the carriage window, Máriam stepped forward and curtsied to Gabriel with exceptional grace.

"Don Gabriel," she said distinctly, her head bowed; she'd come to Spain as a girl, so her Castilian was as fine as any Andalusian lady's. "My name is Máriam. I'm a good Christian and would be honored to serve in your household."

I stared hard at Máriam.

"Of course," Gabriel repeated, flushing, though I heard resistance in his courteous tone. He gestured to the coachman, who fetched the heavy trunk with difficulty; he needed my father's help to set it up on the driver's seat. As the two struggled, Gabriel spoke again to the Nubian. "Do you know where the servant's entrance is?"

Máriam lifted her face to nod politely, and headed on foot across the street as Gabriel called for the driver to take us home.

Neither my father nor husband had mentioned money; if Máriam represented my entire dowry, it was a poor one indeed.

Had I known at that moment the terrible price my father had agreed to pay, I would have bolted from the carriage and run to him screaming. But I was selfish and bitter, thinking only of my unhappiness, not his, and I turned my back to him without a word.

I spent my childhood staring across the street at the Hojedas' Moorish palace, three times the size of my parents' house and at least two centuries older. Many times, I tried to imagine what lay beyond the vine-covered wall separating the property from the street. Now, sitting beside Gabriel, I peered through the carriage window as the side gates swung open before us. A few weeks earlier, I would have been eager to explore these new surroundings—but that night, my curiosity was damped by grief and a rapidly escalating sense of dread.

We rattled onto worn, uneven brick pavement; in the darkness, I got the impression of an immense property that stretched back to infinity. We pulled up to the north side of the house—the side facing the abandoned olive grove where, years earlier, Gabriel had beaten the old Jewish man—and came to a stop beside a one-story covered walkway. Beneath its tile roof, in the glow cast by torches freshly lit after the rain, a young woman in a white veil and plain gray dress curtsied as my husband and I climbed out and approached her. In one hand she held a flickering lamp. Beside her stood a thick-boned, brawny hunchback of about forty; had he been able to straighten himself, he would have been the taller by far. As it was, he barely came to her shoulders, for once his spine left his waist, it swelled outward and then in again so that his face naturally looked down at the ground. He was forced to bend his neck at a harsh angle in order to meet his master's gaze. I looked at his broad, ponderous features and pale, vacant eyes and realized that he was an Hojeda, like my husband, if a less fortunate one. Both of them wore an odd look of terror, as if they wished to warn us of some impending danger but could not.

"This is Lauro," my husband explained, gesturing. "My valet. And this"—he gestured at the young woman, who I guessed was a few years younger than I—"is Blanca. She'll be your chambermaid and provide whatever you need." He looked sideways at me. "Whatever the African—what was the slave's name again?"

"Máriam," I prompted, looking behind us to see whether she still followed the carriage, but she'd disappeared. "She's a paid servant, not a slave."

A thunderous roar drowned out my words before I finished them. "Gabriel! In God's name, with is *this*?"

Gabriel's brother Alonso—known by his monk's title as Fray Hojeda—moved his white-robed, black-caped girth with impressive alacrity to push aside Lauro, while poor Blanca jumped aside in fear. The friar's livid round face was contorted with fury, his mouth drawn in disbelief and disgust.

I had wondered whether Gabriel had told his brother and how he intended to get around the friar's hatred of *conversos*. Or, as their father, don Jerónimo, had called me, *that little marrana*. I wasn't surprised to learn that Gabriel had lacked the courage to confront his brother before the deed.

"What are these women doing here?" Fray Hojeda demanded, as Gabriel's height visibly diminished beneath his brother's full-on rage. In a flash, the friar slapped Gabriel, leaving a bright red mark on Gabriel's already flaming cheek.

Both Blanca and I cringed; Blanca took two steps back, her eyes huge.

"Why does *she* hold those silk blossoms?" Hojeda's hands gesticulated wildly; he loomed toward me to scrutinize me more closely. I did my best not to flinch. "Good God, there is a ring upon her finger! Gabriel—you pathetic fool—you have *married* her! Don't lie: I watched from the balcony. I saw her father leave the carriage, I saw the African bringing her trunk into this house!"

"It's true," Gabriel said, his hand still pressed to his smarting cheek. He clearly intended to sound defensive and determined, but his voice quavered on the second word. "Brother, I have good reason. Please, if you will just listen. . . ."

Hojeda was in no mood to do so; his lip twisted. "Your lust has gotten the better of you! Lust and idiocy! Insanity! We'll go at once tomorrow and have the wedding annulled. What are you thinking, bringing *her* of all people under this roof? You bring dishonor to our house."

Gabriel straightened as he found a modicum of courage; he stepped between me and his brother. "Alonso, *listen* to me."

But Hojeda was beyond listening. "I come here wanting to see my baby brother, and I find him gone at a time that he is always home. Lauro would not tell me where, or why this little piece of work"—he gestured at Blanca without looking at her—"was saying that you'd hired her as a chambermaid when there's no money for it. I was stupid enough to be frightened for you! Frightened! But no! You were in a strange church in front of a strange priest marrying . . ." He gestured at me, unable to find the right word.

Gabriel used the momentary silence to speak. "I made a bargain," he said forcefully. "With her father."

"A bargain?" Fray Hojeda's thick gray brows were still locked

in a scowl—he was a generation older than his younger brother—
but the fire in his eyes dimmed slightly, edged with calculation.
"What sort of bargain?"

Gabriel glanced sidewise at me, then back at the friar. "I know
you're upset—but if you will hear me out in private, I can explain
this to your satisfaction." He nodded down the covered walkway
at the distant great front door. "Let us walk together. We can
speak when we get to the sitting room."

Hojeda said nastily, "You will speak to me of this *now*. I don't
care whether it hurts her feelings."

But he followed his younger brother; as the two headed for
the door, Gabriel looked over his shoulder at me and said, "If you
could give us some distance, please, Marisol . . ."

Lauro scuttled ahead of us, clearly too terrified to remain in
the older Hojeda's presence regardless of what courtesy commanded. Blanca curtsied again to her master; I nodded, shaken
by my reception on my bridal night. With Blanca a deferential
step behind me, I walked several paces behind the men, past sprays
of bougainvilleas and begonias bitten and browned by the cold.

I could hear only snippets of what Gabriel said in a hushed
voice. His shoulders and back, like his older brother's, were
draped in black but were leaner, more muscular; the monk's
were covered with a thick layer of fat. Beside Fray Hojeda's new
wool cloak, Gabriel's looked many years tired, with spots shiny
from wear.

I expected to overhear words of love or lust but heard only
fragments of what seemed to be a business conversation.

"An agreement . . ." Gabriel murmured. "The Holy Office . . .
marriage . . . legal control . . ."

Hojeda rumbled a reply. "... could do without..."

Gabriel countered him. "... but then, Vargas..."

I shook my head and blinked. Surely he hadn't just uttered Antonio's last name; I must have mistaken another word for it, or perhaps he was talking about a different man: There was certainly more than one Vargas family in Seville.

Still tense, Hojeda inclined his head toward his brother. "Still... shame of it..."

"... the property and inheritance..." Gabriel said.

Gabriel continued speaking, now so softly I could make out nothing, and Hojeda fell silent and let him speak without interruption.

By the time we arrived at the great front door, the area lit dimly by a single torch, Hojeda turned toward me with a guardedly civil expression, while Lauro opened the heavy door and held it for us.

We entered a large drafty sitting room which offered few opportunities for sitting—only a pair of stools and one single padded chair with arms, the upholstery faded and torn.

"You there, girl," Hojeda said to Blanca, who curtsied, trembling. "Go and fetch us some wine. And afterward, keep yourself in the kitchen. Anything you might hear you are never to repeat, or God will punish you. Lauro, join her." He then turned to me. "As for you..." He motioned to the padded chair.

I sat—I admit, with an expression of challenge, not compliance, on my face—and watched as my husband took the stool beside me.

Hojeda leaned over me, his owlish gaze penetrating, and extended his hand. "The ring," he said, in a tone that threatened.

Without a word, I pulled it off my finger and handed it to him.

He hid it within the folds of his habit, then, staying on his feet, he began to lecture Gabriel and me as if he, the friar, were in the pulpit.

"What's happened here tonight is to remain secret," he said, his tone calmer but cold. "In the morning, you both will go to have the marriage annulled."

"Marisol," Gabriel said forcefully, stepping in between us. "Blanca will escort you to your quarters now. Stay there until I summon you." He turned to his brother. "Alonso, you must hear me out in private and in full. Then we will abide by your decision, whatever that may be."

"Do you swear it?" Fray Hojeda asked, scowling.

"I swear. Go, Marisol."

Like my father's, my husband's house was *mudéjar* in style, but on a grander scale. The flat-roofed dwelling—large enough to house two wealthy extended families with a plethora of servants—centered around a central courtyard five times larger than the one I grew up with; the traditional fountain was monstrous, with three separate basins. A statue of Santiago Matamoros—Saint James the Moor-slayer—overlooked the tallest center basin. It only made sense that the infidel-hating Hojedas would claim Santiago as one of their favorite household saints.

Usually Saint James was portrayed as a fierce warrior on a fiercer steed, in the act of slaying a Moor. But this particular Santiago seemed expressionless, bland, his horse static. Water bubbled up around the dying soldier trapped beneath Santiago's mount's hooves and spilled down into two other, lower basins, now filled to the brim with rainwater. The left-hand basin was topped by the imperial eagle, recalling the Roman past; the right, by the lion, symbolizing Spain's prophesied Christian king who would come like a messiah to cast out Muley Hacén, the current Muslim sultan of Granada, to our east. In addition to the great fountain, the courtyard featured a long narrow reflecting pond, lined by tall palms that rustled with the slightest breeze.

Blanca escorted me first through a covered entranceway and foyer, then through the courtyard, the lamps above the burbling fountain hurriedly relit after the rains for the wedding party's arrival. We made our way over slick cobblestone paths, past statues, overgrown hedges, and the murky reflecting pond.

The forty-odd windows of the hulking rectangular palace surrounding us were dark, save for a few downstairs and two on the third floor. The light from Blanca's lantern played upon the intricate stone fretwork railing, throwing black lace shadows onto her white veil and gray gown; the glow also revealed thick spider webs in the ceiling corners, and cracks in the pale stone walls. These, along with the worn, uneven stone beneath my feet and the pervasive odors of dust and mold, conveyed a sense of decaying grandeur. We traversed empty, silent corridors up to the south wing on the top floor, where the door to my new chambers lay ajar. By then, Blanca had revealed that she'd been a postulant in the Dominican nunnery at San Pablo and would have taken novice vows had her parents not needed her income.

"Here you are, doña Marisol," she announced in a girlishly high-pitched voice. She gestured with the lamp for me to enter ahead of her, and I stepped into the warm low-ceilinged room. A lamp on an ancient writing desk lit the antechamber; rickety wooden chairs sat beside a pitted ebony table. A fraying, musty-smelling Persian carpet covered worn marble floors, and near the door, the dingy stucco walls sported a single large crucifix, the only decoration.

The bedroom was equally as spare, furnished with pieces from a previous century. To my right was a small fireplace, the stucco above it stained with a half oval of soot; on the wall between the fireplace and window was a door that I assumed led to a closet, but a tug on the handle revealed it was bolted from the inside. To my left stood a very old bed covered in worn dark green brocade, where, I suspected, Gabriel's mother had died giving birth to him. At its foot, my trunk sat open on the floor, its contents neatly folded and ready to be unpacked. The bedspread was matched by long drapes that emanated the same stale scent as the rug out in the antechamber; they covered two rectangular windows as large as the doors.

The instant I set foot in the bedchamber, the blaze in the hearth made me break into a sweat. I shrugged the silk shawl from my shoulders onto the bed and would have gone to one of the windows if Máriam hadn't already been struggling to push one open. Her back was to us as we entered, so that only her black gown and veil were visible. Without a word, I went to her and tried to help.

Behind us, Blanca set her lamp down upon the night table, and cried out: "Forgive me, doña Marisol! I've made the room too warm! It won't open, but I know what to do!"

She went to the other window nearer the fireplace and produced a key. After struggling for a few minutes, she unlocked the window—actually a door leading to a balcony—and pushed her full weight against it until it opened. The fire leapt at the sudden inrush of cool air.

Flushed from her efforts, Blanca turned back toward me; her mouth dropped at the sight of Máriam's dark features. "Holy Mother, save us!" She crossed herself.

"Amen," Máriam replied, and crossed herself as well; she directed a kindly smile at the startled girl. "Don't be afraid. I'm a good Christian, just like you."

Blanca recoiled at the notion. "You're from Africa," she said warily, "so you were born a Muslim. Or worse . . ."

"I was born a Gentile," Máriam said with stubborn cheer, "just as you were. And the Apostle Paul wrote that Christ came to save all Gentiles." Her smile widened. "My name is Máriam, after the Holy Mother. I waited on doña Marisol's mother before my mistress was born."

"You must treat Máriam with respect," I added fiercely. "You can keep my chambers clean and come when I call you; otherwise, Máriam will wait on me. You must always do as she says." To Máriam, by way of explanation, I said, "Blanca was raised at the Dominican convent."

The girl looked at Máriam with dismay and took another glance at my scowling face before forcing a wary smile. "Hello," she said, without conviction.

"Are there other servants?" I asked the girl.

"For you? Or for the household?"

"For me."

Blanca shook her head. "I'm the only one." She directed a faintly resentful look at Máriam. "It's true that I have little experience, doña Marisol. I came from the convent only yesterday. But I'm a hard worker and very honest. I can bring a cot in here to sleep with you, if you like, or out in the antechamber. Or next door."

I was surprised. My mother had had three chambermaids in addition to Máriam, and when I was younger, I had two nurses to watch after me. I had expected many more servants, given such a great house. "Next door will be fine. You can leave now. Come for me when don Gabriel says it's time for supper."

Still owl-eyed, Blanca nodded and made a small curtsy before leaving us. By then, Máriam had pulled the glass-paned door leading to the balcony halfway shut and had discouraged the fire so that it threw off less heat. I walked over to where she crouched poker in hand in front of the hearth. She didn't look up but continued to push logs together to smother most of the flames.

"Máriam," I said softly, as if there were someone nearby who might overhear. "Why did you come?"

I was thinking about the mystery of my dowry—what my father had paid or promised Gabriel—and hoping my father had said something to Máriam that might help me solve it. Nothing in our household ever escaped Máriam's attention—except for one terrible thing.

A long silence followed as Máriam stared hard into the fire, her skin stretched taut over the bones of her cheek and jaw. I looked down at her dark eyes, reflecting tiny golden flames, and was astonished to see them filmed with tears. I'd never seen Máriam weep, and she didn't break down now or let her tears fall but swallowed several times until she was able to speak.

I fought the impulse to kneel beside her and embrace her; Máriam resisted physical shows of affection. Instead, I waited until she finally said, her low, husky voice a whisper: "Your father tried to dismiss me. But I promised your mother I wouldn't leave you."

• • •

Some eighteen months ago, my father brought us the first news of an Inquisition. I remember the day well: Queen Isabel and King Fernando were staying in the Royal Palace—the Real Alcázar in Seville—and all of us were keenly excited for news of the monarchs. It was summer, and I was downstairs in the kitchen discussing the upcoming supper with the cook. Afterward, drowsy from the heat, I went upstairs to the large shaded loggia where my father liked to entertain guests, and sat fanning myself as I watched for my father's return from work.

Our house faced east, and the setting sun had slipped behind it, casting long sharp shadows and coloring the street and the pale walls of the Hojeda's palace across the street a vibrant orange. I recall catching sight of my father as he walked down the dry, dusty street toward home: He was facing north, so that the intense rays struck him from the side, leaving half of him eclipsed by darkness. He was too distant and the glare too great for me to see his expression, but I knew at first glimpse that something was wrong. He had always been a vigorous, energetic man, with forcefully upright posture, but that day, his head was bowed, his face inclined toward the street; his normally square shoulders sagged.

At the sight of him, I stood up in alarm, convinced that someone had died, and hurried downstairs to hear the bad news. But by then, my father had regained his composure. Though his air and voice were sad, he assured me that he was merely tired. But instead of eating in the dining room, he asked the servants to bring a supper up to the loggia for my mother, him, and me, and then dismissed them all, so that the three of us had complete privacy.

Only then did he begin to speak, in a low, carefully controlled monotone. The truth of the monarchs' visit had been made clear to him, he said. All of us had hoped that Queen Isabel had come in response to letters from several of Seville's most respected *conversos*—the mayor, my father, and several of his fellow city councillors included—asking for military assistance against un-provoked, violent attacks in the streets by Old Christians, especially devotees of the preaching of Fray Alonso Hojeda, the Dominican abbot of San Pablo Monastery.

But this was not the case, my father told us sadly. In fact, Queen Isabel had come to meet with Fray Hojeda not to discourage his preaching but to hear his argument in favor of an Inquisition that would persecute any *converso* found to be a "Judaizer."

"But we're good Christians," I countered blithely. Over the years, I'd never caught my mother lighting another Sabbath candle, and it had been easiest to believe that she had kept her promise to be a perfect Christian. At that very moment, her studio downstairs was full of a few dozen glazed white statues, including some large pieces for local churches: Saint Annes, numerous Marys, Jameses, Josephs, and cherubs. She'd been busier than ever with her painting—so much so that I had been working alongside her almost every day.

"We have nothing to hide."

"What are you saying, Diego?" my mother demanded of my father. *"What would such an Inquisition do to us if it comes?"*

He turned to me, his large blue eyes guarded and strangely apologetic. *"Marisol,"* he said gently. *"I'd like to speak to your mother alone."*

I wasn't quite sixteen then and thought that my father was treating me like a child. I rose sullenly, leaving my dinner half-eaten, and went to my room. Within a quarter hour, I heard my parents shouting at each other. Rapid footsteps followed, punctuated by the unequivocal slam of my mother's chamber door.

They didn't bring up the subject again in my presence. Over the next several months, I took to questioning one of the chambermaids, Rosalina, whose brother waited on the councillors at the city hall. The news wasn't good: Queen Isabel had petitioned Pope Sixtus IV for permission to begin an Inquisition in Spain, and the Holy Father had granted it. Yet for a year, there was no more word; the many powerful *conversos* in town felt tentative relief.

And then, this past September, word came that the Inquisitors had arrived among us, gathering evidence in hopes of making many arrests. By October, they no longer hid their presence, but on Sundays made grim religious processions through the streets of Seville, preceded by three altar boys bearing crosses and followed by a small choir from San Pablo chanting psalms of penitence. I watched them from my mother's balcony as they passed by on the main thoroughfare. The Old Christians watched reverently; *conversos*, however, greeted them with hisses. I watched in uncertainty and silent shame.

By then, wagons heaped with belongings had become a common sight on the streets, and even at night, I sometimes heard the rattle and creak of wheels as *conversos*—many of them from wealthy, well-connected families who had lived in Seville for a thousand years—left their homes behind to flee to Portugal, Africa, or nearer sanctuaries in Spain offered by the Marquis of Cádiz and the Duke of Medina Sidonia, the latter of whom had taken a *conversa* for a wife. Men my father had worked with for decades, fellow parishioners at the Church of San Francisco, even servants who worked in our household, disappeared overnight, leaving behind empty, shuttered homes and abandoned properties. We wanted to believe that all of them escaped safely—that the rumors that many of them had been arrested in the night by the Inquisition and sequestered from the public eye were false. Regardless of the reason for their disappearance, the Inquisition's receivers came to claim the properties until the owners could be located or proven innocent.

My father insisted that we were safe; the queen's consort, Fernando, was a *converso*, as were almost all of her closest advisors. We were far too important for her to let any harm come to us. It was only a show put on by the Dominicans, my father said, meant to put a fright into us, and only cowards would run from it. The *conversos* in Seville controlled most of the government and were far too powerful, anyway. I believed him.

My father courageously invited large groups of Seville's prominent *conversos* to his table. I waited on the men alongside the servants, hoping I might learn more about the situation—but always, my father dismissed the servants and me before the real discussion began. Still, I remained close enough to listen to the cadence of the conversation and hear the anger and panic rising in their muted voices. I heard just enough to know that these men—the mayor, the councillors, lawyers, physicians, landowners, and priests, even the *major domo* of Seville's great cathedral—were anxious.

The chambermaid Rosalina, herself a *conversa*, told me that denunciations had already begun, that neighbor was spying upon neighbor and reporting any suspiciously Jewish behavior to the Inquisitors. Priests were compelled to report any questionable information obtained in the confessional, and arrests would come with the new year.

I knew that my father and mother were good Christians, and Rosalina confirmed that we were like all other Catholic families, save for my mother's obvious ancestors. And so I decided that we had nothing to fear, even though there were rumors that the new Spanish Inquisition might be as bloody as the one that had terrorized the south of France a century earlier.

That autumn was tense, and although the street violence against *conversos* and the few remaining Jews in town had lessened, my father hired more men-at-arms to watch the house and accompany him to and from his work downtown; instead of walking, he took to riding a horse. And he announced to me that he had begun to consider suitors looking for my hand—Old Christians only, the better to protect me.

Meanwhile, my mother stopped going to church altogether, making her prayers to the Madonna on the east wall of her bedchamber—the same painted ceramic Madonna that had been the contents of the mysterious bundle she'd been struggling to open on the day that Gabriel had beaten Antonio and the Jew. She was especially fond of the statue, which mystified me because it had been painted by someone much less talented: This Virgin Mary's lips were a gaudy, sloppily applied cherry, her blue eyes unfocused, the black pupils slightly crossed as she gazed down at the chubby white infant in her arms. Her head was crowned by an Andalusian halo—a huge, gilded, many-rayed sunburst. My mother had a wooden shelf built for the statue and began to spend more time praying to it and less time speaking to my father. More and more often, I would go to her room only to find the door bolted shut and her and Máriam whispering inside.

Yet when my mother did admit me to her chamber, I saw the

change in her. She'd always been sweetly obedient to my father's every wish, but independence stirred in her and grew stronger as October and November passed and December came. She began to avoid us and began to take her meals upstairs or in her studio as she painted; I realize now she shunned us because it was easier to hide her pain.

On a cold, dry evening in mid-December, my mother unexpectedly came downstairs to dine with my father and me for the first time in months. Per our custom, I'd waited in the entrance hall to greet him on his arrival home and walk with him to the dining chamber. He had been spending longer hours at work, leaving earlier and coming home a bit later; he'd also lost weight, leaving his cheeks a bit sunken.

When my father stepped inside the foyer that night, I kissed his cheeks; his tanned skin was cold, but his embrace was warm and unexpectedly emotional. As he held me and returned the kisses, his lips cool, he stilled suddenly and inclined his face upward.

I turned to follow his gaze. It rested on my mother, who was coming down the stairs toward us. Magdalena wore a dark blue-green velvet gown with the *verdugado*—what the English called a farthingale—a series of casings that ringed the skirt. These were filled with reeds to make hoops that held the skirt out stiffly from the body. Since the *verdugado* was uncomfortable and made sitting difficult, my mother avoided wearing it except on special occasions. Her bodice was trimmed with indigo lace, and her sleeves were of long, fashionably flaring gossamer silk, resembling butterflies' wings. Her hair was not in its usual braid, but put up with pearl-edged combs and covered with a sheer dark blue veil. Most striking was not her appearance, but something far less tangible—the cant of her head and shoulders, perhaps, or the determination in her eyes.

"Don Diego," she said, pausing halfway down the stairs. *"May I join you for supper?"*

Even her voice had changed. It was no longer soft and whispery, but confident and unapologetic. I remember thinking that this gorgeous creature was not the mother I had known, but someone younger, stronger and far less sad.

Entranced, my father parted his lips and stared at her and slowly nodded. *"It would be my pleasure, doña Magdalena."*

When she reached the bottom of the steps, my father took her hand and kissed it passionately; they shared a look that held adoration and torment. I followed as they walked to the dining chamber, still gripping each other's hand.

My father sat at the head of the table, with my mother on his left and me on his right, facing her; the serving girl was obliged to run to the kitchen to fetch an extra place setting for my mother. When all was settled and the first course—spinach sautéed with chickpeas—was brought, my father dismissed the servants as usual. The room grew very silent. Normally, my father would direct the conversation at this point, but that night, he seemed at a loss for words.

My mother was first to speak. *"Marisol,"* she said, with poorly feigned casualness as she moved her spoon through the chickpeas, *"has don Diego told you that I am under investigation by the Inquisition?"*

Dropping my own spoon, I gasped aloud and looked to my father for verification.

My father too let go a gasp. He stared at my mother with blazing indignation, as if she had just slapped him.

"Lena!" he hissed. *"What are you thinking, speaking of such things in front of—"*

My mother's sudden rage outmatched his; her eyes held a storm of unspeakable emotion.

"Marisol is a woman, not a child!" she interrupted him, and abruptly lowered her voice, realizing the servants might overhear. *"I won't let you keep secrets from her anymore."*

My father stood. *"You aren't yourself, Lena. I won't let you speak so to me."*

Magdalena ignored him and turned to me. *"We must leave Seville. It's not safe for us anymore."*

"Papá," I asked, *"is she telling the truth?"* The thought of abruptly leaving Seville, the only place we had ever known, seemed insane.

Diego's lips trembled with suppressed fury; he stared down at my mother as if she had utterly betrayed him. *"Her imagination is running wild, Marisol, nothing more. Nothing will happen to us, and your mother will be questioned, not arrested. The mayor is a* converso, *most of my fellow councillors are* conversos, *half the lawyers and priests and even the archbishop are* conversos! *And if they attack us, the queen has sworn to protect us. More than half of her courtiers are* conversos, *and the Duke of Medina will protect us, too. . . ."*

"The Duke of Medina will do whatever Isabel tells him," my mother countered forcefully. *"And Isabel wants an Inquisition."*

"Only to get rid of Judaizers—which we are not!" My father stamped his foot. *"How dare you frighten Marisol like this?!"*

My mother jumped to her feet. *"Her innocence won't protect her! I'm proof of that, Diego!"* She looked to me. *"It's only a matter of time now, my daughter."*

I raised my voice to drown out hers. *"Papá,"* I demanded, *"what will happen to us?"*

"Nothing," he answered hoarsely. "Magdalena, hold your tongue! *Enough of this madness!*"

"*They'll take me away to prison,*" my mother said sorrowfully. "*They'll interrogate me, torture me. And then they'll come for your father . . . and you.*"

"Lena!" Diego hissed her name as if it were a curse. "*You'll stop speaking of this* now! *We've done nothing wrong! We have nothing to fear.*"

My mother's lovely features twisted into a grimace. "None *of us did anything wrong! None of us . . . And yet that wasn't enough!*" She looked to me. "*Marisol, just because you've never seen such horrible things, you believe it can't happen to us. But you must know: The most unthinkable things in the world can and do happen, to innocent, well-meaning people. In an instant, no matter how good you are, or kind, no matter how much you pray to God to protect you and your loved ones . . .*"

She choked and began to sob into her hands.

My father rose and caught my mother's wrists. "Lena," he pleaded, "*please be quiet.*"

He looked up at me and gestured sharply with his chin for me to leave the room. I rose and headed for the door, but as I passed my parents, my mother pulled away from Diego's grip and reached for me.

"*No child of mine will endure what I have! Marisol, hear the truth!*" she cried.

My father struck her with the back of his hand. The force sent her staggering backward against the side of her chair, which toppled, causing her to lose her balance and fall.

I moved to my mother, too late to catch her. When I helped her back to her feet, she was wide-eyed, stunned into silence, and pressed a palm to her cheekbone and jaw. Her lower lip was split, and a ribbon of blood trickled down her chin.

In that instant, I hated my father.

Shaking with agitation, Diego stared down at us; a sheen of tears filmed his eyes. As I looked vengefully back at him, the first drop trickled down the side of his face.

"Go to your chambers and stay there until I tell you, doña Magdalena," he said, in a low, ragged voice. *"Go and think on what you have almost done. I forbid you to speak of this again; I can't let your fear destroy us."*

Five

My mother lifted her skirts in fury and ran from the room; my father impatiently brushed his tears away and turned his back to her as he returned to his seat and the now-cold chickpeas awaiting him. I still stood in the open doorway, watching as my mother disappeared up the stairs.

"Marisol," my father said sternly.

I glanced back to see him sitting at the table, staring disconsolately down at his bowl.

"How dare you hit her!" I was seething but kept my voice low, ever mindful of the servants in the kitchen.

My father continued staring down at the chickpeas, his pained expression slowly fading, his face gradually becoming as unreadable as stone. *"It's my right as a husband,"* he said coldly. *"I forbid you too to ever speak of this again. Come sit in your chair. I won't tolerate any more disobedience."*

I resentfully returned to my place at the table and sat, but my tongue couldn't rest. Somehow, I stilled my anger and managed to speak softly.

"You wouldn't be this upset, Papá, if Mamá's fears were all imaginary."

He ran his hands through his thick hair, a sun-bleached brown that was only beginning to show glints of silver, then pressed his hands together to keep from fidgeting. Even then, he wouldn't look at me. *"Your mother's nerves have bested her: She heard a foolish rumor and believes it to be true. Now she's frightened herself so badly that I can't reason with her."*

"What 'truth' is so horrible that I can't hear it?" I pressed.

He shook his head. *"Don't go to her tonight. She's not rational and will only upset you unnecessarily. I'll try to talk some sense into her when she's not so aggravated."*

"I'm an adult now, Papá," I reminded him. *"I don't frighten easily."*

"Your mother was frightened terribly as a child," he said, sighing again and staring slightly above my head at the past. *"So terribly that now she always expects the worst thing possible to happen. I forbid you to see her until I give you permission; it's bad enough that she's upset. I don't want two hysterical women in my house."*

I said nothing more but was obliged to sit and finish supper, both of us silent and keeping our gazes locked on our respective plates. When we had finally suffered through the full-course meal, don Diego gave me permission to leave the table.

I hurried at once to my mother's chambers, to find the door closed but not bolted; this time, not even Máriam would answer my frantic knocking. I drew a breath, and for the first time, entered my mother's room without permission.

I held my breath, not wanting to see what I already knew, as I peered around the corner of the antechamber. There stood my mother, her head covered by the fringed white shawl I hadn't seen in a decade, one she'd promised she'd never wear again. On the little mantel where the crudely painted Madonna stood, two golden candlesticks—ones I believed until that moment she'd given away—sported two burning tapers.

She stood glazed in their light, her profile to me; her lips were moving in the prayer I still remembered: *Baruch atah Eloheinu . . .*

I stepped from the antechamber, one, two, my boot heels audible against the wood. My mother cast the briefest glance over her shoulder at me, then returned to her praying as if I'd been nothing more than a fly. Máriam too must have heard, but she ignored me altogether as she sat, legs tucked beneath her, on a green prayer rug of Moorish design. She held her dark hands up, slightly cupped, in front of her face and whispered the few words in Arabic I knew, as they had been inscribed everywhere on buildings and artwork in the city: *Bismillah ar-rahman ar-rahim . . . In the name of God, the Compassionate and Merciful . . .*

For a long moment, I stood gaping as the women prayed. I told myself I had seen defiance in my mother's gaze—and I knew without doubt that she had lied to me all these many years in order to keep me silent. That Máriam was a liar, too.

Now that the Inquisition had come, she was silent no more.

As I stared, I was torn between affection and rage: How dare these two lie to me for so long? Worse, how dare they expose me to their secret, forcing me to choose between my immortal soul (or worse, my dream of being accepted by the Old Christian world) and my love for them? Did they not realize how they were endangering my father?

In the end, of course, there was really no choice. I'd known from the instant I'd looked on them what I had to do.

. . .

Confused, anxious, and angry, I retired early that night to my bedchamber. My mind was too agitated for sleep, so I sat at the little writing desk, lit the lamp, and tried to reread my father's priceless copy of *The Song of the Cid*, skipping the battle scenes and focusing on the love of Rodrigo for his beautiful doña Jimena. The subject evoked a different sort of pain; I glanced up from my reading to stare at the winter shutters covering the window. Behind them, not far away, stood the tall stone wall that Antonio had dug through so that we could be together as children.

I didn't read long. A quarter hour later, the first drenching storm of winter arrived with a roar. The rain crashed down so hard that, curious, I opened the shutters and stared out at the sheets of water dropping from the sky. They swallowed the sight of the Vargases' house, including the wall; I could see nothing but windswept, watery darkness, and pulled the shutters closed. The wind caused my reading lamp to sputter, and the growing chill near the window finally prompted me to abandon reading for bed. Even then, I couldn't sleep, but lay thinking of Antonio, who should have returned this past June to ask for my hand. I'd waited so long for Antonio, despite his lack of letters, that at seventeen I was almost too old for a bride.

I huddled beneath the covers and listened for an hour to the storm. When it let up quite abruptly, leaving in its wake a profound quiet, I was suddenly able to hear the soft knock at my chamber door. My mother stood on the threshold, still dressed in the blue-green velvet gown with its stiff *verdugado*; her fringed white shawl was gone, and her expression was calm, her tone reasonable.

"Marisol," she said, *"there's something I must ask you, but you must swear to me that you'll never tell your father."*

"Mamá," I countered evenly, *"you know that I can't agree to that."*

"I'm not asking you to keep secret what you saw tonight," she said.

I let her in and silently closed the door. She looked up in frustration at a portrait above my mantel—one of me when I was only seven, an unsmiling, dark-haired, dainty child with too-large eyes, wearing a high collar and a long strand of pearls, like an *infanta.* *"God has cursed me,"* she said, only half teasing, *"with a daughter as stubborn as her mother."*

I didn't smile.

"It's true that I've drawn the Inquisition's attention," Magdalena said, *"because of my appearance, if nothing else. I look like a Jewess. And I fear that you take more after me than your father. I can't stay and bring harm to Diego—and I can't leave you. You're not safe in Seville anymore. You have to come with me."*

I recoiled. *"Where?"*

"I can't tell you just yet," she answered, *"but they'll take good care of us there. We'd be with family. We wouldn't be alone to fend for ourselves."*

Before she could finish, I began to shake my head. *"Mamá, this is crazy! Are you saying that you and I should just leave Papá and go to a strange country?"*

"Yes," she said emphatically. Her eyes held a desperation that unnerved me. *"Your Old Christian father is too trusting of his peers. Do you know what would happen to him if we stayed in the city? Because of me, the Inquisition would take his property and burn him. I can't allow it to happen by staying with him, do you understand? Only don't make me leave you, my daughter. I can bear anything else."*

I stood up, completely undone by the fact that she could even speak of such a heinous end for my father. *"I can't leave Papá!"* I caught my rising tone and forced myself to speak more gently, aware that Máriam was in the next room. *"You're just still upset because he hit you."*

My mother caught my shoulders. *"It has nothing to do with that—I'm trying to save your life, do you understand? You're the daughter of a con-*versa, *Marisol, and the Inquisition has come here to destroy me and you and your father."*

I took my mother's wrists. *"Not Papá and me. Only Judaizers."* My tone was snide, but she was too distraught to register it.

"That's what they say now," she hissed. *"But it will happen as it did before. First, they'll want to punish those in the highest positions of power, and then those with wealth, and then they'll come for everyone. They won't stop until there isn't a single* converso *left in Seville. They want your father because his influence is great. He's always been at odds with the Hojedas."*

I pulled away from her. *"Everyone knows the queen will protect us; King Fernando himself is a* converso. *What you're saying is mad, Mamá. You should hear yourself! Papá said that you're beyond reason now that the Inquisition has come. They're here only to get the Judaizers."* Her words had frightened me enough to make me angry, and I cast about for words to hurt her. *"And good riddance!"*

She gaped at me in silence for a few long seconds; an expression of growing horror crept into her eyes.

Wounded, my mother turned her face from me and shook her head. *"I'm not beyond reason, Marisol,"* she whispered sadly. *"I'm quite rational. It's everyone else who has gone insane."*

I never told my father about my mother's plan to leave, because I couldn't believe that she meant it; even if she had, I felt that her keenness to escape would soon pass. I knew that she could never leave my father and me behind. And I refused to think about whether I should turn my mother and Máriam in to the Inquisition, because I knew I was incapable. It was far easier to believe my father's reassurances that the Inquisition would leave us all alone.

The next weeks brought cool but sunny weather, and my mother began to paint in her studio constantly, producing more ceramics than she ever had. The potter's wagon started arriving at our house almost every day to pick up the pieces she'd finished and deliver new ones—one of which was a massive Saint Santiago. Brother to John the Apostle, Santiago preached the Gospel in ancient Iberia before returning to the Holy Land to be martyred. When Christian fighters returned to Spain to reclaim it from the Moors, they called upon Santiago, who miraculously appeared in the middle of a battle with horse, sword, and shield, and brought the Christians a decisive victory.

This particular Santiago was three times the size of my mother's usual pieces, as large as the Santiago in the Hojedas' courtyard. But this Santiago was a gorgeous work: This Saint James's expression was fierce, his chiseled beard and long hair stirred by an imaginary wind, his muscular steed in mid-gallop, his sword lifted high to rally the troops against the infidel. Beneath his horse's hoof, the crushed Muslim warrior's face reflected the full agony of his death throes. As with certain other grand pieces scheduled for grand fates, my mother would not let me near this Santiago; I respected her artistic eccentricity and never laid a hand on it.

If my mother saw any contradiction between her secret life and her avocation, she never spoke of it to me. If anything, she looked on the Santiago statue with peculiar zeal, eager to start work upon it since she'd not been given much time to finish it, but reluctantly forced to finish her work on other statues first. I remember her looking on it longingly one day and saying to me as we worked, *"Promise me, Marisol, that if anything happens to me, you'll finish him."* I scoffed at her, saying that such a thought was completely ridiculous, that nothing would happen to her. But I wondered why she would ask me to finish it, since she clearly thought it worthy of her hand alone.

During this time, Magdalena never spoke to me again of abandoning Seville, although, when I came to help her in the studio one day, she caught my hand and said with heartfelt remorse, *"I never meant to ruin your life. You should have been married by now, with children."*

I scolded her for saying such a ridiculous thing. *"It has everything to do with Antonio Vargas and nothing to do with you, Mamá."*

Her expression was profoundly serious. *"I hope so,"* she answered. *"And Marisol . . ."* Her tone grew confidential. *"Don't give up hope. Antonio loves you and will come for you. Only wait."*

Before I could answer that such hope was enormously foolish, she squeezed my hand. *"But why worry about things, when there's so much work to be done?"*

And she picked up her brush again with an odd, forced cheer.

Perhaps this was only a new phase of her lunacy. Even so, I was happy that her work kept her occupied—and sad for my father, whose closest friend on the city council, Jorge de Susán, a *converso*, had disappeared along with his wife and children the previous night, leaving virtually all of his possessions behind.

Although I still resented my father for striking my mother, I accompanied him to the bonfires held on the twenty-first of

December, to mark the shortest day of winter and the beginning of the Christmas season. It was a crisp, clear evening, with no winds—the perfect weather for building fires—and as the sun set, the air filled with the scent of burning hardwood.

Flanked by four men-at-arms on horseback, don Diego and I rode in a carriage the few blocks to the great Plaza de San Francisco, the largest public square in all Seville, and the massive whitewashed Gothic structures that housed the church, two chapels, the convent, two hospitals, and a library, all run by the Franciscan monks. In the square's center a vast bonfire—the height of two men and the width of a dozen—burned while a brown flock of monks stoked it. This was flanked on either side by smaller fires, which all the male parishioners leapt over in order to win good health for themselves and their families in the coming year. All but the smallest boys and oldest men could easily make the jump, and my agile-footed father was one of the best leapers. He cleared the bonfire handily, which brought offers of wine and sherry from the other men; he refused none, but proceeded to get unusually drunk and sing Christmas carols with a discernable slur. His guards drank with him, although every *converso* in town was well aware of the fact that, like the other leapers, the Old Christian men at the nearby Church of San Pablo were imbibing heavily and therefore posed a danger. Even so, Diego and his guards had dispensed with caution, and within an hour they stood swaying, cheeks pressed together as they harmonized in the fire's glow, arms flung around one another's shoulders as if they were old friends and not business acquaintances.

I kept company with the women and forced myself to sing along with them. After the carols stopped and the priest emerged to bless the crowd and send us home, my father didn't want to

stop celebrating, but stopped by a half dozen smaller street cele-
brations to demonstrate his nimbleness—which, as he consumed
more sherry, began to suffer.

I'd never seen my father so drunk. By the time I got him
home—with little help from the swaying guards—and sat him
down at the supper table, he could no longer keep his head lifted
and came dangerously close to falling face-first into his soup
bowl. I spooned what I could into him and tried to help him to
his bed, but he grew belligerent, and I was obliged to leave him
slumped in a chair in the second-floor sitting room with a flagon
of sherry. Exhausted and furious at my father for behaving so
childishly, I went to bed and fell into a heavy sleep.

Four hours before dawn on the morning of the twenty-second
of December, I woke to a peculiar state of alertness. Some subtle
noise had wakened me—a door opening in the distance or light
footsteps, perhaps from a fading dream—and I sat up, aware of
my fast-beating heart. I threw on my dressing gown and hurried
out to the loggia; at its southern end, beneath the lantern over
the stairs, I spied a blur of movement, of night-faded color, just
before it slipped down out of sight.

I followed silently, at a safe distance, and crept downstairs. At
the open double doors to the sitting room, I paused to find that
my father was still slumped in his padded chair, his chin resting
upon his chest, his lips puffing outward as he expelled air. The
half-consumed flagon of sherry rested on the little table beside him,
next to an oil lamp with a dying blue flame.

My mother was leaning over him. She was completely awake
and wearing not her nightgown nor her usual black, but the
heavy blue-green velvet dress with the hoops of the *verdugado*. Her
hair was braided, wound at the nape of her neck, and covered by

her best black lace veil; she looked down at my father adoringly as she put a gentle hand upon the inner crook of his elbow.

"Diego," she said gently. *"Diego, my love, come to bed."*

My father snorted and opened his vacant, bloodshot eyes. *"Who is it?"* he growled. He blinked at her and gave a start. *"Lena? Is it really you?"*

She smiled down at him and stroked his cheek with the back of her fingers. *"It is. Let me help you to bed, don Diego."*

She helped him stand—he was very unsteady—and stood on tiptoe to kiss his cheek.

I should have helped her get him to bed. If I'd done that one little thing, perhaps everything would be different now. But I understood nothing, and I was reluctant to interrupt such a tender moment between my parents.

My father turned his head and kissed her on the lips, then grinned at her. *"How beautiful you are . . . you've grown young again."*

She laughed softly and slipped beneath his arm to support him. I hid out in the corridor, behind the open door as they passed by, and waited for their heavy footfalls to fade upon the stairs before following. My father's bedchamber was one floor up, in the same south wing of the house; I got to the landing midway up the stairs and lingered there, listening to the sound of his chamber door opening and closing. I expected my mother to emerge shortly and cross the covered loggia to her room in the north wing, next to mine.

Rather than fade, however, my mother's footsteps grew louder; she was headed back down the stairs. I hurried out of her line of sight, careful to be as quiet as possible, and went back to my hiding place behind the open door of the sitting room to peer through the crack as she neared. For an instant she drew so close—close enough to hear my breath, which I promptly held—that I expected her to fling back the door and expose me.

Instead, she stopped in the corridor a few arms' lengths away, and from a pool of shadow on the floor retrieved a black wool cloak and slipped it on. Accustomed to the lack of light, I watched as a spasm of grief briefly contorted her features, then transformed into an expression of determination. She turned her back to me, raised the hood of her cloak, and melted into the darkness. Gulping in air, I waited behind the door as her rapid steps faded down the corridor and headed—not up the stairs and back to her chamber, as I expected—down toward the kitchen. I gave her a full flight's head start so that I would not be seen and then followed her. Even then I had convinced myself that her winter cloak was coincidental, that she was only going down to the kitchen because she was hungry, that she was not making a foolish attempt to leave. Even if she was, I kept silent; I didn't want anyone to hear us, because I didn't want my father to punish her again.

By the time I made it downstairs and into the kitchen, however, I could no longer tell myself lies: My mother had run silently out onto the patio, unbolted and swung open the front gate, and slipped out into the street. The faint clang of the iron latch alarmed me so that I forgot to lift my skirts as I passed from the kitchen onto the patio, and my slippered foot caught the hem of my dressing gown. My right knee and hands struck the cobblestones with such force that I let go a muffled yelp; yet my mother didn't return, nor did the night guards come to investigate. I pushed myself up on stinging palms to discover that the skirt of my gown had ripped beneath the injured knee, which was throbbing and felt as if the suddenly tight skin would burst. I was hobbled but still unwilling to call for my father and cause another unpleasant scene. Besides, I knew his watchmen outside would never let my mother go running off into the city unescorted, especially at this hour, and so I paused and gingerly eased my weight onto my right leg.

I'll never forgive myself that moment of hesitation.

The pain forced a gasp from me. Straightening the leg made my eyes tear, but I was so troubled by the silence in the street beyond the iron gate—why hadn't one of the guards challenged my mother?—that I forced myself to move, keeping my swollen knee bent and allowing any weight to strike only the ball of my right foot. Teetering and clenching my teeth, I limped as fast as I could over the patio and through the gate, onto the street. Smoke from dead or dying bonfires filled the air, stinging my eyes and throat and veiling the world in an acrid, dreamlike haze.

In the shadow of the hulking Hojeda house, a pair of my father's watchmen sat in the center of the cobblestone cul-de-sac in front of what had once been a blazing bonfire, reduced now to a large pile of smoldering white ash and angry embers. Their bodies were pressed shoulder to shoulder against the cold, their heads bowed—not in prayer, but slumber.

I panicked and squinted through the filmy air, searching for my mother; had it not been for the near-full moon hanging beyond the curtain of smoke, brightening the black sky to indigo, I would never have glimpsed her slight form at the south end of our street, turning west onto the broad thoroughfare of San Pablo Street.

I took in a large breath to call out to the sleeping guards, and choked on the smoky air instead. The men didn't stir at my coughing; I managed to draw in enough air to shout hoarsely: *"Wake up, wake up!"*

One of them was roused and started guiltily at the sight of me. When he scrambled, clumsy from drink to his feet, I called out: *"Get a horse and follow me! Tell the stable master to wake my father! Doña Magdalena is in danger!"*

Ignoring his protests about *my* safety in the darkened city, I turned and broke into a staggering canter after my mother.

I recall only fragments of the chase. I don't remember the cold or the pain in my knee, though both must have been severe, but I recall my frustration over calling out to my mother, running at full tilt two blocks ahead of me, and being unheard, then losing my voice entirely to the smoke. I recall smoldering piles of bonfires on either side of the street and faint catcalls from some of the men lying beside them, too drunk to make good on their amorous threats. I looked through a haze at the back of my mother's wool cloak swinging as she ran down the center of the brick street, past the massive still-flickering bonfire built in the great plaza in front of the Dominican Church of San Pablo, where exhausted monks glanced up with weary curiosity, their faces smudged and golden in the fire's glow. My slippers were coated with horse dung, dust, and ash by the time the street widened markedly as we drew closer to the Guadalquivir River. We passed the entrances of disreputable inns, where shadows of sailors and prostitutes copulated; the square brick armory, stinking of sulphur; lumberyards fragrant with cedar and oak, patrolled by barking curs; and the rope maker's yard, piled high with pale shredded flax.

The moon hung high in the western sky above the river, and its glow limned the harbor and the silhouettes of great sailing ships on the south side of the bridge, their sails furled, their na-

ked masts pointed upward like dozens of black lances. My mother
ran straight toward the docks, as if she planned to board one of
the boats. By then, I was convinced that she had made arrange-
ments with one of the sea captains to help her escape.

But she veered suddenly away from the harbor—where black
rats scrabbled over the worn planks of the docks to and from the
ships—and ran onto the golden sand along the riverbank, where
the poor bathed and fished and drew their drinking water, near
the great pontoon bridge connecting Seville proper with Triana.
It was a place neither of us had ever gone before, as some believed
plague lurked on these shores, brought here by the foreigners in
their big sailing vessels.

With me in breathless, hobbled pursuit, more than a full minute away, my mother turned her back to the moon, the hood of
her cloak still covering her hair, her face hidden in darkness. I
watched dumbfounded as she raised her arms toward the east,
then prostrated her body reverently on the sand. She rose and
chanted quickly: *"Shema Yisrael, Adonai Eloheinu, Adonai Echad . . ."*

I slowed my limping pace slightly, fascinated and terrified at
once, straining to hear over the lapping of water against the bridge
pontoons and the hulls of great ships. My mother's voice was
beautiful and strong.

Perhaps she heard me or saw me in the shadows near the docks,
loping unevenly toward the shore. She broke off, her prayer in-
complete, and, turning back toward the moon, lifted her skirts and
waded quickly out into the river, not even pausing at the stinging
cold water.

I screamed at her. Although my throat was hoarse, my voice
rasping, horror gave it strength; I knew my mother couldn't swim.

I think she heard me, for as I called out to her, she paused for a single breath to stand very still, her skirts and the hem of her cloak floating at knee level upon the water. Rather than turn back to me, though, she squared her shoulders and continued on, the hoops of her skirts rising up around her, floating on the water; soon the water grew too deep for her to maintain her footing, and she paddled farther out. Disturbed, the water around her body caught the lunar light and pushed it outward in undulating, silvered ripples. Her shoulders disappeared beneath the surface, and her chin, and in an instant, her head had vanished, leaving the skirts floating.

I ran across the shore, the pain in my knee no less fierce but entirely forgotten, like the cold, and was about to step into the river when a strong, thick pair of arms clutched me from behind and held me fast.

"*Let me go, let me go!*" I shrieked, and squirmed around to pound my tall, solid attacker with my fists. I expected to see an inebriated sailor from one of the boats.

Instead, Gabriel stared down at me with pity and veiled longing, his pale eyes round, his milky hair a disheveled halo.

"*I'm sorry,*" he whispered.

I struggled frantically in his grip; it enraged me that he spoke as if doña Magdalena were already gone, and I couldn't understand why he wasn't rushing to save her. "*My mother! Stop her! Hurry!*"

Behind us came the clatter of horses' hooves and the sound of my father shouting to one of his guards. Held fast by Gabriel, I surrendered and turned to look back at the river, gesticulating at the spot I had last seen my mother. There was nothing to see now save for the empty velvet skirts, gray against the dark water.

I watched as my father and two guards dashed onto the shore;

all three stripped down to their leggings, casting cloaks and tunics on the sand. My father was first to plunge into the water, but by the time he swam out to where my mother's clothes were still floating, shouting her name, he found them empty; there was no sign of her body. He caught his breath and dove several times, each time deeper; this went on for anguished, interminable minutes, until he finally grew so exhausted and chilled that he could no longer keep himself afloat. Even then, he struggled weakly to break free from the two guards, who pulled him back to shore when it was clear that my mother was gone, lost to the unfathomable depths of the Guadalquivir.

By then, Gabriel had released his hold on me, and I sank down to sit upon the cold sand, unable to think, unwilling to feel. I should have rushed to my father's side when he emerged from the river shivering violently, unable to walk unaided or to speak, only to moan unintelligibly, but I couldn't bear to look at his pain. I ignored Gabriel's proffered hands and leaned forward to bury my own in the sand and caught the coarse grains in my fists again and again, each time feeling them slip easily from between my fingers.

A part of myself went cold as the water and watched events unfold like a disinterested observer. I wept and stormed and lunged again at the river, only to be caught again by Gabriel; at the same time, I watched myself do these things and felt nothing at all. I saw the infinite horror in my father's eyes and noted my conflicting desires to comfort him, to kill him, and was touched by none of these things.

What had just happened was too great and too awful for my mind or heart to comprehend; it was the sort of thing that happens to strangers in cautionary tales, but never to anyone familiar. Crouching there on the riverbank, I knew that the shock and numbness would wear off too soon to leave behind an agony of grief—and that there would be countless bleak days ahead before that grief would ease.

Six

Of the terrible journey home that night, I remember only one image: that of Máriam out in the street in front of our house, the corners of her mouth drawn back in a grimace of pure pain as she let go a ululating wail at the sight of our faces as we returned. In Máriam's dark hand was a small sheet of fine paper—my mother's stationery, the wax seal broken. My shivering father, wrapped in his cloak, saw it and, had he had enough strength to lift his arms, would have taken it from her—but despite my limp, I staggered to her first and snatched it to read:

My name is Magdalena García. I am the wife of Diego García, Seville councilman, and the mother of Marisol García.

As a child, I was orphaned. I remember little of my life before that time. The nuns at the Convent of the Incarnation raised me to be a good Christian.

Because of my physical appearance, I am suspected of having Jewish blood. But my husband is an Old Christian, and in our household, we

have always worshipped Christ and the Virgin Mary as the church in-
structs. I am not a crypto-Jew, and you will not find any more loyal to
the Christian faith than my husband and daughter.

There are those in the Inquisition who would disgrace my husband
for purely political reasons, and they seek to use me against him. To them
I say: My blood is on your hands. I know that they will use torture to
make me invent lies to harm those I love. Let my death serve as my testimony to my family's innocence, and let the Inquisition's suspicion begin
and end with me.

May God have mercy on your souls.

I couldn't stand but sank down to embrace the street, the
piece of paper slipping through my fingers, only dimly aware in
the next moment that my sobbing father was huddled beside me,
the letter now in his hands.

When he could speak, he gasped into my ear: *"Forgive me. Forgive me! I've killed her!"*

It would have been easy to blame him—to believe that my
mother had killed herself because my father had failed to hear
her desperation, to take steps to reassure her, or even, possibly, to
fail to realize that she had been right all along. But I knew that *I*
was the one who truly could have stopped her by agreeing to go
with her.

I caught his shoulders. *"It was me,"* I whispered back. *"Oh, Papá,
it was me and not you at all."*

We clung to each other in our guilt.

Later, in private, I explained to him that Magdalena had
killed herself because I wouldn't escape with her. For my sake,
she had been willing to live without my father . . . but not without *me*.

. . .

Magdalena's body was never found; we held a small memorial service for her in the olive orchard where Antonio and I used to meet. We never spoke of her suicide but told everyone it was an accidental drowning—although our servants and Gabriel, who was there, surely knew better. My father burned my mother's letter so there could be no proof.

Remarkably, my mother had managed to finish painting almost every single piece sent her by the potter; when I could finally bring myself to check her studio, I found it empty of work save for the large Santiago. Her brushes had been freshly cleaned, her paints all carefully stored away.

I waited for Gabriel Hojeda to tell his brother or fellow Inquisitors about my mother's last prayer and the fact that her death was a suicide; I expected the Inquisition to come next for my father, or at least to search my mother's quarters. But to my infinite surprise, Gabriel held his tongue. And when he came to our house with Fray Hojeda, it was only to share his condolences.

Or so I thought at the time. Dazed by sorrow and shock, I never thought to question why Gabriel had been watching our house the night of my mother's death, or why he had followed us in silence to the riverbank, or why—long after his brother Fray Hojeda had paid his condolences and left our house—he remained behind to privately converse at length with my father.

Four days after Magdalena died, my father emerged from his solitary mourning in his room to encounter me in mine. When I opened the door, I saw a man I barely recognized: My father's cheeks glistened with stubble, and his light brown hair stuck straight up in places where it had met the pillow. His entire face and body sagged beneath such self-loathing and misery that I couldn't bear to look at him for long without glancing away.

"We need to speak," don Diego told me. His voice was hoarse and very soft, but his words were clipped and his manner oddly cold.

I gestured him inside; when I moved to kiss him, he turned his face away. I swallowed my hurt and we sat in my little foyer while my father looked grimly down at his hands. Despite his composure, I sensed that he was on the verge of breaking down; his face and upper body were perfectly still, but his feet were tapping with the effort to hold back deep emotion—not just his grief over his wife, but fresher pain from a newer wound.

"What is it?" I asked. *"Papá, what's wrong?"*

He wouldn't look up at me. He spoke in a low monotone, with words that were clearly rehearsed.

"Gabriel Hojeda has asked for your hand," he answered, *"and I've given it."*

I gaped at him. *"This is a cruel joke,"* I exclaimed, *"and not funny at a cruel time!"*

Don Diego shifted in his chair, but his gaze never strayed from the folded hands in his lap. *"It's not a joke. The wedding will be this Saturday."*

I jerked myself to my feet. *"It will not!"* Despite my effort to remain composed, I began to cry out of pure anger as I realized he was serious. *"You can't do this to me, Papá! How can you give me to one of your enemies? To Gabriel Hojeda, of all men! And why now? Now, when things are horrible enough?!"*

He rose, too—slowly, sadly—and when he finally looked

down at me, the skin around his narrowed eyes was twitching with a dark, desperate emotion I couldn't interpret. He seemed on the verge of breaking down, of releasing a torrent of words, but he held them back with a hitching breath, and his features relaxed again into an emotionless mask.

"You'll marry Gabriel on Saturday," he repeated. *"I've given my word. I have only one thing left to say."*

"How can you do this to me? How can you do this now?" My voice shook with hurt and rage; I flung my arms into the air, gesturing wildly. *"Are you mad, Papá? Are you mad?"*

He reached out quickly and slapped my cheek.

His attack was less than halfhearted; the blow stung only a little, and I never wobbled. But the damage to my feelings was devastating: He'd never struck me before.

"Don't ever speak to me so again," he said huskily, and his slightly wild, empty gaze dropped to the floor. *"Don't ever speak to me at all. I'm no longer your father, do you understand, Marisol? And you're no longer my daughter. This is the end of it. You're an Hojeda now. Forget that I ever existed."*

"What?" I gasped at the impact of his words and reached for him. *"Papá, how can you say such a thing to me? You know I love you! You're not yourself. Please, you're upset over Mamá!"*

He lowered his head so that I couldn't read his eyes; his shoulders sagged, and he began to shout with an odd rage, one that left his voice ragged and tearful.

"You'll leave this house and never come back! Do you understand? Never come back! I won't have it! I won't——! You're not mine anymore! You have to get out, do you hear? You have to get out!"

He broke into wrenching sobs and hurried out my door.

I sank to the floor and sobbed without restraint, hearing the silent jeers of the boys out in the street on the day the Jew had wandered into our neighborhood: *Marrana! Marrana! Marrana!*

And I imagined I heard my Old Christian father's voice among theirs. I understood all too well what he hadn't had the courage to admit directly: Shaken by his wife's death, don Diego was marrying me off to Gabriel Hojeda to be rid of me and the danger presented by my tainted blood.

Seven

Standing now in the bedroom where Gabriel Hojeda's mother had died, I stared down at Máriam, who knelt beside me in front of the quieting hearth, her oily brown-black face gleaming. As much as I had always adored and trusted her, I understood why my father had dismissed her and why he harbored doubts.

"So," I asked softly, without emotion, "were there any clues that my mother was planning to kill herself?"

Máriam turned her head sharply to stare up over her shoulder at me. Her great brown eyes were narrowed, the dark, velvety skin beneath them twitching. We had never spoken honestly about how my mother had died.

"Doña Magdalena never said any such thing to me," she whispered harshly, and turned just as quickly back to the fire; she thrust at the white-edged logs mindlessly, provoking as much flame as she discouraged.

"Didn't you ask her," I persisted gently, "why she was making you promise to look after me?"

Her full lower lip thrust forward as she scowled at the flames. "She made me promise that many times when she was close to death after losing a child."

For a moment we remained silent while I struggled to repress all the questions that had tormented me over the past two weeks: *How did she dress without your help? Without waking you? How could you not have noticed when she walked past you out the door?* Máriam was easily awakened, far more so than my mother; I'd never seen her in bed or asleep.

Some painful thought pricked her. She dropped the poker and jerked back toward me, still on her knees.

"Do you really think, doña Marisol, that I would ever have wanted any harm to come to your mother? That I didn't love her as I love myself?" With the word *love*, a tear spilled from each of her eyes, and she didn't stop to wipe them away. "She lied to me. She said—" Her face contorted violently, and she turned back to the fire to compose herself. When she spoke again, staring steadily into the fire, it was in a whisper. "I have no one to care for now, except you."

I sank to my knees and hugged her sinewy arms and bony shoulders, an impulsive gesture that startled her: I hadn't embraced her since I was a child and was still unaware that servants weren't family. Máriam turned her face away, unable to relax into the embrace, and I slowly unwound my arms and rose again.

"I know how you loved her," I said huskily, then turned away myself toward the eastern wall.

A tall, very narrow dresser made of pale creamy olive wood was pushed against the wall. Save for the handsome pattern of burls in the wood, the dresser wasn't notable, but the statue sitting on it was: my mother's Madonna, veiled in blue, her solar halo gilded, her cherry ceramic lips smiling down at the chalk-white child in her arms. Her clumsy grin seemed smug, even mocking.

"Take this away." Even I was surprised at the bitterness in my tone. "I don't ever want to see it again."

Máriam stood, poker in hand, her composure returned. "But it was your mother's, doña!"

"And what good did it do her?" The blasphemous words were out of my mouth before I could weigh them.

Máriam remained firm. "It was very dear to your mother. She wanted you to have it. She asked . . ." A breath of weakness crept into her tone, but she steeled herself. "Every time she asked me to look after you, she told me to be sure you had the Madonna." She lowered her voice to an apologetic murmur, knowing that her lesser status made her wishes of no import. "We prayed together in front of it every day."

I turned my back to it, still wounded. I would have insisted then that she put it somewhere else, where I wouldn't have to glimpse it so often, but Blanca's knock interrupted; she had come to take me to the wedding supper; I was too nervous to ask whether Fray Hojeda had left.

I followed her back across the long courtyard, past Santiago's fountain; the cold and a faint drizzle kept us moving at a fast pace, until we made it to the opposite wing, which housed the dining chamber, kitchen, and public reception areas.

I've always prided myself on being fearless, but by the time Blanca opened the doors to the dining chamber, my legs were so wobbly from fright that I worried they'd give out at any moment.

Just as I'd dreaded, Fray Hojeda was standing inside, a goblet in his hand. My husband paced in front of the fireplace, not far from a near-empty flagon of wine set on a century-old table built to accommodate some forty diners; only a dozen high-backed chairs remained now, all of them set at one edge of the table, above whose center rested a gap in the ceiling covered by planks, suggesting that a large chandelier had been removed. Gabriel's usually pale nose was red as a cherry, indicating that the flagon had been full not long before; he gripped the stem of his goblet as if it were a lifeline. For once, the friar was not quite scowling, though it was clear that not doing so strained him.

"Doña Marisol," he said, in his commanding bass. *Doña*, he called me—the polite title of address for a married woman— and though his tone could not be called welcoming, it was civil. While he was not completely drunk, there was a slight slur to his speech; it had apparently taken more than just Gabriel's words to soothe him. "I apologize for my earlier show of temper. Don Gabriel has something he wishes to give you."

Startled, I looked to Gabriel, who was trying his best not to seem too pleased at his victory over his older brother. He nodded at my right hand, and when I lifted it, he held it and, smiling faintly, slipped the thin gold band back on my finger. Fray Hojeda could not bear to watch; he averted his eyes, his lips twitching with the effort to suppress his outrage.

"I wish to welcome you to the family," Fray Hojeda said woodenly as he set his goblet on the table. "I see now that I was wrong to treat you as I have." He paused, and his tone grew adamant. "I will not have the marriage annulled—on one condition: that you do not indulge in marital relations for at least one month. This marriage was made in far too great a haste to be consummated immediately; let the month serve, if you wish, as a period of betrothal. Gabriel has already vowed to maintain celibacy for the time. I must insist on the same from you."

"Of course," I said, perhaps too eagerly; I hoped my voice didn't betray the infinite relief I felt. "I vow the same."

"Good." Fray Hojeda finally looked me in the eye. "Then I would ask one more thing from you, doña Marisol: that you let it be known that Gabriel and I have shown you great kindness and have taken you under our roof to protect you from those who are not as . . . tolerant as we are, who might do you harm because you are a *conversa*." He lowered his voice. "There is no need, of course, to mention the vow of celibacy to anyone."

His words about protection made no sense to me. Still, I was grateful for his change of heart, although I couldn't imagine what Gabriel had said that could have caused it.

"I must return to the monastery," Hojeda said, "so I will leave you two to your supper. I wish you both goodnight." With that, he strode from the dining room without a further glance at Gabriel or me.

I turned to Gabriel in disbelief. "What did you say to him?"

I asked the question uneasily. For my entire life, I'd lived across the street from the man who was now my husband, but my only personal exchange with him had occurred years earlier, when he'd attacked the elderly Jew.

Gabriel smiled with a hint of timidity, although he was clearly pleased with himself. "You mustn't blame him, doña Marisol. He has his prejudices—we all do—but if he is to succeed, he must learn the difference between a *converso* and a crypto-Jew."

I stared at Gabriel in disbelief; had his beliefs truly changed so much over the years?

With his goblet, he gestured me toward the table, where a small silver candelabrum sat between two place settings near one end of the table. Save for the small area lit by the candles and fireplace, the room was dark, the bulk of its interior hidden from scrutiny, but given the echo of Gabriel's steps off the walls, it was clearly vast and mostly empty.

I was grateful that the place settings were at the end of the table closest to the hearth, where a recently lit fire struggled to catch hold; the room was still so chilly I could just see my breath in the gloom and rued the fact that I'd left my shawl back in my apartment. I moved toward the hearth and fought to repress a shiver as I rubbed my upper arms.

"Poor doña Marisol, you're freezing," Gabriel said, and hurried to set down his goblet. He'd had enough sense to throw a wool cape over his tunic, and he undid the clasp, removed the cape from his shoulders, and draped it around mine. His body had heated it, and I gathered it around me, grateful for the warmth.

"Thank you, don Gabriel," I said.

"Look at you, you're damp," he said kindly. "It must be starting to rain again. No wonder you're cold."

He reached toward my face as if to wipe the droplets away. For an instant, his palm hovered above my cheek, but he resisted the urge to touch it, as if it were a forbidden object, and instead directed his attention to refastening the clasp at my collarbone. He fumbled nervously; I put my cold fingers over his, guiding them until the clasp snapped shut, but when I tried to drop my hands, he caught and held one of them. I had to bend my neck backward in order to see the fast-spreading blotches of color on his cheeks. In his eyes burned the same flicker of desire I had seen when I'd shouted for him to stop hitting Antonio.

At the same moment, I realized that Blanca had disappeared without a sound. Had Gabriel so quickly forgotten his promise to his brother?

"Doña Marisol," he half whispered, still clasping the hand I yearned to pull free, "you're so beautiful tonight. I can't believe that you're under my roof at last." His breath was warm and smelled of wine. Tipsy, he took an unsteady step closer, until our bodies grazed each other, the black silk over my breasts gently brushing his rib cage. I could feel the heat of him and hear his quickened breath.

I averted my gaze and my face, hoping he would think modesty, not disgust and horror, caused me to do so. He read my dismay, slowly released his grip, and stepped back.

"Your hands are so cold, my wife." He used the term of address with a shyness that might have been charming under different circumstances.

"They'll warm soon enough," I replied tonelessly.

"Come to the table, then." He pulled out a chair at the table for me, as if he were a servant. When I had settled in it, he walked through the gloom away from the fireplace, toward the distant glow of the kitchen, and unceremoniously called for supper before returning to his place across the table from me.

We sat in uneasy silence until Blanca came to refill the flagon and set food in front of us. It wasn't what I would have expected for a wedding supper: watery soup, a leg of cold greasy mutton, olives, sheep's cheese, and tart, sour wine. Gabriel drank copiously, and I fought not to grimace as I swallowed as much wine as I could; the unpleasant encounter with Fray Hojeda had unnerved me.

We spoke little during the meal, save to comment on the

weather and the suitability of my quarters. Eventually Blanca arrived, not with the traditional sponge cake studded with almonds, but two pieces of sweet shortbread known as *polvorón*,
purchased from the baker. Once she had served us, Gabriel requested strict privacy and dismissed her. I halfheartedly nibbled
my piece, which was crumbly and dry, while Gabriel swallowed
his in two bites, then pushed aside the plate and folded his huge
hands upon the table.

"I'm sure you've heard that Queen Isabel appointed me civil
prosecutor for the Inquisition here in Seville."

I nodded, accidentally inhaling a piece of *polvorón* and muffling
a wheezing cough with my fist, glad that it allowed me to hide my
expression.

"It's a great honor," he said proudly. "Ideally, the post would
go to a Dominican priest or monk, but Her Majesty has allowed
me to serve because of my degree in canon law." He hesitated. "I
want to apologize for my brother's bad temper. He's very proud
of my position and feared our marriage might jeopardize it."

"Won't it?" I asked bluntly.

He gave a faint smile. "I should think it wouldn't, given that
Queen Isabel is herself married to a *converso*." His expression grew
serious. "I hope my brother didn't insult you with his insistence
on our remaining celibate." He studied my reaction intently.

"Of course not," I said. "You needn't say any more about it."

"You're not offended?" He looked up at me, his tone suddenly
wistful. "Not . . . disappointed?"

I shook my head and took a swallow of wine to wash away the
last of the *polvorón* crumbs stuck in my throat. When I set down
my goblet, Gabriel was watching me with an eerie light in his eye.

"I'm very tired," I said, trying to sound casual. "May I retire to my chambers for the evening?"

Without answering, he rose and walked around the table in order to pull back my chair, a gallant gesture. But when I stood up and turned to leave, his body blocked me; his breath was coming hard, causing the muscles in his chest to strain against his tunic.

I was frightened but refused to show it. "Thank you for the use of your cape," I said, as I slipped it off my shoulders. Without meeting his fixed gaze, I held it out to him.

He reached toward it, let it drop to the floor, and grasped my hand, hard, before I could pull it away.

"You're so beautiful, Marisol," he whispered. "Surely you know I've loved you for such a very long time."

I tried to free myself, but he tightened his grip, leaned down, and swept the dishes in front of me aside with a sharp, violent sweep of his other arm. Pottery, silver, and glass clashed and clattered; my goblet cracked where the bowl met the stem and toppled, spilling wine that ran off the table's edge onto my skirts. The candelabrum teetered dangerously, spewing hot wax that hissed as it met the alcohol.

Gabriel seemed to register none of it. He caught my other hand and squeezed it until I flinched with pain.

"Let me go!" I struggled, but it only inflamed him more. He pulled me to him again until our bodies touched; his was shaking.

"I thought perhaps you had come to care for me. You know I've always wanted you," he whispered, almost angrily; his lips were parted, his eyes wide. He looked down at my face for a response, but I refused to give him one.

I stilled my own trembling; he was more than twice my size and could easily have taken me. But remembering his initial reluctance to attack the elderly Jew until his fellows urged him on, I feigned confidence and straightened until I inhabited as much space as possible.

"Let go of my hand!" I snapped, in my best imitation of the late don Jerónimo. "Have you forgotten your vow of celibacy so quickly?"

Fury sparked in his eyes, threatening to turn into a blaze; his breath came rapidly through his open mouth. It stank of the sour wine, and I wanted to turn my head away, but my father taught me never to turn my back on a dog that bites. Instead, I scowled as hard as I could and stamped my foot.

"Don Gabriel! What would your brother say, to see you now?"

His gaze dropped, and the fair skin of his neck and cheeks turned a mottled red; slowly, he released my hands, which bore the marks of his fingers. "You would tell him?"

"I would. A promise must be kept."

"Then never speak to anyone of this," he hissed.

By the time I looked up from my aching hands, he had disappeared into the darkness, leaving behind only the sound of his rapidly receding tread.

Máriam was startled by my early return; she had changed into her nightgown and dressing gown and was standing at the basin in the antechamber, peering into the mirror. She'd always slept in my mother's room, and I'd never seen her without her turban. Her matte black hair was parted in the middle and braided in tiny rows, like a farmer's carefully tilled field. Dozens of slender little braids fell almost to her shoulders, and she was replaiting one of them, at whose end was a cloud of dark hair.

Her amazing hair intrigued me, but what caught my attention most was the right side of her scalp: A palm-size swatch of skin above her ear was completely bald, though she had tried her best to cover it with the braids. Lamplight reflected off a series of raised, shiny scars that looked like pink-red tiger's stripes.

As I entered, I drew in a breath at the sight of the scars. Máriam grabbed her long black scarf on the dresser, but I instinctively reached for her old wound before she could cover it.

"Oh, poor Máriam! What happened?"

"It happened a long time ago," she said. "It doesn't hurt anymore." She got hold of her scarf and carelessly tied it back on, despite the fact that it was almost time for bed.

"But what . . . did someone hit you?"

She clearly hadn't intended for me to see the scar. For a long moment she studied me guardedly and then looked past me at something too distant to be contained by the Hojedas' walls. Whatever she saw caused her eyes to narrow; she recoiled slightly, but soon lifted her chin, defiant and resolute.

"My hair caught fire," she said at last, watching me carefully. When I nodded to encourage more explanation, she motioned me to the bedchamber. I went obediently, and when Máriam gestured at the chairs in front of the hearth, I sat in one. She took the other and stared into the flames. When she spoke again, it was at the measured pace of a storyteller.

"It happened thirty years ago this coming summer, doña. I was thirteen years old and worked as a laundress for the Convent of the Incarnation; I'd shown myself to be a hard worker and was given much responsibility—in the form of more bedding to wash from their hospital and orphanage.

"They allowed me to farm the work out and gave me an allowance to pay for it. They never asked where I took it, but they knew, as I did, that the cheapest labor could be found in the Jewish Quarter.

"I found a woman there—a lady, actually—who was fast and reliable. She always took the time to get the stains from every sheet and scrubbed them until they were white again. Her name was doña Raquel. She lived in one of the nicer homes in the Quarter and was well-spoken. She had a charming eight-year-old daughter called Raquelita, 'little Raquel,' and three older sons. Her husband, don Moisés, was a rabbi, a very learned man whose study was always filled with books.

"Unlike most, they didn't look down on me for being born a Muslim and an African. They always shared food with me, especially during their holidays: Doña Raquel always worried that I was too thin and worked too hard. I began to give her more and more work, because although she and her husband came from aristocratic families, the laws made it almost impossible for Jews who weren't bankers to make a living. Even so, doña Raquel was always taking food to the poor."

I couldn't look at Máriam anymore. I stared into the fire along with her and fought the urge to put my fingers in my ears. I didn't want to hear any more sad stories about Jews. I wanted to put my mother's past behind me and to forget how cruelly I had rejected her for it; at the same time, I couldn't stop listening.

"Doña Raquel was not only generous and kind but a very beautiful woman," Máriam continued. "Had she been a Christian, she would have married well and lived a pampered life. But she remained faithful to her religion—a very brave thing to do—and she loved and respected her husband. And she treated me like a friend, as if I were a real Spanish lady like her. For two years, I delivered laundry to her twice a week, and I became very fond of her and of little Raquelita, who helped with the laundry and was always grinning and playful. Raquelita told me my skin was beautiful and was always stroking my arm just to touch it; I used to lean down so that she could pat my hair, because she loved how soft it was."

Máriam smiled fleetingly at the memory, but her tone soon darkened.

"But I worried about them, too. Attacks on Jews were as common then as now. And one afternoon I was carrying a bundle of dirty laundry to doña Raquel. Her house stood on a corner in the *judería*, and I always knocked at the servants' side door. Normally I wouldn't have turned the corner to see the front of her house, but that day I heard angry shouts out in the street, so I peered around the side of the building.

"A group of seven men, maybe more, stood out in front of doña Raquel's house—all Old Christians, all laborers or poor. There was a butcher in his bloody apron with a cleaver in his hand, and a blacksmith with his sleeves rolled up and his sledge-hammer resting on one shoulder, and a man with a burning torch." She closed her eyes at the mental image. "You probably don't know how narrow all the streets are there—not wide enough for me to lie down crosswise. The men pressed together around doña Raquel's front entrance.

"One of them was saying terrible things about Jews, calling them names and blaming them for a missing boy. And I could hear don Moisés calling back that he would never harm a precious child. But the other man yelled, 'All Jews are filthy liars! You're the rabbi; either you or one of your flock has him! Give him back—or at least give us his body!'

"If doña Raquel hadn't been so good to me, I would have run away; I knew there would be trouble. But I went back the way I'd come and pounded on the side entrance.

"No one answered, so I opened the door and called out to doña Raquel and her daughter. They didn't answer, but I could hear the girl crying in the front of the house.

"I followed the sound and found Raquelita clinging to her mother's skirts in the kitchen. Doña Raquel was staring out at don Moisés, who had stepped out into the street. It was hot and the window was open; we could hear every word and I could smell the men's sweat. The two older sons must have been off working, but the youngest son—maybe ten or eleven—was standing in the threshold just behind the rabbi. He was frightened but also red-faced with anger for his father's sake. 'Devil worshipper,' they called don Moisés, 'swine' and 'stinking Jew,' even though he was a very clean man and they were the ones who stank.

"Doña Raquel was trying to hush her daughter, and when she saw me, she put her fingers to her lips and touched my shoulder to keep me from getting too close to the window; we stood back in the shadows so the men outside couldn't see us.

"One of the men demanded that don Moisés let them into the house so they could search for the missing boy. The rabbi politely refused, saying the only children inside were his own and that he didn't want them to be frightened. He said, 'My God and yours forbids us to kill. We are good people and obey the ten commandments. My family is just like yours.'

"For that, the man stepped forward and spat in don Moisés's face, and another pulled his beard. His son couldn't stand it and pushed past him to strike the man who'd spat at the rabbi.

"It was a child's clumsy blow and did no real harm. Some of the men laughed, but two of them grabbed the boy and forced him to spread his hand out against the whitewashed stucco wall. The butcher came forward with his cleaver and was going to chop the boy's fingers off, but don Moisés became surprisingly strong. He pulled the men off his son and pushed the boy back inside the house. Doña Raquel rushed forward and caught her son before he could run back out, and I held Raquelita fast and tried to soothe her.

"Doña Raquel pleaded with her husband to bolt the door and run out through the side entrance, but don Moisés instead ordered her to go herself with the children, quickly. His tone was stern, but his voice caught; by then, the men had started beating on the door to come in, and don Moisés braced himself against it, trying to hold them off. A look passed between them, one of such pain and love that I lowered my eyes to give them a final moment's privacy.

"But doña Raquel refused to leave don Moisés. She told me to take her daughter and son and run with them. I tried to take the boy's hand"—Máriam's voice grew husky with sorrow—"but he pulled away from me; he wouldn't leave, either. And the men were at the door shouting.

"They broke down the door"—Máriam clutched her elbows and leaned forward in her chair, her liquid black eyes reflecting the orange hearth light—"with the blacksmith's hammer, and except for the rabbi, we all screamed when the wood splintered. In an instant, the door was open and the men rushed in and—"

She broke off and let her forehead touch her knees. Her voice muffled by her skirts, she moaned, "Oh, Marisol! What makes people capable of such evil?"

I put a hand on her strong back and stroked it the way my mother used to stroke mine when I needed comfort. Máriam shook with so much grief and guilt that I struggled against the impulse to weep with her.

After a moment, she lifted her head and sat up with an unsteady sigh and wiped her eyes on her sleeve. Her voice became unnaturally calm and dull.

"They killed don Moisés with one blow of the sledgehammer. I looked away after the first second, but I saw the instant it struck the crown of his head, and heard the horrible crack. Saw the blood flying through the air, and the bits of . . ." She couldn't finish the sentence.

"And the blacksmith hit him again, again . . . with those awful sounds. Before I could move, a man with a torch ran toward us. I turned to run with Raquelita, but not before the attacker thrust his torch at my and doña Raquel's heads. I was a girl then and had let my hair fall free and uncovered, so it caught fire immediately. Raquelita was screaming, too scared to run, but she was small, and I picked her up and ran without even thinking about the pain. By then the curtains and doña Raquel's skirts were burning, and smoke began to fill the house. Doña Raquel and her boy wouldn't come with me, but as I dashed into the other room with my hair on fire, I could hear her over the men's shouting. She wasn't screaming or frightened; her voice was strong and calm and she was singing a prayer."

Gooseflesh lifted the hairs my arms. I shifted my body in the chair to face Máriam. "What was the prayer?"

"Aleinu l'shabeach l'Adon hakol . . ." Máriam said. "I can't remember the rest. Do you want to know what it means?"

A thrill coursed through me. Judaism was wicked and of the Devil; I'd rejected my own mother for uttering such prayers. Yet I suddenly wanted to understand with all my heart—even knowing that if our conversation was overheard here in the Hojeda house, our lives would be at risk.

Máriam pressed her lips to my ear and recited: " 'Let us praise the Lord our God, King of the Universe, Who has commanded us to sanctify His name in public, Who has not made us like the nations of other lands, nor like other families of the earth.' It's the Jewish martyrs' prayer."

I listened, rapt. When Máriam drew back to study my reaction, I whispered a question, fearing the answer.

"What happened to doña Raquel and the boy? And Raquelita?"

She shook her head sadly. "The mother and son perished in the fire, if the men didn't kill them first. And the next day, when I went back, their home had been burned to the ground. I don't know what happened to their older sons; I pray they heard the news and fled to safety.

"I took Raquelita to the Orphanage of the Incarnation," she said, suddenly scrutinizing my expression. "I didn't tell the nuns where I found her, but I'm sure they knew. They were kind to her and gave her a new Christian name, and since I worked at the laundry nearby, I visited her whenever I could. To me, she was like a little sister. And I felt I owed it to her mother.

"And when Raquelita grew older and got married, I went with her to live in her household. With her and her husband, don Diego. Except that she wasn't called Raquelita anymore."

I couldn't speak. I couldn't breathe. I saw clearly the source of my childish shame that made me loathe what I was: I had been foolish enough to listen to men whose God was too small, too humanly jealous and tyrannical. I stood up and opened my arms.

Máriam stepped into the embrace gratefully. We held each other tightly while tears and grief and love seeped from me like water from an underground spring.

When I could finally talk, I kissed her and drew back, my palm pressed to her soft, soft cheek. Surely Máriam's pain was the worst of all: She had rescued Raquelita from her tormentors, only to see them claim her life after three decades. But I was still here, living proof of a lowly servant's courage.

"Thank you, Máriam," I told her. "Thank you."

Eight

That night, with Máriam asleep in a cot at the foot of my bed, I dreamed of my mother. I had once seen a drowned neighbor girl fished from the river after two days; her once-agreeable countenance had become a grotesque death mask, her cheeks and neck so bloated that her face was no longer the shape of an oval, but a pear. Her skin was ghastly, waxen white save for a blush of blue-gray over the closed eyelids and the swollen, parted lips; a clinging rivulet of hair traced an uneven diagonal from her left brow, across one eye and her slightly open mouth, to her puffy jawline.

When I'd set eyes on her, I had been too shocked to scream or cry, but had rushed away, thinking I was going to be sick. Instead, a visceral panic overcame me, and I sank to my haunches, struggling to breathe.

In the dream, I saw that face again, close up—only it metamorphosed into my mother's horrific yet beautiful face. But before I could become anxious, I realized that I was suddenly looking at it from very far away. I was on the eastern bank of the

Guadalquivir near the docks, and my dead mother was standing, her hair and clothing twisted and bedraggled, on the opposite shore. I shouldn't have been able to recognize her; the river was so broad that a person standing on the west bank should have appeared no larger than a fly, but in the dream I saw her clearly. Eerily, the wooden bridge spanning the water had disappeared, and there wasn't a single sailing ship or fisherman's boat in the river to block my view. The water was still as glass, reflecting the bright sun like quicksilver.

And then her corpse opened its eyes, and the blue-gray lips curved upward as it smiled at me.

For some reason, this didn't frighten me—quite the opposite. As my mother waved to me, her frightfully tangled hair fanning out in the triangular space between her shoulder and lifted arm, I felt a rush of pure relief and joy, to the point of tears. I understood now why she had behaved as she did, and wanted only to ask her forgiveness and to apologize to God for thinking that He could ever be less compassionate than I was, that He could damn such a good-hearted woman to hell for all eternity.

Even asleep, my beliefs shifted away from those endorsed by the *converso*-hating preachers toward those of love and tolerance.

I began to laugh, and my mother laughed, too; it had all been a great mistake. We had thought she had died, but here she was, alive. My first impulse was to go get my father, who would be overjoyed at the sight of his wife, but then I realized that I should simply take doña Magdalena home instead. Yet with the bridge gone, I couldn't reach her; the water was too deep and dangerous to swim all the way across.

As I puzzled over this, studying the river and the bizarrely empty docks, something on the opposite shore caught my eye. I glanced back again at my mother; she was looking more herself with each passing second, but now she wasn't alone.

Antonio—his red-gold hair dazzling in the light—was standing next to her, smiling.

He was a hand's span shorter than Gabriel, but the top of my mother's head didn't quite reach his shoulder; his presence restored her fully to life and beauty. I had forgotten how handsome Antonio was as a man, how brilliant his smile. At the realization that I saw him, he too lifted his arm and began to joyfully wave.

The next morning, alone on the lumpy feather-and-straw mattress, I opened my eyes to the gray light and saw Máriam in profile, kneeling on the carpet in front of the olive-wood dresser, where the bright ceramic Madonna rested. Somehow Máriam had dressed and rewound her black scarf without waking me.

From her reverent posture, it was clear she was praying, but her lips didn't move and her hands were lifted in front of her face, shielding her eyes from the sight of the Madonna.

I rose quietly. She was startled when she heard me move and dropped her hands to regard me warily, as if I were a viper that had slithered into the room. I didn't answer the question in her eyes with words, but, still in my nightgown, padded barefoot from the bed onto the worn carpet and stood beside her.

I didn't reach for my rosary as usual, but knelt down next to her, crossed myself, and folded my hands in prayer. Except that after the first Hail Mary and Our Father, I began speaking silently to my mother.

What could I have done to save you? Why didn't you trust Papá to take care of us? Why did you feel that you had to die?

I knew the answer to the last question: My mother had convinced herself that her death was the only thing that could save us from the Inquisition. I couldn't blame her or Máriam or my father for it. I could only blame myself.

If I hadn't stumbled that night . . . If I'd run a little faster . . .

If I hadn't rejected you . . .

I thought of the jeering boys in the street crying *Marrana! Marrana!* And I understood that the pain I felt at their rejection—and at my father's rejection of me—was no worse than the pain my mother had suffered for years when I had turned away from her.

If I hadn't been so frightened of their judgment . . . If I hadn't been so weak . . .

If I hadn't, if I hadn't, if I hadn't.

Kneeling, I relived my mother's death a thousand times. When I was done, I glanced at Máriam beside me and didn't flinch at the sight of her hands still blatantly shielding her eyes from the Madonna's face. Instead, I responded to her second challenge by crossing myself, rising, and leaving her to pray as she wished.

The days that followed between Christmas and New Year's were dismal ones, even though the weather turned sunny and clear. I spent them walking the Hojedas' huge courtyard, trying to outpace loss and rejection. In fresh daylight, the grounds looked even more rundown; the triple fountain with Saint James Matamoros, the patron saint of the Lion King, looked as though it had been drizzled with blackish green mildew, and the water in the basins was opaque with mud. No flowers bloomed on the property; only clumps of weeds and tangled, sickly boxwoods lined the paths, full of debris from the recent rains.

The walls in all the rooms were dingy and cracked, the floors dirty and uneven from wear. The grand dining chamber and hall were empty of all but the most immediately necessary furniture for the home's inhabitants; obviously, no one had entertained here in years.

I'd been raised in a household with some thirty servants, and my father wasn't considered as rich as the Hojedas, but when I learned that there were no other servants besides an old chambermaid named Miguela, Lauro, and the recently hired Blanca, I began to have doubts. We'd all assumed that don Jerónimo had held on to his wealth, but the estate clearly hadn't been well cared for in decades.

At breakfast on the day after our wedding, my husband had looked wan and pained; I never mentioned the incident at our wedding dinner, and Gabriel answered my few questions about my household duties with meek, weary monosyllables. To my frustration, he refused my offer to be of use, saying that Lauro went to the market and did all the gardening, and that he, Gabriel, preferred to handle the finances. I had no allowance but was to depend on Gabriel to provide for me and was to make no decisions. Since I was in mourning, I was not expected to leave the house on errands unless it was to church or some necessary destination, in which case, Gabriel would take me.

I was, in essence, imprisoned on the estate and sentenced to boredom.

"Most of all," Gabriel said, ducking his great head at the table to stare shyly down at his bread and hard cheese, his voice dropping to a whisper, "you aren't to speak of last night. To anyone, especially my brother."

I looked up at him, trying to keep my smile fixed and my gaze innocent-looking—even though I'd just learned where a possible source of power in my otherwise helpless position lay. "Of course, husband," I answered sweetly. "Of course."

Gabriel went off to be with his brother on New Year's Eve Day. I was allowed to attend Mass with Máriam at my family's Church of San Francisco, a spare but massive brick sanctuary built in the shape of a Latin cross and twice as large as San Pablo. My father was surely there among the throngs, but I kept my gaze fixed on the worshipper immediately in front of me, purposely avoiding an encounter.

I had few conversations with my husband, who preferred to keep his own company outside of breakfast and supper. Our meals tended to be mostly silent, with me occasionally asking questions about how things were done in the Hojeda household, and Gabriel providing shy if curt answers. He never again accosted me the way he had at our first supper.

But in the early dark hours of the New Year, Gabriel returned home from celebrating with his brother at Fray Hojeda's fine quarters at the monastery. Asleep in bed, I woke to the sound of his tread, slow and heavy on the stairs and then shuffling out in the loggia as he made his way to his room. On the way, he passed mine, and his footsteps suddenly stopped as they reached my door. I froze, listening, and after an instant of breathlessness, released a sigh as he moved on to his own quarters, his unsteady footfalls betraying another night of overindulgence in wine.

I fell back to sleep. Sometime shortly afterward, I woke again, this time to a drawn-out hissing sound, which made me start, thinking at first in my drowsy stupor that a snake was in my bed.

Almost immediately I realized that I hadn't heard a snake at all, but sliding of the bolt on the other side of what I'd thought was a locked closet door.

I sat up quietly. Máriam lay in her cot at the foot of my bed, her faced turned away from me, toward the fire; I couldn't tell whether she was awake and didn't want to risk making noise by calling to her. Instead, I remained frozen, clutching my blanket, and in the ebbing hearth glow saw the door between the fireplace and the western wall open no more than a sliver, only to have its rectangular shape immediately outlined by an interior light. The wood groaned and let go a sharp snap; I sensed a presence on the other side of the door and drew in a breath, steeling myself.

But the door never opened farther. Instead, someone on the other side began moving stealthily away. The light emanating from the crack dimmed at the same time.

I slipped from the bed, dashed on tiptoe toward the door, and pressed my ear to the wood. I could hear treads receding into the distance; surprised, I wormed a finger into the crack, thinking to enlarge it so that I could peer in without being noticed.

My plan failed. Improperly hung, the door swung wide open into my room, forcing me to take a step forward and grab hold of the jamb to keep from falling.

In front of me, a narrow windowless passageway led from my wing to Gabriel's. Halfway to other entrance, a retreating hulk held a lit candle.

As I recovered from stumbling, Gabriel turned toward me and lifted the candle, the better to see me; caught by his breath, the small flame flickered, causing his shadow to loom and writhe against the stucco walls. The corridor was cramped and the ceiling low, forcing him to crouch. Even so, his body, pale as a marble ruin, its edges fading into the dimness, reminded me of a Roman gladiator's: naked and powerful, its torso a broad V that narrowed at the whittled waist and spread to its broadest point at the shoulders, which were so heavily muscled that he couldn't turn his thick neck without his chin brushing against them. His legs were equally as sculpted.

As much as I disliked him, I was still young and aching from lurid dreams about my lost Antonio, and never having seen a fully naked man, I was curious. Gabriel's body was beautifully sculptured. I stared frankly at the thatch of golden hair at his pubis, and the erection, straight as a white arrow, emerging from its center. I should have run away for modesty's sake, but I was too entranced to move; the sight brought a giddy rush of warmth, a stirring between my legs.

I parted my lips, fascinated, and held my ground: Part of me wanted nothing to do with Gabriel, but another part of me longed to be touched by a man, to rut there, on the floor of the airless, musty corridor. For a long instant, Gabriel and I stared wide-eyed at each other, he panting so that the shadows on the cracked stucco jumped up and down with the candle in his hand, and I praying that he would take me then, while hoping just as fervently that he would not.

I broke free from the sensual spell and came to myself at the realization that Gabriel's stare had become narrowed and fixed, his breathing ragged; he seemed about to lose control.

"On the night my mother died," I whispered suddenly, "you were watching the house. Why, Gabriel? And why did you follow?"

The question caught him off guard, so much so that he blurted out an answer without thinking.

"I've always been watching you, Marisol. I've always hoped . . ."

The slurred words made me shudder, but they broke his trance. He became suddenly embarrassed by his confession and his nakedness and turned away, revealing dark stripes upon his otherwise white shoulders. In an instant, he disappeared back down the dark passageway. I waited a moment to make sure he was gone before stealing down the corridor to see what lay at the other end.

It led directly to his bedchamber. He'd left the door slightly ajar so that I could see one corner of his room, but not him. I didn't press my luck, but stopped well before the threshold to linger, listening, in the dark passageway.

His breath came harshly enough to hear; I started as he let go a sharp whimper. The sound almost made me turn away in disgust, until I heard the whistling of a many-tailed whip, followed by Gabriel's cry of genuine pain.

A moment of silence was followed by a prayer uttered so rapidly, it seemed all one word: *"Lordhavemercyuponme, a poormiserablesinner! Christhavemercyuponme . . ."*

As the lash sung again, I tiptoed back down the passageway. The door could only be bolted from Gabriel's side, but I shut it as tightly as I could and dragged a chair over to block it.

By then, Máriam was awake and standing by the hearth. She asked no questions, and I volunteered no answers, but crawled back into bed and pulled the covers over my head.

New Year's Day passed uneventfully; I never saw Gabriel, who slept late. I went to Mass with Máriam at San Francisco and took my supper in my room. Several times that day I looked out the window at my family home, hoping to catch a glimpse of my father: As furious and hurt as I was, I still worried about him. On the previous New Year's, his house had been filled with guests and song, but now it was dark and silent.

On the second of January, 1481, I awoke the hour before dawn to see Máriam sitting straight up in her cot. She slept between me and the hearth, and the glow of the dying fire behind her kept her features in shadow but provided a crisp silhouette, right down to the few downy, riotous hairs at her temple that had escaped her braids. Her body was motionless but tensed with dread, as if a great spider were crawling on her arm and she dared not move lest it bite her.

I sat up, too. "What is it?" I hissed.

Her face, invisible in the shadow, turned toward me. "Don't you hear it?"

Even before she finished the question, I heard the progressively nearing drum of hoofbeats and the rumble of wooden wheels. Over this came the occasional drone of men's voices.

"It's an army," she said. With that, she flung aside the covers, found her neatly folded clothes, and began to dress rapidly. When she had wound her scarf around her head, she looked over at me, still sitting in the bed.

"Up," she said. "Let's get you dressed."

I was too exhausted to share her urgency—until I went to the window, pulled back the drape, and wiped the condensation from the cold pane.

In the street below, the men-at-arms who had once guarded my father were standing out in front of the Hojedas' protective walls—but now there were more than twice as many, some armed with long sharp pikes, others with swords. Another dozen stragglers, pikes in hand, were still hurrying down the street toward the house, while three mounted men, their horses pawing the cobblestones nervously, shouted commands at them.

The sight made me catch my breath and step out onto the balcony, forgetting I wore only my nightgown. To the south—my left—at the intersection of our cul-de-sac with San Pablo Street, eight soldiers sat on horseback, two of them bearing torches whose light revealed red-and-white caparisons beneath their saddles.

One of the men down below hooted in amusement at the sight of me in my nightgown. I retreated back into the room.

"There *is* an army," I said. "They're wearing the royal Castilian colors. And my father's guards are surrounding this house. I'm going to ask Gabriel what's going on."

"Ah, no!" Máriam called after me, grimacing. "Not *him!*"

It was too late; I was out the door and almost collided with young Blanca in the loggia. She was dressed and smiling, unfazed by the soldiers and weapons outside our walls.

"Good morning, doña Marisol," she said cheerfully, with an awkward curtsy. "Don Gabriel sent me to tell you to stay inside today. He's going downtown."

"Did he say why? What are all the soldiers doing outside?"

"I believe it has to do with the Inquisition. They're making an announcement in the public square," Blanca replied.

Half an hour later, I watched from my window as Gabriel rode off in his carriage, surrounded by an escort of several mounted men-at-arms. I tried to obey his command to stay inside, but my curiosity was too great. And the tolling of the bell meant that tens of thousands would hurry to the square; my chance of being detected in such a huge crowd was slim. For my father's sake, and my own, I wanted to hear what the Inquisition had to tell us—and I didn't trust Gabriel to tell me the whole truth when he was clearly holding back some of the reasons he'd married me.

Lauro, it turned out, was easily bribed into harnessing horses to a wagon for us. Both Máriam and I covered ourselves in black shawls, hiding our faces; fortunately, she knew how to drive, and together we set out for the square.

At the bell's summons, hundreds were swarming out of houses, churches, and shops into the street. The constant stream of pedestrians caused other carriages and wagons on the broad avenue to slow; before long, our way was blocked by a stalled mass of bodies and vehicles with cursing drivers, and our wheels creaked to a stop.

A good quarter hour passed before our carriage lurched and began to move again. At last we made it to the intersection of San Pablo Street and the broad thoroughfare leading to the great Plaza de San Francisco. With each creak of the carriage wheel, my dread increased, but I forced away all thoughts of the Inquisition and looked out at the city.

The day was cloudless, and the low risen sun was already casting off the chill and gilding the buildings, including the variegated clay brick walls and the tall crenellated watchtowers surrounding the Franciscans' compound, larger than a city block and almost as sprawling as the magnificent royal residence, the Real Alcázar, which lay farther southeast. By the time we finally rolled into the monstrous brick plaza in front of the western entrance to the compound, at least ten thousand citizens had already gathered.

We navigated past monochrome flocks of Benedictine friars

all in black, Carthusians in all white, Franciscans in gray or brown, and townsfolk in the full spectrum of color. Eventually we made our way close enough so that, standing on the wagon bed, we could see the front platform pressed against the compound wall, where public announcements were made. That day, a black-and-white Dominican banner—a fleur-de-lis cross above the motto *Laudare, Benedicere, Praedicare* ("Praise, Bless, Preach")—hung behind the dais.

City soldiers with pikes ringed the platform two men deep in a large half circle, within whose guarded perimeter stood scores of black-clad priests and of Dominican friars sporting the white habits, black capes, and broad-brimmed black hats of their order. Their gazes kept returning to a spot near the base of the platform, where two other monks and an elderly judge stood talking.

After another quarter hour, the bell finally stopped tolling. A hush fell over the great plaza as several armed local police, swords unsheathed, mounted the stairs leading up to the platform. Behind them, two Dominican friars ascended. The first was a short, slight, elderly man wearing an engaging smile; his partner was a full head taller and too well fed. The smaller of the two set a large sheaf of papers down on the podium and gripped its wooden edges with the confidence of a practiced orator as he surveyed his audience. The taller friar, his clasped hands hidden from the chill by his long sleeves, waited motionless behind the speaker.

The podium faced east, so that the speaker squinted almost directly into the rays of the rising sun; he shaded his eyes with one hand and with the other gestured at the glare and quipped over his shoulder to his partner: "The light of God."

He chuckled and the other monk laughed politely.

"In nomine Patris, et Filii, et Spiritus Sancti," the speaker intoned.

Despite his small size, his ringing tenor filled the air. His manner was relaxed, even jovial, as if half the crowd listening to him were not *conversos* waiting to react angrily.

"Good morning," he said pleasantly. "My name is Fray Miguel de Morillo; I am the vicar of the Dominican Order in Spain. I address you today at the behest of the monarchs, Her Royal Majesty Queen Isabel of Castile and León and His Royal Majesty King Fernando of Aragón. May God keep and bless them both. I will read to you first a letter from the monarchs appointing myself and my good brother in the faith here, Fray Juan de San Martín, prior of the Dominican monastery in Burgos"—he acknowledged the taller man with a quick smile—"as Inquisitors for the Holy Office in Castile. This letter will be posted on the plaza wall for those who are able to read it for themselves. I will also read a papal bull from His Most Blessed Holy Father, Pope Sixtus, as well as two edicts—one from the Inquisition and one from our royal monarchs. Afterward, the town magistrate, The Most Honorable Judge Diego de Merlo, will read a third edict dealing with civil matters."

Fray Morillo checked to be certain the papers before him were in order and reached into his cloak to retrieve a pair of spectacles; the light glinted dazzlingly off the lenses as he put them on his face. He cleared his throat, and when he spoke again, it was with a stern authority that negated his earlier display of goodwill.

"From the hand of the Monarchs," he said, glancing down at the pages on the podium, "Her Most Esteemed Royal Majesty Queen Isabel and His Most Exalted Majesty King Fernando, published this second day of January in the year of Our Lord Fourteen Hundred and Eighty-one. To the people of Castile and the city of Seville in particular.

"In order to stamp out the heresy that has been growing unchecked in Castile and León, and most noticeably in Seville, we, the Monarchs, being zealous for the faith, do hereby appoint the venerable fathers Fray Miguel de Morillo, Vicar of the Dominican Order in Spain, and Fray Juan de San Martín, Prior of the Dominican Cloister of San Pablo in the town of Burgos, as Inquisitors. We commend to them the task of combating a peculiar heresy promulgated by certain persons who are Christian in name and outward appearance only, but who, after being baptized of their own volition, chose to turn away from the true faith and cling to the Jewish superstition and its rituals.

"We have instructed the venerable fathers to proceed with an Inquisition against these infidels, and have full faith that Fray Miguel and Fray Juan will carry out their duties diligently until the heresy is banished.

"However"—Fray Morillo's tone went dark—"should these men fail in their duty, we Monarchs have obtained permission from His Holiness Pope Sixtus to dismiss them and appoint others in their stead."

At this, a rumble traveled through the crowd, from the front of the plaza to the back. Near us, an Old Christian peasant cried out: "Fuck you, *marrano* swine; your days are numbered!"

From a safe distance, another voice called back: "Fuck you, Dominican liars! May God send you straight to hell, where you belong!"

Stray shouts followed; the guards surrounding the dais lifted their pikes, ready to fend off attackers in case of a riot. In front of them, battalions of city soldiers had stationed themselves in case the crowd became unruly.

Fray Morillo miraculously raised his voice above the noise.

"Please!" he exhorted. "Anyone here today who raises his hand in violence against anyone else for any cause will be struck down by Christ Himself! Did not Jesus say, 'Pray for your enemies, and bless those who persecute you'?"

What Fray Morillo did not address was the terror that had been born in the heart of every *converso* listening; no ruler in Christendom had ever been given the right to direct an Inquisition. That power had always rested in the hands of the pope, because of the obvious danger that a king might be swayed more by domestic politics than church law.

Fray Morillo finished reading the letter, which ended in a prayer that God would keep the Inquisitors of Spain steadfast and guide them in their holy task. Afterward, he set the letter at the bottom of his sheaf of papers and began to read a papal bull—one that had been signed by Pope Sixtus more than two years earlier.

The bull was in Latin. I knew enough Latin to follow the gist: In recognition of the Spanish monarchs' sincere devotion to the faith, Pope Sixtus had granted Isabel and Fernando the power to appoint Inquisitors to quash the "Judaic deviation" that had infected Seville and other areas of Spain. Again, he reiterated that Seville was filled with so-called Christian converts who remained "practitioners of Hebrew traditions" and "emulators of Jewish ritual."

Until that moment, the bull had been only a rumor and easily dismissed. The pope had always been our ally, as church law had specified for more than a millennium that every Christian—recent convert or not—was the same in the eyes of God. My father hadn't taken fright when the Inquisition first arrived in Seville, because any Inquisitor was bound to report directly to His Holiness in Rome, who was obliged to uphold canon law to the letter. Sixtus had shown himself to be highly tolerant of Jews and befuddled by the distinction made in Spain between Old Christian and New. And we had counted on the pope's support.

Now it had just been withdrawn from us.

To all accounts, Isabel was not only extremely intelligent but a devout, compassionate ruler. It was said that she and her husband loved each other dearly. True, she was not saying all *conversos* were guilty of Judaistic heresy—but by allowing secret denunciations, she had taken away our strongest legal protection.

Morillo began to summarize the text in Castilian, which brought fresh reaction from those who had not understood the Latin.

"There is much more," he said sternly, to quiet the Old Christians' jubilation, as he retired the bull to the bottom of the stack of papers on the podium. "Hear now, city of Seville, the edict concerning those suspects who fled the Holy Office of the Inquisition and those who harbor them."

Frowning at the sun's glare, he began again to read: By order of the Spanish monarchs, the crypto-Jewish sympathizers the Duke of Medina Sidonia and the Marquis of Cádiz, rulers of Andalusian territories to our south—both of whom had provided refuge to "scores of thousands of heretics fleeing the Inquisition in Seville"—were hereby commanded to immediately eject these refugees from their lands and use all means to assist the Crown in returning them to the city. These *conversos* had confessed their guilt by leaving and were therefore subject to arrest and trial.

Should either the duke or the marquis fail to assist the Inquisition in this regard, they would themselves be subject to arrest, immediate excommunication, and seizure of their domains.

Old Christians greeted the announcement with cheers; this time, the *converso* faction was too stunned to respond. Never before had the queen threatened a noble in this way, nor had any large group of *conversos* been publicly denounced as heretics.

"Next," Fray Morillo announced, straightening his round spectacles as he studied his audience, "let me speak of the Edict of Grace. Along with God's judgment comes grace. In that spirit, we extend an invitation for the next thirty days: Those who come to us admitting freely that they have been guilty of such heresy are guaranteed that they will not face excommunication and execution for their crimes, but will be forgiven and, after a period of repentance, accepted back into the church.

"Those who confess their deviation from the faith must be prepared to testify against all other heretics of whom they are aware, as proof of their genuine repentance. Also, we exhort all true Christians who have any reason to suspect others of practicing Judaic rituals in secret to denounce them. Do not shirk this duty, as it is better to denounce your neighbor than to let him practice his heresy in secret and lose his soul to the Devil.

"But we also recognize that the threat of retribution might deter you from reporting what you have seen to the Inquisitors. The Holy Office has therefore decided to guarantee all witnesses complete and total anonymity. You will not be required to testify in person against the accused, nor will your name ever be made public. You are free to speak the truth without fear."

Uneasy murmurs rippled through the crowd. Before now, the accused always had the right to confront his accuser face-to-face.

It was simple common sense, intended to discourage a man's enemies from lying against him. Suddenly this protection was gone, and there was nothing to stop bigots from accusing every *converso* they knew of crypto-Judaism.

"With that," Fray Morillo said, turning his head and nodding to the old magistrate who had made his way up the stairs and now waited, parchment in hand, for his turn to speak, "I shall say God bless you and keep you, and make His light to shine upon you in these difficult times. These documents shall be published upon the plaza walls for all those who wish to read them for themselves. I now welcome Judge Diego de Merlo, who has an announcement."

He made the sign of the cross over the assembly, gathered up his papers, and with his fellow Inquisitor, hurried off the platform and down the stairs to disappear into a Dominican sea of black and white.

Judge Merlo was white-haired and gaunt, a man whose age had conferred on him a dulled awareness of his surroundings and a complete lack of self-consciousness. For a moment he stared blankly out at the massive crowd and then he started and squinted at the parchment, as if surprised to see it in his hand, and began to read without preamble. His voice was wavering and much weaker than Fray Morillo's.

"By order of the Monarchs Queen Isabel of Castile and León and King Fernando of Aragón," he said without emotion, "all Jews remaining in the city of Seville and her surrounding territories are expelled until further notice, so that their wicked influence over those Christians weak in the faith is removed and the Inquisition may do its work without impediment. They must be gone no later than three days hence, and may take with them neither silver nor gold, but only such items as are required to keep body and soul together.

"Nor are they to sell their properties. They are to leave them in the capable hands of the Inquisition's receivers, who will make an accurate record of such property and protect it until such time as the Monarchs give the owners leave to return."

He let go a phlegm-filled cough, and after several seconds of sniffling, added, "Her Majesty says to the Jews: 'I give you my protection as you leave. No one is to harm or obstruct you, or they shall answer to my wrath. The evacuation is to be peaceful and orderly.'" He wiped his nose with the back of his hand. "This is the edict of the Monarchs. It will be upheld by the police, the local militia, and Her Majesty's army, and will be posted on the plaza wall shortly."

He rolled up the parchment and shuffled away from the podium without a word of farewell. The square filled with noise as thousands of onlookers began to speak impassionedly to each other; at the same time, the Dominicans at the foot of the platform, including their head, Fray Morillo, headed swiftly inside the heavily guarded watchtowers of the Franciscan complex. Gabriel was no doubt among them. As they hurried to safety, Máriam and I retook our seats in the wagon and began—at a frustratingly slow pace, given the crowd—to make our way out of the plaza.

We were in motion when I spotted Antonio. He was in the group of Dominicans leaving the area in front of the podium and had turned to look at the crowd behind him. Something had prompted him to remove his broad-brimmed black hat, similar to those of the monks, but he wore a layperson's garb; the morning sun made his bright hair incandescent.

I had convinced myself by then that I had seen him the night of my wedding only because I had wanted to see him so badly— just as I had "seen" my dead mother for the past fortnight in the faces of passersby who matched her height and build enough to make my heart skip a beat. But the sight of him today brought me no joy: All of his natural cheerfulness was gone, and the face that looked past the scores of milling bodies separating us was paler and sadder than I remembered. His lips had parted in surprise on seeing me, but they soon closed, and he turned away without any gesture of acknowledgment.

Shaking, I put my head into my hands. Every person with power over my life was infected by the madness that had overtaken the Dominican Order. And my dearest friend, whom I had loved my entire life, had now joined the Inquisitors against me.

Nine

When I returned home that day, I was desperate to see my father—so much so that I slipped from the Hojeda house and crossed the street. I entered the gate and, for the first time, knocked on my father's door as if I were a stranger.

My father's valet answered the door. Don Diego hadn't responded to the city bell but had remained home. I waited on the threshold while the valet went back to fetch my father and was mortified when the valet returned to say that don Diego was indisposed and could not see me.

I told the valet about the Edict of Grace, the Jews' supposedly temporary expulsion from the city, and the pope's surrender of his power over the Inquisition to Isabel and her husband. I explained my concern over the Inquisition's willingness to accept secret denunciations, and I urged the valet to explain all of this to my father and tell him that I wanted badly to see him.

Crushed again by rejection, I went home, but not without

pausing to stare at the Vargases' house. Antonio had probably been sleeping there for some time without my being aware.

I kept myself up most of the night wondering why Antonio had never contacted me, even after arriving back in Seville. He had been watching silently in the Chapel of the Fifth Anguish as I was married off to Gabriel, and he hadn't uttered a sound. The thought gnawed at me until I rose from bed, careful not to wake Máriam, who slept as soundlessly as the dead.

I stepped over to the window and drew the curtain aside. Across the street, my father's house stood next to Antonio's, the windows of both dwellings dark and unrevealing.

I pressed a palm to the cool glass—hard, as if by doing so I could somehow break through the barriers that separated me from the two men I loved most—and let go silent tears. Physically, I was only steps from either, but I might as well have been a sea apart.

I was grateful that, for the next two days, Gabriel's work preoccupied him; he left early before breakfast and didn't return home until dark. We shared only one conversation at a late supper when he was clearly exhausted. Yet he was in good spirits, and after the meal, he asked me to sing for him, whatever I liked.

I was a bit taken aback. "How do you know I sing, don Gabriel?"

He dropped his gaze shyly, smiling. "You and your mother sang often out on the balcony. You have a very beautiful voice, Marisol."

I drew in a breath and began to sing an old ditty my mother

had taught me, one that gave humorous advice to newlyweds. I sang only one verse, then paused because the second mentioned the marriage bed, a subject I preferred to avoid.

Fortunately, Gabriel interrupted. "Do you play an instrument, Marisol?"

I shook my head.

My answer made him smile. "Oh, but a woman must learn an instrument! Then you can play for me when you sing." His grin broadened. "You must learn to play the lute!"

"If you wish," I answered automatically. I averted my gaze, as the question made me think of Antonio's serenade.

"Then you will," Gabriel vowed. There was an odd smirking playfulness in his tone and smile that I'd never seen before, but I thought no more about it.

Before the sun rose the next morning, Gabriel left for work, his carriage surrounded by mounted guards; he left word with Blanca that I was not to leave the house under any circumstances. By then, I'd been up for hours, unable to forget what day it was.

Máriam and I said not a word to each other but dressed in silence, grim and distracted. The morning was warm for January, and when the sun first peeped over the horizon, I threw a light shawl over my shoulders and went downstairs. Máriam went with me, and together we paced rapidly through the scraggly court-yard with its mildew-stained fountain capped by the statue of Santiago, patron of the Catholic monarchs, impaling a Moor on his sword. The sky lightened quickly; it was blue and cloudless, and the sun was strong.

We'd been striding aimlessly for almost an hour when we heard a shout coming from the cul-de-sac outside the house, from one of the guards keeping watch.

"They're coming! They're coming!"

Máriam and I shared a swift look and stole out the front gate. By then, the men-at-arms guarding the Hojeda house were all headed for the corner, where our little street intersected San Pablo's broad thoroughfare. I followed them, but not without staring at my father's house, where a coil of smoke coming from the kitchen chimney revealed the cook was already at work. Smoke rose from two of the chimneys at Antonio's house; the sight brought fresh pain.

We were not the only two hurrying to the intersection. The hunchbacked Lauro lumbered behind us, and Rosalina, my father's stout, square-jawed chambermaid, hurried out of Diego's house. A half dozen servants and I joined the men-at-arms, who stood with swords sheathed at their hips, their heads turned eastward toward the heart of the city. A cool brackish breeze came off the river, lifting dust from the cobblestones.

Despite the guard's calls, the eastern half of San Pablo Street was eerily empty on a weekday, but the rumble of wheels and clatter of horse's hooves filled the air; the stones beneath my slippers began to vibrate.

The soldiers, five abreast on fine horses, led the procession. They wore breastplates that glinted blindingly in the sun, and helmets with fine red plumes; each bore Isabel's shield of the red lion against a white background—for the legend of the Lion King, and León—alternating with the image of a yellow turret against a red background, the symbol of Castile. These were the queen's troops, and their horses rode side by side in perfect alignment.

As they neared, I could see an apparently endless parade of open wagons behind them. A young rabbi in black, the red circle pinned to his breast, drove the first, his wife sitting beside him holding on to a squirming toddler. In the wagon bed behind them sat a pair of silent, frightened children amidst blankets, bedding, plain kitchenware, worn clothing, water and oil jars, and flour sacks, all bathed in bright sun. The wife's face was lowered; she looked at no one but wept steadily onto the top of her impatient child's head while her husband stared grimly ahead.

As the rabbi's wagon rattled past us, the crippled Lauro shrieked, with such volume and ferocity that I started.

"Filthy Jews!" he screamed. "Child killers!"

"Go back to the Devil and never return!" one of the men-at-arms shouted. This caused a second guard to cup his hands around his mouth and call:

"Good riddance, Jewish scum!"

None of the Jews reacted at all, even though some of them walked alongside wagons that were too full to allow passengers. A youth my age—short and thin, his eyes wide with shock—marched past us on foot, flanking a wagon in whose center sat a very old hairless man, his skin gray from illness, his mouth open and drooling; I'd never seen eyes so frighteningly vacant.

At the instant the youth walked by us, barely two arms' lengths away, Lauro leaned forward, ignoring the scattered mounted soldiers that policed the edges of the parade, and spat at him.

The wad of mucus struck the young man's cheek and clung, glistening, on the coarse dark hairs of his sparse beard. His eyebrows rushed together as it struck; outrage rippled across his features, but instead of turning to look at his attacker, he shut his eyes. When they opened again, they were blank and fixed firmly

on the road ahead of him. Unwilling to acknowledge his tormentors, he didn't wipe the spittle away, but trudged onward.

One of the queen's soldiers monitoring the perimeters of the
procession saw the incident and cantered up behind the youth;
his hand on the hilt of his sword, the soldier gazed fiercely down
at Lauro.

"Someone tell this idiot there's to be no violence!" he called,
and rode off.

The second he was gone, Lauro and the men-at-arms began
to shout at the next wagon, so laden with personal belongings
that the owner led the pair of horses by the reins. He too looked
to neither side of the street—now lined on both sides with
onlookers—but kept watching those directly in front of him.

A beautiful young Jewess flanked the wagon on our side of
the roadway. Dressed and veiled in deep blue cloth shiny from wear,
she bore herself elegantly, proudly, despite the swaddled infant
in her arms. A crease of stark determination had formed between
her black brows, and although she had carefully fastened her eyes
on the horizon, her dark, intelligent eyes were narrowed with
hate, her delicate mouth a taut line that tugged downward at each
corner.

I couldn't help but stare. Though small of build, she was vo-
luptuous and full breasted, with features so like my mother's that
grief caught me unexpectedly.

"Don't ever come back!" Lauro screamed beside us, so loudly
that I grabbed Máriam's hand out of fright.

Beside him, one of Gabriel's men-at-arms hooked his little
fingers in his mouth and let go a piercing, derisive whistle at the
sight of her.

It was noisy, given the crowds, the rumbling wheels, the clattering horses, and her young husband, walking ahead of her, didn't hear. But the Jewess did.

She lifted her handsome chin and looked on the whistler with such defiance and scorn that I drew in a breath, terrified for her safety. But our guards only laughed raucously, pleased to have gotten her attention. As she shifted her attention from them, her gaze caught mine and lingered there. The fury faded immediately from her expression; disbelief took its place, followed by astonishment, then pity.

Pity at the sight of me—at my dark, unruly Semitic hair and features, at my dark eyes. As if she knew that she had already lost everything of value but was managing to escape Seville alive to go to a place where she would be free; as if she knew that her misery was almost over, but mine, a *conversa's*, had yet to really begin. My sheltered sense of reality crumbled. I, a heretofore insistent Christian, could no longer deny that there was no difference between us, no right or wrong religion, no good or evil save that found within the human soul.

The Jewess averted her eyes and moved on. I suddenly remembered my mother's hopeful story about Sepharad. The last lines repeated themselves in my head:

Can the Lord God move through a woman?

Surely He moved through Queen Esther. And perhaps He can do so with Queen Isabel, who made us weep with joy when she wrote the Jews of Seville, saying: "I take you under my protection and forbid anyone to harm you."

... We look to our Visigoth queen with hope and pray for her success and the time when we can raise our voices again in the streets of Seville.

I looked again at the soldiers' shields and the images of the lion and the castle tower. Surely Isabel, the most pious ruler in all Christendom, was simply unaware that her orders were bringing about such suffering; surely she would have wept had she learned of my mother's unnecessary death, and would weep now to see the pain in her Jewish subjects' eyes.

I swallowed hard at the abrupt, unwanted welling of tears, knowing they would make me an outcast among the Old Christian hecklers. Behind the young Jewess, the parade of human suffering stretched to the horizon; in it, I saw the enormity of my cruelty toward my own mother and broke.

The next afternoon, Fray Hojeda arrived at the mansion, his stern visage bright with anticipation. Gabriel conferred privately with him in the sitting room for a few hours, during which time I was obligated to remain in my quarters. Supper was served late as a result. When I came down, Gabriel informed me that I would need to be ready to go with him the following morning for what he described, with a furtive smile, as a "surprise." His little smile seemed ingenuous enough, but Máriam and I trusted him not at all.

The next morning, I had Máriam lace me into the nicest of my mourning gowns and together with her went downstairs to meet my husband with feigned enthusiasm. His grin, as he wished me a good morning, was as forced as my own.

"Are you ready for your surprise?" he asked in a strangely playful tone.

I could only nod, wide-eyed and solemn.

Ever since the Edict of Grace had been read in the city square, Gabriel rode in the carriage surrounded by men-at-arms each time he went out. That morning was no different, and when our carriage turned west toward the river, I tensed; Gabriel's preoccupied silence during the ride did little to ease my dread. By the time we slowed in front of the Church of San Pablo, I felt a cold thrill, and when we passed behind the walls surrounding San Pablo's monastery, I clasped my hands in my lap to still their trembling. I couldn't bring myself to look at Máriam, who was surely just as terrified. Was Gabriel taking us to be questioned by the Inquisition?

Our carriage rolled past a vast brick dormitory three stories tall, one that was rumored to serve as a prison for those arrested on suspicion of heresy, although only those who had been inside knew for certain. Its windows were shuttered, its delicate turrets unrevealing; built centuries earlier under Islamic rule, its once-smooth stone exterior was pitted with age. The lower floors featured rows of slender archways with beveled stone edges, mullioned windows, and a half dozen armed guards standing watch at each entrance; the upper floors featured lacy wrought-iron balconies covered in rust, and three-dimensional spirals of tiny bricks that bloomed in magical bas-relief from the stone walls. It was warm that day, and the breeze through our open carriage window carried the stench of overstressed latrines.

I put a discreet hand to my nose to block the smell as the carriage came to a stop in front of a nearby outbuilding, a small, one-story rectangle of wood and plain, whitewashed stucco that had probably once served the Dominicans as a storage facility. Gabriel instructed the driver to take us around to a back entrance, one hidden from the larger building's view. Once we rolled to a stop, he turned to me.

"Are you ready?" he asked. His manner and voice were pleasant, but his eyes held strong emotion; anger, I thought at first, but it was something more complex.

"For what?" I asked, almost too shaken to speak at all.

"Your lesson," he admonished, as if it had been obvious. "With the lute, of course. Remember?"

"Oh." I gaped at him an instant. When he seemed irritated by my hesitation, I quickly added in a more cheerful tone, "Oh! What a wonderful surprise, don Gabriel!"

"I'm glad you're pleased," he answered tersely, in a tone that said he was not. "Stay in the carriage; I'll be back in a moment. There are monks and priests inside who would be unsettled by a woman. I'll make sure the way is clear." He moved, stooping, as the driver opened the carriage door; as Gabriel's hand caught the edge, he looked back over his shoulder at me.

"Remember, my brother and I have been kind to you: I offered my house and protection to you, to save you from Old Christians who are not as fair-minded as I am."

"Of course, I'll remember," I said, confused.

"Lower your veil. There are monks inside," he said.

Gabriel lingered in the doorway, watching until I covered my face.

My world grew darkly filmed, visible only through gaps in the black lace cutwork. I could make out only one of Gabriel's pale eyes and part of his sunburned nose; I listened to his stern voice as his invisible mouth said, "Stay here until I come for you."

I obeyed. Máriam and I were too tense to utter a word until Gabriel returned a few minutes later and led us into the small building. The smell of refuse and urine grew stronger as I climbed from the carriage; I held my breath as I glanced at the prison windows, unrevealing in daylight. Once we stepped over the threshold of the smaller edifice, I took in the smell of fresh whitewash and sawdust.

Happily, the hallway was empty and very narrow; to my right, unpainted wooden walls had been hastily erected to create small, separate rooms in what had once been a large open area. Gabriel led us to the closed door of the room nearest the back entry, knocked, and motioned for us to enter ahead of him. I stepped inside, with Máriam close behind.

And there was Antonio.

He stood alone at a reading pedestal, staring down intently at a sheaf of notes. Beside him, stacks of papers rested on a brand-new desk equipped with wooden compartments for holding files. The office was small, with one tiny window overlooking the kitchen gardens filled with parsley, bright green from the rains. Although the wooden interior walls were new, the exterior ones were old, with dust-covered spiderwebs veiling the corners of the ceiling.

Antonio glanced up as we three entered. Once again, his deep-set eyes stole my breath; they were the dark, impossible blue of lapis, startling against the contrast of his pale skin and generous red-gold brows. His lips remained tightly pressed together; they didn't part in astonishment, as mine did beneath my veil. He scarcely glanced at me but instead exchanged curt nods with Gabriel.

We hadn't seen each other in almost two years, but it may as well have been a decade: Antonio was only twenty years old, but his dark, solemn air made him seem far older, as if his father's death and other sorrows of life had aged him too soon. The light streaming through the open window caught the first lines in the pale, delicate skin at the corners of his eyes, where they crinkled when he smiled. But Antonio wasn't smiling now. His expression was sad and darkly serious; whatever he was reading made him sadder. His tunic and leggings were black, as if he were in mourning or a priest or monk; the color was too harsh for his coloring and made his skin look chalkier than it was.

I stared at him—at his broad turned-up nose, his generous lips, and oval clean-shaven face, all conspiring to make him neither too pretty nor too plain, but pleasant to regard. He wore his golden red hair brushed straight back now, revealing his fair forehead and a widow's peak; thick waves fell against his long neck to just below his collar and curled around the backs of his ears.

At once I was swallowed by the memory of the kiss we'd shared the day of his father's burial. He'd seemed so childlike then, so lost, although he fought to master his grief. At the funeral, he had wept openly, his arm around his frail mother's shoulders. Later that afternoon, he and I met alone beneath the huge olive tree in my father's yard. His eyelids were swollen, the rims red, but by then he had spent his tears and was dry-eyed, if dazed.

I had put my hand on his shoulder and let him talk. He didn't look at me, but instead stared out toward the river, at the distant horizon.

"I failed him." His voice was naturally musical and soft, and that day, it was even softer, almost a whisper. *"I was gone too long without visiting. . . ."*

"You were at university," I said, caressing his shoulder. *"You were doing what your father wanted you to do."*

"You don't understand." His lips stretched thin and then began to twitch; a grimace passed over his features as he struggled to contain himself. *"My father suffered. He suffered greatly for a long time, and I wasn't there. And by the time I came to him, I couldn't help. There was nothing I could do. . . ."* His voice trailed; he lowered his head and closed his

eyes. *"I wanted only to ease his pain."* A tear spilled onto the sunbaked earth.

"Oh, Antonio." I slipped my hands beneath his arms and embraced him, pulling him toward me, and nestled my head in the hollow of his chest.

To my surprise, he gently lifted my chin with his finger. *"Life goes on,"* he murmured. *"I know only one thing, Marisol: that I want to spend it with you."*

He lowered his lips slowly to mine.

A muscle tugged involuntarily between my legs, igniting a fire that traveled upward through my spine, past the pit of my stomach, and up to my breasts. The hairs on my arms lifted, as if lightning had just scorched the air. I put a hand behind Antonio's head and pushed him closer until I felt the hard outline of his teeth beneath the flesh, until our breath steamed the gaps between our faces. I peered through the faint dark tracery of my lashes to see his eyes open a slit, like the crescent moon, the sunlight reflecting off irises as dark blue as water.

Just as quickly as it had come, the memory of the kiss evaporated, but as I stood staring at Antonio in his tiny office in the Dominican outbuilding, the fire and lightning lingered. Antonio observed decorum and addressed Gabriel first, his manner one of scrupulous propriety, his startled gaze careful not to light on an unfamiliar young woman.

"This is the cousin you mentioned, Gabriel? I was expecting a young man. . . ."

Antonio failed to use the word *don,* an honorific reserved for nobility and those well established and respected in the community, even though his household servants had taken to calling him don Antonio years earlier. Undoubtedly he used Gabriel's given name in an effort to be neighborly, but Gabriel chose to be sullen.

"Not exactly, Antonio," my husband responded, pointedly emphasizing the name and thus the lack of honorific. Gabriel gestured to me with one hand, while the other, hanging by his side, curled and uncurled into a fist; his jealousy was palpable. "This is my wife."

I lifted my veil.

Antonio flinched as if struck. His features slackened, causing his mouth to gape slightly for a heartbeat before he mastered himself and closed it. Even then, his eyes remained wide, and his lips worked a few times to form my name before he managed to expel the word:

"Marisol." He cleared his throat and looked, stricken, at Gabriel, both of whose fists were now clenched, his downcast face violet. Antonio cleared his throat and repeated hoarsely, "Marisol . . ." He looked owlishly at my husband. "*She* is the student?"

Gabriel nodded, disabled by rage, unable to look up at either of us. "She wants to learn to play the lute," he said between gritted teeth.

Antonio's eyes narrowed beneath thick golden red brows. "And *you* brought her here?"

"With a chaperone," Gabriel countered defensively. He thrust a chin in Máriam's direction; her dark face remained impassive, her gaze artfully innocent, although a bit more of the whites of her eyes showed than usual. "You told me that no one comes back here except you. That *is* the truth, isn't it?"

"Of course," Antonio said. "Only rarely does someone else come back here; if Fray Morillo needs me, he rings for me."

Still in shock, he nodded a greeting to Máriam, whom he'd known since childhood; the gesture conveyed wistful regret that he couldn't welcome her more properly. Máriam's rosy brown lips curved faintly upward in reply.

Then Antonio looked to me. I lowered my face, aware that, like Gabriel, I must have been flushing brightly.

"The driver will be back for her in an hour," Gabriel continued stiffly, scowling down at the papers on Antonio's podium. He looked over at me, his eyes imploring yet threatening. "See to it you remember what I told you," he muttered at me, and ducked from the room, closing the door behind him.

For a long instant, I stood frozen, listening to Gabriel's receding tread in the hall, followed by the sharp slam of the outbuilding's rear door. Only the faintest murmur of voices emanated from the front of the building, where the rest of the occupants dwelled. Antonio's office was so distant from the others that when Máriam wandered to the far corner of the room and turned her back discreetly to us, it was as if we two were alone.

Ten

I stood staring at Antonio as he came around the reading stand toward me, my expression cold.

"Perhaps you don't want to see me," I hissed, remembering the honest distress in his voice when he'd asked Gabriel, She *is the student?* "Perhaps I should follow don Gabriel and leave now."

I wheeled about, thinking to do just that. But before I could lift my skirts to run out, Antonio stepped in front of me and put a polite if sympathetic hand on my elbow—the platonic touch of a stranger, not a friend.

"I was so sad to hear of doña Magdalena's passing," he said, lowering his already-soft voice. "I am so sorry, Marisol."

I pulled my arm away, as if his touch stung. "And did your friend Gabriel tell you how she died?" My tone was scathing.

He recoiled; the look of pained sorrow on his features made me darkly jubilant. "Marisol," he said sadly, simply. "Marisol, I *am* sorry."

He moved toward me, arms open to comfort me, but I took a step back and held up my hands to fend him off.

"Why do you care?" I taunted him. "The Dominicans are happy she's dead. You work for them now."

Antonio closed his eyes to hide the painful emotion in them as he slowly lowered his arms.

For once I was glad to see him suffer, and I tried to land another verbal blow. "Aren't you afraid the other Inquisitors will see you hugging a *conversa*?"

His eyes snapped open. "I'm not an Inquisitor; I've taken no vows of celibacy. I serve as secretary and scribe to Fray Morillo. I manage the case files of the accused."

Fray Morillo, the tiny, powerful head of the Dominican Order in Spain, had read the papal bull and Edict of Grace in the town square. I turned my head in disgust at the sound of the name.

The sympathy in Antonio's expression transformed to distrust; his voice became an accusatory whisper. "Why are you angry with me? I wasn't the one who married someone else. I saw you with him in the chapel, Marisol."

"After you deserted me," I responded coldly.

He gaped as his red-gold brows rushed together. "How did I desert you?" My retort so surprised him that he forgot himself and asked the question in full voice.

I whispered an angry reply. "Where *were* you for those eighteen months? Or should I ask *with whom*?"

He shook his head in disbelief at the question and lowered his volume. "How can you say such a thing to *me*? You know where I've been. It's you who abandoned me." His tone hardened. "To think that you would marry Gabriel—of all people."

I bristled, remembering the young Antonio sitting beside me in the old olive tree, saying: *You're New Christian, I'm Old—and together, we could make a bunch of little Christians.*

"You have no right to criticize me," I said.

Antonio's mouth thinned to a slash, one corner slightly tugged down.

I glanced at the papers neatly arranged in the wooden cubbyholes on his desk, and knew that each of the dozens of sheaves represented a life, like my mother's.

"I bear no grudge against Gabriel," he said softly. "But I don't understand why he brought you here, to me, and left us alone. Aren't you curious as to why?"

I was but had no intention of discussing it with Antonio; I thought that perhaps Gabriel was punishing us both out of spite, although I couldn't explain why he would leave me alone in the presence of a man who made him quake with jealousy. Instead, I walked over to the window and nodded at the lute carefully propped against the far corner of his desk. Sunlight glistened off its shiny lacquered soundboard, in whose center was carved a round rose, as delicately intricate as the finest Moorish stone fretwork on now-Christian cathedrals. I had seen this very lute in Antonio's arms before, when he'd serenaded me at my mother's window.

"I'm here to learn to play," I said shortly. "I think we should focus on that."

He lingered, watching me unhappily for a few seconds, and then drew a long breath.

"All right," he said. "I'll teach you. Here."

He pulled a stool from behind the desk; Máriam reminded us of her presence by hurrying to bring a second chair from the back of the room. She set it down near the desk and ducked her head shyly, smiling as Antonio thanked her, then hurried back to her distant corner, once again turning her back discreetly to us. She'd always loved Antonio; her smile and courtesy to him irritated me, as I considered them disloyal.

Antonio kept the chairs at a discreet distance. I sat with my back to the window with the light from the window streaming over my shoulder. Antonio lifted the lute with practiced care and sat on the stool, settling the instrument into his embrace, and strummed the strings.

"All right," he said. "First I'll play a simple tune with only a few chord changes. This first time around, just watch the position of my fingers."

He began to play a popular song, one I knew well, about a long-lost love returning. He'd plucked out the first phrase when I felt a flush of heat on my cheeks and neck; he stopped abruptly, realizing what he'd done, and launched into a different melody.

It was a bright, cheerful song with a driving rhythm, and I shifted my weight in the chair, relaxing a bit as Antonio sang softly in his whispery baritone.

The first line of the ditty always made me smile; it was supposedly the wife of an innkeeper singing, chiding her amorously neglectful husband and explaining why she strayed. I fought to ignore the lyrics and keep my gaze on Antonio's fingers, but it was difficult.

I hang my sausages in the kitchen with care
And feed you and our guests the same
But you so rarely stroke my hair
Or call me loving names.

The song continued on, with references to handsome young travelers and, of course, the sausages in the kitchen, comparing the husband's "wanting portion" to the more generous ones served to the male guests at the inn. As children, we'd sung the song to our elders and they had smiled patronizingly at us, thinking we missed the double entendres.

I fought to pay attention to his long fingers as they moved over the strings at the fret, but I soon found my attention wandering to his face. Antonio's gaze was lowered, fixed on a spot on the aged stucco wall behind me. Whatever he saw in his mind's eye was pleasant; the somberness lifted from his expression, revealing the old cheerful Antonio behind it. I felt my resistance melting despite myself.

> *Oh, how I could resist*
> *His sausages, well stuffed?*

As Antonio sang the line, the corners of his eyes crinkled, and a spark of joy lit up his face; his lips stretched into a faint crescent. I didn't intend to smile myself; the expression formed against my will, just as my right foot began involuntarily to keep time. I sang the next two lines with him:

> *Oh, how could he insist*
> *Our tryst should be so rushed?*

Antonio looked shyly up at me, his smile deepening; he nodded in gentle approval and looked away again, losing himself in song. And for a moment, just a moment, I allowed myself to forget everything—my mother's death, my father's rejection of me, my marriage to Gabriel—and let my voice soar, as strong and as clear as my mother's once was. I dissolved into the present, remembering only that I was singing again with Antonio, that he was alive and well and we were together, and that the rollicking music was balm for my wounded heart.

As we launched into the third verse, the door was flung open, startling all three of us. Two Dominican nuns in white habits topped by black cloaks and veils appeared in the doorway. One was quite old, with a deeply wrinkled face and thick spectacles that magnified her eyes. A young sister held her elbow supportively and led her into the back of the room without a word to Antonio or to me. Immediately, they knelt in deep curtsies—the older woman doing so with some difficulty, leaning heavily on the younger. They were bowing not to us, but to someone in the doorway.

I turned in my chair. A third woman stood on the threshold, surrounded by a group of Dominican monks in white and black. She was taller than most of the men next to her, large boned and stately in a modest black silk gown, the casing for the *verdugado's* hoops in velvet, her bodice trimmed with the finest black lace I'd ever seen. Her matching lace veil covered straight, thick auburn hair, parted in the middle and pulled back into a thick, silk-wrapped braid, and a small gold crucifix rested on the shelf of her prominent bosom; she wore no other jewelry save a thin gold wedding band. She was plain, with a long, horselike face and a nose too long and too thin, with pinched nostrils; her lower lip was very full, her upper bowed and thin. Although she was far from old, perhaps thirty, there was already a fold of flesh beneath her weak chin; her dark blue-green eyes, shallow and heavy lidded beneath slight overplucked brows, exuded a jaded air.

Yet she was smiling, baring the considerable gap between her two large yellow front teeth and clapping in time to the music.

Antonio looked on her and rose so quickly that the lute slipped from his grasp and struck his stool, causing the instrument's wooden belly and strings to protest. He set the lute on the floor so carelessly it rattled, and he offered a sweeping bow, keeping his eyes fixed on the ground.

I jerked to my feet, unclear as to exactly who the woman was, but I too curtsied and dropped my gaze.

"Oh, don't stop!" the woman encouraged us. "Rise, rise! Keep singing!"

"Of course, Your Majesty," Antonio replied, and promptly picked up the lute.

Standing, he gracefully tucked its wooden belly in the corner of his right arm and caught the neck with his left hand. And I, fool that I was, straightened and began to tremble from pure nerves as I realized that I looked on Her Majesty doña Isabel, Queen of Castile and León, the most powerful woman Spain had ever known. It seemed impossible that she should be here, in Seville; she rarely traveled this far south, but preferred to stay near her palaces in the Old Christian strongholds of Toledo, Segovia, and Madrid.

"Your Majesty," I gasped, so overwhelmed that I could scarcely utter the almost-inaudible words. I found myself staring at her and immediately looked away at Antonio. He caught my eye as he began to play the opening notes of a more sedate, formal tune.

"No, no," doña Isabel called, still grinning toothily. "Play what you were playing before!"

Antonio's eyebrows lifted, and a spark of merriment shone in his eyes as he began to pick out the melody, adding embellishment this time. At the same time, he shot a polite, sidewise glance at the queen; she noted the whimsy in his gaze and responded by widening her gap-toothed grin and nodding.

In an instant, she was clapping again to the rhythm with a childlike lack of restraint, ignoring the perplexed expressions on the faces of the nuns and monks, most of whom lifted their arms but could not bring themselves to clap in time along with her.

But I clapped and somehow managed a smile, and when Antonio launched into the music again, singing harmony to my lead, I gave my voice free rein and let it soar as high and loud as it wished.

> *I hang my sausages in the kitchen with care*
> *And feed you and our guests the same . . .*

Doña Isabel and I kept time; she sang with us, her voice low, soft, off-key. I should have remained terrified, but the queen's manner was so irresistibly friendly and engaging that I thawed at once, realizing that my teacher wouldn't be punished for having a female student in his office. So did Antonio, and together, we gave a remarkable performance, perhaps out of sheer relief, winking and gesturing at each other when delivering the more-suggestive lines.

> *Oh, how could I resist*
> *His sausages, well stuffed?*

Doña Isabel laughed aloud and nudged the monk standing beside her. "Clap, Fray Tomás!"

Fray Tomás was half a head taller than she, so motionless and so quiet that I hadn't noticed him at all. He was altogether ugly: His tiny hazel eyes were embedded in folds of flesh; his hair, mostly gray with a few streaks of dark brown, was excessively curly and shaved in a monk's tonsure, so that only a riotous fringe, as soft and cloudlike as Máriam's, encircled his otherwise bald skull.

His head was large and square, his eyes, ears, and mouth very small in proportion. His huge nose eclipsed his face: It was thick and bulbous, with large, broad nostrils and several bumps in the bridge. Unlike his queen, the monk didn't smile. His lips were entirely invisible, leaving only a taut, thin line of flesh against flesh for a mouth, tucked into the folds of his ponderous cheeks. His skin was brown and mottled with age—very dark for an Old Christian's, if he indeed was one.

As I glanced at Fray Tomás, he caught my gaze. His was like a freezing draft in an otherwise cozy room; his eyes were dead as frost.

In the next instant, he turned back to doña Isabel with a look of mild reproach and intentionally disregarded her command. I expected the queen to lose her temper at such insubordination, but Isabel merely shrugged her shoulders and ignored him, instead returning her attention to the music.

> *Oh, how could he insist*
> *Our tryst should be so rushed?*

The queen clapped again, keeping time as Antonio and I harmonized and began another verse. By then, I had noticed that behind the regal Fray Tomás stood Fray Hojeda, his plump, owlish profile revealing a forced smile.

The queen was obviously pleased and enjoying our music, but just as we were launching into the rousing chorus, Fray Tomás leaned down suddenly and spoke into her ear. Doña Isabel's smiled thinned, and her eyes hardened with faint irritation at the monk's words. She lifted her hand into the air, like a priest ready to make the sign of the cross; Antonio and I broke off in mid-note.

As Antonio hushed the strings with the flat of his fingers, Her Majesty doña Isabel smiled, her gaze bright, intent, and focused solely on me. I didn't know if anyone could tell my lips were trembling; I widened my grin, stretching them more tightly, hoping it would still them.

Doña Isabel spoke; her voice was deeper and huskier than I expected, her tone pleasant and infinitely self-assured.

"My wise confessor, Fray Tomás points out that this is not a place for rejoicing, but the more serious business of routing out heresy. But you sing so beautifully, my dear! Who are you?"

Before I could answer, Fray Hojeda leaned forward. "This is Marisol García de Hojeda, Your Majesty," he said quickly. "My sister-in-law."

Isabel eyed him skeptically. "Your sister-in-law? Really?" Neither mentioned the word *conversa*, but both were thinking it.

"Yes," Hojeda replied eagerly. "My brother, Gabriel—your civil prosecutor here in Seville—saw that she was in need of protection. I, of course, granted them permission to wed."

Looking unconvinced, Isabel moved into the room, her steps mincing, as if her shoes pained her. Once she was no longer braced by the doorway and Dominican friars in black, her thick waist and wide rib cage were visible, but other than the fold beneath her chin, there was no excess fat on her. Several other monks, including the two who had appeared at the town square for the Edict of Grace—Fray Morillo and Fray de San Martín—surged into the room behind her, along with a scattering of elderly nuns, until Antonio's little office was overcrowded.

"Well, doña Marisol García de Hojeda of Seville, you must explain to your husband that you are going tonight to the Real Alcázar, the Royal Palace, to perform at the court of Isabel, your queen. Your voice is lovely and pleases us. Where do you live? We will send a coach this evening. Come hungry."

I hesitated, but not overlong. "Off San Pablo Street, Your Majesty. On the Calle Hojeda."

"I and my brother will make sure she is ready, Your Majesty," Hojeda proffered quickly, apparently seeking an invitation.

But it was not forthcoming. "Very good," the queen said, pointedly refusing to glance in Hojeda's direction; his expression did not change, but his eyes narrowed at the snub. Her Majesty continued to address herself to me. "My coachman will come for you. I'm in the mood for cheerful music and will see you later this evening, doña Marisol. Bring your lute."

Still frozen in the curtsy, I caught my breath. It was presumptuous to speak to royalty unless given permission. Fortunately, doña Isabel noticed my desire to say something and hesitated the instant before turning away.

"Yes?" She lifted her dark, rust-colored brows at me; I forced myself not to quake at the faint impatience in her tone.

"I don't play the lute, Your Majesty. It isn't mine."

"Then bring your lute player," she said, with a swift gesture at Antonio, and turned her back to me dismissively.

"Your Majesty," Fray Tomás said, and waited until she nodded for him to speak. "The lute player happens to be the young man I mentioned to you—Antonio Vargas of Seville. Don Antonio recently received his degrees in both canon and civil law from Salamanca." Sotto voce—just loud enough for Hojeda to hear—he added, "The one I recommended replace the current civil prosecutor."

Replace Gabriel, that is. Hojeda directed a spiteful glare at Fray Tomás. It was humiliating enough that the queen had failed to invite Gabriel or Fray Hojeda to the palace; Fray Tomás's comment added fresh injury.

"Ah, the lad with the double degree," Isabel said, warming a bit as she addressed herself to my lute player. "Impressive. We've heard good things about you and look forward to seeing more of you during our visit, don Antonio." Her tone grew faintly sarcastic. "So he must be the reason you led me back to this closet, Fray Hojeda?"

She turned to smile at Hojeda.

"I did not expect to find him here with my sister-in-law unescorted," Hojeda countered. "Your Majesty."

The queen's smile never wavered. "The fault lies not with don Antonio, then, but with your brother, does it not? He should learn to be a more conscientious husband."

Hojeda flushed scarlet.

"I've seen enough," the queen told him. He bowed, nodding so vigorously that the waddle of flesh beneath his chin jiggled.

Isabel sailed past him. As he moved toward the door after her, I caught the look he shared with her confessor. Unnoticed by the queen as she stepped into the corridor, Fray Tomás lingered, regarding Hojeda with an air of contemptuous superiority, while Hojeda, his lips still curving in a frozen smile, shot the other monk a purely hostile look.

Fray Tomás turned his back to the abbot Hojeda with pronounced dismissiveness, and instead glanced at Antonio, who still clutched the lute.

"It's good to see you again in the flesh, don Antonio," the Inquisitor said, his tone far warmer than his manner toward the local abbot. "I trust your journey here was unremarkable?"

Admirably poised, Antonio gave a single long, gracious nod that served as greeting and answer. "I trust yours was as well, Fray Tomás, although I must admit I'm surprised to see your traveling companion. No one told me Her Majesty was coming."

The corners of the monk's lipless mouth curved upward, revealing small gray teeth like jagged merlons against a black sky, but the muscles around his eyes never moved. "I look forward to speaking with you tonight," he said silkily, "after you perform for Her Majesty."

"It will be my pleasure, sir," Antonio replied. Although he treated the Dominican with the courtesy due a stranger, the familiarity in his tone disturbed me.

"Fray Tomás!" the queen called sweetly out in the hallway. When the monk failed to respond at once, her tone grew faintly irritable, her manner of address less polite. "Torquemada! I am waiting!"

Even then, the Dominican's features failed to shift. He neither tensed nor hastened but glanced back at Hojeda to hold his venomous gaze an instant longer, his own once more so breathtakingly cold and predatory that I lowered mine rather than risk meeting it.

I'd heard the surname before. The famous Dominican cardinal, Juan de Torquemada, had died when I was a little girl. I knew of him because he was greatly admired by my parents and

Antonio and his family. That Torquemada had vigorously defended the *conversos* in the northern city of Toledo, successfully reminding Catholic officials in Spain that, under the church's own ancient laws, recent converts and Old Christians were equal in the eyes of God. Juan de Torquemada admitted that *converso* blood ran in his family.

I looked at Fray Tomás's hazel eyes and dark complexion and decided he was likely related. The name was an uncommon one.

"Torquemada!" Isabel snapped again. Only then did the monk respond by walking slowly out into the corridor to join his queen, his movements as regal and unhurried as hers, his air one of such limitless power one might have thought he was the monarch, not she.

With a dark glance at Antonio, Fray Hojeda held the door open as the others filed out; the tiny office emptied almost as quickly as it had been filled, leaving the two of us and poor Máriam, still owl-eyed and stiff after holding a low curtsy for so long. Hojeda shut the door behind him with a resounding slam.

My lute player and I remained silent until the footsteps receded into silence.

"The Hojedas are using you, you know," Antonio said with quiet anger.

I studied him coldly. "How so?" Admittedly, I had decided that Fray Hojeda had permitted the marriage only because Gabriel would inherit my father's property one day—but I was confused by the friar's sudden eagerness to claim me as a relative.

"Isabel's official reason for not appointing Hojeda as Grand Inquisitor—for not giving him *any* position, in fact—was that he is too radical. He claims all *conversos* are heretics by virtue of their 'unclean' blood. As King Fernando is a *converso*, Her Majesty took offense."

"So," I said slowly, "Hojeda was trying to prove to her he'd changed."

Antonio nodded. "Especially since she's traveling with Fray Tomás—Torquemada. Rumor has it she'll soon appoint him Grand Inquisitor—the position Hojeda thinks he deserves."

I believed Antonio but lifted a brow and pretended to be unconvinced. "Why should I believe you?" I countered. "Obviously, you're trying to take Gabriel's job away."

"Not I. Neither Fray Morillo nor Torquemada feels Gabriel is competent—and of course, there's bad blood between the Hojedas and Torquemada, who has the queen's ear." He paused. "The real question you should be asking is why Gabriel chose to bring you here at precisely the time Isabel was touring this building. And why Fray Hojeda brought Her Majesty back to this office when there is nothing to see but a clerk and his files."

"To see me, I suppose," I answered.

"And to show me neglecting my duties by entertaining a young married woman. With the door closed."

When we were sweethearts, I'd rarely heard Antonio utter a negative word; to hear him speak about such disgusting politics made me want to cover my ears.

"I've heard enough about the Hojedas and Torquemada," I said stiffly. "The queen has commanded us to perform for her tonight. Shouldn't we be preparing?"

Something very like embarrassment rippled over his features. "You're right, of course," he said softly.

Antonio and I didn't share another unnecessary word. The

unexpected encounter with Isabel and the realization that I had just received a royal summons to perform left me too shaken to cling to my rage, despite the fact that my tutor's friendship with the Dominican Fray Tomás disturbed me deeply. Instead, Antonio and I agreed on what songs we would play that evening for the queen and quickly rehearsed the tunes and lyrics. Antonio admitted that he had twice been at the queen's court in Valladolid, a day's journey from the university at Salamanca, and instructed me on the basics of proper behavior around Her Majesty. By the time my husband's driver returned to take me home an hour later, I had yet to deal with my sense of shock over all that had happened.

Máriam and I retreated to my chambers, where she immediately stripped me of my mourning gown, helped me bathe, and unbraided my hair. I was dazed during the process; seeing Antonio reopened an old hurt that made me want to weep. Together with my still-raw grief and my nerves over the thought of singing for the queen, it made me want to run across the street to my real home and find comfort in my father's arms—but those were now closed to me.

Instead, I fought to steel myself and listened to Máriam rattle on about whether I ought to dispense with black mourning, as it hardly seemed appropriate for a royal performance; I nodded without really hearing what I was agreeing with. Before I knew it, she had pulled out a dark blue velvet dress—one I'd had made back in the fall intending to wear this past Christmas—and spread it out on the bed to ease the wrinkles.

At one point, I found myself sitting in one of the rickety chairs in front of the basin in the antechamber, staring into the mirror as Máriam brushed out my hair. By then, I was dressed in my finest white silk chemise and Máriam had convinced me to put on my mother's sapphire teardrop earrings. A knock came at the door, and Máriam answered it to tell Blanca that I would be coming down for dinner that evening with don Gabriel, as I needed to speak with him about the summons from the queen.

Out in the corridor, Blanca let go an ear-shattering squeal. "The *queen*? Queen Isabel?" She peppered us with questions: How did Isabel look? What did she say? What was she wearing? Did she have a gold crown, or, as the simple and pious rumored, a halo like the Madonna? Was she as saintly as everyone said? Who was with her?

Blanca leaned forward in the doorway, watching as Máriam pulled out a long strand of my loose hair, holding it at the ends in order to gently brush the tangles out. Reflected in the mirror above Máriam's shoulder, Blanca's pale face was flushed, her features animated with excitement. For some reason, the sight made me break from sheer strain: Pampered and primped, my hair black tentacles in Máriam's fingers, I dissolved into wracking sobs, unsure precisely which emotion—heartbreak, rage, grief, anxiety—had pushed me over the edge.

I remember Blanca's eyes in the mirror, round and blue and thoroughly puzzled, as she recoiled quietly back into the hall. I was far from the joyful creature she expected, and she disappeared as I dropped my chin and let my tears drip onto the breast of my fine silk chemise.

Even then, Máriam was undeterred in her preparations. Once my damp emotional storm quieted, she put a cloth soaked in cold water on my face and made me lie quietly for several minutes. In the end, I saw myself transformed from a red-eyed, hiccuping girl into the same sort of gorgeous dark-haired, velvet-clad creature my mother had become the night of her death.

Gabriel was late coming home that evening. Half an hour after he was due, wheels rumbled against the cobblestones outside my bedroom window. I parted the curtains with my fingers and peered down at the black coach riding in through the gate. At first I worried that Isabel's carriage had arrived early for me, but before it passed out of sight, I glimpsed the crest painted on the door: the black-and-white fleur-de-lis formed into a cross above the motto *Laudare, Benedicere, Praedicare.* Dressed in the dark blue velvet gown with seed pearls lining the stiff matching cap and a few pearls woven into my uncovered braid, I stepped from my bedroom through the antechamber and peered from the covered loggia across the courtyard. Fray Hojeda—a great, thick blur of white topped by a black cape—hurried along the covered loggia from the driveway to the dining hall at a rate of speed admirable for his size. Even at that distance, the slam of the heavy dining-room door betrayed his mood. Gabriel wasn't with him.

I let Máriam put a matching blue cloak around my shoulders—it wasn't particularly cold, but the sky was overcast and a few halfhearted raindrops splattered against the dust—and hurried off across the desolate courtyard to the halls. I left Fray Hojeda undisturbed in the dining chamber, choosing to linger in a nearby sitting room with the door open so that I could watch my husband pass by when he returned home. The sitting room was off the kitchen; with the door pulled one-quarter ajar, I was hidden in shadows, able to see only the dining-hall entrance and hear those inside. I listened as Fray Hojeda called impatiently for wine; Lauro's lumbering steps in the kitchen followed, along with the tinkling of glass and liquid, and finally his shuffling progress into the dining hall.

"When will Gabriel be home?" Fray Hojeda demanded, and Lauro gave an inaudible reply. This was followed by Hojeda's insistence that Gabriel come immediately to the dining chamber upon his return and not stop to wash his face and hands for supper.

Lauro shuffled back to the kitchen.

By then the sun was beginning to set, taking the heat with it. My tiny sitting room lacked a fireplace, and I jiggled my legs to keep them warm, unwilling to close the door and block my ability to hear what transpired between the brothers. A quarter hour later, a second carriage rumbled onto the brick driveway. Soon Gabriel emerged onto the covered loggia, his head down, his mood dark and distracted. He would have turned toward the courtyard to head for his chambers first, but Lauro came out of the back kitchen entrance to intercept him.

Lauro stood a dozen strides away with his back to me. His stooped spine made him the shorter, allowing me full view of my husband's pallid, scowling face set atop a gladiator's too-thick neck and shoulders. Lauro's words caused Gabriel's scowl to deepen; he let go a hiss of frustration before turning and entering the dining hall.

Within an instant of Gabriel disappearing behind the door, Fray Hojeda began to speak earnestly, in a low, steady tone.

Not another sound came from Gabriel, however, until he rang for Lauro a few minutes later and asked him to summon me. Rather than wait for Lauro, I hurried to the dining-hall door and knocked timidly before entering and bowing to my husband and his brother.

Gabriel was standing staring into the fire, still in his cloak. Hojeda stood an arm's length away facing his brother's shoulder. At the sound of my approach, Gabriel turned; when he saw me, he let go a soft gasp. I was beautiful and knew it. I lifted my skirts and twirled slowly around so that he could enjoy Máriam's handiwork, thinking of how my mother had so often done the same for my appreciative father.

I smiled at my husband and greeted him cheerfully.

Carnal appreciation glimmered in Gabriel's eyes. "You look lovely, Marisol."

As the friar turned toward me, Gabriel went to the long dining table and sat down. Hojeda pulled a chair from the table across from Gabriel and gestured for me to sit as well. I did, and forced myself not to flinch or recoil as the friar put a hand on the back of my chair and lowered his round, massive head to the level of mine.

"You do look quite nice my dear," Hojeda said, but there was little sincerity in his tone; it galled him to treat me kindly. His breath smelled of raw garlic and the sour wine resting in his goblet on the mantel. "It's modest enough to suit the queen. But have you decided yet on what you'll perform for her?"

I nodded and explained that Antonio and I had taken advantage of our lesson period to rehearse what we would sing at court. I even mentioned the songs.

Hojeda listened carefully and gave a grudging nod. "You must understand," he said, "you'll be going alone. Not even a chaperone from your household." Squeezing the wooden edge of my chair, his fingers twitched at the notion.

I understood, all right. Fray Hojeda, who was most responsible for convincing Queen Isabel of the need for an Inquisition in Seville, wasn't invited to court tonight, even though his *conversa* sister-in-law was. His clouded gray-green eyes, the whites yellowed from years of excess, were narrowed with frustration at not being able to control my every move in front of the queen.

"That's why it's important that you remember everything," Hojeda said. It took all of my resolve not to turn away from his sour breath. "This Fray Tomás, this Torquemada . . ." He spat out the name, then forced his tone to become more pleasant, though his words were anything but. "He's an interloper, trying to steal power that doesn't belong to him. He was abbot of the Dominican monastery in Segovia, and quite by luck became the queen's confessor. He had nothing to do with the Inquisition—but now he's trying to steal everything, to become Grand Inquisitor, by manipulating Her Majesty's sincerity for the faith. Do you understand?"

I nodded; I knew raw jealousy when I saw it.

"For Isabel's sake, for the sake of Holy Mother Church," Hojeda said, "Torquemada must be stopped." He smiled unconvincingly at me. "But you can help us all, Marisol. Tonight, when you go to court, watch all the interactions between Queen Isabel and Torquemada that you can. Listen when you can and report back to me. If possible, you can put in a good word for me as your brother-in-law." He stressed the last three words. "After all, who understands Seville's problems better than I do? I called for an Inquisition before anyone else!" He paused to scrutinize me a long moment.

"You'll be playing with Antonio, of course," Hojeda added finally. "And it was clear today that he and Torquemada are well acquainted. Anything you can learn about that relationship would be very helpful." He paused. "Regardless of what happens tonight, remember that we protect and support you; remember that you are Gabriel's wife."

The friar's great round face was still only inches from mine. I looked down at the dining table's dark, pitted surface, caught in an arc of candlelight. "I'll do my best," I answered softly, although I had no intention of speaking to Antonio if I could avoid it.

Hojeda sensed my reluctance; he crooked his fat forefinger and used the knuckle to lift my chin so that I was forced to look into his murky eyes.

"Yes, you will, Marisol," he said, his smile hardening. "And you'll be sure that the queen comes to love us. Because"—he shoved his face closer until our noses were a mere finger's span apart—"your father is still under investigation by the Inquisition, and I know you'll do whatever's necessary to spare him imprisonment and torture."

Eleven

Two hours later, with an opal moon shining full in the night sky, the royal carriage arrived—ordered, as the queen had requested, by Hojeda himself. The coat of arms of Castile and León—the golden castle against a red background, the crimson lion against white—was painted on the carriage's lacquered black doors. As Lauro caught my elbow to help me climb inside, I saw my chaperone sitting inside on new leather cushions.

In the light of the carriage's lamps, I could see that she was matronly, her flesh hanging slack at the jawline, the swell of her ample belly visible beneath her bodice. Her hair, medium ash blond divided into two braids coiled over her ears, was more than half white, draped by a pale mauve veil held in place by large silver combs. Had she not been so old, one might have thought she was pregnant instead of overfed. Yet traces of faded beauty were still visible in her now-jowly face, in the upward slanting pale eyes hidden in folds of flesh, in the freshly pinched lips that smiled coolly at me. Her gown was far more magnificent than the simple black silk the queen had worn. It was made of gray brocade, its raised pattern of twining vines and leaves shot through with a glittery mauve sheen that flashed deep purple when the torchlight caught it right. Blue-gray velvet lined the edges of the full bell sleeves with the gossamer "butterfly wings," and the low, square collar of the bodice, which revealed pale aged breasts lifted as high and pushed together as hard as possible beneath her chin. The sight shocked me. I would have expected such immodesty of the French or Italians, but not from anyone at the pious Isabel's court.

"I am the Marquesa of Valladolid, but you may call me doña Berta," she said, her full cheeks dimpling. Her tone was so oiled and languidly aristocratic that at first I thought she was making fun of herself, and I let go a short, nervous laugh, only to realize in the next instant that her posh accent was no joke. She patted the cushion beside her with a hand that was impossibly white, small, and weighed down by jewels. "Come sit next to me, dear."

I slid in and settled beside her, fighting not to cough at her overpowering perfume, a mix of rose, jasmine, and sweet orange blossom. I felt suddenly uncertain as to whether a marquesa merited a curtsy and whether I should attempt one now that I was already in the carriage. My decision was made as our vehicle took off and we were thrown back against the cushions.

"I'll be your chaperone tonight," doña Berta said in her unctuous Castilian accent, and she launched into a summary of royal protocol, most of which Antonio had explained earlier. I was to stand when the queen entered the room, to curtsy, to speak only if spoken to, to address her as "Your Royal Majesty." I was never to touch her person. I was to keep my gaze downcast in her presence.

I listened to it all—including instructions as to what I should

do with myself when the queen had had enough of my singing—
as we rode through town, headed away from San Pablo Street,
past the Franciscan complex and the town square, toward the
southeast corner of the city where the Real Alcázar, the Royal
Palace, lay. The streets were empty after nightfall, save for one or
two carriages of the wealthy and a few drunken soldiers singing
on their way back from the brothels and taverns near the river
docks.

As we made our way toward the richest neighborhood in Seville, the crowd of now-closed shops, hovels, and modest houses
lining the streets thinned, giving way to orchards, private gardens, and the occasional well-lit mansion owned by nobles or
wealthy clerics. Soon we passed by the cathedral—the largest in
the world, built atop a ruined mosque, its fortresslike walls thick,
unrevealing save for a few high square windows that flickered
with faint internal light. Flanking its eastern side stood the
Giralda, the tall, ethereal minaret that now served as a bell tower.

By then, I could make out the tall, thick walls enclosing the
back of the sprawling palace grounds, over which rose slender
ancient palms, black against the indigo sky and swaying with the
slightest breeze. The wheels of our carriage rumbled off the uneven cobblestones, growing muted as they met the polished flagstone surrounding the Alcázar. We soon made it to the palace's
eastern side, lit by sconced torches and guarded by soldiers in
bright new armor, standing at attention beneath freshly unfurled
banners of Castile and León, red and gold and white.

A turn west, and we arrived at the front gate—a broad archway situated between two towers. The wall joining the towers
was painted the eye-popping red of my mother's geraniums. Just
above the arch itself was a crowned golden lion with a serpent's

forked tongue, the Lion King. It held up a Christian cross in its forepaw, a reminder that the monarchs of Spain were ordained by God to fight the infidel. No matter that the bricks beneath the paint had been laid three centuries earlier by Muslim hands, just as Muslim hands had planted the slender palm trees, now taller than the towers.

Beneath it, a score of carriages waited in line as the guards ascertained who was in each one.

I stared in awe. I'd seen the front of the Alcázar only twice before in my life—once when I was so small, my mother held me up in her arms so that I could see my father, along with other Seville notables, bow to King Enrique on a podium as he confirmed their appointments as city councillors. The second time, a few years ago, I'd stood cheering beside both parents to watch as litters carried Queen Isabel and King Fernando toward the Lion's Gate.

Doña Berta leaned out of the window and whistled at the guards in order to be heard over the clatter of hooves; the gesture was so at odds with her formal manner that I grinned before I could stop myself. Doña Berta caught the gesture and flashed a row of small gray teeth at me.

One of the guards heard the whistle and saw the royal crest on our door; he motioned for the other carriages to pull aside so that ours could roll through the gate. The long driveway beyond was of the same smooth, polished stone, this time flanked by trimmed, stately junipers surrounded by boxwood hedges. At its end, we passed beneath another archway of fine *mudéjar* fretwork; it opened out onto a courtyard the size of a small town square.

"And this is the Patio de la Montería," doña Berta recited, as if she'd said it a thousand times before, "where the hunting party meets."

There were no signs of a hunt now, only carriages emptying of passengers or exiting toward the stables.

I huddled in the carriage doorway as the driver helped doña Berta out. The patio was enclosed on three sides by the two-story palace. The red, white, and gold banner of Castile and León hung from every second-floor window, next to sconces lit above every slender colonnade. It was warm for a January night, with just enough of a breeze to keep the impossibly tall palms undulating, and the sound of music, crashing fountains, and conversation floated out into the courtyard. There were bright white, red, and gold paper lanterns and more lit sconces than I'd ever seen in one place; the play of the torchlight cast intricate patterns from the delicate stonework onto people's faces.

Once the driver helped me down, I paused so long to take everything in that doña Berta chuckled with glee.

"So, my darling," she said. "This must be your first visit to the castle. We have time for a little tour. Would you like to see some of the rooms few others get to see?"

I didn't need her narration to recognize the bleached red-brown stone facade directly in front of us, or the glittering white marble threshold. I still remembered how my father, on describing his first visit inside, had spoken of the reverence he felt as he stepped on the white marble at the entrance to old King Pedro's Palace.

Pedro the Cruel, they call him now—but my father said they hated Pedro because he protected the Jews and was too tolerant of Muslims. I craned my neck back and looked up at the white-washed third-floor tower perched atop Pedro's palace. Beneath the white tower was a thick stone cornice, and beneath the cornice was a frieze. The outer edges of the frieze had Gothic words carved into the stone; the center consisted of shiny dark blue tiles arranged in Kufic script, a stylized written form of Arabic.

I blinked my eyes at the sight, remembering how my father had relayed the experience with relish and how my mother and I had sighed with envy. As Berta beckoned me along and my feet touched the white marble threshold, I felt a wave of grief, wishing that I could share this experience with my parents.

We passed by more soldiers still as statues, their backs pressed to the walls as if they supported them, their armor so assiduously polished that I had to look away or be dazzled. Doña Berta led me past another archway into a huge high-ceilinged reception room, where more soldiers lined the walls, which sported bright blue, green, and yellow azulejo tiles arranged so that they created elaborate medallion designs; even the steps leading up into the room were trimmed in colorful tiles. Servants liveried in red, white, and gold served wine and food to the guests, who made their way to long tables covered in red linens. A group of pipers played in one corner, softly to allow conversation; the center of the room was open for dancing and for mingling. The earliest guests were already sitting in sparse groups at the tables with food and drink.

Antonio was standing and chatting at one of the tables with a seated elderly man, a well-known noble in town. At the sight of me, Antonio excused himself from the conversation and hurried over. Like me, he was dressed all in dark blue—a fact that embarrassed me, as it made us look as though we had planned it. But the color made his lapis eyes even more striking and brought his red-gold hair to life. Even with his lute hung by a strap over his shoulder, he managed to bow gracefully to the middle-aged doña Berta, who giggled as he solemnly took her plump, bejeweled hand and kissed it. He was resoundingly handsome and as poised as a courtier, despite the fact that he had nicked his chin shaving.

"My lady," he said with a flourish. It was the proper term of address for a marquesa, and doña Berta didn't fail to be flattered. "I am Antonio, the lutist for doña Marisol."

Doña Berta put her kissed hand to her heart and grinned at Antonio with senile lust. I, on the other hand, could scarcely bear to look up at him. It had been hard enough earlier that day to be in the same room with him. When I failed to greet him or smile, doña Berta lifted a thin plucked brow.

"So," she said, with childlike eagerness. "Have you visited the palace before, don Antonio?"

"I have," he replied.

Berta sighed with disappointment. "Well, at least follow me to where you'll perform," she said, crooking her finger flirtatiously at Antonio, and took off at full stride.

We followed her through another archway out into a different courtyard. A long, narrow reflecting pool ran through its center, flanked on either side by flagstone walkways. The walkways were in turn flanked by sunken gardens—that is, long strips of grass planted with miniature orange trees in full bloom. Nearby, water spilled from a flower-shaped fountain, thrumming like rain as it splashed into the basin, filling the air with a cooling mist. Berta led us to a nearby cluster of potted palms at one end of the reflecting pool. The shaded loggia surrounding the patio's perimeter boasted walls covered in bright glittering tiles, broken by a continuous ring of arches and slender colonnades, each archway leading back to another arch inside the palace, which in turn led to another distant archway, giving a sense of infinity.

"The Patio of the Maidens," Berta announced proudly, as if she'd had a hand in its creation. "When I tell you, come right here to this spot"—she pointed at her feet, and arranged herself in the position we should face—"and when I signal, begin to play."

I'd heard of the Patio of the Maidens. Everyone knew the old legend that the Muslim rulers supposedly claimed a hundred virgins from the kingdom of Iberia every year and that they were brought here for inspection. A few like the Hojedas said the women were sacrificed to the Devil, while most believed that the women were forced into the royal harem. Others, like my parents, were more skeptical. "History is written by the victors," my father would say, and shake his head.

"How soon will we play?" I asked. "A few minutes? An hour?"

Doña Berta grinned frankly at the question.

"The queen will be ready when the queen is ready," she answered lightly. "Don't worry. I'll find you when the time is right and let you know when to begin. You have at least an hour, maybe two. In the meantime, you and I will continue our little tour."

She led Antonio back to the reception hall, saying he should be sure to remain there and not wander off.

"And now, my darling doña Marisol, let me show you a few rooms you might not have the chance to see tonight."

She led me through a maze of corridors, each grander than the last. We wandered over floors of white marble, then black-and-white tile, through rooms connected by an apparently infinite series of archways. At last we came upon a chamber connected to the others on either side by three arches supported by slender black marble columns. I thought I had already taken in all the glories the palace had to offer in the front room of King Pedro's Palace; I was mistaken.

"The Salon of the Ambassadors," Doña Berta said with smug pride. "Her Majesty reserves this room for her most important guests."

I took one step through the archway and could go no farther; the sheer glory of the room stopped me cold. It was lit not by a hearth or sconces, but by several massive gold candelabra, taller than I, placed along the walls and corners. A faint film of smoke hung in the air, conspiring with the dim light to soften all edges; what lay exposed in the candle glow seemed unearthly, unreal. This was not a room but a piece of jewelry, a work of art that had taken many *mudéjar* craftsmen many years of demanding labor.

Beneath a high ceiling, the lower quarter of the four walls consisted of glazed white tiles covered in interlinking blue-and-green geometric patterns: hexagrams, triskelions, circles, and bars. The tile, which ended just above my shoulders, was impressive enough, but what lay on the walls above it made me gasp.

Every bit of space was adorned with delicate raised plaster-work that looked like carved stone, formed in a riotous collection of intricate designs: medallions, curves, scrolling vines, arches—all geometric patterns, as the Muslim rulers who built the palace believed that representing the human form was forbidden. The raised plaster was stark white, its every curving edge gilded so that the wall glittered like a gem. Bits of pale blue and green paint had been sparingly applied in spots to give a hint of color. In the flickering half-light, the patterns shimmered and seemed to shift. There was no place for the eye to rest save the polished marble floor, no spot that failed to catch the light and gleam.

"Beautiful, isn't it?" Berta crooned. "You're lucky to have laid eyes upon it; most Sevillians are born and die without ever seeing it or knowing it's here."

I would have remained several minutes longer, but Berta was mindful of the time and hurried me along. "One more place that you would *never* see otherwise," she said. She took me down another long corridor—this one going farther back, toward what I assumed was the private royal part of the palace—to a narrow staircase of dark wood. Berta lifted her skirts high so that she wouldn't stumble, and I followed suit, suddenly worried that we might be caught in the queen's private rooms.

The worn, shallow steps led up to a small choir loft overlooking an altar in a grotto next to walls that rose to cathedral height. Impossibly high chandeliers burned above dark wooden pews and above the altar, dominated by a massive, magnificent portrait of the Virgin, the infant Christ in her arms, as she was being crowned by a pair of cherubs.

For a long moment, we admired her—and the gold appointments on the altar, which gleamed bright against the dark wood. Finally, Berta said, "Time to go."

She returned me to the reception hall where she had left Antonio. By then, the crowd had swelled, and half of the seats had been taken; the volume of conversation now matched that of the pipers, who were playing a spirited tune. Once Berta had gone, Antonio took my cloak—it was warm now that the room was full of people—and delivered it to a servant for safekeeping. He then led the way to a chair, which happened to be next to the elderly gentleman he'd been speaking with earlier.

I had no desire to kill time by making small talk with Antonio, but I was too flustered to do anything other than follow him; I didn't feel like sitting alone among strangers or those city luminaries who knew my father and would ask awkward questions. The elderly man jumped to his feet at once and pulled the chair

out for me. It was at the very head of a long table, at an end occupied by a small group accompanying the old man.

"Thank you," I said, bowing from the shoulders.

"Don Francisco Sánchez at your service," he replied, bowing
himself. Don Francisco was small, stooped, and skeletally thin. I
pegged him as seventy, although his voice and movements were
those of a younger, vigorous man. He wore no beard, but his full
white moustache was neatly trimmed at the lip, if long and curl-
ing at the ends; his thin white hair was oiled and brushed straight
back, candidly revealing a large bald patch at the front. His eyes
were large and dark brown, set above deep pockets of flesh
framed by purplish half circles; his flesh was dark olive, the real
mark of a *converso*, and browned by the sun. His thick, mostly
black eyebrows and his large fleshy nose were his most prominent
features. Sitting next to him was a middle-aged man I assumed
to be his son or nephew, and two finely dressed women, who were
too engrossed in their own conversation to take note of me. Men-
at-arms, dressed in black and clearly not part of Isabel's guard,
hovered nearby to keep an eye on their master.

Don Francisco's introduction wasn't necessary; I'd already
encountered him a few times. He attended the Franciscan church,
and we occasionally saw him there, surrounded by his family and
bodyguards. He always greeted my family warmly, especially my
mother, but he never had cause to address me by name, nor I him.
Even though my mother had always smiled back, and my father
seemed to want to be friendly, something held him back, as
though some ancient disagreement had made it impossible for
them to be friends.

Even though my father never invited the old man to his fre-
quent parties, he never spoke ill of him. And it was impossible to

grow up in Seville and not speak of the well-respected Sánchez clan, whose members had converted from Judaism during the pogroms of the previous century. Despite the taint of *converso* blood, the Sánchez family had become the richest and most influential in Seville, and don Francisco was now the largest landholder. *Sitting on a hidden mountain of gold,* our servants used to say, claiming the old man had a royal fortune in gold coins buried on one of his many properties. Yet they said it without resentment, because don Francisco was famous for his incredible generosity to the poor and the sick. Many of the churches and almost all of the hospitals—including those run by the Dominicans— relied on his donations; not even Fray Hojeda dared bring up the man's name during his anti-*converso* sermons, lest he anger his listeners.

I let Antonio make the introduction. It was fitting, since Antonio's family had socialized with the Sánchezes and he was at ease with don Francisco. "And this is Marisol García, my neighbor."

"Of course, of course," don Francisco murmured politely. "We've met before."

As I moved to sit, don Francisco took a step forward, blocking me, and suddenly took my hand in both of his. His flesh was surprisingly warm, the bones of his fingers warped by age, his touch light as a bird's.

"Doña Marisol," he said urgently, "I was so saddened to hear of your mother's tragic passing. Please accept my heartfelt condolences and those of my family." He squeezed my hand.

There was authentic emotion in don Francisco's tone, in his touch, and I felt distantly angry with myself for the unwanted tears that welled up in my eyes.

"Thank you, don Francisco," I managed, and glanced at him, at Antonio. "Please, gentlemen, sit down."

Don Francisco sat while Antonio waved down a servant to bring the two of us food and drink. A plate was set in front of me, heaped with lamb kidneys sautéed in sherry, slices of cheese, and a smoky, garlicky sausage that smelled tempting. When it came time to take a bite, however, my stomach cramped and a faint wave of nausea overcame me. I addressed myself instead to the wine. Before the rim of the brass goblet met my lips, the intense aroma made my mouth water, and when I took the first sip, I knew I'd never again drink a wine so fine. It bore no resemblance to our tart local brew; it tasted of blackberries, earth, yeast, smoke, and a thousand other delicious things that lingered on my tongue long after I'd swallowed.

"It's good, yes?" don Francisco said, smiling a bit smugly. "I procured it for Her Majesty from France."

"Very good," I answered, and spent the next hour making small talk with Antonio and the Sánchez patriarch and shifting in my seat several times because of the stiff, uncomfortable hoops in my gown. Don Francisco called my father "a very good man" and inquired after him with the same apparently genuine concern. We spoke of the weather, of don Francisco's family, including his wife, Nelda, who had died a decade earlier and for whom he still wore mourning, and of his granddaughter, who had married the previous year and was now pregnant. Don Francisco kindly invited me to come visit his family—in fact, he insisted I do so soon, I suppose out of kindness because I'd lost my mother—and I responded politely in the affirmative, though I never thought for a moment that the old man was serious.

I let don Francisco and Antonio do most of the talking while

I nursed my wine—which Antonio kept refilling from a flagon at the table—and proceeded to get intentionally tipsy for the first time in my life. The alternative was to choke and lose my composure while speaking of my father or my mother. And so I chose to drink—not, in the end, a very good idea, because it made the roiling jumble of emotions harder to contain. But at least it made my nose and feet tingle and relaxed my muscles.

Given the background din in the now-full reception hall as the pipers played and other guests chattered, I had to strain to hear the conversation. The men-at-arms watching don Francisco made sure that no one came near our end of the table, except for servants bringing or carrying away food and wine, and the discussion strayed toward more political topics. Don Francisco began to speculate—only after all servants were gone and then at a volume only Antonio and I could hear—as to why Isabel had felt obliged to make a secret visit to Seville.

"Her Majesty wouldn't make such a long, arduous trip without good reason," don Francisco murmured to Antonio. "Especially to a city as dangerously divided as ours."

Antonio glanced casually over at the queen's guards posted all around the room's perimeter. "Hence the army," he said, a faint smile on his lips, as if he were speaking of the pleasant weather.

"Hence the army." Don Francisco nodded thoughtfully. "A very long way for her to come indeed."

"Perhaps the royal treasury needs fattening," Antonio suggested. I didn't follow his logic, but don Francisco understood perfectly.

"I should know by the end of this evening," the older man replied with a wink, and the two grinned knowingly at each other. "But if it's not that, then . . ."

"Her Majesty attends carefully to details, does she not?" Antonio asked lightly.

Don Francisco laughed. "No greater understatement was ever made." He sobered a bit. "She's no doubt having everyone in charge of her Inquisition investigated and tested herself. Alonso Hojeda and his idiot brother must both be going wild with jealousy, to see you and that Dominican abbot from Segovia"—he referred to Fray Tomás de Torquemada—"so favored by the queen."

Antonio had hardly touched his wine, but at those words, he gave a small, inscrutable grin and suddenly took a large swig from his goblet to avoid meeting my gaze. I took another swallow of wine, too; a tiny, insincere smile froze on my lips as I stared at don Francisco. Fortunately, Antonio said nothing about my marriage, as don Francisco leaned closer to me and said into my ear, "It's always a matter of money, my dear. Like the Crown, the Inquisitors themselves get a percentage of the property and money seized."

I couldn't believe what I'd just heard. "Are you serious, don Francisco?"

He nodded. "Why do you think the abbot Alonso Hojeda is so mad with jealousy where Torquemada is concerned? Why he was so desperate for his younger brother to get even a temporary position with the Inquisition? He maintains a lavish lifestyle at the monastery—so lavish I fear he's run up so much debt, he can't keep up appearances much longer, unless his brother Gabriel is able to convince the queen to let him keep his job. But Her Majesty and Fray Tomás want Antonio to have it, as he's clearly . . . how shall I put it kindly? More capable, more intelligent. There are rumors that Isabel brought Fray Tomás to Seville in order to evaluate all the locals involved in the Inquisition. The queen isn't fond of the idea of the Inquisitors lining their pockets. Or paying bribes to get more denunciations. And she knows Hojeda is not only a spendthrift but the greediest of them all. So she has cut him out of all the money to be made by the Inquisition. And then there is the convenient excuse that he insulted King Fernando by the way he has spoken of *conversos.*"

I listened to this wide-eyed, thinking of the lack of servants at the Hojeda mansion, and the board on the ceiling in the dining hall, where a large chandelier had obviously been removed. I thought of the sour wine, the untended grounds, Gabriel's miserliness, and Fray Hojeda's desperation.

"If I were you, I'd take care around the Hojedas," Sánchez said, turning to Antonio. "Especially Gabriel, who realizes that you will soon take his place unless he can prove himself more capable. You were always too trusting, don Antonio, too quick to think the best of others."

"I'm not that way anymore," Antonio answered, his tone and eyes suddenly hollow.

I looked down at the garnet liquid in my cup, trying to hide my disgust. Did don Francisco, the most respected *converso* in town, even know that Antonio was now working for the Inquisition? Was he aware that Antonio had cruelly jilted me? Most everyone in Seville knew that we had been sweethearts. Perhaps don Francisco thought we still were.

I lifted my chin, intending to announce that Antonio was now working as secretary to the head Inquisitor, Fray Morillo, just in case don Francisco hadn't known, and that we were only here together because the queen had ordered us both to come. But as I turned to look at the head of the Sánchez clan, doña Berta came hurrying up behind him, her movements fast and deliberate, her gaze focused sharply on me.

"Come," she ordered, her hand raised, the back of it toward us as she beckoned imperiously with a jeweled finger. Only then did I realize that the pipers had fallen silent and disappeared.

Both Antonio and I jerked to our feet. Don Francisco rose with us and suddenly clasped my hand as he put his lips to my ear.

"You will come see me?" he asked quickly, and when I nodded, added, "May I send a carriage tomorrow?"

I stared at him in disbelief—I'd thought his earlier invitation was polite banter, and that his sudden insistence on such an imminent visit odd—until Antonio plucked my sleeve. I nodded quickly, and with murmured apologies to don Francisco, hurried with Antonio to follow Berta out onto the Patio of the Maidens. Many guests had carried their goblets outside to enjoy the pleasant night air, now that all the warm bodies had overheated the reception hall. Berta took us to the spot near the pool and potted trees, where we were to play; an unlit torch, smelling of rancid oil, was positioned next to us.

"Don't worry," Berta said, just loud enough to be heard over the revelers, and pointed to the liveried servant standing beside a sconced lamp near one of the archways. "When I give the signal, he'll light the torch. Once it catches, that's when you're to begin to sing."

Antonio appeared, as I did, to listen carefully, calmly. I wondered if his heart was stuttering in his chest as hard as mine was, and I drew a breath as we got into position and fell still in the relative darkness.

Beneath the loggia, two servants in red and gold carefully climbed two different ladders and ceremoniously lit a huge chandelier hanging above the now-closed doors leading back to King Pedro's Palace. Once convinced that the small area was lit up like a stage, they removed the ladders as gracefully as possible and flung open the doors.

At once, a dozen or so young women came spinning out of the doorway onto the patio in choreographed movements that couldn't quite be called a dance. They were all young—all maidens, judging from the loose-flowing hair beneath their gossamer veils—and dressed in fine bright silks in shades more suited to spring than winter: rose, pale green, lavender, pale yellow, robin's egg blue, cream. Fair flowers all, in scandalously low-cut bodices and simpering smiles. They twirled into position to form a wide V whose pivot was the well-lit threshold, and in unison, dropped into full curtsies and held the pose, heads bowed and gazes demurely lowered.

The crowd let go a sigh of approval and might have applauded the pretty ladies had four trumpeters not marched through the doorway onto the patio, horns blaring briefly before they too moved aside.

"Citizens of Seville," a booming male voice announced dramatically, "Her Majesty doña Isabel of the House of Trastámara, Queen of Castile and León."

Along with everyone else on the patio, I held my breath and focused my eyes on the spot beneath the chandelier, in front of the doorway.

Isabel sailed gracefully into the circle of light. She stood alone, dressed in the same black silk gown with velvet *verdugado* casings, this time with bell sleeves so wide and long their edges almost swept the ground. Her dark red hair was braided loosely in the back, wrapped in white silk—an informal look for a queen, but Her Majesty's court was itinerant, ever on the move, and Isabel famously disapproved of unnecessary vanity. On her head rested an equally austere stiff band of plain black silk. Again, she wore no other jewelry save a small gold crucifix.

Her face was just as long and as equine as it had been earlier, the folds beneath her weak chin just as unflattering. Yet in the spotlight, Isabel exuded a charisma so magical, so compelling, that those gathered on the patio fell utterly silent. She was too skilled with an audience to be hasty, but remained soundless for several seconds, her posture and facial expression so noble, so poised, so magnificent that the crowd released a collective gasp of appreciation before bowing.

This was, after all, a woman who as a girl had twice refused her half brother's, King Enrique's, order to marry men not to her liking, a woman who had fought for her brother's, Alfonso's, right to the throne. A woman who, after her beloved brother died of plague, went against the king's orders and escaped Segovia to se-cretly marry a man of her choosing—Fernando, now King of Aragón.

And she married Fernando in order to do the unthinkable: win enough followers to claim the throne of Castile and León for a woman, despite ancient laws that forbade it—and to unite Spain into one kingdom. This was a woman who'd thought nothing of jumping onto a horse when pregnant and riding to meet her hus-band in battle, a woman who knew war and privation and shrank from neither.

No one on the patio lifted his head until Isabel cajoled us.

"People of Seville," she called, in the same ringing voice she must have used to rally her troops, "rise and hear my words!"

She waited until the rustling ceased and every eye was fixed on her before continuing. I could have sworn that she had grown taller and more physically imposing since I saw her in Antonio's office, her features almost handsome. The candlelight caught the hair around her face and glinted bright auburn.

"These are difficult times for your city," she proclaimed with fierce passion, "difficult times for Spain. But know that I care for each of you as I do my own children. My little Isabel, my babies Juan and Juana, they cried when I told them their mother had to leave them again. But I explained that I am also mother to my people. And when a city weeps, I come to dry its tears.

"I am here myself at the outset of this Inquisition to ensure all is done fairly and properly, in accordance with the laws of Mother Church and Spain. I will not permit even the lowliest citizen to suffer unjustly. That is my sacred vow to you, Seville. Know that you are in my prayers and that I beseech the Lord daily to protect all Christians of goodwill, and to reveal those few who debase our holy faith.

"With that aim, I have taken care to appoint only the humblest of men to inquisitorial posts, men whose only earthly goal is to glorify the name of God. Rest assured I hear your concerns, my people, and my thoughts are of you." She suddenly beamed. *"Sevilla, no me ha dejado!"*

We all roared. *No me ha dejado*—"You have not abandoned me"—was the city's motto, created by King Alfonso after his son tried unsuccessfully to steal the throne. Alfonso lived in the Alcázar and was so grateful to the citizens of Seville for their loyal defense that he made the phrase official. Over time, *No me ha dejado* came to be written NO8DO; the number 8 represented a skein of wool, a *madeja*. When read aloud, *No madeja do* sounded the same as *No me ha dejado.*

When the cheering eased, Isabel cried out, "But for tonight, leave your cares behind and enjoy my hospitality!" She spread out a long arm, her fingers as artfully arranged as a gypsy dancer's, and made a flourish in our direction.

At Antonio and me.

At the same time, the servant who had carefully lit the chandelier appeared with a long candlesnuffer and put out several of the tapers above Her Majesty, causing the area around her to dim. Near me, another torch caught and flared audibly, casting Antonio's and my sharp shadows onto the flagstones in front of our feet. Panicked, I looked around for doña Berta in the shadowy crowd and couldn't see her.

Antonio apparently did, for he strummed his lute dramatically, drawing the attention of the crowd, and stamped his heel in time. And then he began to pick out the initial strains of the first duet we had chosen to perform. Immediately, I saw the brilliance of his choice.

I became suddenly senseless to all save the music, a song about a foreign trader sailing on a great ship upon the Guadalquivir, returning to Seville after a long absence, during which he met and lost his true love. I sang of the strong sun and clear sky, of the curving river widening at the port, of the famed towers of silver and gold along the banks, of the high palms swaying in breezes off the river or the dustier southern winds from Africa. The man speaks of his grief, which is eased by the sight of Seville, the city that has stolen his heart.

Singing with Antonio was as magical as the sight of Isabel, only more so. I fell into the same blissful space I'd found earlier that day, where there was no queen, no friars, no audience to judge us. There was no past where Antonio had shattered me, where

my mother had died and my father disowned me, where the Inquisition hung over us like the sword of Damocles. There was
only Antonio, my friend, whom—unhappily—I realized that I
still loved, despite my fury at him, and we were together, singing.
I sensed that there would be little happiness left for me in life
beyond this moment, so I let myself pretend with all my heart
that I lived in a simpler world where Antonio loved me, where we
were not forced to be apart.

I turned my body toward him. I met his gaze and tried not to
melt when Antonio reflected my attitude back to me, his expression adoring, his dark blue eyes glistening with heartfelt emotion
as we came to the chorus.

> *"Sevilla, mi alma*
> *Sevilla, corazón*
> *Con tus brisas suaves*
> *Dolores calmados son.*
> 'Seville, my soul
> Seville, my heart
> Your gentle breezes
> Ease all pain.'"

The queen stood off to one side of the entrance, no longer
brilliantly lit, but visible enough so that I could tell she was clapping and grinning broadly. Her subjects immediately began to
clap with her, and some softly joined in on the chorus; I think
Isabel would have sung, too, had she known the words.

After several verses, the citizens were all patriotically roused,
and Antonio played a slower love ballad. I sang the woman's verses
and Antonio, the man's, and we harmonized on the chorus.

Meanwhile, the queen gradually made her way around the perimeter of the courtyard, greeting guests. We sang four more songs after that but scratched the tune about the innkeeper's wife and her sausages, judging it to be a bit too scandalous given Isabel's sedate but stirring speech.

Just as we finished the fifth song, doña Berta stepped up to us and caught my hand. She was beaming.

"Congratulations, my dear!" she said, and squeezed my hand with an enthusiasm that took me aback. "Her Majesty was charmed by your performance! She's asked that you visit her in a little while in the Salon of the Ambassadors for a more private reception. It's quite an honor to be invited. I'll find you when it's time."

She glanced over her shoulder to see the queen moving our way. "Oh!" Berta hissed at us. "Here she comes!" She immediately turned around and took her place beside me. As the queen approached, Berta curtsied far lower than I could manage.

"Doña Marisol," Isabel called as she made her way toward us along the empty walkway between the reflecting pool and the sunken gardens. She was followed by the women dressed in spring colors; they in turn were braced by a quartet of soldiers in dress uniform with sheathed swords. "You have the voice of an angel."

The crowd surrounding us on the loggias was silent out of respect. Isabel's words carried easily on the night air, and I felt myself blushing.

"Thank you, Your Majesty," I murmured, my hot face turned toward the smooth flagstone.

"Up, up!" The queen gestured with jovial impatience for the three of us to rise. "I should like to see who I'm talking to!"

My cheeks must have been violet, but I rose with the others and faced the queen, hoping my expression didn't reveal my nervousness.

Even if it did, Isabel smiled kindly at me. "You have pleased us, doña Marisol, and we are disposed to treat you kindly. If ever you have need of anything, only ask me."

I'd suffered so many catastrophes in the past year that I couldn't believe something this wonderful was happening. I stared at Isabel in disbelief until doña Berta's discreet elbow found my ribs.

"Thank you, Your Majesty. You're too kind," I breathed, and—uncertain what to do next in the face of such royal generosity—curtsied again.

If it was a breach of protocol, no one seemed to notice. "And you, Antonio Vargas," Isabel said, "you've pleased us as well. We hope to see you later this evening."

"I am honored, Your Majesty," Antonio said with marvelous composure, and bowed as the queen moved off with her entourage.

He and I both turned and watched as she approached the elderly don Francisco, who had come out onto the patio with his middle-aged son and two of his bodyguards. Isabel grinned broadly at the old man and held out her hand to him. He genuflected with real grace for such an old man, and kissed the proffered hand. The queen responded by pulling him to his feet and linking her arm in his.

"Don Francisco, my friend! How long since we two met in the flesh?"

The head of the Sánchez clan smiled, apparently at perfect

ease in the royal presence. "A few years, doña Isabel. Yet you've aged not a day."

Doña Isabel, he called her. Not *Your Majesty, doña Isabel,* as might have been proper for a queen's familiar. But *doña Isabel,* which only King Fernando had the right to do. And Isabel's gap-toothed smile never wavered, which meant that she'd insisted at some point that he dispense with her title, which was extraordinary.

"Come, my friend." Isabel patted Francisco's hand, now in the crook of her elbow, and drew him away from his son and his disgruntled guards. "We have much to catch up on...."

The noise on the patio soon drowned out her words, as the two headed away from us, toward a side entrance to the palace, leaving the queen's pretty, colorful maidens to entertain the guests on the patio. Before she and don Francisco disappeared inside, Isabel cast a quick glance over her shoulder. I followed her gaze to the now-half-dimmed chandelier, beneath which she'd addressed her guests. If don Francisco noticed her lapse in attention, he was too polite to turn his head to see who she was looking at.

Fray Tomás de Torquemada—an unlikely guest for such a festive event—stood beneath the loggia in the exact spot where Isabel had spoken, dressed in his white Dominican habit and worn black cape. I'd forgotten how homely he was, with his squashed thick nose and mottled skin. He looked completely out of place among the seductively dressed young ladies and wealthy guests; his stiff posture, coupled with the judgment in his gaze, showed his contempt for all present save the queen. I couldn't imagine why Her Majesty's confessor would be at a party this time of night and not in his cell, praying.

Her smile vanishing, Isabel shared a swift, subtle glance with
him. He replied with a slow, barely perceptible nod; the coldness
in his tiny eyes stole my breath. Isabel turned back to don Francisco, her grin carefully back in place.

To my dread, the friar Torquemada headed directly toward
us, taking care not to notice the pretty young women or acknowledge anyone else on the patio. I caught the edge of Antonio's long
sleeve, trying to get his attention so that we could escape. To my
frustration, Antonio wouldn't move but met Torquemada's gaze
and acknowledged him with a faint half smile. As the monk
stepped up to him, he bowed.

"Fray Tomás," Antonio said pleasantly. "A pleasure to see you
again."

Torquemada returned neither the gesture nor the greeting.
"Don Antonio, I wonder whether I might have a word with you
in private."

"Of course, sir," Antonio said, slinging his lute over his shoulder and, after bowing to me, walked off with the Dominican into
the palace.

Twelve

After Antonio abandoned me, I was in no mood to socialize. Because of their connection to my father, I knew some of the guests here—mostly city officials, including the mayor. But I had no desire to answer questions about how my father was faring after my mother's death, or why he had failed to escort his only daughter to the palace to hear her sing for the queen.

Instead, I wandered back the way doña Berta had brought me, into the front halls of King Pedro's Palace, empty of all but a scattering of soldiers. They stood motionless, eyeing me as I moved slowly through the vast rooms, admiring the walls and their amazing tiles. The stonework over the archways was unlike anything I'd seen before. Light and frothy, more air than earth, it resembled nothing more than a honeycomb sculpted by an artist instead of bees, each comb an ornate repeating design. It was impossible not to touch the cool stone with my fingers to be sure it was real; fortunately, no guard challenged me.

Away from the press of bodies, it was cool and quiet, save for the sound of music and conversation drifting in from the patio. As I studied the centuries-old palace walls, I tried unsuccessfully to forget Antonio's association with the Inquisition and Torquemada, to quash the question that ate at me: What had happened to him to make him join forces with the Dominicans after all these years?

When the question threatened to shatter my pretense of calm, I forced myself to remember the happier fact that the queen had said she owed me a favor. My first instinct was to ask Isabel to tell the Inquisition to leave my father alone. Yet if I did so, was I then drawing unwanted attention to my father and the fact of my mother's suicide? Would I be endangering him more?

I wandered for almost an hour. Now that the royal performance was behind me, the wine's effects were more noticeable. I'd been too nervous to realize that I was still a bit drunk and ravenous. Remembering the delicious-smelling sausage I'd rejected earlier, I slowly made my way back out across the crowded Patio of the Maidens toward the reception hall and food. Just as I was walking through the open archway into the reception hall, I heard a voice calling my name.

"Marisol! Doña Marisol!"

I turned. Doña Berta stood behind me, looking a bit wilted but no less in charge. She gracefully wiped the sweat from her forehead with the back of a bejeweled hand and smiled toothily at me.

"And now comes your reward," Berta murmured into my ear. "Trust me, you don't want to fill yourself up here. Come, eat and drink at Her Majesty's private table."

My eyes must have grown huge at the thought, because Berta laughed aloud at my reaction before catching my elbow and steering me back onto the Patio of the Maidens. I noticed suddenly that one of the archways leading back into the palace had been closed off by two thick wooden doors inlaid with Kufic script. Six soldiers in crimson and gold barred the door.

Berta didn't approach them but led me through an open archway, down corridors that looked very familiar. Soon I could no longer hear the pipers in the reception hall; their reedy wail was replaced by the sound of lutes playing a vigorous dance tune.

This time, when we approached the three arches resting on slender black marble columns, half a dozen soldiers stood guard. They never stirred as we approached nor acknowledged Berta's little nod as they made way to let us pass by them beneath the horseshoe arches.

"Who would have thought you'd have the opportunity to see the Salon of the Ambassadors again?" doña Berta asked gaily. She had to raise her voice in order to be heard over the music and laughter.

As the doors to the outside were now closed, the film of smoke had thickened. Bedazzled once more, I followed doña Berta into the room and breathed in the scent of hot candle wax and overpowering orange blossom. The air itself had been perfumed, perhaps to mask the base note of perspiration. Berta and I wormed our way through the close press of bodies along the room's perimeter—greeting the mayor of Seville, councillors, judges, and their wives in their best finery along the way—and arrived at a table heaped with food and drink near the massive wooden doors shutting out the Patio of the Maidens. The crowd was so thick and I so short that I couldn't see the front or center of the room.

"Eat," Berta half shouted into my ear in order to be heard

over the music and conversation. "All of my charges are usually starving after the performance. And you *must* try *this* wine; you've never had anything like it in your life. Drink it while you may, my dear."

I had no desire for more wine, but Berta sailed easily to the front of the line, where thirsty revelers were waiting, and gracefully extended her arm across the table until her hand, with its flashing rings, rested palm up in front of the servant pouring wine.

"The wine from Champagne," she called, loud enough so that her voice carried above all the others. "A goblet, please."

A few seconds later, she handed me a cold silver goblet filled to the brim.

"Taste it," Berta said into my ear as she led me toward the food. "Go ahead. And don't waste a drop. This is what the queen prefers to serve her most honored guests. It's His Majesty don Fernando's favorite, and your reward for a fine performance." It was public knowledge that Isabel never touched alcohol, considering it an unseemly indulgence for Christian women.

I looked into my glass and was surprised. The liquid was neither white nor red as I expected, but pale pink—a color of wine I'd never seen before, much less drunk, although I'd heard of it. I lowered my face to it and drew in the fragrance of raspberries and roses; I drank and tasted the same, along with yeast and a bright, slightly fizzy astringency that tickled my tongue and nose.

It was so delicious that I immediately took another sip while doña Berta watched, smiling at my delight. She then managed to charm the man first in line at the table full of food so that he allowed me to cut in front of him. I stared at the king's feast in front of me. Local delicacies from the River Guadalquivir included small delicate crayfish in their boiled-red shells, mussels sautéed in garlicky olive oil, whole baked fish with saffron, and roasted ducklings. There were snails with butter sauce, peacocks reassembled with their bright, uncooked feathers and stuffed with rice and pine nuts, and my favorite, *ortiguillas*, briny little anemones fried in oil. There was an array of pastries, some of which looked like the jeweled, gilded walls of the salon. My stomach was still uncertain despite my hunger, but I requested a small portion of mussels and one of the pastries, a small almond sponge wedding cake. Unlike the dusty *polvorón* I'd eaten under Gabriel's roof, this cake was moist, soaked in syrup fortified with brandy and intensely flavored with almonds. Like the wine, it was one of the most delicious things ever to touch my tongue. When combined with a sip of wine, the cake's flavor grew more intense, producing yet a third taste in my mouth that left me craving more. Before I even tried the mussels, I went back for a second helping of cake.

The second piece of cake required me to drink more wine in order to enjoy the mix of flavors that lingered on my tongue, which led quickly to my being far more inebriated than I'd ever been. Soon the garlicky smell of the untouched mussels made me a bit queasy. I handed my plate to a passing servant and wandered alone toward the front of the stuffy room in search of fresher air, leaving doña Berta to chat with another guest near the tables.

At the front of the crowd in the room's center, three pairs of young courtiers danced. Two of the couples consisted solely of the queen's fair flowers, the pretty young maidens dressed in scandalously diaphanous gowns in spring colors. The third featured another maiden paired with a handsome young man with short blond curls in a tight-fitting doublet and leggings that showed off the sculpted muscles in his chest and legs, not to mention his well-packed codpiece—an immodest Italian style no native of Seville would dare sport on city streets. The two were performing a stately court dance, one that required a slow procession about the dance floor followed by exaggerated bowing to one's partner.

Several strides beyond them, at the wall opposite where guests were being served, stood a podium covered entirely in red velvet. A single high-backed padded chair rested atop it, covered in the same red velvet, and on that chair sat Isabel of Castile.

Her black gown and veil were gone, replaced by a deep blue brocade gown heavily embroidered with bright thread of gold. A small golden crown rested atop her veil of sheer dark blue silk, light as air and threaded with gold ribbon. The colors couldn't have suited her auburn hair and eyes better; naturally blue-green, her eyes reflected only the hue she wore, making them look almost as startlingly dark blue as Antonio's. Her square collar now revealed a bit of her white décolletage, although it was not as scandalous as her dancers' or even doña Berta's.

What caught my eye most was her jewelry. Around her neck hung a king's ransom: at least a dozen heavy gold necklaces, one laden with sapphires and diamonds, another strung with rubies, yet a third sporting large perfect pearls. A cascade of diamonds and sapphires spilled from her ears. Like doña Berta, the queen wore a ring on every finger save her thumbs: emeralds, rubies, sapphires, and pearls were set in the brightest, purest gold I'd ever seen. The simple little crucifix she'd worn at the Inquisitors' offices and earlier that evening was gone.

"Hear, hear!" Isabel called to the lutists, who immediately

stopped playing. "Enough formality. This good city has endured enough suffering. Play something lighthearted. Something... rustic, a country dance." She winked at one of the lutists. "Giovanni, my darling, you know what your queen likes to hear!"

Giovanni, the head lutist, nodded and picked out the first few notes of a tune. His fellow musicians quickly joined in, and many in the crowd roared happily as they recognized a popular Andalusian drinking song. Most started clapping and joined in the singing; I stood swaying and grinning drunkenly at the dancers, who organized themselves into a circle and began clapping their hands in time to the music. Other male courtiers magically appeared, most of them dressed in the Italian style, in tight doublets and in leggings with the codpieces scandalously exposed. This was a far cry from Spanish custom, where older men wore tunics hemmed below the knee and complained about the young men who dared wear tunics that fell mid-thigh.

Still clapping their hands, the dancers began to move around the perimeter of the imaginary circle, each man paired with one of the lovely flower women, whose layers of sheer skirts partially revealed the shape of their comely legs. I wasn't as familiar with drinking songs and didn't know all the words, although I was inebriated enough to try to sing along. The lyrics were at least as scandalous as the tune we'd sung in Antonio's office, focusing on the fine white breasts of a fisherman's lover and how he far prefers them and her company to that of his boat and the sea.

Isabel too began to clap in time to the music, and suddenly hurried down from her throne to replace one of the men and join in the dance with one of the flower women as her partner. She was agile, with a light step—a natural dancer—and being one of the few in the room who was completely sober, she was the most graceful of the lot. The fact that Her Majesty had joined the dance compelled everyone in the room to turn toward her and join in the clapping.

When the second chorus sang again of the lover's white breasts, the most handsome of the male courtiers reached out with both hands and seized the breasts of his female companion. I held my breath, waiting for Isabel's outraged reaction.

The queen laughed. Not a small chuckle but a laugh straight from the belly, and she covered her mouth and flushed. This led to all of the dancers giggling through most of the dance, and the male courtier with his revealing codpiece repeated the act every time the song mentioned breasts. Isabel laughed heartily each time.

She was no weakling and remained on the floor for a total of six vigorous dances, all of them with earthy themes. She wouldn't allow the lutist to slow the pace, despite the fact that her fellow dancers were gasping for breath. Unwisely, I'd made my way to the front row of the spectators, where the wine made me forget myself and clap and sing with drunken enthusiasm.

After the sixth dance, as Isabel was thanking the musicians and her fellow dancers before returning to her throne, she caught sight of me in the crowd. Her Majesty grinned suddenly and motioned to me.

"Doña Marisol, you have pleased us," she said. "Come and dance! Enjoy this night while you can."

As she moved back toward the red velvet podium, I handed my goblet to a passing servant and, filled with panic at the thought of dancing in front of such illustrious company, moved out onto the smooth marble floor.

"The sausages!" Isabel called to her musicians. "Do you know a song about sausages?"

The head lutist looked at her blankly as Isabel hummed the first line in an off-key alto; the queen immediately looked to me.

"Doña Marisol!"

I nodded, showing my understanding so that she need not finish her command, and sang the first few lines of the song. The lutists nodded and began playing the introduction. The male courtier with the most impressive codpiece and tightest doublet immediately caught my hand.

"Marisol, is it?" he said in my ear. His tenor was high-pitched and his intonation rather feminine; his accent was faintly Italian, as if he'd been born in that country and come to Spain in his youth. He was possibly the most handsome man I'd ever seen, with golden curls, pale gray eyes, and a flashing diamond in his ear. His clean-shaven face revealed his dimples, one in his chin and two others bracing his mouth. The latter flashed attractively whenever he spoke or smiled. "My name is Marco."

His refusal to address me as *doña* was incredibly forward, as was his gaze, which took me in frankly from head to toe. I blushed and lowered my eyes as Marco pulled me into the circle.

"You're my partner now," he said, waving away his previous one, dressed in pale yellow silk. His tone was bluntly flirtatious. "And the most gorgeous young woman I've ever seen. Come dance with me, beautiful Marisol."

The dancers weren't slow to please the queen. They'd already quickly organized themselves into a wide circle, each male paired with a female, and were launching into the first steps of a country dance, the *chiarantana*. I hurried with Marco as all the participants suddenly closed the circle by walking to its center, so that everyone met. Just as quickly, we all retreated out to the circle's perimeter and moved briskly around the circle.

I'd been nauseated earlier by the smell of the garlicky mussels; three glasses of the pink wine from Champagne in France hadn't helped matters. As I began to revolve around the circle, the room began to spin, slowly, and when I closed my eyes to blot out the dizzying sight, I could still feel everything moving around me. I opened my eyes, but they wouldn't focus; instead they twitched, unable to rest on a single object.

I gritted my teeth and continued through sheer will. Back on her throne, Isabel was clapping and crowed happily at the lines *Oh, how could I resist his sausages, well stuffed?* At that point, one of the other male courtiers grabbed his female flower and began to simulate the marital act, slowing those of us moving around the huge circle's perimeter.

"Oh!" Isabel called from her throne, her hands to her cheeks in mock dismay. "Hurry and get my confessor! My ladies are supposed to be virgins!"

Her words prompted a chorus of raucous laughter.

I reminded myself that I'd lived a sheltered existence, that such crudeness was to be expected in royal courts. But it was hard to hear the sarcasm in Her Majesty's voice. I'd been taught as a child that Isabel was a saint who spent her days and nights in prayer and kept company only with nuns and monks.

Once the dancers began to move again, Marco caught my hand and spun me around. The act caused the room to start revolving again, this time faster. Unable to catch my breath in the hot, airless room, I felt a flush of uncomfortable warmth, then a chill, followed by the sickening, unmistakable urge to empty my stomach.

I let go of Marco's hand and staggered off the dance floor, with my hand clamped firmly over my mouth, and pushed my way rudely through the crowd toward the horseshoe arches and black marble columns where soldiers stood guard. They parted easily to let me rush past, as if they were accustomed to drunk guests needing to make hasty exits.

I ran past a dizzying blur of patterned tiles, white marble, and arches within arches within arches. Soon I found myself lost in a corner, clutching the busy walls. Despite my efforts, a bit of the almond cake made its way up—but I was already so ashamed at leaving the dance while the queen watched, and so desperate not to be sick inside the Alcázar, that I forced myself to gag it back down, my eyes tearing as the acidic bile burned my throat.

A gentle hand suddenly supported my elbow. I looked up through streaming eyes at doña Berta, her pale eyes full of pity.

"Poor child," she said. "Come."

I let her lead me, even though moving made me start to feel sick again. By the time Berta got me outside and into a deserted corner of an unlit garden, I could no longer control myself and heaved the remnants of the exquisite wine and cake onto an oleander bush. Another servant appeared in the darkness with a basin and towels, and when I finally came to myself, I was alone again with doña Berta, who was gently wiping my face with cold water.

"My fault, I fear," she murmured. "I keep forgetting that you local young ladies aren't as accustomed to drink as our courtiers."

As soon as I could move, Berta steered me away from the oleander so that I wouldn't have to watch the former contents of my stomach dripping from it. The breeze was delightfully cool, the air fresh, the gentle rustling of palms restorative. I lifted my veil and let it dry the perspiration on the back of my neck as I listened to Berta lecture me on how to recover. I must sip cold water slowly and make sure that I drink plenty, but not too fast, that night. In the morning, I must eat a raw egg. If symptoms persisted past the morning, a glass of sherry or brandy would ease them.

"Your husband will never forgive me," she said, "or Her Majesty." When I protested that the blame was mine, Berta shook her head and said shortly, "You're *my* charge."

We sat half an hour out in the dark garden, until I felt recovered enough to walk again. "Time to go home," Berta announced. "Can you walk to the Patio de la Montería?"

I nodded, even though part of me wanted to find Antonio again before I left. I'd probably never have the chance to see him alone again. Despite my anger at him, singing with him had brought the only real joy I'd felt since he'd left Seville. At the same time, I feared the feelings it had stirred. That and the lingering nausea and headache convinced me to give up and go home.

Keeping my gaze downcast, I let doña Berta lead me haltingly back into the palace and out again onto the Patio of the Maidens. As we neared the spot where the queen had addressed the crowd—right in front of the doors leading back into King Pedro's Palace—I remembered that I had left my cloak in the reception hall. Berta left me leaning against one of the archways in order to run back and get my cloak for me. I'd been waiting only a minute when someone stepped in front of me, blocking my view of the retreating Berta. I looked up.

Antonio and Fray Tomás de Torquemada stood in front of me. Although they were matched in height, Torquemada seemed to loom over the younger man. Antonio was uncharacteristically tight-lipped and grim. He took a step back from the monk, as if to distance himself; he wouldn't look directly at me, daring only to cast me an occasional sidewise look. Someone who hadn't grown up with him might have thought he was simply avoiding me, but—I thought—I could still read him well enough to know that he was nervous, desperate to be rid of Torquemada and doña Berta.

Fray Tomás' tiny eyes focused with unsettling intensity on my face and would not look away. There was no kindness in them, no human warmth, only the cold amusement of a cat toying with its prey.

"Doña Marisol García de Hojeda," Antonio announced with terse formality. "May I introduce you to Fray Tomás de Torquemada, the prior of the Dominican monastery of Santa Cruz in Segovia?"

Torquemada bowed without a sound or a smile. When he rose he said, in a voice almost as soft as a whisper, "Doña Marisol, I should like to have a word with you alone, if I may." His tone was as unctuous and polished as any courtier's, yet it held a dangerous undercurrent; he took a half step closer to me, and as his robes shifted, they revealed that his broad, large-boned skeleton held hardly any meat. Yet he pulled himself straight in such a way that, gaunt or no, he was as physically imposing as possible. For some reason, I flashed on the memory of Gabriel, his arm around Antonio's neck as he pounded the latter's head mercilessly.

"I'm ill," I croaked. "I have to leave. Doña Berta is getting my cloak and will be right back."

Torquemada tucked his chin and slowly lowered his gaze to mine, taking a step closer so that he towered over me. "Antonio will stay here and tell her where you've gone," he said slowly. "I would think you'd be far more concerned about pleasing Her Majesty."

Puzzled, I looked again to Antonio, who was busy examining the flagstones near his feet.

"Please," I said. "I'm not well enough for conversation."

"Only because you allowed yourself to become drunk," Torquemada countered scathingly. "God's work doesn't wait because of sin. Come."

Antonio remained silent as I let myself be intimidated into going alone with the monk. I followed Fray Tomás through a different archway, down different corridors lined with more dizzyingly patterned tiles and up a staircase. At last we arrived at the door to a small, private chamber deep in the palace interior, where the music and drone of partygoers grew muted. Walking so quickly made me feel sick again, but fear proved a good distraction.

Torquemada motioned for me to enter the chamber ahead of him. It was windowless and mostly dark, lit by a single thick taper burning in a brass wall sconce. A carved wooden crucifix hung nearby; beneath it sat a rickety prayer bench, on whose upper shelf rested a small statue of Saint James. In one corner, a wooden plank, the height and breadth of a man, lay on the floor beside a folded, many-times-mended blanket. The monk entered after me and pointed to a chair beside a small plain desk. Once I sat down, he took the chair behind the desk, facing me.

He made no effort to smile or set me at ease. Instead he sat silently, studying my face intently for long, torturous seconds until he finally spoke.

"You and Antonio Vargas seem quite taken with each other," he said, and waited.

I curled my hand into a fist and pressed my fingernails hard into my flesh, hoping to distract myself from flushing violently at his words.

"I don't know how he feels," I said coldly. "I'm certainly not taken with him. We were sweethearts, but then he went off to university and forgot me."

"Someone watching the two of you sing together wouldn't think so," Torquemada countered.

I shrugged. "It was an act for Her Majesty, so that she would enjoy the song."

"You're both quite the performers, then. I was entirely convinced." He paused. "Is there anything you would like to tell me, doña?"

The tone of his question was intended to unnerve me, shame me. I narrowed my gaze and frowned curiously at him. "Regarding what, Fray Tomás?"

"Regarding the Edict of Grace. Did you go to the square and listen to the edict and bull that Fray Morillo read?"

I nodded.

"You're a *conversa*, the daughter of a *conversa* who drowned in the river not long ago. There is much gossip in town regarding the circumstances of her death. You may be skilled at dissembling, Marisol, but your hair and eyes and flesh betray you."

I felt a blast of heat on my cheeks and dropped my gaze to the desk. Its unvarnished surface was scratched and pitted from decades of wear; like Fray Tomás, it seemed out of place in such glorious surroundings. I glared at the burls in the wood furiously. I despised Fray Tomás for the ease with which he spoke of my mother's death, for the way he referred to her as nothing more than a *conversa*, as if she'd been something less than human.

When I looked back up at him, I wondered whether the depth of my hatred showed.

"One might say the same for your hair and eyes," I said softly. I was tempted to bring up the cardinal Torquemada who had confessed to being a *converso,* but the monk's expression stopped me.

His lipless mouth twisted in disgust, his eyes narrowed to slits beneath a thunderous scowl. "Don't insult me!" he hissed. "God is not fooled, Marisol García. I must know: Did your parents ever pray together on Friday evenings, or light candles and keep them burning until Saturday night? Did you ever celebrate Passover?"

"Of course not," I lied, my tone ragged with outrage. All I could think of was my mother, Magdalena, leaning over to light the Sabbath candles, her profile luminous in their golden glow.

He spoke over me, raising his voice to drown me out. "Your father has been denounced and is under investigation."

The end of my gasp coincided with his last word. For several seconds, I couldn't draw a breath.

"You've heard the Edict of Grace. It's your solemn duty, Marisol, to report all heresy that you witness. It would be wise to tell me everything you know about your father, now. You would not only be saving his immortal soul, you would spare yourself from being interrogated as a witness. You could save yourself from suspicion."

"My father's an Old Christian." I was angry with myself for not being able to keep my voice from shaking. "He's always attended Mass and confession regularly and brought me up in the true faith."

The friar lifted a grizzled brow. "He never prayed facing

East? Never uttered a foreign word when he prayed? Did he eat pork?"

"No. Of course we ate pork. We're Christians."

Torquemada narrowed his eyes at me, unimpressed. "Then surely your mother did not, and your father protected her. Others have said that your father is a Judaizer. Some say he's the head of a planned uprising against the Crown."

"They're lying!" I leaned forward over the desk, my nerves partially forgotten; no one had been more loyal to Isabel than don Diego. "Who says that my father's done such a thing? Who accuses him? We've always been faithful to the queen!"

"Their anonymity is guaranteed by law." Fray Tomás's smug tone goaded me. "You know, if my father were under investigation and in danger of being arrested, I'd do everything possible to help him. I'd cooperate with authorities. Especially knowing that those who are arrested undergo extremely painful torture if they don't willingly confess."

"Is my father going to be arrested?" A sickening chill settled over me. It was one thing to hear such things from my mother's lips, quite another to hear them from Torquemada's.

"Much depends on you, Marisol." A corner of his lipless mouth quirked upward. "For example . . . there is the case of don Francisco Sánchez. Not just the wealthiest man in Seville, but a *converso*, like you. Except that both of his parents were *conversos*, and he's long reputed to be a Judaizer. How well do you know him?"

"Not well at all," I answered honestly, my anger eclipsed by a desperate desire to protect my father. "My parents knew of him, though he never dined at our table. I was just introduced to him formally this evening."

"He seems to have taken quite an interest in you."

"He was just being polite. As you pointed out"—my tone hardened—"my mother recently died. He was sharing his condolences." I paused. "You'd be far better off talking to don Antonio about don Francisco. His family was better acquainted with him." It was cruel of me to single out Antonio, but Torquemada was already kindly disposed to him.

"I see." The Dominican looked at a distant spot on the wall behind me and nodded as if my answer vaguely pleased him. When his gaze refocused on me, he spoke again, this time in an easy, relaxed manner, as if his previous efforts to intimidate me had been in jest. "You could be of great help to Her Majesty, doña Marisol, and especially to your father, if you got to know don Francisco well."

In my mind's eye, the birdlike Sánchez patriarch stood next to me, clutching my hand and whispering *May I send a carriage tomorrow?* Perhaps I should have mentioned it. Perhaps Torquemada already knew. But I had no desire to endanger a man as kind as don Francisco, and so I said nothing. When my hands began to shake again, I withdrew them hastily from the table and clutched them in my lap, hoping the friar didn't see.

"I will," I answered huskily. "To help my father, of course I will."

Fray Tomás's mouth stretched into a black, cavernous smile. "Yes, doña Marisol. Of course you will."

After extracting my promise of cooperation, Torquemada remained vague as to what I should do next, saying that things would soon become clearer to me. I followed him meekly back to the Patio of the Maidens, where doña Berta stood waiting beside Antonio, who held my cape over his arm. At the sight of Fray Tomás, Berta nervously averted her gaze, waiting until the silent monk had disappeared before speaking.

"Poor child," she murmured as soon as he was out of earshot. She'd brought another rag dampened with cool water and discreetly passed it over my brow. "And you feeling so ill!" This latter was a criticism of Torquemada, although she was careful not to be more specific.

"I'll take her home," Antonio said eagerly. He had put on his cloak to leave, and his lute was hanging again from a strap slung over his shoulder. As he spoke, he unfurled my cape with a snap and set it over my shoulders.

Berta pulled herself up to her full, plump stature and shot him a disapproving look. "I should say not!" she countered. "Her Majesty appointed me the girl's chaperone, and I have no intention of surrendering her to an unmarried young gentleman at this point, especially one as handsome as you. I'll see her home. The driver's waiting."

She put a maternal hand beneath my elbow and began to steer me back inside the reception halls that opened onto the Patio de la Montería. Antonio stepped in front of her.

"You don't understand," he said earnestly. "Doña Marisol and I have been friends since we were children. Our houses stand side by side. As her neighbor, I feel responsible. . . ."

Berta lifted both pale brows in disbelief. "I saw the way you two were eyeing each other during the performance; responsibility isn't the name for what you feel. No one's that good an actor."

A short, stout juggernaut of propriety, she pushed past him. I felt too queasy, too exhausted and distraught over Torquemada's threat against my father to care whether I rode home with Antonio or not. But I was still making plans to steal over to my father's house that night and speak to him secretly. My mother had been right: We'd been fools not to leave town sooner.

I let the indefatigable Berta lead me back through the handsome reception halls to the Patio de la Montería, where a number of carriages were still parked, the drivers drowsing in their seats. We found our carriage and rumbled out past the Lion's Gate into the city. The farther away we got from the Alcázar, the darker and more deserted the streets.

"I hope you'll be feeling better by tomorrow evening," Berta said. "Her Majesty enjoyed your singing and asked that you come to the palace tomorrow for a more private celebration. I'll come for you again at the same time."

It was impossible to say no; I nodded, overwhelmed. Afterward, doña Berta fell silent and began to drowse.

Battling thirst, hunger, and nausea, I fell into a trancelike state as my mind worked to figure the fastest way out of Seville. The police were patrolling the streets at night because of the number of *conversos* escaping the city; those caught were presumed to be heretics and were promptly arrested—or killed if they resisted. I thought of all the sailing ships anchored at the harbor. No one had stopped my mother the night she ran to the river; the police were looking for people in wagons with belongings. Perhaps, if my father and I were willing to leave everything behind—except for enough money to bribe a sea captain . . .

I couldn't risk letting my father stay in the city another day. Even if he hated me, even if he shouted for me to leave him, I had to find a way to convince him to leave. Tonight.

I leaned my forehead against the cool glass of the carriage

window and closed my eyes as our coach rounded the corner onto the cul-de-sac where the Hojeda house lay. I was still puzzling over the precise words that would make my father listen to my scheme when I heard doña Berta let go a little cry of fear and surprise. I lifted my face and looked out at the street.

The Hojeda mansion was dark, save for a feeble sputtering lamp that hung at the carriage entrance. Gabriel's men-at-arms had multiplied in number; at least two dozen stood in small groups circling the outer front walls, peering out like vultures from the shadows. The windows at Antonio's house were likewise black, making the house look as though it were unoccupied. But the front entrance of don Diego's home was bright as day in the glow of torches held by a wagon driver and one among three deputies. Along with Seville's sheriff, a man who had often visited our table, the deputies stood in a row in front of the iron gate leading to our front patio, marking a path from the gate to the back of the open wagon.

My father staggered in front of them. Shoeless, he wore only his rumpled lawn nightshirt and leggings, his hair wildly disheveled; his hands were shackled in front of him at the wrists. A Dominican monk walked ahead of him, leading the way to the wagon, and a fourth deputy with a drawn long sword walked behind him, prodding him with the flat of it when he lagged.

I shouted for the driver to pull over in front of the Hojeda house. Before the wheels creaked to a complete stop, I pushed open my door, jumped from the carriage, and ran shouting to don Diego.

Thirteen

"Papá!" I cried. "Papá, I won't let them take you! I won't let them take you!"

I don't know how I got from the carriage so fast in heavy skirts and a long cloak—faster than the distracted guards could react. I wound my arms around my father and pressed my cheek against him. I drew in the scent of his skin at the juncture of his jaw and neck, which I'd been so homesick for, the smell of his shirt and even the wine on his breath. The heat of a torch on my back, the sting of black smoke, the slither of long swords being unsheathed—I cared about none of them. I wrapped my arms awkwardly around my father and squeezed with all my strength, meaning never to let go.

In that instant of contact, his chest shuddered; the men's shouts drowned out the sound of his sob.

"Get away!" my father raged at me. Or pretended to: Torchlight glinted off the shiny tears trailing down his cheeks as he writhed in my grip, unable to lift the heavy shackles high enough to push me away. "Get away. I don't know you anymore! I disown you!" His voice cracked on the last words.

Stronger arms caught mine from behind and pulled until the pain grew intolerable. A man's body pressed against my back as his fingers dug deep into my gut on either side of my navel, forcing me to yelp. My trembling muscles gave way, and they pulled me from my father. I shouted at them to let me go and kicked backward with full force, causing one of the men holding me to stumble. I lunged, but the other caught me at once.

"Papá!" I screamed again as they took don Diego away. While he'd been sleeping earlier that night, the back hem of his nightshirt had been pressed up into an awkward fold, revealing his right thigh up to the curve of his right buttock; I wanted to strangle his captors for submitting him to such public humiliation. The sole of his leggings caught on a stone and he stumbled, brushing against the sheriff's shoulder. Distracted, my captors eased their grip, and I lurched forward toward him, wanting only to touch him again. Two deputies converged to block me with their bodies, but I launched myself off my feet, brazenly grabbing their shoulders to pull myself up, to at least see him for another fleeting second.

Framed between two flaming torches, my father clambered with his legs as the sheriff pushed him up into the back of the wagon, where the black-and-white Dominican sat waiting. When the wagon began to roll away, the deputies recruited two men-at-arms to hold me back.

"Don't worry!" I shouted, before don Diego was completely out of earshot. "I'll come for you! I'll get you freed!" And when he'd rumbled out of sight, I murmured to myself, in a spasm of foreboding, "I love you."

The instant the wagon disappeared onto San Pablo Street, a fiercely strong hand clutched my elbow, pulling me off balance, forcing me to stumble forward rather than fall. Gabriel towered over me in the carriage lamp's wan glare. Rage etched deep grooves in his brow; his arm was lifted, palm up, ready to strike. He was hissing my name.

I bared my fingernails like a cat and lunged at him, aiming for his eyes. Although I didn't succeed, the longer nails—hard and strong, like my mother's—caught the promontory of his cheek, just beneath the eyes. I felt them sink into his flesh and withdrew them to the sight of blood, pleased.

But the image was far too fleeting. Before I could take another breath, the side of a huge hand blotted out everything to my left. First came the blinding flash of light and with it, a flare of pain along the left side of my face. In the next instant, the right side of my head met the ground with a force I knew would make me faint, and there was nothing to do but yield to the darkness.

I woke to find Máriam perched, spine straight, on the edge of a chair pulled up next to my bed. Her black gown hung on her spare frame, and her dark skin gleamed in the light of the oil lamp on the little night table. The instant she realized I was awake, her scowl transformed into a grin.

"Marisol," she said, leaning over me. She looked genuinely relieved and happy to see me, but her voice was oddly faint, as if she were speaking on the other side of a thick glass window. I had to strain to make out each word. "How do you feel?"

After a second of silence passed, I realized I couldn't hear well because of the roaring in my ears—that, and Máriam seemed to be whispering. I didn't remember where I'd been or what had happened; the right and left sides of my skull throbbed so badly that I decided I had a fever or even plague. I tried to move my head and soon realized that if I continued, I'd be violently sick, so I lay very still. But I kept blinking, because the details of Máriam's burnt-umber features kept blurring into her black veil, and both occasionally blurred into the trembling shadows gathered on the dingy wall.

"Terrible," I croaked at Máriam, but my tone was darkly cheerful, and her smile deepened a bit. Then she started as she heard something I couldn't, and glanced over her shoulder at the open doorway leading to the antechamber. Her frown returned, and her eyes narrowed with a hatred so deep and dangerous, I grew frightened. She turned back to me, her scowl easing, and put a long, elegant finger to her lips. Someone was in the other room.

In the next instant, Fray Hojeda, his eyelids heavy from want of sleep, moved into the room. Gabriel was right behind him.

Hojeda pushed rudely past Máriam, displacing her, and shoved the chair behind him. Then he planted his feet at the level of my waist and leaned over me, the light catching his odd profile with its bridgeless, downturned nose. I tilted my chin down to see I wore only my best chemise; the silk clung immodestly to my breasts, which were full, like my mother's. I pulled the blanket from my waist up to my neck and wished I could leave the room. After years of publicly manifesting wrath on cue, Fray Alonso Hojeda had no difficulty working himself into a rage before my eyes, despite his sleepiness. His eyes blinked rapidly; the muscles around his mouth twitched and drew the corners back into a grimace.

But my nominal husband seemed determined to speak first. Although he didn't force his older brother to shift the position of his feet, Gabriel sidled up tightly against him until he stood near my shoulders.

"Move aside!" the friar snarled at him.

Gabriel was oddly unmoved. I tilted my head back and saw the blood drying on the curve of his cheek just beneath one clear green eye, where three of my fingernails had gouged a pattern not unlike those made by the graceful arches surrounding the Patio of the Maidens.

"I hate you," I said to Gabriel. I didn't care if he hit me again. If I'd been able to move, I would have gouged out his eyes. "Why didn't you warn us? Why didn't you stop them from arresting him? Go save him! Now!"

Gabriel's eyes were bright with fury. "There's a more important issue. You shamed me out in the street, screaming and carrying on. And when I corrected you, you were going to strike me."

I looked at him in disbelief. "My *father*," I repeated. "You have to save my *father*. Tonight. What if they hurt him or torture him? He's an innocent man, a good Christian. You have to help him!"

"You forced me to hit you," Gabriel accused. His eyes were burning cold. "You caused a scene."

It taxed my will to swallow so much rage, but I did it for the sake of don Diego. "What if it were your father being dragged to prison, don Gabriel?" I asked softly.

He fell silent; his expression grew perplexed. I thought suddenly of old white-haired don Jerónimo, shouting at his son. *Come away from that filthy little* marrana! Gabriel had disappeared behind the gate, only to yelp in pain as don Jerónimo struck him. I tried to imagine life without my parents' constant affection, one where there was only scorn and abuse.

I pressed. "I love my father, and he loves me. I'd die to save him. Please, help him!"

The beginnings of compassion flickered in Gabriel's eyes. Fray Hojeda took advantage and pushed him backward, forcing him to stagger. As Gabriel found his balance, the friar stepped up to my bedside again, blocking my husband's access.

"I'm exhausted," Hojeda announced flatly, his face haggard, "and you'll answer my questions now, so that I can go to bed. You've no right to be angry, Marisol. You should instead be on your knees praying that your own heart is pure. You heard the Edict of Grace, and if you've failed to divulge any heretical practices you're aware of . . ." He let the thought dangle for a few seconds before adding, his tone ridiculously wheedling, "You can tell me. Denounce your father. Tell us what you know. It will go easier on him that way."

I turned my face from him, gritting my teeth as the bruise left by Gabriel's fist met the pillow. "My father's innocent. He's an Old Christian. He's never had anything to do with the Jewish religion or with Judaizers. He raised me in the church. He's saintlier than the rest of you!"

His eyebrows rushed together in a thunderhead of self-righteous judgment, but he no longer had the energy to muster sufficient outrage at the insult. "But he married your mother," Hojeda said nastily, softly, which wounded me far more than any show of anger could.

My expression must have revealed my pain; the friar calmed, pleased, and said, "You can help us by telling me what happened at the Alcázar when you saw Her Majesty. Did you put in a word for me? For Gabriel?"

My head hurt too badly to shake it. "No," I said. As Hojeda's owlish scowl deepened, I added, "There were so many people pressing to see her. I had no chance to speak to her, except to thank her for her public praise and her kindness. She invited me to the Salon of Ambassadors afterward. Doña Berta—my chaperone—said that the queen liked my singing and asked me to come sing again at the palace tomorrow night." I felt a wave of panic. "It's not tomorrow night already, is it?"

"No, no," the monk soothed. He was completely changed, his frown traded for the suggestion of a smile, his eyes suddenly wide and bright, his demeanor warm. "Don't worry, doña Marisol, you have plenty of time to rest now." He spoke over his shoulder to his younger brother, who stood simmering behind him. "Gabriel, have the African slave find Lauro and tell him to bring some fresh meat from the larder. You can spare it. We want Marisol to look pretty for her performance tomorrow. We don't want any bruises on the side of her face." Fray Hojeda turned back to me with a feigned half grin.

"My dear," he said pleasantly. "Was Antonio Vargas there? Did you see him?"

I averted my gaze. "Yes. He played the lute while I sang."

"Did you speak to him?"

"Only as much as was necessary."

His brow furrowed a bit. "You didn't speak to him or anyone else about his relationship to Fray Tomás de Torquemada, the abbot who spoke to him in his office?"

"No."

Hojeda sighed. "Then you will remember to try to put in a good word on my behalf and Gabriel's to Her Majesty tomorrow without fail. I may not be a member of the Inquisition, but I *am* the abbot of San Pablo, and I have a say as to how prisoners are treated in the jail on the monastery grounds. I can be of much help to you. And of course..." He glanced over his shoulder briefly at my brooding husband. "Don Gabriel has great influence with the Inquisitors and the judges. Be good to us and we will be good to your father. Do you understand this, Marisol? Will you try to remember its grave importance?"

For a long moment, I couldn't bring myself to answer.

"Yes."

After Fray Hojeda left, my mind cleared a bit; I saw that my rage was pointless and possibly harmful. I had to get control of myself in order to plan quickly; one night in jail, and my father would die of humiliation, if grief didn't kill him first.

"I'm sorry, don Gabriel," I whispered to my husband. "I'm too heartbroken over my father to know what I'm saying. Please, is there anything you can do to help him? Now?"

The muscles in his face shifted as some crafty scheme occurred to him, but any pleasure he felt at his cleverness soon faded and was replaced by uneasiness. "Perhaps. If you're willing to give me something in return."

I hid my dread. "What would that be?"

Gabriel leaned closer, bringing his face toward mine. The lamp's steady yellow glow made the fair skin around the edges of his nostrils and the tip of his nose translucent. A few stray hairs around his face caught the glow and glinted dazzlingly, fine strands of lightning.

"Get closer to Antonio," he said, and dropped his gaze—but not before I saw the shame and jealousy in it.

Those few words so startled me that I spoke without thinking. "Closer? What do you mean?"

A dark red flush traveled upward from his neck to just below his eyes. His voice grew low and raw. "Don't make me say it," he whispered.

I stared at the fine tracery of veins on his cheeks, on his half-lowered eyelids, and gaped at the realization that my so-called husband was asking me to have an affair. Seconds passed before I collected myself enough to speak. "I can't believe you would ask me to jeopardize my immortal soul," I said, my tone hard. "I want nothing to do with Antonio Vargas."

That caused him to lift his head and return my stare with one colder and far more intimidating. "You ask the price of your father's life. I'm telling you: Get to know Antonio's secrets. And all you can about Torquemada's infatuation with him." Gabriel lifted his face again as anger rose in him, coloring his entire face. He looked right at me, but his focus was beyond me, on someone else. The taut skin around his eyes twitched with hatred, and I thought of the vicious youth with one arm wound around Antonio's neck, pummeling his head.

"If you were to denounce him," Gabriel said slowly, deliberately, "I swear to you on my father's and mother's souls, all your problems would be solved."

"Denounce Antonio?" I whispered ingenuously. "He's an Old Christian! He works for the head Inquisitor!"

"He loves you," Gabriel said tightly. "You must use that." He paused to give his words weight. "If you want to help your father."

I stared hard into his clear green eyes and saw the depth of his hatred, of his icy resolve. When it came to Antonio Vargas, immortal souls were irrelevant. Truth did not matter. Gabriel might have married me out of lust and affection—but these weren't the only reasons. He also wanted revenge.

Before I could answer, he turned away and strode from the room as if he didn't trust himself to stay a moment longer.

"I'll do whatever you want," I called after him, not caring that it made my head hurt beyond bearing, not caring that it was a bald-faced lie. "Only free my father tonight!"

The only answer was the sound of his footsteps retreating out in the loggia.

"Bastards," Máriam hissed. I started at the sound; she'd been so quiet that I'd forgotten she was there. She moved from the corner to where Fray Hojeda had stood, her dark face gleaming.

I pushed my palms hard against the lumpy feather-and-straw mattress in an effort to rise.

Máriam pushed me back against the bed. I cursed as I realized that I was too weak to fight her and fell back against the pillow.

"You have to go to Gabriel. Please—you know that the shame is killing don Diego," I begged. I caught Máriam's shoulder and attempted to dig my fingertips into it. "I can't rest knowing that he's in prison."

"Hush," she soothed. She gently took hold of my wrists and lowered them to the bed. Then, when I had stopped struggling, she lifted my right hand and pressed it to her heart in a stunning display of affection. "Sweet child, hush. There's nothing for you to do right now except rest. Don Diego isn't forsaken." Her dark eyes glittered in the light. They'd always been difficult for me to read, but that night, I looked in them and saw hope, reassurance, and certainty. "Do you understand? And will you trust me?" Máriam asked quietly, her features softened by love and sorrow, just as they'd been on the day she'd told me how she'd rescued my mother as a child. "Your only task now is to rest until morning."

Clasped over mine, her hand was warm and dry; I flattened my palm against the hollow of her chest, where her heart beat strong and slow beneath the breastbone, and trusted her rather than become insane.

Even then, the hours before dawn were long and torturous. Máriam insisted on remaining at my bedside rather than going back to sleep on her cot, although from time to time, her chin tucked itself, allowing her head to bow forward as she dozed. I was alone with the aftereffects of the wine and my memories.

I closed my eyes and remembered my father the night he had come to my room to announce that he'd given my hand to Gabriel.

I'm no longer your father, do you understand, Marisol? . . . You're an Hojeda now.

I understood at last: Everything my father had done had been to protect me. Just like my mother, he'd known the arrest was coming. He'd rejected me and forced me to marry Gabriel Hojeda with a single purpose in mind, the same purpose my mother had hoped to accomplish by killing herself and leaving a note exonerating her family: to save my life. Their love for me had never wavered. They'd hidden their terror and grief, all for my sake. And I'd been selfish and angry in return.

I squeezed my eyelids together hard, glad that Máriam was sleeping and couldn't see the tears sliding down my cheeks.

. . .

Dawn finally arrived, and an hour later, Gabriel, fully dressed, stopped by my room to confirm my promise that I would "get closer" to Antonio. I agreed, so long as he would find a way to free my father—to which he answered cryptically, "In time. First you must fulfill your part of the bargain."

Somehow, I managed to keep from screaming at Gabriel; every minute my father spent in prison was another moment of torment for him, another moment closer to interrogation and torture, even though Máriam tried to keep me calm by telling me that nothing would happen until later that morning.

Soon after, my husband left for the courthouse. Despite nursing my first hangover—eased by some sips of the tart wine from the kitchen, which tasted vile after drinking from Her Majesty's cup—I insisted that Máriam help me dress. I was determined to find a friendly high-ranking judge who could release my father; although we all feared the Inquisition, it relied solely on civil authorities to enforce its power. Gabriel had taken the carriage, but there was still a wagon. I would have walked if necessary.

Just as Máriam finished helping me with my hair—pulled forward along the sides of my face, with my veil, to cover the bruises left by last night's encounter with Gabriel—Blanca rushed up to the half-open door opening onto the loggia. She paused on the threshold to wave a piece of paper sealed with black wax at me.

"Doña!" she gasped, her fresh young face flushed pink. "There's a carriage downstairs! A royal one, with the queen's banners! The driver asked me to give you this note and is waiting for your reply!"

I bolted from my chair in front of the mirror, hurried over to her, and snatched the letter from her. "Who was inside?"

"I don't know," she breathed, awestruck. "The windows were veiled. But the coach is so new and shiny, and the horses are so beautiful—" She broke off, suppressing a giggle; it must have been heady for a poor girl like Blanca to be this close to wealth and royalty.

I clenched my teeth so they wouldn't chatter. My fingers shook so badly that I couldn't open the note; I expected an inter-rogation summons from Torquemada. Fortunately, Máriam had followed close behind me; she took it, wormed a finger between the folds, broke the seal quickly, and handed it back to me.

Holding my breath, I opened it and read, holding it so that Blanca could not see.

> *To the esteemed doña Marisol,*
>
> *Forgive me for the surprise, but I was saddened to hear of recent events. I know that time is of the essence. Will you come to see me now, as you promised yesterday evening? I will help.*
>
> *P.S. Please forgive me for my unkind remarks about your husband and brother-in-law. I have since been made aware of your marriage.*

The note was unsigned; the writing was large and rounded if unsteady in places, as if penned by an arthritic hand.

Careful to keep my expression unchanged, I looked back up at Blanca.

"Yes, it's the Crown," I lied. "Her Majesty has summoned me. I suppose she wants me to sing again."

Thrilled, Blanca put her hand to her heart as if to keep it from leaping out of her chest. Cursing my aching head, I threw a shawl over my shoulders and—after sharing a cryptic glance with Máriam—hurried out the door, the note still in my hand.

The carriage was freshly lacquered, with appointments as fine as the one I'd ridden in the previous night; the only difference was that the royal tower and lion weren't painted on the door. Instead, cloth banners sporting the tower and the lion had been carefully draped from the windows, which were open but covered by gauzy dark curtains. The well-groomed driver wore spotless black livery and bowed low before opening the door and helping me inside. The interior was empty—a shocking sight, as women in Spain never traveled unescorted.

But the driver wasn't about to wait for me to decide whether I trusted him or not. He slammed the door behind me and, before I'd fully settled, urged the horses on, causing me to fall back against butter-soft leather cushions.

We rolled to a stop at the intersection of our cul-de-sac with San Pablo Street. The Royal Palace lay to the southeast; so too did don Francisco's estate, which I understood lay outside the city walls.

To my dread, the carriage turned west instead, toward the Dominican monastery and jail. The hairs on the back of my neck lifted as a thrill coursed through me: It had been a trap. Torquemada had tricked me.

Fourteen

I stared out at the darkly filmed street, forcing myself to remain calm enough to think. I had to convince Torquemada of my father's innocence; I decided my best chances lay with begging the queen for mercy, or—by far the less desirable path—asking Antonio to lobby the Inquisitors to have my father released. By the time the coach drew near San Pablo Monastery, my ability to concentrate deserted me, and I still hadn't settled on the proper strategy to ensure an audience with Isabel.

Just as quickly our carriage rumbled past the entrance to the monastery and jail. I stared back at it, stunned, then looked ahead at our destination, the River Guadalquivir. Just before we rolled onto the docks, the carriage took a sharp right turn, heading north, onto a dirt road running parallel to the shore.

I took the edge of my long bell sleeve and pressed it to my nose like a kerchief, recoiling at the dankness and the stench of open latrines. The poorest of the poor dwelled here, along with vermin, rabid dogs, and the plague; the sheriff and his men refused to patrol the neighborhood, making it a haven for thieves and murderers. I shrank from the windows, staring out through a film of dark gauze and dust as we flew down the narrow trail, past crowded miserable shacks made from river flotsam and rotting planks, past naked filthy children playing in the dirt, gangs of hard-bitten youths who yelled curses in our wake, and a young woman in ragged skirts with a basket of wet laundry, her face hauntingly worn and broken before her time.

The ride over the uneven trail was rough, and the stink never eased; my teeth rattled as I clutched the edge of my seat and fought the nausea brought on by the carriage's rocking and the wine's lingering effects. After several minutes, the tight cluster of shacks gave way to open land along the shore, dotted with clumps of grass and schools of ducks that flapped off into the blue sky as we approached. The land here flooded too often to farm and was still muddy from the winter rains. The smell eased, and because we were far from prying eyes, I lifted the gauze curtain and breathed in fresher air gratefully. Despite the mud, the trail was blessedly flatter here, and within minutes I spotted our destination: a solitary large storage shack of wood and metal, built on a mound of earth to protect it from floodwaters.

The driver brought the horses to a stop in front of the shed, jumped down, and slid open the wooden door. Soon, the carriage was inside the shed, and the driver pulled the door closed over us. In an instant, he pulled the royal banners free, revealing that the carriage was unmarked.

When we emerged from the shed again, we headed east back into the city. But instead of heading south toward the Alcázar Real, our carriage went north, toward the city quarter known as

La Macarena, named for the daughter of Hercules. We were clearly headed outside the city walls toward the Sánchez family home. I calmed down enough to ask myself why a man like don Francisco would be interested in me or my father, and why he would still be friendly to Antonio, knowing that he was one of Torquemada's favorites.

Antonio, who had betrayed me by not warning me last night of my father's impending arrest. He was secretary to Fray Morillo, the head Inquisitor, and had access to every case file. He had to have known.

The carriage rolled through working-class neighborhoods of small churches and tiny stucco houses crowded together, the yards full of billowing laundry hung out to dry. Soon we passed by the northernmost city walls out into open country, most of it flat beneath a blindingly sunny sky. The street gave way to dusty trails and buildings to almond and orange groves, their leaves still bright after December's heavy rains. A gentle promontory rose in front of us, home to a large stand of ancient olive trees, their trunks gnarled and plaited, their silvery leaves spread to the sun. I pushed aside the curtains and caught the window's edge as the carriage's wooden wheels met brick paving with a lurch. In front of us, a long driveway curved out of sight behind a green knoll.

The driver shouted encouragement at his horses, who pulled us up the mild incline without complaint. Soon I could see the high, bleached walls, so old that bushes had rooted themselves in chinks in the crumbling masonry and grew unchecked. The driver rode alongside the walls for a moment, revealing that the estate was completely encircled by an olive grove. Soon we reached a heavily reinforced wood and iron gate, where no fewer than two dozen men-at-arms stood guard. They stepped aside as they recognized the driver; one of them waved for us to pass.

We did. I counted four residences in addition to the stables, barn, and several other outbuildings. Our destination was the great house—twice as large as the other three, set on the highest part of the promontory—which was limned by the curving driveway. The house's entrance looked onto a patio of stone inset with the occasional blue and yellow azulejo tile. A fountain featuring a large bronze dolphin stood at the patio's center, flanked by pots of geraniums and a broad squat palm tree.

The carriage came to a stop near the fountain. By the time the driver hopped down and opened the coach door, two women had hurried out onto the patio to meet me.

I caught the driver's proffered hand and stepped down to their level. Despite the cloudless sky, the strong breeze was cool; it caught the fountain's spray and drove it into my face. Before I blinked, I caught a breathtaking view: From the swell where the main house lay, most of Seville was visible, including the delicate Giralda, the bell tower that flanked the great cathedral. I could see the merlons on the walls surrounding the Alcázar, and even glimpse the armory near the docks. The Sánchez family had situated the estate so that they could see attackers coming for miles in any direction.

I wiped the water away with the edge of my sleeve and curtsied to my hostesses.

"Marisol," one breathed, as if it had been a prayer. Her brown eyes were wide with adoration and disbelief, as if she had just laid her eyes on an angel or saint. She was quite short—shorter even than me—and tiny waisted, despite the solitary streak of gray in her black hair. She was dressed like most proper Spanish matrons, in a high-necked black grown with a tiny crucifix at her heart; for some reason, she looked terribly familiar.

"Marisol," she repeated, her slack expression transforming into a radiant smile. "My name is Alma. I'm don Francisco's youngest daughter." Not *doña Alma*, as would have been proper for a stranger, but the far more intimate *Alma*. "And this"—she moved aside to gesture at the woman next to her—"is my youngest daughter, Luz."

Luz's welcoming grin was unfeigned. She was roughly my height, with black hair and dark eyes and a nose like my mother's; she might have been my sister had it not been for her tight natural curls, which formed a riot of ringlets around her face, and for the fact that she looked to be ready to give birth at any time. Her swollen belly strained so hard against her emerald brocade gown that it showed the outline of her out-turned navel.

"Marisol!" she exclaimed, as if meeting a long-lost friend. Shifting her weight, she leaned forward and reached out to take my hand. I stared down at hers uncertainly; it was spotted in places with faint layers of wet clay drying to dust, the hand of a potter, and she politely withdrew it at once.

"We're sorry," her mother Alma said. "We don't mean to overwhelm you. I know this is a terrible time for you. Come."

I followed her and Luz past delicate, decorative iron gates that led onto an inner patio planted with a dozen orange trees, where a white-haired woman wielding a broom displayed a gap-toothed genuine grin. The house reminded me a great deal of the Hojeda's massive estate, except that it was kept in far better repair. We passed by *mudéjar* archways balanced on slender marble columns, and went through the front double doors into an open sitting room large enough to accommodate hundreds of guests. It was high ceilinged and airy, with pale marble floors and many windows to let in the sun. A wide curving staircase inlaid with azulejo tiles bisected the room; dozens of padded brocade chairs and settees lined its walls, along with shelves of ceramic saints. My mother had painted some of them; I recognized her hand. Although it was early, the smell of roasting meat and onions wafted from the invisible kitchen. I drew in the smell and was immediately homesick for my parents and every meal we'd shared.

I wondered where my father was at that instant—what he'd had to eat since they'd taken him, whether he'd been able to sleep at all, what he was setting his eyes on right now. It didn't seem fair that I was free, breathing sweet air, and looking on such beautiful things.

"Let me rouse don Francisco; I'm sure you have many questions for him," Alma murmured, turning to leave.

"Oh, no," I countered thoughtlessly, "don't wake him on my account."

"Nonsense," Alma said. "He's anxious to speak to you. I'll be back shortly."

She lifted her skirts and hurried up a broad spiraling staircase, while Luz led me over to a padded chair facing a huge rectangular mirror in a gilded frame over the marble mantelpiece and offered me food and drink. I was cotton-mouthed, so Luz rang for a servant, who brought me a sweating silver goblet of heavily watered wine. To my delight, it was the same I'd drunk the night before in the royal reception room. I took a few grateful sips as Luz settled her bulk into a chair opposite mine.

"I was so sorry to hear of doña Magdalena's death," she said sweetly. "You have my condolences, and those of my family. We were so saddened to—"

"I don't know you," I interrupted, a bit too harshly. "And you didn't know my mother." I was suddenly angry at Luz for what I decided was feigned sympathy. Although the love and pity on her face seemed to be real, not even don Francisco had had a real relationship with my mother. And this young woman, despite her kindness, could not have known her at all.

Luz flushed, but her expression remained kind and sad. "No, I didn't. But we all admired her so. And I know how awful it must be for you this morning, after what happened last night." She lowered her voice on the last sentence, even though we were alone in the vast room.

Her words so startled me that I forgot my anger. "You know about my father?" I gasped.

She lowered her gaze and smiled sadly at me. Only then did I notice the crease between her brows as she struggled to keep her eyes fully open. She was exhausted, as if she'd slept little, and I realized suddenly that her mother had looked drawn as well.

"My grandfather knows everything that happens in Seville." She paused, and her little grin faded. "I know you must feel very alone, Marisol. But you're not. You've never been."

She had no idea how I felt: Her mother hadn't killed herself; her father hadn't been arrested. But my efforts to hate her were failing. She was a *conversa*—like me marked by her hair, features, and dark eyes—and although she was gazing on me with pity now, it was only a matter of time before the Inquisition destroyed her family, too. I couldn't let myself think how Torquemada would deal with her and her unborn child if I exchanged her life for my father's.

As I looked at her, my gaze fell on the mirror. I saw myself, pale and desperate, and the back of Luz's body and head, covered in a sheer veil. From her build, it could have been my mother sitting there against the backdrop of the opposite wall's reflection. Her head was at the level of the wooden shelves, with their pantheon of ceramic saints. The front entrance, with its double wooden doors, was reflected as well; to their right, a small, special double shelf had been erected. On the very top sat a ceramic Madonna. She stood out from the other household saints not only because of her special post by the entry, or of the score of lit votives on the lower shelf, but because, of the dozens of figurines, she was the worst looking. The bright cherry-red paint missed part of the fullness of her lower lip and escaped the borders of her upper; the black dots that served as pupils for her flat blue eyes made the latter looked crossed. Her veil was a paler shade of the same blue, and behind it was a massive solar halo, with long gilded rays emanating from it. The child in her arms had been painted stark white and was overly fat.

I blinked several times, but the impossible apparition remained. It was a perfect copy of my mother's ugly Madonna, the one that she was so fond of, the one that Máriam had insisted on bringing into the Hojeda house.

It was no doubt coincidence that an identical ugly statue resided in don Francisco's home; I couldn't afford to yield to emotion and trust him or anyone else, however badly I wanted to confide in this sweet girl. I closed my eyes and struggled for control while Luz waited patiently. When she reached out to pat my hand, I pulled it away.

"My parents and I have always been alone," I said. "No one helped us when she died."

"She is a hero," Luz said vehemently. "Had it been safe for you and your father, we surely would have visited you after she passed."

"Did you know her?" I asked.

"We never met." Luz turned her face toward the windows. Rays of sunlight bathed her features, revealing a glaze of unshed tears over her brown eyes, flecked with gold; for the first time, I noticed that their rims were red, the lids puffed and swollen. In the mirror, her beautiful face appeared beside that of the homely Virgin. "But I knew *of* her, of course, just as she knew of us."

"How——" I began, but was interrupted by the arrival of doña Alma.

"Don Francisco is thrilled that you are here," Alma announced, glaring at Luz as if she had said too much. "Will you follow me, please, to his study?"

I obeyed. Unsmiling, I nodded a good-bye to Luz and followed Alma upstairs to a long corridor. We made our way to a closed door, where Alma knocked lightly, then opened the door, which swung inward, and turned to me.

"I realize that it's inappropriate," Alma said in a low voice, "but I'm afraid don Francisco has forbidden me to come inside during his discussion with you. But I'll be right outside the door." She put a tentative, reassuring hand on my shoulder and managed a wan smile; her eyes, too, were red, as though she had been weeping all night.

I stepped over the threshold and heard the door close behind me with a click. Now that the sun was climbing, the day was turning warm, but the fire in the study hearth was still blazing, and the room smelled of smoke. I breathed in a lungful of over-heated air and immediately began to sweat.

The small, low-ceilinged room held little furniture. There was a pair of padded chairs with arms, a writing desk with ink-well and quill and a stool, and a velvet chaise longue with a sleep-ing pillow and rumpled blanket lying on it. The pillow still bore the imprint of don Francisco's head. Near the desk, a massive tome sat open on a reading pedestal. Wooden bookcases that spanned floor to ceiling held more books than I'd ever seen col-lected in one place, books in Castilian, Aragonese, French, Ital-ian, Latin, Arabic, and Greek. Some were leather bound, some scrolls, others unbound stacks of paper or parchment. My eyes widened at the sight of them all, and then don Francisco stepped into view.

The old man was bleary-eyed and stiff; he straightened with a faint groan, but greeted me warmly. "Doña Marisol. I'm so glad you could come." His eyes were not as red as Luz's or Alma's, but he seemed to have aged a good deal overnight. His manner was grave, his tone hushed. "I'd hoped to have far better news for you this morning. We hoped to warn your father in time so you could both escape, but unfortunately, we couldn't stop the arrest—nor the wagon that took him to the prison."

"Yes," I answered quickly, without really hearing what he'd said. "You know then, that he's there. Can you help him?"

Don Francisco tilted his head to one side and let go one of the longest, weariest sighs I'd ever heard—the sigh of Atlas, bearing the weight of the world. "Doña, I know how you loved your mother and how you love your father. For this reason alone, I've told you as much as I dare. But I first must know: What did your mother tell you about me?"

"Nothing."

"Nothing at all?" He lifted a disbelieving brow.

I shook my head; interestingly, he seemed relieved.

"But can you help my father?" I persisted.

"It will be far more difficult now, if not impossible." His tone switched from apologetic to stern. "I'd meant for you and your father to leave Seville together last night. I'm sorry I could give you no warning; you won't be able to take anything with you. But it's imperative you leave Seville. Now."

"Leave Seville?" I gasped. "Where would I go?"

"I can't tell you that." The old man shifted his weight uneasily; I realized that standing was hard for him and I immediately sat down in a chair so that he could do the same. "The carriage waits now," he continued. "You'll be well provided for; money won't be an issue. You'll go where there are people who will care for you."

"There's no one I know outside of Seville," I answered, "and even if there were, I wouldn't leave the city without my father."

"Doña Marisol, I trust you enough to tell you that if you leave, your father won't be deserted. But if you stay, you might well be captured yourself."

I shook my head, vehement. "Let me make it clear, don Francisco. I know the danger and I don't care. I'm not leaving Seville without my father."

He watched me carefully throughout our exchange. His

forehead grew furrowed as I spoke; my last words seemed to res-
onate with him. His watery eyes narrowed with pride.

"I had expected nothing less than courage from you," he murmured. "You are indeed Magdalena's daughter." I flushed at the
compliment as he continued. "I'm afraid that danger to you and
others has required me to be oblique up to now, so let me be
completely clear. Had it been possible, I would have had both you
and your father escaping today."

"You would have rescued us both today? Why?" I asked.
"Why would you do something so dangerous? Why would you
risk everything for us?"

"Because I love your mother," he said.

I thought suddenly of my father's behavior around don
Francisco—polite, but doggedly distant. I thought of how my
mother would smile shyly at Francisco in public without greeting
him, and immediately lower her eyes.

"I'm afraid that's all I can say at this moment," the elderly
patriarch added. "If you're not leaving Seville now, it's better that
you know as little as possible. I urge you to go home and stay
there or find someplace to hide. We can provide a place for you
here if you like."

"No," I said. "I need to help my father. Is there anything else
you can do for him?"

Don Francisco glanced up and to the right, at something invisible and ugly. He fingered the curl of his moustache absently
as regret crossed his features, only to be replaced by faint hard-
ness. "Not today, I fear. Not while the sun shines."

"Then I'll go to Queen Isabel and beg her for mercy. She told
me last night she liked my performance and would grant me a
favor."

He shook his head. "The queen is good at making pretty speeches. But she's a ruthless decision maker. I've known her for years, Marisol."

The back of my throat tightened until it ached. "I'll get Antonio's help then. Maybe he can speak to his superior, Fray Morillo."

"Hmm," don Francisco said. "Do you think it's wise to get don Antonio involved? Do you trust him?"

I hesitated. "No," I said. "He deserted me. We were supposed to marry, but . . ." I glanced away at the flames snapping in the hearth. "He stopped writing to me. I suppose he found another girl in Salamanca. We pretend that we're still friends, but—" I broke off. The world I knew had just changed. Perhaps it was all an act, but I trusted this man and these women who spoke so kindly of my mother. And even though I was still desperate to save my father, I felt a wild rush of hope. "Torquemada questioned me last night. About you."

Don Francisco managed a faint grin. "Did he?"

"He wants me to get to know you so that I can inform on you. The Inquisition wants your property and wealth."

He let go a feeble chuckle. "You're not telling me anything I haven't known for some time, my dear." For a long moment he studied me intently, then spoke again, his tone sharper. "Marisol, the Inquisition will come for you next. Considering that the queen is disposed to listen to Fray Tomás de Torquemada over Fray Alonso . . ."

"I want to help you," I said, with half a heart. Yet at the same time, I didn't know these people very well, and I knew I lacked the resolve to keep their secrets if it meant my father had to die. "But I have to do what's necessary to free my father. So I don't

think we should meet again, don Francisco. I shouldn't have come here."

All trace of humor fled the old man's features. For a long time, he gazed on me solemnly, sizing me up; I knew he sensed my lack of determination. Finally he answered, "Perhaps not. But I would ask one favor of you."

I lifted my brows questioningly.

"Honor your mother by finishing her work. See that no statue remains unfinished."

"Why?" I demanded.

He remained silent.

"But her work is locked up in my father's house; I can't get to it."

A longer pause followed. At last he said, "You're intelligent enough to figure out a way. And stay on good terms with don Antonio. I'll make sure he does you no harm." He paused again. "You alone can finish the work she began for us. But I must know that you are sincere. . . . You and she never spoke of me or my family?"

"Never," I said, with a bit of shame. "I . . . judged her harshly for being a *conversa*. It was cruel of me to do so."

"I see," he replied sternly.

Before he could utter the next sentence, I interrupted. "You speak as though my mother's work were somehow important."

Don Francisco frowned. "I've already told you too much. Any more would put you and us at higher risk. Go home. And if by chance you decide to share this conversation with Torquemada—be aware it's grounds for *your* arrest, as well. Don't worry about your father. Just remember . . . my offer to help you escape still stands."

I nodded but inwardly had every intention of going to see Her Majesty as soon as I could to beg for my father's life . . . and of figuring out the secret that my mother and don Francisco had kept.

Fifteen

On my return from don Francisco's house, the driver let me out of the unmarked carriage on San Pablo Street a good walk from my house. I was glad he did; the instant I turned the corner onto the Hojeda cul-de-sac, I saw another black carriage waiting in front of Gabriel's house, this one bearing the standard of the Inquisition—a wooden cross flanked on its right by an olive branch, on its left by a double-edged sword, the whole set beneath the Crown of Spain.

The sight made me quail. I was tempted to turn around and run from it—but the thought that my father waited at the other end of the ride made me steady myself and walk up to it.

Blanca, her eyes starkly wide, stood out in front of the house walls beside Máriam. Her pale features conveyed suspicion. "How can there be *two* carriages for you in one day? And what am I to tell don Gabriel if he returns home and you're not here?"

I shrugged. "What will you tell the queen, the Inquisition, if I don't go?"

Máriam stepped up to me and put a tentative hand on my elbow, a bold move for her. "I won't leave you, doña Marisol."

"You will," I said shortly, and not at all nicely, despite her show of loyalty; it was the only way to show her I was serious.

I waited as the driver climbed down and opened the coach door for me. As he helped me inside, I started at the sight of Antonio Vargas, again dressed all in black. The color leached away the ruddiness of his flesh, but not the intensity of his red-gold hair.

"The world is determined to put us together," he quipped wryly at my dismay, twisting one corner of his mouth to reveal a dimple. He reminded me so much of the old Antonio that I gave a short, humorless laugh despite myself.

But when he offered a hand to steady me as I settled on the seat beside him, I pulled away coldly. "Who sends you?" I demanded.

The light left his eyes. "Fray Tomás de Torquemada," he answered. "He wishes to question you himself." He cleared his throat. "My superior, Fray Morillo, has given me leave to attend to Fray Tomás while he is visiting. You're a person of particular interest to him."

"Only because don Francisco took a liking to me last night. Torquemada wants his hands on the money." Anger welled up in me. "I swear to you, he'll never get his hands on anything belonging to my father."

Antonio turned his face sharply toward the window. "Ahh, innocent Marisol. Did they not tell you?" He glanced back at me, his lids half lowered with an emotion I decided was shame. "Your father's property and money has already been seized by the

Crown. Even if he's found innocent, it's unlikely he'll see any of it returned."

The Inquisition had no right to ruin my father's life forever over a baseless charge. Even the most feared Inquisition in France, a century earlier, respected the accused's rights. "But that's impossible! Illegal! Surely Queen Isabel—"

"Isabel knows what is going on," he said. "She and the king are deeply involved in the workings of the Inquisition." He focused his eyes on the sights outside the window.

"How can you know that?" I demanded. "The queen is a very pious Christian: She came all the way to Seville in secret to make sure the Inquisition was carried out properly."

He shrugged. "Believe what you wish, doña."

"I believe you're jaded from listening to the Inquisitors. And I believe the queen is a good person who would be scandalized by the greediness surrounding her."

Antonio shrugged again. We both fell quiet as he again directed his attention outside. I didn't speak until our carriage pulled alongside the Church of San Pablo.

"So," I said coldly, "you've betrayed me twice."

He quickly drew his attention back from the scene beyond the window. "I never betrayed you," he said evenly. "You abandoned me."

"Liar!" I snapped. "You're—"

He interrupted. "You never answered my letters. Not one of them—"

I talked over him. "You never sent me any letters. I sent you dozens!"

"—and I returned to Seville to discover you were marrying

Gabriel Hojeda. What was I to think, Marisol?" He stopped abruptly as my words registered.

"I told you," I said heatedly, lowering my voice. "I wrote you and never heard back. So one of us is lying."

His expression was perplexed. "Or neither."

That gave me pause. It didn't matter, I told myself bitterly. I could never love a man who served as Torquemada's lackey.

We didn't speak as we rode past the church and through the monastery walls, up to the three-story dormitory near the outbuilding where the Inquisitors worked and where I had met Antonio and the queen. The dormitory windows were still all shuttered, holding in the day's warmth but not the wafting stench of human waste. It seemed wrong that a building of such graceful design, with its rows of archways and slender turrets, should contain such misery.

Our carriage rolled to a stop in front of the main entrance; a guard hurried over to make sure of our identities and that I was not carrying a weapon. Antonio shouldered a satchel of papers before following me inside the building; I felt both oddly reassured and unsettled that he was accompanying me.

Finally we were allowed to pass beneath the central archway—flanked on either side by a pair of guards—into the prison, where the smell grew so foul I pressed a kerchief to my nose. Antonio seemed not to notice. A guard led us down a broad corridor with doors on either side. Clearly, the rooms had previously served as cells for monks, as the archways above the doors were painted with religious tableaus: the Nativity, the Crucifixion, the Assumption of Mary. But now the heavy wooden doors were fortified with black iron bars and padlocks.

Near the end of the hallway, one of the doors sat ajar. Here the guard stopped and gestured for me—but not Antonio—to enter. I felt a thrill of panic. What if I was being tricked—and being arrested now, at this moment?

My nerves weren't helped by the fact that Fray Tomás de Torquemada was sitting behind a small desk, waiting for me; behind him—as if he needed protection from me, a mere girl—stood a burly man bearing a long sword.

"Come," Fray Tomás said, in the warmest, most inviting tone he'd used yet. "Please, doña Marisol, come sit and talk with me." He noted my reaction to the guard standing behind him and gave a short, insincere laugh, more like a bark, as the guard stepped around us to close the door behind us, leaving Antonio standing in the corridor. "Don't let Ignacio cause you any concern. He's simply here as a chaperone. Please, sit down."

Reluctantly I obeyed and sat on the stool across the desk from him.

And he smiled at me, the penetrating, lipless smile of the serpent in Eden. I was surprised yet again by how ugly he was—his tiny eyes embedded in a face full of flesh that looked like a child's clumsy effort to throw a lump of clay on the potter's wheel; his nose thick, pockmarked, and shapeless; his head crowned by the coarse, curly silver and brown fringe encircling his grayish white scalp.

"I mean you no harm," he said pleasantly. "You're of far too much use to us to be in any danger."

If he meant to reassure me, he failed; I was more concerned about someone else. "Where is my father, Fray Tomás? What have you done with him?"

"You'll see him presently." He leaned forward over the desk, and his homely features shifted from welcoming to subtly intimidating. "First, I have a few questions for you. Remember, I am questioning you as a member of the Holy Office of the Inquisition; if you lie, therefore, you are not only committing perjury, you are endangering your immortal soul."

I sent up a quick prayer to God, asking that He would protect those I loved from any careless remark I might make, and then braced myself for questions about my family. But Torquemada's first question caught me off guard.

"How well do you know Antonio Vargas, doña?"

I started, but controlled myself quickly; Torquemada missed none of it. "Not well at all," I said, feigning more scorn and outrage than I actually felt at the moment. "We played together when we were children. But he went off to university and never communicated with me again."

"Hmm." Something I'd said caused a light to flicker in his narrow eyes. "I had heard that he had told you he would marry you when he returned from Salamanca . . . ?"

"That's true," I admitted after a pause. "But he stopped writing me a few years ago. Long enough for me to realize that he was a liar."

"So you have no feelings for him?"

"No," I said emphatically, cursing my burning cheeks.

He rested his elbows upon the desk, hands folded as if in earnest prayer, and brought his face uncomfortably close to mine; his gaze was breathtakingly cold. "So if you believed him to be guilty of a crime against Mother Church and the Spanish Crown, you would report it to me at once?"

"Yes, of course," I said, with an ease that made me proud. I neither flinched nor looked away but held his gaze fast, knowing at that instant that I could never do such a thing to Antonio unless he had also committed a heinous crime against humanity. My childhood friend had betrayed me, hurt me—but I had no intention of doing the same to him.

"And you would come tell me if you suspected anyone else of heresy?"

I nodded eagerly.

"Then why," Torquemada pressed, his tone suddenly icy with contempt, "did you not report your own mother for your entire life?"

I stared at him.

"Her suicide—for that is what rumor says—is itself an admission of guilt," Torquemada said. "Otherwise, what had she to fear from us? Why kill herself unless she was trying to hide something from us?

"It is your duty, Marisol, to tell us why your mother felt she had to die."

A clever man, Torquemada. In only a minute, he'd brought me to the edge of tears.

"She drowned accidentally. But of course, anyone with Jewish blood would be afraid of the Inquisition. Her parents were killed by Old Christians. . . ." The minute the last sentence was out of my mouth, I regretted it.

Another sudden spark in the tiny hazel eyes. "And her parents' names would be . . . ?"

"I don't know," I answered. "I don't know. I only know they died violently."

"A pity," he responded, in a tone so devoid of feeling it would have been infuriating if it hadn't been so chilling. "Be that as it may, let me suggest a course of action to you. It seems that Francisco Sánchez has taken a sudden liking to you. That he invited you to his home. Is this not true?"

I became aware of my rapid heartbeat and forced myself to draw a deep breath. I meant no harm to don Francisco or his family, but it was very possible that a spy—even Antonio, despite Torquemada's attempt to cast suspicion on him—had witnessed the warm exchange between don Francisco and me at the queen's palace. Or worse, had somehow learned of my visit to his home that very morning. And so I was forced to tell the truth, in hopes of playing along for a little while.

"Yes," I told Torquemada.

He leaned back, and the ghost of a smile crossed his features.

"I would suggest, doña Marisol, that you consider denouncing don Francisco in order to save your father's life. We have more than enough evidence to convict your father and sentence him to death. But you could change that—and save your own skin as well—by gathering evidence against don Francisco."

I struggled to keep my tone from sounding ragged. "What sort of evidence?"

The friar didn't hesitate. "That don Francisco engages in crypto-Jewish practices. More importantly, that he is funneling large amounts of gold, silver, and gems belonging to himself and other *conversos* out of Seville. And helping fellow *conversos* escape. All these are mortal crimes against church and Crown, punishable by death."

I forced myself not to flinch; I'd heard enough as a girl about the terrible Inquisition just to the north of Spain, where hundreds if not thousands had been burned alive at the stake—a slow, hideous death.

And then I realized it could actually happen to my father if I wasn't willing to make don Francisco die.

I lifted my gaze to see Torquemada studying me with an intense predatory but pleased expression; no doubt he'd read my thoughts all too well.

He signaled to the guard. "Ignacio. Would you bring the prisoner in, please?" His tone was faintly gloating.

Ignacio obeyed, and when I heard the door creak open, I couldn't sit still but jumped up and turned around to face the open doorway, where my father stood.

Flanked by Antonio on one side and a tall, wiry guard on the other, my father seemed barely recognizable. Don Diego's shoulders had always been strong and square, but now they had buckled and his head had bowed beneath the weight of shackles on his wrists and ankles. He shuffled into the room like a man thirty years older. As he neared, I could see that the skin around his pale eyes was taut and quivering; that, along with his tense posture revealed the severity of his physical suffering. Always clean-shaven, he now sported all-silver bristles on his face; there was a streak of pure white in his uncombed light brown hair, which hadn't been there the day before.

I wanted to run to him but managed to hold myself back. My father croaked emotionlessly, "Don't touch me. I have lice."

He showed no joy at the sight of me; his gaze was so guarded that he showed no reaction at all. For a fleeting second, I was hurt by his rejection, but then I understood why he had married me off to Gabriel and had pretended to disown me, why he would not look in my eyes now. It was all calculated to protect me and to refuse to give Torquemada joy at the sight of our torment.

For the first time since my mother's death, I felt pride and uncomplicated love for my father. And because I wanted him to take pride in me, I straightened my shoulders the way that he could not, banished all emotion from my features, and turned from him. I retook my place on the stool across from Torquemada and forced myself not to look at my father's face.

Torquemada scowled first at my father, then at me.

"You show little interest in your fate, don Diego," he said. "Are you still determined to be burned alive at the stake, or will you take pity on your daughter here and give us the names we want? Else she will join you soon."

"Marisol is strong," my father answered tonelessly, "and I will not dishonor her or her mother by becoming a liar this late in my life. I denounce no one—for I know of no one guilty of your charges."

"You married a Judaizer!" Torquemada thundered. "For that alone, you deserve to die. But we will spare you if you confess"— and now Fray Tomás's ugly gaze fixed itself on me—"or if your daughter confesses."

"I am innocent and have nothing to confess," my father breathed. "And I am ready to die. As for my daughter, she has no business being involved in the matter, as she is entirely innocent and naive."

I wanted to beg him to do precisely as Torquemada asked. But he was honorable, like my mother, and truly did prefer death to causing the slaughter of innocent others. I couldn't force him to go against his own conscience.

"Doña Marisol," Fray Tomás snapped, clearly irritated with both of us. "Remember: Your answer could save your father's life. Was your mother a crypto-Jew? Did she pray on Friday nights? Observe Passover?"

"No," I said, with a vehemence that made Torquemada lift his grizzled brows.

"Well, then, have you nothing to say to your father?"

"Yes," I said. "I wish to tell him that I love him." Despite all my efforts, my eyes brimmed and a single hot tear spilled from my cheek into my lap.

"Love him enough to help save him?"

"Yes," I whispered, and Torquemada gave another smug grin.

My father spoke dispassionately. "I wish to tell my daughter that I love her no matter what she chooses. And I bid her farewell."

Torquemada jerked to his feet.

"That's enough from you, don Diego! I'd hoped the sight of your daughter would bring you to your senses, but that's clearly not the case. Ignacio, take the prisoner back to his cell."

My father allowed himself one brief, longing glance at me before the guard caught his elbow and forced him to turn his back to me and shuffle from the room. Only after he was gone and the door closed behind him did I notice that Antonio was standing in a corner, busily writing notes on our conversation.

"And now, Marisol," Torquemada said, once he was settled again on his stool, "I will offer you a second chance to save your father's life. Will you befriend don Francisco and gather enough evidence—quickly, in a matter of two days—against him for us to convict him of smuggling valuables and *conversos* out of Seville?

"Otherwise, doña, enjoy your performance tonight for Her Majesty, as the next time I allow you to meet with your father again . . . it will be in the torture chamber. Perhaps that will change both your minds."

I looked to Torquemada, to the unreadable Antonio, and couldn't find my voice.

Fray Tomás repeated the question about gathering evidence against Sánchez, this time with far less patience.

I drew a long breath, feeling as though I were sinking fast beneath the weighty waters of the river. I couldn't bring myself to betray the entire Sánchez family at that moment—but I feared, as the time grew shorter for my father, that I would do exactly that.

"Yes," I said at last, avoiding both men's eyes. "Yes, I'll get your evidence."

Sixteen

I rode home in the carriage, but I didn't see the fine leather appointments, the black silk drapes; nor did I see the dormitory receding behind us, or the Church of San Pablo, or even Gabriel's house when the coach finally stopped in front of it. Instead, I saw my mother, dipping her spoon into her soup bowl, asking, *Has don Diego told you I am under investigation by the Inquisition?* I no longer wanted to cry; instead, I was caught in that horrible moment of futile rage, when my mother was drowning and Gabriel held me back.

I hated Torquemada now as I hated Gabriel then, yet I could not in good conscience turn in don Francisco, any more than I could bring myself to turn in Máriam as a *morisca*, a Muslim heretic.

I saw only one possible way out: to speak to the queen.

After I returned home, while Máriam unlaced my bodice and helped me into my housedress, I did my best to answer her concerned, discreet questions. But I could only reply in the tersest sentences.

I was home barely an hour when yet another carriage arrived for me. This one had the royal insignia painted on its glossy black doors and bore doña Berta, who insisted on remaining in the coach until Máriam finished helping me dress yet again. I put on the same dark blue velvet dress—my finest—that I had worn the night before to the palace, but I felt no anticipation, no excitement or anxiety over my upcoming performance.

When I was finally ready and let the driver take my elbow to help me up inside the carriage, doña Berta sat, her protruding belly draped in aubergine silk, a waist-length sheer lilac veil covering her coiled ash-and-white braids. She lifted a hand heavy with amethysts and diamonds and gestured, saying in the courtliest Castilian, "Of course, you know your neighbor, Antonio Vargas." She giggled suddenly like a child, breaking the formality. "He certainly looks handsome today, doesn't he? Almost, I dare say, as much as you look beautiful."

I started a bit when I saw Antonio sitting across from doña Berta. It only made sense, of course—he must have come home to change clothing, and lived across the street—and had I not been so distracted by thoughts of my father and Torquemada, I might have been flustered by his handsomeness. He wore a silk tunic of an amber hue that made his bright hair and lapis blue eyes come alive. I caught myself staring at him—as much out of hatred for his participation in my father's humiliation today as out of lust.

"What a handsome couple you two make!" Berta said. "Her Majesty will be so pleased. She asked for you again, as she wishes to be entertained before her supper. No crowds tonight, only her immediate court. I thought we would bring you early to the palace so that you could rehearse with Her Majesty's musicians and learn a few new songs."

Antonio managed a politely interested smile as Berta chattered on, giving instructions, repeating herself. I doubt my wan effort at a smile was anywhere as convincing; my heart was with my father and the curiously kind don Francisco.

Once again, as I rode through the streets of Seville—this time southeastward, toward the Real Alcázar, I failed to notice the sights and sounds, including doña Berta's near constant droning. I remained lost in memories: My father embracing me joyfully as he returned home from work; my mother teaching me to hold the fine paintbrush, the one for creating eyes and lips, for the first time: *Just so, my darling, between your little thumb and forefinger . . .*

When we finally rattled onto the property of the Royal Palace and through the Lion's Gate, our carriage came to rest in front of King Pedro's Palace. I exited the carriage first, then drew doña Berta aside as we waited for Antonio to descend.

"Please," I whispered, "I desperately need to speak with the queen privately today. Would it be possible?"

Berta's expression remained kind, but she studied me cagily. "The queen isn't holding audiences today."

"I don't mean to be rude," I said, "but it has to do with my father's life."

Her pale, nearly invisible eyebrows lifted. "In that case, perhaps . . . but it depends on the subject matter."

Fully emerged from the coach, Antonio stepped off to one side and allowed us a bit of privacy.

"My father has been wrongly accused of a crime," I said.

Berta laid a jeweled hand on her large, crepey bosom. "Oh, dear. But what crime has he been accused of?"

"Heresy. He's being held by the Inquisition."

Berta slowly lowered her hand; the pity in her eyes cooled to distrust. I may as well have admitted to having the plague.

"I will speak to her," she said stiffly, "but it depends on her mood, you understand."

"I understand," I said. "Thank you."

I couldn't allow myself to yield to fear at Berta's cold reaction; I stubbornly decided that Queen Isabel, being far more pious, would also be far more compassionate and open-minded.

With Antonio beside me, I met the other musicians. They were three permanent courtiers, all from the north, like their queen: a mandolin player, a flutist, and a drummer. No doubt they thought my pained, distant smile arose from the same type of disdain they felt toward outsiders. But Antonio won them over and managed to cheer even the mandolin player, a woman who was enormously jealous over the fact that I would be singing the solos.

Our repertoire was to be different that evening. There would be no lusty tavern songs, no love ballads with earthy innuendos. When we went at last to perform for the queen, I understood why: She was surrounded by a sea of black and white, all Dominican priests, monks, and nuns. The long dining hall had been decorated with tapestries depicting scenes from the life of Christ, giving the sense that we were in a chapel or monastery, not a pleasure palace. The effect was enhanced by the fact that all the diners faced us, as if in a Last Supper tableau, and Isabel herself sat at the very center of the long dining table.

She wore what she had when I'd first met her: an exquisitely tailored black mourning gown and no jewelry save a small gold crucifix. Her behavior—although more assertive than the nuns'—was solemn and prim.

The Mother Superior of the local Dominican convent sat to her immediate left, Torquemada to her immediate right; beside him sat Fray Morillo, head of the Dominican Order and Antonio's immediate superior.

This time, we musicians weren't announced or applauded; it was our job to play and sing softly enough not to impede conversation among the diners. Because they kept their voices low and we were obligated to play at some distance from the table, I couldn't make out what they were saying. But the somber expressions on the faces of the three having the most intense conversation—Isabel, Torquemada, and Morillo—betrayed the subject matter.

Hojeda had been invited as well—this looked to be a gathering of all the upper-level Dominicans in Seville, and as head of San Pablo, he could not be ignored—but he had been placed at the very end of the right side of the table, separated from the queen by several male diners so that he couldn't hear the conversation or catch the queen's attention, much less be heard himself. The look of frustration on his round, owlish face was comical.

After we musicians began our musical foray with a stirring—if more sedate than the previous night—tribute to the city of Seville, we launched into a psalm:

Whither shall I go from thy Spirit?
Or whither shall I flee from thy presence
If I ascend up into heaven, thou art there;
If I make my bed in hell, behold, thou art there.

The mandolin player and I launched into a sweet, high harmony.

I prayed with my entire being, with an intensity that made me ache, until I knew I had reached something, something I caught and held fast, not even certain whose God I was praying to:

Please let Queen Isabel free my father. Please soften her heart. I can't lose him too, O Lord.... Please, I'll do whatever You ask of me for the rest of my life. Only grant me this....

Through each song I prayed with all my strength, all my will. And at one point doña Berta finally appeared and genuflected apologetically to the queen for interrupting her supper. She leaned over and whispered at length into Isabel's ear. Both the queen and Berta looked hesitantly out at me.

And then Isabel drew a weary breath, shook her head, and dismissed Berta with a flick of the royal fingers.

I was devastated but kept singing. I could not, would not, let my father's life be dismissed so easily.

When the meal was at last over, Her Majesty took her leave, accompanied by Torquemada and a single bodyguard; the rest of the guards remained with the Dominicans, who shuffled out of the room slowly. Meanwhile, Berta approached me, her plump, jowly face glum, her eyes faintly guarded.

"I am so sorry," she began, but I held up my hand.

"Please, doña," I said raggedly. "It's bad enough news. I don't need to hear the actual words."

"Poor girl," she clucked. "It's not *that* bad. Her Majesty is engaged today and cannot speak to you. Perhaps tomorrow. So go to the kitchen with the other musicians and get your fair share of something to eat."

As if I could think of food under such circumstances. Berta made a poor liar; not only did her expression reveal it, but Queen Isabel's utterly dismissive gesture had indicated no possibility of a second chance. But I nodded sadly and followed Antonio and the others at a far distance. Once out of the dining hall and into the narrow corridor, I waited until they and Berta were out of sight . . . and then intentionally followed what I suspected had been the queen's footsteps.

God would either help me now or I would be thrown into jail for daring to trespass in the Royal Palace.

I took off my slippers and hurried as fast and as quietly as I could down the tiled corridors, cold against my bare feet; there were few rectangular doors, only graceful archways opening onto other archways into seeming infinity. Soon I could just see the backs of the guards and the slowest-moving Dominicans; I thanked God silently that all but one of the guards had chosen to accompany the guests. I followed quietly, ducking behind corners when they presented themselves, until the guards herded their charges around a corner to the left—the way that led out to the open square in front of King Pedro's Palace.

Once they were out of sight, I quickened my pace until I just caught sight of Torquemada and Queen Isabel, rounding another brightly tiled and gilded corner, with the solitary guard following at a discreet distance so as not to intrude on their conversation. I waited for the guard to disappear, then ran to the corner and carefully peered beyond it.

The queen and Torquemada stood in front of a pair of heavy dark brown-black doors; I realized at once that they led to the Gothic chapel and that I'd just trodden the way that doña Berta had led me the night I first performed for Her Majesty.

As Torquemada swung open one of the great tall doors, Isabel turned to the guard and uttered something softly. The guard bowed and began to return back down the corridor, the way he'd come—the way that he would surely see me.

I checked my first impulse. If I ran, I would be immediately presumed to be up to something nefarious, and, besides, the slap of my bare feet against the tile would alert him. I knew I couldn't run fast enough to hide behind yet another corner.

On instinct, I pressed myself against the wall and tried desperately to think of an excuse, one that might win me an audience with Her Majesty.

I tensed, inhaling sharply and not breathing as the guard approached the corner . . .

. . . and to my intense relief, he didn't turn but continued straight ahead, his attention on something other than the small young woman flattened against the perpendicular wall.

I exhaled deeply once he'd passed and peeked around the corner again to catch a glimpse of Torquemada closing the door behind Isabel.

If I threw myself and my father on the queen's mercy while Torquemada was there, there was little chance of convincing her to take pity on my father. But there was no way to predict how long their conversation might last; in the meantime, I was too exposed standing in the hallway—and that's when I remembered the choir stall overlooking the chapel.

Quickly, silently, I found the stairs leading up to the stall and ascended them. I crouched low, trying to still my breathing; fortunately, Torquemada and the queen were too engrossed in conversation to notice me. They stood in front of the great altar, where a painted, gilded Virgin held her man-infant as angels set a crown upon her head. This was recessed into a panel of dark, ornately carved wood—the same dark wood of the choir stalls and pews. Happily the altar was placed acoustically so that I could hear their every word.

Isabel stood beneath the huge flickering chandeliers; her tone was venomous, her words echoing off the high domed ceiling: "... lied to me! I don't know why I should be so surprised when dealing with their kind. Had the gall to put me off to my face. A week! A kingdom can be won or lost in a week. Doesn't he realize what it takes to sustain a war? How could I ever win Granada if I can't even secure my western kingdom? ..." She trailed off, then grew freshly agitated as another thought occurred to her. "Yes, it's the largest amount I've ever asked for, but he surely has it! How dare he make excuses to *me*?"

"Your Majesty," Torquemada said emotionlessly, "he is indeed lying to you; his kind simply can't speak the truth. I swear to you upon my soul that Sánchez is planning to smuggle at *least* as much as you asked for, if not more, as soon as he can. He stalls you so that you will never receive a single coin. Rumor says he has already smuggled at least that much to his family in Portugal."

I expected Isabel to burst into a fresh tirade, but instead she grew quiet and paused a long moment before asking solemnly, "Are you certain of this, Fray Tomás? Don Francisco has long been a friend to us and supplied us with funds."

"You'll see all of those funds," Torquemada countered, "and all of his vast properties if you are patient another day or two.

Trust me, Your Majesty, and trust God. The young girl, the singer who asked for an audience with you today—her father has been denounced and arrested. Don Francisco has befriended her—unfortunately for him. She will crumble soon and give us evidence. And if she will not, Antonio Vargas will."

"Who?"

"Vargas, Your Majesty. The redheaded lad who serves as secretary to Fray Morillo. He is a Sevillian, and he and his parents were long friends with don Francisco and the rest of the Sánchez family. I shall give him an opportunity to prove whether his true loyalties lie with us or them."

Isabel snorted. "Let us hope he chooses wisely, then." And she switched the topic to battles she was still fighting against the traditionalists who couldn't bear the thought of a woman on Spain's throne.

It didn't matter; I'd heard enough. No matter how prettily I made my case, Isabel would never free my father. Antonio had been right: She was far more interested in the profit she could make off his estate. And how could I be sure don Francisco wasn't manipulating me as a pawn, too?

I stole down the choir stall and fled down the hallways until I found my way out of the palace to an aggravated doña Berta and the waiting coach. She believed my story that I'd briefly taken ill and had gotten lost trying to find the water closet—or at least, like everyone else, she pretended to.

By the time I made it home in the carriage, I was overcome by rage—against the queen, against Torquemada, and most especially against God, who had resoundingly ignored my heartfelt prayer and had instead shown me how hopeless my father's situation was.

When I arrived back at Gabriel's house well after sunset, he and Fray Hojeda were waiting in the dining hall to interrogate me: Did I put in a good word for Hojeda and Gabriel with the queen? Yes, yes, I answered, irritable and impatient; that night I didn't care what either man did to me if they learned I wasn't telling the truth.

Gabriel asked, "Did you do as I asked with Antonio?"

"Yes," I lied nastily. "Yes, I kissed him and he kissed me back. And we enjoyed it. So are you happy, pious man, to have your wife play the harlot?"

With that, I turned my back to both men without permission—catching a glimpse of jealousy on Gabriel's hawkish face and suspicion on Fray Hojeda's—and stomped off across the courtyard to my apartment.

Máriam was in the bedroom praying in front of my mother's ugly ceramic Madonna. She was kneeling on the floor, her dark hands held at a distance, covering her eyes; as I entered, she looked up slowly, her expression inquisitive.

"Stop praying and get up!" I snapped, not caring who overheard. "God doesn't listen. He doesn't care."

Máriam finished her praying and rose gracefully, calmly.

"They will kill my father," I half shouted, "and probably me too. It's all for money, do you understand? All for money!"

In my rage, I stood on my tiptoes, grabbed the ugly Madonna from her shelf, and dashed her to the floor. Máriam moved to catch it, but in a heartbeat, it lay broken between us: The Madonna's face had cracked in two diagonally, from the top of her head to her blue-veiled shoulder. The Christ child in her arms was intact, but a second shard had come loose on her face, leaving a gap where her crossed blue eyes had been.

In that gap lay wool wadding, wrapped tightly around something at the statue's core. My anger transformed into curiosity; I had never seen a ceramic figure stuffed in this way. Everything my mother and I ever painted had been hollow.

Máriam stood perfectly still, her gaze riveted on me as I knelt down to examine the broken statue. I pulled gently at the wadding, only to realize that other items were wrapped inside. But the broken gap in the Madonna's face was too narrow to pull all the wool through; I struck it against the floor until her entire head split off at the shoulders.

Only then was I able to pull out all the wadding and see what was inside: a rolled-up letter, yellow with age, and a slender object, no taller than my hand from wrist to fingertip. It was carved from olive wood, with an image near the top that resembled three lit candles joined by a thick line at the base. Most of the wood had been badly scorched, except for the letter; the lower edges had been completely charred.

Oddly, Máriam showed no interest in it but sat down in a corner while I examined the treasures. I couldn't fathom what the olive-wood object was for, so I set it aside in order to carefully unroll the old letter. It read:

My dearest Raquelita, for that is your true name,

It is I, your uncle, don Francisco. Do not think that because we have not been in contact with you that we have rejected you. Far from it; you remain in my prayers and those of my beloved family every morning and night. But given the insanity that overtook Seville in the days and weeks after your parents' deaths, we decided that it was far safer for you to be taken in by an orphanage, and renamed, lest those who took your loved ones go searching for you.

Herein is hidden a treasure, one salvaged from the rubble by your mother's good and true friend, who is now yours. It is the mezuzah that graced the front door of your father's—my brother's—home in the Jewish Quarter. I pray you will keep it near you always, as it will bring you blessings and strength.

For out of great darkness, an even greater light always arises. I believe that light dwells strongly in you and your daughter.

You should know, if you were too young to remember your mother's stories, that you are a daughter of the renowned Abravanel clan, and niece to my brother, the famous don Isaac Abravanel, known for his wealth and philanthropy. Rather than change his religion or his name to Sánchez as I did, he fled Seville for Portugal, where he practices his faith openly and serves as benefactor to all Jews in Spain, regardless of whether they were forced to be public Christians and Jews in secret. My calling is a different one: to stay in Spain and help rescue our people and our sacred objects of faith. I send them to my brother in Lisbon, who sees to it that their every need is fulfilled.

The day will come soon, I suspect, that you and my family will be forced to join him in Portugal. I do not weep for any properties lost; I will be glad to freely rejoice in our faith as my heart bids me, without fear. And I will rejoice in the arms of family and friends who have escaped before us.

Until then, I have a great favor to ask of you: I have seen your incredible talent for painting religious figurines. When we lost your father—may his soul slumber peacefully—we also lost many priceless artifacts of gold and silver, precious to us not only because of their cost, but their religious significance.

To prevent this from happening again, we have decided to hide the remaining religious items inside Christian statuary in order to smuggle them to safety. But as you can see from our little Madonna, we do not know anyone of your talent who can easily produce and sell many such items without arousing suspicion.

Will you help us, dear niece? If your answer is no, say nothing. But if you wish to help, merely say the word yes—nothing more—to your neighbor don Pedro Vargas, and he will give you the name of a potter in Triana who will send you glazed items with hollow bottoms, ready for painting. Return them to him, and we will deal with the rest.

In the meantime, know that I and my family love you and your family dearly and pray for you daily, as we do our own. But in public, let us remain strangers; it is the safest way.

Only know, each time you gaze on the Madonna, that you have never been separated from the Lord's love or from your family's.

Until I can greet you properly in the flesh, may the Lord bless and keep you. May He make His face to shine upon you, and grant you peace. Amen.

Your loving uncle,

Francisco

P.S. It is imperative, for your safety and ours, that you burn this letter at once.

Seventeen

I knelt on the floor, cradling the letter and the mezuzah in my lap, all my anger evaporated. In its place was a very deep love and sorrow that caused me to lower my face into my hands.

In my mind's eye, I saw Luz—don Francisco's beautiful and pregnant granddaughter—saying of my mother: *She is a hero.*

I understood now. My mother had chosen to die rather than risk exposing don Francisco's family and its operation to the Inquisitors. I could only pray that she had kept it secret from my father as well as she'd hidden it from me.

I remembered too the very day the Madonna had come into our house a decade earlier—the day the aged Jew had delivered the bundle, only to suffer a beating from Gabriel. Antonio alone had fought to rescue him. I remembered the sting when old don Jerónimo had called me *marrana,* that ugly word for *converso* that meant "swine," and how the pain intensified when the other children in the street took up the cruel singsong: *Marrana! Marrana!*

It was the same day I had rejected my own mother—and my own heritage—for being the same. Because I was a coward.

Honor your mother by finishing her work, my great-uncle had said. I was needed to finish the Santiago statue. But I knew that if I did so, I was exposing my father and myself to even greater danger.

Herein is hidden a treasure, one salvaged from the rubble by your mother's good and true friend, who is now yours.

I looked up at Máriam. "My mother's good and true friend," I whispered, "who is now mine."

At that, Máriam went to her knees, sat beside me, and wrapped her lean, strong arms around me.

"Always," she said.

"You saved the mezuzah and gave it to don Francisco."

She pulled away from me grinning, showing white, evenly spaced teeth, minus a canine. "As a laundress, I had many clients."

"But you're a Muslim," I breathed. "Why would you risk your life to save Jews?"

Her grin softened to become an enigmatic smile. "There is only one God, but a thousand different ways to find Him. The love is the most important thing. You know in your heart, Marisol, what love wants you to do."

I looked down at the letter in my lap. "I must become a hero, just as my mother was."

I hid the mezuzah in the deepest corner of my trunk but fed don Francisco's letter to the flames in the hearth. Máriam said my mother was adamant about saving it.

"She had a premonition that this day would come . . . that she would be gone and you would need to see it." She paused. "So what will you tell don Francisco?"

I drew a deep breath. "I need to see him now. Right away. To tell him I'll help him, that I'll paint the Santiago, now that I know what it's for."

"And your father?" Máriam prompted softly.

I pressed a hand to one temple, as if trying to blot out the thought of what I might be tempted to do or say if I saw my father tortured. "Don Francisco told me he'd try to take care of him, to save him. I believe him. Besides . . ."—my voice thickened with emotion—". . . even if I told don Francisco no and gave Torquemada everything he wanted . . ." I let the devastating thought linger unspoken.

"Then I'll go now," Máriam said, with sudden brisk authority. "Because as you said, there isn't much time. I'll be half an hour, and then a wagon will come for us."

The instant I opened my mouth to pepper her with questions, she lifted a long, slender finger to silence me. "Hush. I know that you are my mistress, doña Marisol, and that I am your lowly servant. But in this case, it's wisest to let me lead."

Máriam waited until well after the bells of San Pablo and San Francisco had struck the hour of Compline, night prayers, knowing that both Gabriel and Blanca would retire to bed immediately after. She slipped out silently in her bare feet despite the cool weather, and true to her word, reappeared after half an hour.

"Now we wait," she said, and stood near the cracked-open window, listening, until she heard the town crier announce half past midnight.

By then, she'd outfitted us both in hooded black cloaks, instructed me to carry my boots despite the weather, and refused to listen to my pleas for a lantern.

"There's a moon out, and your eyes will get used to the darkness soon enough," she insisted. The urgency of her manner convinced me to fall silent and do as I was told.

I followed her silently off the Hojeda estate into the unlit street. A handful of men-at-arms guarded the front of the house; we avoided them by heading around the back, walking close to the rear wall encircling the estate. We made our way through a long-abandoned olive grove, where the land was uneven; I stumbled a few times and had to grab onto Máriam for support.

At last we made our way out of a narrow alleyway onto San Pablo Street. Rather than head west toward the monastery and prison, Máriam made her way east, toward the intersection with the great boulevard that led to the public square in front of the Church of San Francisco. I was grateful to encounter no traffic— most of the drunken sailors and brigands congregated behind us, in the western quarter near the river—but I soon heard the clap of horse hooves against cobblestone.

A solitary driver, cowled and cloaked like us in black, drove a single-horse flatbed wagon. A plague wagon. There had been rumors that plague had been found in the wealthy southern neighborhood near the Real Alcázar; I turned away at once, thinking to flee.

But Máriam held my upper arm with an iron grip and dragged me in the direction of the wagon, which gradually slowed its pace until it came to a stop in front of us.

I couldn't see the driver's face, but he and Máriam nodded at each other like old acquaintances. I was vaguely annoyed that the driver wasn't gentlemanly enough to help us up into the wagon, but Máriam managed to push me up into it before climbing in herself.

"Lie down," she instructed tersely, and I obeyed, looking up at the near-full moon and the stars. Soon the spires of churches disappeared from my view. I suspected we were headed northeast, away from the river and into hilly country, but the wagon took so many turns that I lost my sense of direction.

The rhythmical rocking had lulled me into a drowsy near-dreaming state, which was interrupted when the wagon lurched, then rolled to a complete stop. Máriam and I scrambled to our knees to discover the driver half fallen out of his seat. Thinking he was drunk, I grew angry.

Máriam had an altogether different reaction. "Dear God!" she hissed, and jumped out of the wagon; I followed.

Together we lifted the barely conscious driver into the wagon bed. Máriam unfastened his cloak and pulled it off him, revealing a blood-soaked bandage on top of his shoulder.

I, however, was too busy staring at his face: the skin frightening pale, the red-gold hair now a bright shade of gray in the darkness and damp with sweat, the eyes open a slit, their focus uncertain.

"Antonio!" I cried. Máriam hissed at me, a warning.

"Fool," she muttered at Antonio. "What were you thinking, not telling me that it was this bad?"

I dropped my voice to a whisper and put a hand to his cool brow. "Can you hear me? What happened?"

He murmured an unintelligible reply, one that left me doubting he'd heard me.

"Don't waste his breath or yours," Máriam ordered, as she

tore a strip of cotton from her chemise. I cradled Antonio's head and shoulder in my lap while Máriam quickly rebandaged his wound—a deep, plunging one.

"Here," Máriam said kneeling. She pressed a hand forcefully against the cotton-wrapped wound, the edges of which were starting to turn crimson. "Keep your hand against it hard, like this. If it soaks through again, tear a bandage from your clothes and replace the old one." She looked up to gauge whether I understood the seriousness of the matter. "Otherwise, he could bleed to death."

I pressed my hand to the wound with all my might. "We need to get him to a place of safety, to a midwife or barber. . . ."

Máriam was through with explanations. Before I'd even finished speaking, she crawled into the driver's seat, and we took off again.

I half reclined in the wagon, Antonio in my lap like the dead Christ in a pietà. Máriam drove the wagon at fever pitch, and each time the wheels found rocks or holes in the dirt road, Antonio groaned.

After one particularly deep pothole, he blinked up at me, then closed his eyes. "Marisol?" he whispered. "Am I dead or in prison?"

"Neither," I told him. "You're here in the wagon with me."

"Then I'm in heaven," he sighed, and closed his eyes.

As the old wagon rattled on, I sat beneath the stars and realized, to my amazement, that for the first time since my mother had died, I felt something resembling happiness. Blessedly, Antonio hadn't bled through Máriam's makeshift bandage, and best of all, he was alive and in my arms. Being next to him brought me such bliss that it no longer mattered whether he had deserted me or joined with the Inquisitors; the simple fact was that being this close to him brought me joy.

The wagon hit a great bump. Antonio groaned again.

"Marisol? I'm sorry I failed you. Sorry I failed your father. . . ."

"It's all right, Antonio. Everything is all right now."

We didn't head, as I expected, toward the Sánchez estate; instead, Máriam guided the horse surely into the untilled countryside. When we arrived at the edge of a mature orange grove, she brought the wagon to a stop. The trees were tall with age, each so full that its leaves touched its neighbors, making a thicket impossible for the wagon to navigate through.

Máriam climbed from the driver's seat and turned to look at Antonio and me. "How is he?" she asked, her tone hushed.

"Better I think," I answered, and Antonio opened his eyes. "The bleeding's stopped."

Máriam gave an approving nod. "Don't move. I'll be back." And she disappeared into the foliage between the trees.

"Why did you marry Gabriel?" Antonio whispered up at me.

I pushed the damp hair from his brow. "My father insisted. He meant to protect me from the Inquisition."

"It won't help you. They mean to use you as a pawn," he murmured. "If only you hadn't married him . . . The sight of you two together hurts me. . . . I always thought that I would be the one. . . ."

I blushed. "We're not really married. Not *that* way."

Despite his weakness, his eyes widened slightly. "Tell me that means what I think it does."

I smiled. "It does. I've never been with him."

"Thank God," he sighed. "I didn't mean to hurt you, Marisol. It's true I sent you letters and never got yours."

"Gabriel?" I suggested. "Do you think he intercepted them?"

"Most likely. I didn't give up trying to contact you until my fourth year—after I'd met don Isaac Abravanel. I traveled to Portugal, learned he was your mother's kin . . . and accidentally realized that he and doña Magdalena were working together to bring the extended family and its sacred objects to Portugal, where they're free to worship. I wanted to help. To save him so that he could join your . . ." His voice trailed as he closed his eyes, exhausted.

"Hush," I said, and leaned down suddenly to kiss him, his head cradled sideways in my lap. His lips were cool and damp; he smelled sharply of sweat and blood. None of it was unappealing, because it was of Antonio, and because I had waited years for this moment, however desperate the circumstances.

Best of all, he raised his uninjured arm and held the back of my head, pressing me closer to him.

We held the kiss until his hand trembled violently and he had to lower it; even then, I kept my face low, close to his.

"The marriage can easily be annulled," I said.

Antonio's reply was interrupted by the sound of crashing in the foliage. Two strange men and Máriam, bearing a lantern in her hand, appeared. The taller of the men—with curly pale hair, a wiry beard, and a barrel-shaped midsection—easily hoisted Antonio up beneath his arms. The other, smaller, dark-haired man caught Antonio's legs. The two managed to climb out of the wagon with him, Antonio muttering a weak protest, saying he could walk; fortunately, both men ignored him.

Máriam led the way with her flickering lantern through the

thicket of leaves for a few minutes, at which point, a large, unpainted old barn appeared in a clearing. Although the door was
closed and the windows all shuttered, a dim light shone through
the cracks.

Máriam set down the lantern to pull open the sliding door.
Inside, the vast interior lay hidden by darkness, save for the small
yellow arc of light cast by a single lamp on a crude table. The
only inhabitant was a hunchbacked elderly man sitting upon a
stool in the arc of light; shadows obscured his face so that, with
his gnarled limbs, he looked like a sort of monster—until he
stood up and revealed himself to be don Francisco.

"What news? Is don Diego with you?" he called out to the
men—the tone of his first question eager, the tone of his second,
dismayed at the sight of Antonio.

"Here, here..." don Francisco directed the two men with
their burden to a pile of clean straw bedding.

"Wine and water," the curly haired giant demanded, as he and
his partner settled Antonio down on the straw. Máriam carefully
set the lantern down nearby. "Needle and thread, if the wound
is deep, and clean bandaging."

A flagon of wine, pitcher of water, and a goblet rested on the
rickety table, along with the tools of surgery: a knife, a skein of
thread, a roll of bandages, and a hooked needle that looked designed for catching fish, not sewing human flesh. While Máriam
fetched the latter, don Francisco hurried to mix the water and
wine in the goblet, then handed it to Antonio and settled next to
the injured man.

Tenderly, as if Antonio were his own son, he cradled Antonio's
head in one hand and with the other, brought the rim of the cup
to Antonio's lips. Antonio drank haltingly, but don Francisco

coaxed him into taking a bit more each time he stopped. When the curly headed man approached to make use of his surgical tools, don Francisco waved him away.

"Can you talk?" don Francisco asked Antonio.

The latter nodded, and don Francisco eased Antonio's head back onto the straw.

"We failed," Antonio rasped. "Don Diego is still a prisoner."

I stiffened, riveted by shock.

A look of sorrow passed among the men, leaving the mood even more somber.

"Jorge betrayed us," the injured man continued, "else we would have succeeded. He tried to kill me, but I managed to slit his throat first."

"But where are the others?" don Francisco demanded.

"All dead. Killed by guards when Jorge cried out and betrayed us. He must have gone to the Dominicans to get a larger bribe."

The curly haired surgeon and dark-haired man crossed themselves; don Francisco braced his forehead and cheek with a hand and began to weep silently.

"I escaped without exposing my identity," Antonio added hoarsely.

"Our five best men. May God give them eternal rest," don Francisco said somberly, wiping away his tears. He nodded to the surgeon, who knelt down beside the patient, unwrapped the wound, and bathed it with wine, pouring straight from the flagon.

At the hiss of pain that emerged between Antonio's gritted teeth, I repressed my urge to run to him. Don Francisco rose from the straw and drew me away from the scene. "He'll be fine, Marisol. Carlos is a very able barber."

"You tried to save my father," I said, "and Antonio was wounded, and men I didn't even know died." Despite my best efforts, I began to weep. "Won't their families be in danger now?"

"None of them were married," don Francisco answered. "None had any traceable connection to me or anyone else here."

"But why would you risk so much for my father and me?"

"I would do nothing less for one of my kin," don Francisco answered gently, "and surely your father came to know, over the years, what his wife was doing for us, but he has chosen to keep silent. Why would we not risk all to save him and to prevent the possibility that our secret would be divulged?"

"Thank you anyway," I breathed. I kissed him solemnly on each cheek.

Behind us, Antonio let go a yelp as the surgeon began the work of sewing up the wound. I started. Don Francisco distracted me.

"Will you work for us, then, Marisol?"

"Anything," I replied, and meant it.

He managed a wan smile. "Then come and see the task before you."

He led me to the back of the barn, where the lantern's glow revealed a long worktable draped in nubby black silk. "Here," don Francisco said, and threw back a corner of the fabric.

I let go a faint gasp at the work of art before me, dazzling in the light. It was in the shape of an inverted warrior's shield, though half the size, created from the very purest gold. Carved into the center were Moses's two tablets of the law, flanked by great bas-relief pillars of fire. Beneath the tablets, two lions lay curled; above the tablets was an ornate three-dimensional crown. Three chains held it fast atop something.

Don Fernando lifted it reverently. "This is a Torah breast-plate," he said, then nodded at what lay beneath: an old scroll, the parchment brown with age, with bright golden finials.

"And this is a Torah—the Book of the Law. There is another one that your grandfather, a rabbi, kept for his congregation. That one is many centuries old and irreplaceable: To the Sánchez and Abravanel clans, it's far more priceless than any jewel."

I stared at it in wonder, imagining that, as a little girl, my mother had listened to her own father read from such a sacred manuscript.

"You lied to me," I told Máriam. "You told me everything in their house had burned down, was rubble, that the entire library was lost."

She shrugged, her gaze fixed on the Torah scroll. "Sometimes," she said softly, "it's necessary to lie in order to protect the people and things that you love."

Don Fernando cleared his throat. "It's far too difficult an operation to move people along with such heavy belongings. Better to smuggle out treasures one at a time. Which is what we have done with your mother's help. And now, only this one—and the most precious one—remains. You can help us save the one that belonged to your grandfather's congregation."

"But how?" I asked.

"By finishing your mother's work. By painting the large statue of Santiago. We'll need it tomorrow."

"But Torquemada has demanded I go to the prison tomorrow," I protested. "And if I'm arrested . . ."

Nearby, the dark-haired smaller man cleared his throat. "Our spy told us earlier that the queen and Torquemada fled Seville a few hours ago. One of the guards at the Alcázar fell sick with plague and had to be carried out."

"Don't rejoice too soon," don Francisco warned me. "Torquemada will surely leave your interrogation to someone else, such as Fray Morillo. I wouldn't even be surprised if Fray Hojeda uses this event to gain some control of the Inquisition." He hesitated as if trying to decide whether to continue. "Gabriel and Alonso Hojeda are incompetent and none too bright. But they are nonetheless dangerous to you."

He trailed off and his tone grew matter of fact. "The auto-de-fé will be held in two days. Despite the danger, Marisol, will you paint the statue of Santiago for us now, tonight, knowing that it will carry your family's sacred Torah to a safe place? Even knowing that we cannot afford to make another attempt to rescue your father?"

"You can't save him?" I countered, aghast.

"I lost five fighters and Antonio is wounded. The Inquisition will no doubt put extra guards around your father. And on the day of the auto-de-fé, there will be even more protection around the prisoners. I won't lie to you Marisol; there is little hope of our saving him."

I covered my face in my hands.

When I finally looked up, I saw that the old man's gaze had grown piercing. "Don Antonio says you have been summoned tomorrow to watch your father be tortured. It's why we chose tonight to attempt to rescue him. If you cannot hold your tongue tomorrow . . . then we will *all* die. Not just your father. Do not make the mistake of thinking that confession will protect you or anyone else. They will use it to damn you, Marisol."

My eyes burned with tears as I said, "On my mother's soul, I swear to keep silent."

"Good," he replied. "The Santiago statue must be painted before daybreak, so that you can return to don Gabriel's house without him being the wiser. The Torah shield is packed firmly inside with wadding so that the treasure cannot fall out. Once you have finished, don Antonio will bring it to us on the day of the auto-de-fé." He paused, his expression grown sympathetic but still firm. "You cannot stay behind and expect to survive, Marisol, whether your father lives or not."

"Don Francisco," Máriam said respectfully, "there are two things that Marisol should have with her tonight as she paints the statue."

He raised a brow, questioning.

In response, Máriam pulled the black silk back farther, revealing other religious relics as well as a neatly folded white prayer shawl and a pair of gold candlesticks.

I cried out softly at the sight of the last two: They had been my mother's.

"Tonight *is* Shabbat," Máriam said softly.

Don Francisco's eyes grew liquid; so did mine. "Please," I asked, "may I take them with me tonight? I won't disrespect them."

"Of course," he replied huskily. "Of course, Marisol."

Máriam reverently lifted the candlesticks—both with white, unused tapers in them—and wrapped them in the prayer shawl.

As she did, don Francisco took me aside and said in his sternest voice: "There is something I must tell you now that I share with all of my true friends. Remember it well, for it can save you in times of great danger. Do you understand?"

"Yes," I answered solemnly.

"If trouble befalls you, go to the river docks near San Pablo Street. Get there by whatever means necessary. If the danger is extreme..." He paused, eyeing me. "I had best let Antonio tell you when the time draws nearer. The less you know now, the safer you are."

I didn't want to hear more: It seemed as if he were mocking my mother's death. I turned away, upset, just as I heard Antonio calling out my name.

The surgeon was just rising, carrying away with him a clean cloth on which the fishhook and bits of black thread rested, and a bloodied cloth.

"How is he?" don Francisco asked, referring to the patient.

"It was a deep cut, but I cleaned it well," the curly haired barber answered. "With luck, he'll survive."

"Will he be able to fool them all tomorrow?"

"Probably. So long as he's the kind the poppy doesn't make too queasy. He needs rest and water now, and something to eat when he's able."

Don Francisco let go a grunt of relief. "Good. Don Antonio, you rest now. We need you strong so that you can pick up the statue the day after tomorrow. Carlos will take care of you tonight and see you back to your house when you are strong enough. Don't worry."

Antonio's red-gold hair was still dark with sweat and stuck to his forehead, his complexion still chalky. His eyelids were half closed and his mouth stretched into a faint but decidedly inebriated smile. He said, "Oh, I'll deliver the statue on time. And I can never worry about anything again! She's not really married!"

I blushed as the others smirked.

"Drunk on wine and the poppy," the curly haired surgeon

said knowingly. "He'll be feeling little pain for the rest of the night."

"Come," don Francisco said softly to all but the patient and me, "let's give them a moment alone. They deserve it."

The others didn't leave the barn but instead went to the back, disappearing into the shadows so that it really did seem like Antonio and I were alone.

I went and knelt beside him on the straw; although he still seemed rather weak, his mood was decidedly better. His head was supported by a small bale that served as a pillow; his unwounded right arm was next to me, the freshly bandaged left arm mostly hidden from my view.

He caught my hand in his right one and squeezed admirably hard; I met his pressure with my own, and he grinned hugely.

"Marry me," he said.

"You're silly drunk," I countered. "You probably won't remember this conversation tomorrow."

"Oh, yes, I will," he retorted. "Just like I remember when I was fourteen. Hanging upside down on that old olive tree in your father's orchard. Do you remember?"

I smiled, remembering Antonio at fourteen, his limbs gangly and long at that age, his voice beginning to deepen. I recalled too how comical he had looked that day, his straight strawberry hair hanging beneath his reddening face with its upside-down, toothy grin.

We could make a bunch of little Christians!

"I remember," I said, a bit embarrassed that the others were listening. "How can you ever forgive me, Antonio? I thought you betrayed me."

"It doesn't matter, Marisol. None of it matters. There's only right now."

He grinned lopsidedly at me until I couldn't keep from breaking into a full, affectionate grin myself. I finally said, "That day when you were hanging from the tree—you asked me to stay with you forever."

"And I asked you to marry me," he said, slurring a bit. "And you said . . ."

"That all our children would be considered *conversos*."

He laughed weakly. "Where we're going, Marisol, no one will care if our children are *conversos* or Christians or Jews. So. When you have this sham marriage-that-isn't-a-marriage annulled . . . will you marry me? Only if you love me, of course."

I drew a deep breath and let it out, deciding that I no longer cared who heard or saw. "Of course. Of course, I'll marry you, Antonio. Of course. I love you."

I bent down and kissed him, and he kissed me back with an enthusiasm unexpected of a frail, wounded man. Despite don Francisco's promise of privacy, the other men in the barn roared their approval; even so, neither of us faltered, but kept our lips pressed together fast.

Eighteen

Máriam and I left Antonio, the surgeon, and don Francisco behind in the barn, while the small dark-haired man, Martín, drove us back toward town, while we were covered beneath a tarp in the wagon. Once we entered the city proper, Martín left us on a small side street not far from our neighborhood.

From there, we made our way to the western side of Antonio's family property—through the scraggly remnants of an ancient olive grove. At last, we came upon the tall stone wall that enclosed the family house. Despite the darkness, Máriam had no difficulty finding the single large stone that came loose when she pulled on it.

We squirmed through the opening, and Máriam led me unerringly across the large property toward the house, pausing not far from the old tree where Antonio had first proposed marriage to me; I could see the dark outline of my parents' now-abandoned house over the top of the fence.

Máriam began to brush the ground with her foot until she

came upon a scattering of gravel; soon, I heard her boot heel connect with something more solid.

"Help me," she whispered, bending down to touch the earth.

I reached down, my fingers sifting through earth and stone until they found the edge of something thick and wooden. Once we had pulled upward enough so that the outline of the trapdoor became clear, Máriam and I swept away enough of the heavy dirt and gravel so that we could get the trapdoor open.

I admit, I was terrified making my way through the narrow, airless tunnel—particularly after Máriam closed the door behind us, blotting out even the faint light of the moon and stars, leaving us in total blackness. But she caught my hand firmly and dragged me onward, not pausing at the eerily silky sensation of spiderwebs on our faces and shoulders, or the muted squeal of rodents.

Soon we emerged through another trapdoor into my mother's ceramic workshop, beneath one of the large worktables she normally kept covered with a tarp. By then, my eyes were so accustomed to the darkness that, even with all the parchment-colored shades drawn, the room looked sad and abandoned. There were no ceramic works left except the magnificent half-painted Santiago, sitting upon the largest worktable. Don Francisco had been right; his granddaughter Luz could never have finished the statue properly, because although the easier sections of the defeated, crushed Moor had been finished, Santiago's windswept hair and fierce expression—and the fiery eyes of his mount—were still unpainted.

While Máriam hurried to cover the windows with black cloths to blot out any stray speck of light that might escape, I carefully undid the bundle tied to my waist, containing my mother's prayer shawl, tapers, and golden candlesticks. I unfolded her prayer shawl and put it over my head and shoulders, grateful for the added bit of warmth, as all the fireplaces in the house had gone unlit.

I waited until Máriam finished covering the windows. Then I moved in the darkness to where my mother kept her flint and tinder wood and worked until I got a spark.

Máriam was quick to set the tapers in the candlesticks and place them on the worktable so that I had to face east in order to light them. Before I did, she brought over the Santiago statue and set it midway in front of the candles. At first I was surprised to see her stagger beneath its weight, given that the statues were all hollow. When it stood before me, I pushed against it and realized why my mother had never let me near it: The treasure had already been hidden inside. Clearly, the potter from Triana who had delivered it was part of don Francisco's conspiracy.

I lit the first candle, then the second and stepped back; in front of them, the white of the unpainted statue glistened. I looked down at Santiago's cape and the horse's muscular flank, and saw my mother reflected there.

I blew out the tinder stick and smiled inwardly as the words of my childhood came back to me. They weren't the right ones for kindling the Sabbath light, but I knew in my heart that they would do.

I raised my hands before my eyes, reverently blotting out the light as my mother had done before me, and whispered: *"Shema Yisrael, Adonai Eloheinu, Adonai Echad."* Hear O Israel, The Lord is our God, The Lord is One.

I looked upon the light and smiled. And on the shining white surface of Santiago's unpainted features, I saw my mother smile back at me.

The work itself did not take long; my mother had already crushed the semiprecious stones and earth-based pigments to powder. All that remained was to mix them: dull gray for Santiago's armor, brown for his hair and eyes, crimson for his flapping cape, real silver for his sword.

As I painted, I could see how the statue had been made precisely to fit the Torah shield, how extra room had been made for it by Santiago's body leaning forward to press against his mount. And as I continued working, I began to sing—soft, low, and hushed—a song my mother used to sing to me long ago:

> *"Durme, durme, querido hijico*
> *Durme sin ansía y dolor*
> *Cerra tus chicos ojicos*
> *Durme, durme con savor.*
> Sleep, sleep, beloved child,
> Sleep without fretting
> Close your little eyes
> And sleep peacefully."

And for the first time since childhood, I began to believe that it might be true: that even though my beloved mother had perished, I might yet live to see Sepharad with my own eyes.

Máriam left the tunnel uncovered by gravel so that Antonio could more easily retrieve the finished statue, and we stole back to the

Hojeda house without incident. I lay exhausted in bed but couldn't sleep, vacillating between horror over my father's likely fate and the joy of knowing that Antonio had always loved me. But any joy failed to linger long before the dread and terror returned. Don Francisco's honesty—that he and his men could not make another rescue attempt to save my father—had shattered my heart.

I finally dozed off toward dawn and woke sometime later with a start at the sharp rapping at my antechamber door. I bolted from bed and struggled into my dressing gown as I heard Máriam answer the door, and I listened to the short exchange between her and don Gabriel.

She returned with orders for me to dress as soon as possible. Within an hour, I was riding, bleary-eyed, next to my so-called husband, headed for the Dominican prison.

When we arrived, Gabriel remained at my side as we were ushered in, and led me not to the same room where I had spoken with Torquemada, but to a chamber deeper in the bowels of the prison, whose stink grew fouler with every step.

Gabriel finally stopped and opened a large wood-and-iron door. I moved past him and a pair of armed guards into a small antechamber of stone, with a single high, barred window.

As don Francisco had suggested, Fray Hojeda was waiting there. He looked on me with the delight of a glutton being presented with the next course of a feast, but immediately forced his owlish visage into a more threatening expression; his thick gray brows rushed together in a thunderous scowl.

"Doña Marisol," he said, more a rebuke than a greeting. "Let me explain to you that I am now in charge of your father's case, and my brother don Gabriel is here as witness for the court. Let me also make it clear that *you* are in command of the proceedings about to commence. At any point, you can make the activity stop simply by offering to tell the full truth of what you know."

He turned and led me back to a larger inner chamber, one that smelled of piss and vomit. In one corner of the room stood what looked like a ship's wheel bolted to the ground. Someone had firmly tied ropes attached to the gears on the wheel, then thrown the ropes over a metal rod on the ceiling; shackles had been attached to the end of each rope. In another corner sat a chair, from which more empty shackles dangled; beside it on the floor sat an assortment of gruesome pincers and pokers, not far from the hearth.

But what held my attention was a device the width of a small bed, though greater in length. In place of a mattress lay a number of barrel-shaped horizontal rollers, and atop those rollers lay my father, naked to make his humiliation complete. The flesh of his sun-browned face and neck turned white at the collarbone. A triangle of thick golden brown hair, the pinnacle of which touched the spot equidistant between his nipples—as if pointing to his heart—thinned just enough at his waist to reveal his umbilicus. There the triangle reversed to a delta, its base above his exposed genitals. His arms, the muscles straining, were extended over his head, his wrists chained to a movable bar with a long wooden handle that served as a lever; his ankles were tied to a fixed wooden bar at his feet.

"Papá!" I cried out, before I had a chance to hide the anguish in my tone.

"I am not ashamed, Marisol," he replied weakly. "Or afraid. Nor should you be."

Gabriel's expression was timid and reserved; he lowered his

eyes, clearly embarrassed by my father's nakedness, and moved behind his brother, whose expression was openly gloating.

"I should remind you both, don Diego and doña Marisol," Fray Hojeda said, "that the auto-de-fé takes place tomorrow morning. Don Diego will be marched through town wearing the mark of a heretic; he will be called on to repent and confess, then his sentence will be read aloud to the public. At that point, he will either be turned over to the church for rehabilitation or to the civil authorities for execution."

I stared hard at Alonso Hojeda. And saw not a dedicated servant of God, one who regretted inflicting pain in order to save a soul, but rather the same sort of creature as Torquemada: soulless, heartless, rejoicing not in a sinner saved as much as one lost whom he could torment, whose life and happiness he could destroy simply because he relished doing so.

Hojeda addressed my father without a hint of compassion. "I can tell you, sir, based on the raid on the prison by your now thankfully dead cohorts, today is the last chance we shall give you, and to my mind, you do not deserve even that. Confess and spare your daughter the agony of watching you suffer."

"I will suffer then," my father said, "and die with honor. My daughter will not yield; I have raised her to be truthful and strong."

With that, Hojeda turned to me and said with poorly hidden delight, "Listen carefully to what you are about to hear."

A pale-faced young man with auburn hair stood with his hands resting atop the wooden handle attached by ropes to the shackles on my father's wrists. The lad might have been pleasant looking, were it not for the deep numbness in his eyes.

Hojeda nodded meaningfully at the young man, who used

both arms and a great deal of strength to pull on the wooden lever; the barrels rolled, and the wooden frame near my father's head inched upward, along with his shackled wrists.

There came the most horrible combination of sounds: the muted twang of sinews pulling free from bone, the ripping of muscle, as if a butcher had torn meat from a beast's carcass with his bare hands, the muffled cracking of bone—and, most awfully, the loud pop of thigh bones and arm bones being pulled from their sockets.

Added to that was my father's involuntary scream. Stretched grotesquely beyond his bearing, he could not move.

I fought tears. For a single turn of the lever had brought not only pain—marked by the horrific rictus on my father's face— but also suffering and deformity to last a lifetime. Sinew ripped from bone could not repair itself, and crippled joints could not easily mend.

Yet there was a wicked genius to it: The shredded muscles beneath my father's skin were bleeding, his snapped bones weeping blood and marrow. He was torn up inside, as if some beast caged beneath his flesh had been freed to attack with tooth and claw. So much damage, all cleverly covered by his skin, so that the abominable crime of what was done to him remained his tormentors' secret.

"Stop it!" I shouted.

The ghost of a grin played at the corners of Hojeda's plump lips. "You can make it stop by confessing the truth: that you and your father are crypto-Jews. You can make it stop by denouncing Antonio Vargas and admitting that you have had an affair with him, that he is no longer fit to serve the Holy Office."

"But we're not crypto-Jews," I protested. "And I have never wanted anything to do with Antonio Vargas. He's one of your own, working for the Inquisition."

"He's always been good friends with your family," Hojeda insisted. "We all know he was going to marry you." He paused. "I've heard you were consorting with don Francisco."

I straightened and asked, sounding nervous to my own ears, "When?"

"At the palace, when you sang for the queen," Hojeda said. "If you were to denounce him as a crypto-Jew, I would release your father today."

My father groaned. "Marisol . . . don't believe him. Your 'dowry'—I agreed to denounce myself to Gabriel . . . to protect you from the Inquisition."

Enraged, Hojeda instantly signaled the torturer, who applied full force to the lever, his muscles straining, the dull look in his eyes grown ghoulish. I covered my ears at the sound of a deep, terrible crunch inside my father's body, at the sound of his scream.

Hojeda sensed my weakness and leaned forward to whisper in my ear; his breath was putrid.

"Decide now, Marisol . . . or face watching your father suffer more now, and die at the stake tomorrow."

"Let me die, Marisol," my father said. "Make me proud."

It was the one thing he could have said to give me strength. This time, when the torturer applied his full body weight to the lever, I did not cover my ears, but composed myself.

And when Hojeda asked, "Will you confess?" I did not look away but shook my head and stared straight ahead.

"Tomorrow will be too late," Hojeda threatened again, but I countered him with an announcement of my own.

"I am leaving now. I have nothing more to say."

"Walk away if you wish," Hojeda said. "Only bear in mind that *this*"—he nodded at my father upon the rack—"doesn't stop when you leave. Every moment you breathe, walk, or enjoy a meal—at that moment, your father is suffering horribly because *you* will not stop it."

But I left, head held high, the way my father wanted me to, the way he wanted to remember me.

I spent the rest of the day unable to rest as I began to mourn for my father. He would spend a long, anguish-filled night—a sleepless one, not only because of pain but because of the all-night vigil and procession around the prison that the Dominicans had planned.

I stayed in my room until well after sundown and the supper hour, until Blanca came to announce that the master was coming to see me—and he did *not* want Máriam in attendance. Máriam left reluctantly, and I sat waiting in one of the small chairs in my antechamber.

Minutes after, Gabriel entered, his cloak still bearing the chill of evening, his body and tunic faintly reeking of the prison. His expression wasn't stern but complicitous, even abashed.

"I had to speak to you alone," he said urgently. "You realize that if there is no intervention, your father will be found guilty and executed tomorrow?"

I looked away, in the direction where the now-broken ugly Madonna had once stood. "My father's life was my dowry. You always meant to destroy him—to secure your position with the Inquisition."

Gabriel took no offense but pressed with a strange gentleness: "If there was something that could be done to save him, would you not do it?"

I slowly turned my gaze on him and lifted a brow.

"I am not as cruel or controlled by my brother as you might think," he said. "While the head of the Inquisition, Fray Morillo, despises my brother, he is more kindly disposed toward me. And I have influence with Judge Diego de Merlo, who will be handing down the sentences given by the Inquisitors and seeing that they are implemented.

"Judge de Merlo is easily bribed. For a reasonable sum, your father could be rehabilitated by the church instead. It would spare him death at the stake."

He trailed off, and we looked at each other for a long moment, my gaze penetrating, his, oddly self-conscious.

"Why are you telling me this?" I demanded. "Why would you suddenly tell me to go bribe Judge de Merlo after keeping my father's arrest secret from me, after forcing my father to suffer what he did today?"

He blushed. "I am not suggesting you bribe the judge. Being who you are, he would spurn or even report you. But he has accepted 'gifts' from me in the past readily enough. Once de Merlo has publicly announced your father's innocence, there is little my brother or Morillo could do to hurt your father."

Incredulous, I stared at him. "You would do this for my father *now*?"

"For you, Marisol," he said, with sudden heat. "Forgive me; my brother forced me to arrest your father. I did not want to, and I am sorry for it now. I truly care for you."

I hid my revulsion. "And the price for my father's life?"

He brightened; his pale eyes widened with hope.

"One encounter," he whispered. "Only one. And we would keep it secret—both the bribe and the . . . encounter—from my brother. He would seek revenge on your father if he knew we'd broken our promise of chastity."

His breathing quickened as he spoke. By the time he fell silent, he was trembling, but not with fear.

I maintained a neutral expression. "How certain are you of success?"

"Completely certain." Gabriel didn't hesitate, didn't flinch under my scrutiny.

"You swear upon your father's soul?" I demanded.

"I swear upon my father's soul," he parroted, but it was not good enough for me.

"May his soul be damned to hell for eternity if you are lying," I pressed.

Gabriel was expressionless. "May his soul be damned to hell for eternity if I am lying."

He said it with such conviction that, for love of my father, I felt my self-respect slip all too easily from me, like silk from my shoulders.

"Come," Gabriel said, holding out his large hand.

God forgive me, I took it—took it and let him lead me out of my quarters and down the loggia to his closed chamber door. He opened the latter onto gloomy quarters, more Spartan, if possible, than the rest of the crumbling estate. Black curtains were pulled shut over two different sets of windows, closing out the stars and moon, leaving the corners of the room swallowed by darkness.

An oil lamp—the only source of light—burned on a narrow

ledge beside the surprisingly small straw bed, with no linens save a worn blanket. There was no night table, but instead, upon the wall, a hook from which hung a small multilashed whip. Above the hook and whip rested a large shelf, which held, in separate gabled shrines, fine ceramic statues that looked to have been painted by my mother. One was of the Virgin Mary exposing a crown of thorns encircling her heart, another a bold Santiago, perhaps one-third of the size of the one I'd painted, with his dark hair and his horse's white mane stirred by an imaginary wind.

These—along with a small wardrobe—were all that stood in the room. There was no mirror, no chair, no table, not even a carpet on the cold stone floor. The hearth was unlit, adding to the chill and gloom.

The light glinted off the Virgin and Santiago as Gabriel took off his cloak, set it beside him on the bed, and sat down.

Thinking he had set the cloak down for me, I moved to sit down upon it.

"No," Gabriel said. His voice quavered, but this time not from timidity. An arc of light from the lamp captured his face—lips parted, eyes wide and focused intently on me, just the way they had looked on me when I'd tried to stop him from beating the child Antonio.

"No, Marisol. Come stand here."

Still sitting, he leaned forward and caught my arms gently but firmly and pulled me into the arc of yellow light.

"Take off your clothing."

I tried not to shudder. "I can't without help," I said bluntly. "My bodice laces in back."

Without reply, he got to his feet and guided me to stand

sideways, then fumbled with the back laces until they were finally undone.

"Now," he said, sitting back down on the edge of the bed, "undress yourself."

I saw no choice but to obey, for my father's sake, and I prayed for God and Antonio to forgive me.

My bodice hung loose, but I let the weight of my overdress hold it in place. First I slowly unlaced each heavy sleeve; when I let the first one slip to the floor, Gabriel gasped aloud at the sight of my bare arm.

"So beautiful," he said. "So white."

I doubted that my olive-colored arms, though long shielded from the sun, could ever be as pale as Gabriel's skin and hair, now colored a garish yellow by the oil lamp.

Another sleeve hit the floor, and another gasp came from Gabriel. Soon I struggled to pull my black overdress over my head, then the unlaced kirtle, until I stood in front of him in my chemise, my arms and décolletage revealed. As it was winter, I wore not sheer white lawn but opaque ivory silk. The silk clung to the outline of my body—and since the room's chill was pervasive, the tip of my breasts could clearly be seen.

Gabriel watched, still fully clothed in his black tunic and leggings; seated with a wide-legged stance on the edge of the bed, he lifted the tunic's edge and began to run his hand over his swollen codpiece. As I slipped first one shoulder, then another, from my chemise, he fumbled madly with the codpiece laces and freed himself. I had never seen a man erect at such close distance and decided that Gabriel's genitals must have been homelier than most: His penis was pinkish white, bent to the right, with a purplish foreskin gathered in tight folds beneath what appeared to be the cap of a rosy mushroom.

I wavered, holding the chemise over my breasts, bile rising in my throat.

"Drop it," Gabriel commanded, his voice suddenly harsh. The strange light in his eyes was blazing now.

I let go of the slip; it fell with a sigh, and I stood perfectly naked before him.

He groaned again, this time louder. He was breathing hard, his mouth gaping, his brow furrowed in an intent scowl as he took in the sight of me. For a long moment, there was no sound save that of his labored breathing, and then he said:

"Come here."

I took a step closer so that my legs were between his, pressed against the prickly straw of the bed. Entranced, he touched my breasts, cupping them clumsily at first, then pressed his palms flat against them, then examined the erect nipples with his fingers.

"You tremble," he breathed.

I dared not open my mouth, lest I show my disgust. Gabriel was trembling, too, though not for the same reason as I.

"Touch it," he whispered.

Forgive me, I thought to everyone I loved, and reached for his genitals. The shaft of his penis was hard as oak.

He pulled me by the shoulders to him. "Sit," he breathed into my ear, and tried to push me down. My shadow fell sharp over him, covering his face in darkness.

He pulled his knees together, and I half sat, clutching his penis between my thighs tightly, so that he almost, but could not quite, penetrate me; fooled, he thrust against my legs with bruising force, groaning with pleasure while I struggled to keep him from taking my virginity. Just when I thought I could hold him back no more, he roared the name of God. Hot liquid spurted on my legs as Gabriel bucked away from me, his eyes rolled back into his head.

I leapt off him quickly and used my chemise to wipe his seed from my thighs, then wadded up the chemise and slipped back into my kirtle and overdress as best I could, though the unlaced bodice hung loose.

Gabriel lay on his back upon his bed, gasping; when his breath slowed a bit and his eyes finally opened, I stood over him and said, "May your father's soul be damned to hell for eternity if you are lying."

With that, I hurried off to find Máriam and the basin.

Nineteen

I did not sleep that night. Gabriel's brother had sent a coach for him hours before dawn, leaving the carriage for me and Máriam; my husband was insistent that I attend the auto-de-fé.

As Máriam dressed me, she begged: "Please, doña! It's not necessary to force yourself to go through with this."

I dismissed her. "This will be the only chance I have to set eyes on my father again."

She pressed, clasping her hands as if praying to me. "Marisol, of all days, this is the safest one for you to escape. Do you see?"

"No, you don't understand," I countered sadly. "If there's any hope—if there's any chance my father might be spared—I *have* to know. Even if there's not, I can't desert him.

"Then I will go with you," Máriam said. "But we should return before your husband and the guards do." She looked about carefully, then peered through the chink in the wall that looked into Blanca's bedroom. Satisfied, she said, "Antonio will have the

Santiago and the wagon waiting for us. Today is the day we must leave everything behind. Are you ready?"

I nodded, reluctant.

The driver pulled us to the front of the crowd near the podium where Fray Morillo had first read the papal bull announcing the Inquisition, and Máriam and I climbed to the top of the carriage in order to get a better view.

After the encounter the night before with Gabriel, I had dared nurse some hope; now, as I watched the sun rise over the distant spires of the great cathedral, lightening the gray sky to rose and then blue, I grew more frightened. Those in the crowd were somber and spoke in hushed voices. Even those who earlier would have jeered at *conversos* and applauded their mistreatment held their tongues, silenced by the solemn atmosphere.

The procession from San Pablo Prison approached from a distance. The armed guards came first, cloaked in black, their long swords drawn to make the crowd give way. Behind them followed the civil magistrate, Judge de Merlo, and the civil prosecutors, including Gabriel and the mayor—a *converso* himself and friend of my father. This group was flanked by more guards. Then came the Dominicans: Fray Morillo and Fray Hojeda and a flock of black-caped monks in white habits.

Behind them came the prisoners—nine in all, including three females. They were shackled at the ankles, making their progress even more tedious combined with their invisible wounds. Each one's broken body was covered by a garment known as the *sambenito*. For three of them, the loose tunic was bright yellow with red crosses and an appliqué of upside-down flames. The rest

wore black *sambenitos* with regular flames and serpents, also red. All the accused wore the same pointed, conical hats and bore lighted candles; each was flanked by a guard, as if the prisoner had the strength to break free of the shackles and present a physical danger to the crowd.

My father was among those wearing black. Pain and despair showed in his hobbled movements, in the slump of his shoulders and cast-down face, just as they showed in every prisoner in the gruesome parade. Two guards supported him entirely, dragging his feet on the ground.

The magistrate and the Dominican Inquisitors took their places upon the platform, in a specially constructed box near a podium. Behind the podium, on a pedestal high enough to be seen by all in the crowd, stood a wooden cross the size of a man, painted bright green and draped with a black cloth.

The guards clustered around the platform's base, facing the crowd and the prisoners, who were obliged to stand clutching their burning candles.

Most remarkable was the silence as the procession took place, such that the clanking of the shackles could be heard. As the last prisoner and last guard took their places, every eye in the crowd fell, expectant, on the podium.

Fray Hojeda, his step slow but his manner ebullient, if weary, lumbered to the podium, he so massive and tall that the structure looked undersized. He grasped its sides with his huge hands and beamed at the crowd.

"Fellow Christians," he announced, his tone giddy with victory yet uncharacteristically weak, "this is a day of great rejoicing! For the Devil has been defeated, and those who have done his bidding will be purged from our flock. Thanks to our wise and pious monarchs, Her Majesty Queen Isabel and His Majesty King Fernando, the Holy Office of the Inquisition has ferreted out the heretics among us. Let all those who would betray the sacred tenets of our faith heed and take warning!"

And he grinned broadly, pausing to look out at his listeners to judge the effect of his words.

Immediately, a woman screamed with terror in the middle of his audience; her cries were instantly echoed by others nearby. A section of the crowd parted, leaving a widening circular gap. I stood up atop the carriage to get a better view and spied a child's motionless body lying on the cobblestones at the circle's center. A rumbling began and soon carried over to the place where I stood.

"Plague! It's plague . . . from the Dominican monastery!"

"Here now," Fray Hojeda ordered. "Silence! Get control of yourselves!" His voice cracked with the strain; he wiped his forehead wearily, and the sunlight caught his face, revealing its sheen of sweat.

The rumbling did not stop but grew louder and more hysterical until his voice was drowned out. Hojeda was forced to hold his tongue until the child—who appeared to be lifeless—was removed from the plaza by wagon. So great was the fear provoked by this incident that a third of those in attendance forced their way out of the square, causing a tide of bodies to swell out into the streets. Their flight caused wild disruption, impossible for Hojeda to contain. Máriam and I were forced to sit and hold tight to our carriage, which swayed as frantic pedestrians rushed past us.

After several minutes, the now-smaller crowd was silent once more, and Hojeda resumed his preaching, his mirth undimmed.

"Such is the power of God," he cried out, "that He has struck down an evildoer who managed to escape our grasp. Do not be fooled: This is not Satan trying to disrupt us; he has no power here in this godly place! Rather it is the hand of a vengeful God showing us His might!

"For I say unto you that those who turn against the true faith have been revealed this day; those who have repented and turned back to Mother Church will be saved, but those who scorn and reject Her will find themselves in the Devil's grip and suffer the eternal torments of hell.

"Rejoice, Christians! For today we witness the judgment of a just and faithful God!

"And now, I take my sermon today from the book of Ezekiel: 'Yet if thou warn the wicked, and he turn not from his wickedness, nor from his wicked way, he shall die in his iniquity. . . .' "

A matron in a black *sambenito* fainted and was prodded back to consciousness and onto her feet by a guard.

Hojeda did not pause. But the all-night vigil had exhausted him; he began to lean more heavily on the podium as he spoke.

At last, the friar ceased preaching and offered up a prayer, that God's will might be done; and I thought that surely God's will could never be so cruel or so evil as that of these men.

After the prayer, Hojeda announced that the time had come for the prisoners' sentences to be handed down. Old Judge de Merlo rose, white-haired in his official robes, and shuffled up to the podium. Despite his frailty, he managed to look imposing, even threatening.

A pair of guards led the first prisoner, a quivering black-haired young man dressed in one of the yellow tunics with red crosses, to stand in the space immediately below the judge and his podium.

"Miguel de Madrid," the judge thundered. I knew the man; he was an architect who had worked with my father on the design of many public buildings—a pleasant, handsome fellow who had yet to marry. "You stand accused by anonymous witnesses of heresy against the church, of practicing the filth known as Judaism secretly in your house; of abstaining from the eating of pork; of celebrating Passover and the Jewish Sabbath secretly; of uttering prayers to the Jewish God Jehovah in the Hebrew tongue, blaspheming our true Lord and Savior Jesus Christ. What say you to these charges?"

Don Miguel's voice was too weak to carry.

Judge de Merlo repeated his words for the edification of the crowd. "The prisoner confesses freely to his crimes and begs for forgiveness and mercy from this tribunal, from the church, and from God Almighty." He frowned down at his victim.

"Do you swear before God and this assembly never to repeat these crimes, but to hold steadfast in the Christian faith for the rest of your life?"

A short pause followed in which don Miguel undoubtedly answered in the affirmative.

The judge seemed mollified. "Hear now the sentence handed down by the Holy Office of the Inquisition: Your possessions remain forfeit to the church and Crown. For a period of no less than two years, you are not to leave your house without wearing the *sambenito* to Mass and in public, so that all Christians will be reminded of your heresy and take warning, lest they fall into the same error. You shall also be given penance, which you are to perform daily, by your priest. In this manner, you are reconciled to Mother Church."

At this pronouncement, one of the monks sitting on the platform rose and removed the black cloth draping the great green cross.

Don Miguel fell to his knees, sobbing; too overwhelmed to walk, he was gripped by his guards and dragged back to his place among the prisoners, where he was compelled to stand, bowed by emotion.

Another prisoner—this one a young woman, also dressed in yellow—was brought before Judge Merlo. Again, the prisoner confessed to all charges of Judaizing, and again was accepted back into the church, the major penalty being loss of wealth and the wearing of the *sambenito.* Yet a third prisoner—the last one wearing yellow—came before the judge with the same result.

And then came my father, in his black tunic adorned with flames and serpents, to stand before the judge. It served my father nothing that he had known de Merlo all of his life and had consulted with him on the city council and had broken bread with the man. De Merlo stared down at him as if he were an alien creature, one that he had never set eyes on before.

"Diego García," de Merlo intoned. "You stand accused by anonymous witnesses of heresy against the church: of practicing the filth known as Judaism secretly in your house and of encouraging your wife to do the same; of celebrating Passover and the Jewish Sabbath secretly; of uttering prayers to the Jewish God Jehovah in the Hebrew tongue, blaspheming our true Lord and Savior Jesus Christ. You are also brought before me upon the civil charge of fomenting rebellion against Her Most Christian Majesty Isabel of Castile. What say you to these charges?"

My father managed to straighten himself a bit, but his voice was an unintelligible whisper.

De Merlo scowled. I looked quickly to Gabriel, who sat upon the podium next to his gloating brother. And he—having spotted me earlier in the crowd when he ascended the platform—looked to me as well, then coldly, resolutely, turned his gaze away.

I found myself unable to draw a breath.

The judge summarized my father's words. "The prisoner refuses to admit to his crimes, despite testimony to the contrary. He clings to his error and refuses the forgiveness and penance offered by the church. Nor will he admit or beg forgiveness for his rebellious acts against our queen.

"Hear now the sentence handed down by the Holy Office of the Inquisition and by this court: You are remanded this day to the civil authorities, to be taken outside the city walls and burned at the stake until you are dead, with your body refused Christian burial."

My father did not fall to his knees nor cry out nor speak a word. Unashamed, he stared directly at the judge until the guards led him back to his place.

I began to weep. Máriam called down to our driver to take me home, but he could not leave until we crawled down from the roof and into the carriage. I refused—and though it was considered a gross lapse of propriety for a servant to touch her mistress uninvited, Máriam put her hands on me and tried to pull me.

I would not go. I struck her full in the face, and she drew back, her expression grief stricken and perplexed.

I shouted for the driver to remain and clambered down from the carriage, propelling myself into the crowd, pushing through the press of perspiring bodies and shrieking for them to make way, until I arrived at the line of guards that separated the accused from the onlookers. I tried to reach past them toward my father. One of them drew his sword to block me.

"Damn you to hell!" I screamed at Gabriel. "And damn your father's soul to eternal hell!"

Gabriel looked down coldly from his lofty seat. He had deceived me intentionally, knowing that this moment would come.

Had the guards realized I was screaming at the Inquisitors and not a prisoner, they would have arrested me. My father, several arms' lengths away, heard and recognized my voice and understood. He half turned, unnoticed by his distracted guards, and looked at me.

I quieted at once, and we two stood staring at each other for an instant. He was still strong enough not to let his own grief and torment overshadow the moment; instead, his courage spurred him to consider only my good.

And so he directed at me a warning scowl, one that held not the slightest hint of sorrow or affection, with a face slack with weary resignation. With the same intent, he had disowned me. I knew what he wanted: for me to fall silent and return to the carriage, lest I be arrested myself.

For love of him, I obeyed. I fell silent and let my flailing arms drop. Still, I would not return to the carriage but remained near him, as if my presence could somehow mitigate his suffering.

Five more prisoners in black were escorted before Judge de Merlo—two women and three men, one of whom had sat on the council with my father. And after the last guilty sentence was proclaimed, the head Inquisitor, Fray Morillo of the spectacles, took the judge's place and questioned those prisoners who were to be spared on the tenets of the Christian faith: whether Christ had died for our sins and ascended into heaven; whether He, along with the Father and the Holy Ghost constituted three, yet were still one God; whether baptism and confession were sufficient to save one's soul, and the like.

And the so-called innocents answered in unison to each question "Yes, I believe"; and each individually publicly renounced his or her crimes at length and swore never to repeat them. Fray Morillo led the crowd in singing a psalm: *Miserere mei, Deus*, "Have mercy on me, O Lord." This was followed by the hymn *"Veni Creator Spiritus."* Through it all, my father remained silent, until Morillo granted absolution to those spared, and then Judge de Merlo reappeared to order that those sentenced to die be immediately taken outside the walls for execution.

Those reconciled to the church stood aside as the guards began to march the condemned out of the great square; the magistrate and Inquisitors slowly rose and descended down a set of back stairs to a secure place hidden from the public. The crowds, eager for the final act of the grisly circus, came alive, chattering gaily as they slowly moved out of the square. The guards made a protective wall around the prisoners, reinforced by drawn swords.

I began to follow them. Soon I spied Máriam, who had abandoned the carriage, jostling her way through the mob until she reached me and caught hold of my elbow.

"Don't go," she said, her voice raised so it could be heard over the noise. "It won't help, it will only make it harder for you and for him." She lowered her voice. "Doña, we must leave now, please! Antonio will be taking the wagon with the statue—it is our best chance to escape."

I pulled free of her grip and began to follow the guards escorting my father as closely as I could. Máriam paused only a second before following me.

The sun was high, and the sky blue and cloudless; the air had warmed since dawn, and the presence of thousands of bodies added to the closeness and heat. The procession through town to the northwestern city wall took three-quarters of an hour, given the condemned's slow pace and the size of the crowd. It slowed matters that two of the prisoners fainted. One—the woman who had earlier fallen during the auto-de-fé—could not be revived and had to be carried by her captors, like my father.

We made our way under the watchtowers outside the city, surrounded by grandparents and parents with their children, who laughed with excitement. The mood had grown festive, even though the black carriages of the Inquisitors—including that of Gabriel and his brother—had appeared to watch the final outcome of their work.

Our destination was a berm of heaped-up earth, dry and dusty given the absence of recent rains. Atop it were six wooden stakes as wide and tall as a man, set in the ground at equal distances. At each stake were a set of black iron chains, kindling sticks, and piles of straw. Off to one side a small fire already burned, tended by one of the executioners, a heavyset older man; the other executioner—none other than the young auburn-haired man who had tormented my father at the rack—moved from stake to stake, pouring oil over the kindling and straw. A solitary priest waited, a small vial in his hands.

The guards and prisoners neared the berm. Nearby, a pair of

Franciscan monks, their brown hoods pulled up to hide their faces, led a trio of horses pulling a flat wagon covered by a tarp: a death wagon, to carry off the bodies of those executed. One of them bore a lit torch even though it was only late afternoon, as if he expected to keep vigil through the night.

Shouts came from the more virulent Old Christians: "Die, Jew! Now the Jewish pigs shall roast! Death to *marranos!*"

Máriam clung to my arm, comforted as much as comforting. We followed on the soldiers' heels until they reached the berm. Before they began their ascent, the majority of them encircled the rise, swords drawn so that none could pass. The remainder prodded the prisoners, each to his own place in front of a stake.

But before the prisoners had taken their places, a shrill, deafening whistle blasted my ears. Startled, I looked to its source— the wagon led by the Franciscans. A loud boom followed, and a light flashed overhead, a beautiful starburst of red and white. The two monks held on to two of the rearing horses, which somehow had come unhitched, but the third horse ran terrified toward the center of the berm, scattering pedestrians and guards as the wagon careened dangerously behind it.

A second ear-shattering whistle came, and a third, followed by two consecutive booms, as flares of blue and white light splashed dizzyingly across the afternoon sky.

Fireworks. The poor mad horse dragged a wagon full of exploding fireworks behind it, onto the berm and across, desperate to escape its burden while painting the sky green and gold, in bright globes that expanded quickly, then faded to nothingness.

Everyone was screaming except the two Franciscans, who held calmly on to the bridles of their astonished steeds, then mounted them quickly. I watched with heart-pounding gratitude as they galloped up onto the berm. One of the monks wielded a sword, fighting off the confused guards on foot, while the other rode, his brown habit flapping, directly for my father and tried to pull him up onto the horse.

Caught by surprise, the guards nonetheless soon rallied and enclosed the berm once more. The armed horseman managed to fight his way free, actually running down a trio of guards. But the second man lacked the strength to pull my heavily shackled father up onto the saddle in time. Within seconds, guards surrounded them and took hold of the rider's bridle. The horse reared, and my father slipped and fell to the ground. By that time, the horseman drew a sword, but it was too late; one of the soldiers seized his arm and pulled him from the horse.

My father lay helpless beneath his chains while a guard struck the Franciscan with the flat of his sword, causing him to drop to his knees. One of them pulled back his brown hood.

It was no monk, but Antonio.

A soldier kicked Antonio in the head; he fell onto his side and was dragged back onto his knees again. They bound his hands behind him. One of them took his horse and chased down the renegade wagon.

The soldiers laid claim again to the berm, swearing at the crowd until the screaming stopped and a form of calm descended. The majority of the guards once again encircled the rise, their swords drawn so no one could pass.

The remainder prodded the prisoners, each to his own place in front of a stake. There my father was made to strip off his black tunic, leaving him naked. The same was required of each prisoner, at which point all were forced to kneel in the kindling— this so that death would come faster, either from the smoke or the roasting of the internal organs. The auburn-haired executioner lifted the heavy iron chains and forced my father to put his hands behind him, an act that evoked a cry of pain from him. The executioner bound the chains around my father's wrists and oddly dangling arms, binding him fast to the stake.

But one of the victims cried out before the chains could be applied: "I confess! I abjure my sins! I admit to all and beg the forgiveness of the church! Please, not the fire!"

This caused a stir among the guards and executioners. The auburn-haired one hurried over to the fearful victim, as did the priest. And after the male victim—wild-eyed, his dark hair disheveled, his shoulders visibly dislocated so that his arms dangled in peculiar fashion—was allowed to stand and answered several questions posed by the priest, the latter anointed his sweating forehead with holy oil and administered extreme unction.

After the priest had finished his prayers and benediction, he nodded to the executioner. The auburn-haired man produced a narrow rope from his belt, and the other, heavier executioner fastened the chains around the prisoner's arms, binding him fast.

In a thrice, the younger man slipped the rope around the vainly struggling victim's neck. As the crowd watched, entranced, he strangled him. The prisoner struggled mightily against his chains for several seconds, turning crimson faced, until his eyes and tongue protruded. After a great shudder, he sagged against the chains and fell still.

A man in the crowd let go a great cheer, echoed thoughtlessly by the children. But as soon as their cheers died, one of the victims—a woman—cried out feebly:

"Aleinu l'shabeach l'Adon hakol, latet gedulah l'yotzer b'reishit."

"The martyr's prayer," Máriam whispered in my ear.

The woman's cry broke off abruptly as one of the executioners struck her full in the face, but it was soon echoed by one of the doomed men:

"Aleinu l'shabeach l'Adon . . ."

He too was struck silent. The executioners then finished fastening each prisoner to a stake. When this was done, and no one else cried out for forgiveness, the priest departed while the other two men finished their grim business. Each fetched a pole, at the end of which was tied an oil-soaked rag; these they lit in the small fire. And when each rag had caught sufficiently, they began to walk to each prisoner, lighting the kindling.

Máriam and I held each other as my father's kindling was lit. For a time, it smoked, covering his face with dark billows. They eased, revealing soot covering his cheeks and brow as his pale eyes streamed. He began to groan uncontrollably as the fire caught in earnest, searing the flesh of his knees and shins. Soon, the cries of the suffering muted the sounds of the onlookers, who stood entranced by the spectacle.

The executioners went from stake to stake, adding more kindling and dousing each fire with oil; the flames around my kneeling father leapt up, singeing away the hair on his chest. His eyebrows melted away, and the skin of his face turned red, as if it had been boiled.

When at last the hair on his head caught and flared brightly, he seemed a living candle, and all those on the pyre looked like flaming tapers on a gruesome candelabrum.

Most called out the name of God, but my father's only words were: "Magdalena! Magdalena!"

I do not know how long I watched, how much time passed since the fires were lit. I only felt that my heart, like the skin on my father's bones, was bubbling and darkening and sloughing away, poisoned by smells that should not have been: that of roasting human flesh, of burning hair. But in time, when my father ceased crying out and slumped, bald and blackened, against the stake, Máriam tugged at my arm.

"Come away," she said, sobbing. "Come away; there is nothing more to see." She tugged again, this time with all her strength, forcing me toward her. "Come away—don Gabriel will be looking for you now. And they have captured don Antonio. We must hurry quickly to save the statue and take it to don Francisco. There is no time left."

"I can't leave Antonio," I whispered. "I can't. . . ."

"They've already taken him."

Disbelieving, I looked to where Antonio had been kneeling in the dirt, bound and under guard. Somehow, during the executions, they had taken him away.

"Who will rescue the statue of Santiago?" Máriam hissed in my ear. "He would want you to do it."

I did not answer her. I turned away from the horrible sights—not back toward the carriage, but the other way on foot, as it was far faster to make our way through the crowds. She understood and followed me.

Part of me longed to surrender to the grief, to let myself be taken, to join my mother and father in death. But another part found me lifting my skirts and running in earnest for the living, back beneath the archway of the city wall, down the broad avenue only half filled with pedestrians who had chosen to avoid the crowds by leaving early.

Sorrow dulled my perceptions: I do not remember traversing the distance to San Pablo Street, but soon we were there and running into the large overgrown grove behind Antonio's house. I remember a blur of images: of Máriam pulling away the stone in the old fence where Antonio and I had played as children; of the dark, stifling tunnel beneath the earth; of emerging once again into my mother's workshop, where the spiders had been spinning their webs unimpeded.

The statue of Santiago—his killing sword brandished above his head, his expression one of righteous wrath toward the heretic he slew—sat on the dusty worktable where I had left it. I clutched it with both arms—it was heavy with the Torah shield inside and required effort—and clung to it as if it held the spirits of my mother and father. Still dazed, I followed close behind Máriam and obeyed her gestures.

Soon we were in the wagon Antonio had left behind for his own use; I nestled the Santiago statue beneath a tarp left on the wagon bed, while Máriam harnessed the horse she had brought from the near-empty stable. The only gate, however, led us back onto the cul-de-sac and past the Hojeda mansion.

As Máriam drew open the gate, she said grimly, "Pray we encounter no one."

The gate opened onto the dusty cobblestones not far from where Antonio and Gabriel had fought years before as children, where Gabriel and his cohorts had attacked the hapless Jew—no doubt one of my relatives—who had left the Madonna with my mother.

Máriam gave the horse the whip; it was a strong young gelding, shining and black, and the wagon rattled as the creature lurched forward out into the cul-de-sac. We had barely made it past my father's house and the Hojeda mansion, when Gabriel's familiar carriage rolled into the intersection at San Pablo Street.

My husband leaned out the carriage window and yelled a command at the driver; immediately, his carriage hurtled toward our wagon, then pulled to a fast stop sidewise, blocking our way. Máriam barely managed to rein in our horse before we collided with the carriage; our wagon spun about, kicking up dust, and came to an abrupt halt.

Gabriel and Fray Hojeda climbed out of the carriage, their expressions contorted with self-righteous rage, and called to the driver to accompany them. The latter moved to seize our horse's halter, but Máriam coaxed the horse to move just beyond reach, and made the wagon spin around in an arc as she prepared to make a run past them. Dizzied, I clutched my seat, huddling low in order to keep from falling off onto the cobblestones as the wooden wheels groaned with effort.

Even in my disorientation, I called to Máriam to remain with the wagon at all costs, to abandon me if need be. When Gabriel managed to capture the reins, holding our neighing horse in place, I tucked the Santiago statue more firmly beneath the tarp— foolishly giving away its location—and stood at the edge of the wagon, preparing to jump off.

"Take me!" I shouted. "I'm the one you want!" I looked back to Máriam, silently urging her to take flight in the wagon, but Gabriel still held the halter fast.

Fray Hojeda, sweating and pale, ordered the driver to examine the wagon. The man headed directly for the covered Santiago, but before he could find it, I pulled it from under the tarp and jumped from the wagon, barely managing to stay on my feet without dropping the statue—though how I expected to outrun the three men with my heavy burden, I do not know.

While Fray Hojeda stayed close to the carriage and watched with the driver, Gabriel seized the statue in my hands. I would not let go and made an impossibly strong effort to hold on to it—but inevitably, Gabriel was stronger and pulled it from my grasp. I gave him such a fight, though, that the Santiago slipped and fell to the cobblestones.

I watched in horror as the statue that my mother and I had painted with such care shattered—revealing first the wadding and then, as Gabriel and the driver pulled it free, the golden Torah shield.

Gabriel stared down at it in amazement—at the gleaming gold hidden beneath the yellow wool wadding covered with shards of broken ceramic—then looked up at me wide-eyed.

"It's *true*," he breathed. "You *are* a crypto-Jew!"

"And you are a monster!" I slapped him with all my strength. "God damn you to hell!"

Behind him, Fray Hojeda called out in a quavering, panicked voice. "God help me!"

We all turned and watched him as he vainly clawed the side of the carriage for purchase; he slid to his knees and loosed black vomit onto the cobblestones before finally falling down.

"*Plague*," the driver said, crossing himself and staring at both Gabriel and his brother accusingly. He rushed back to his master's carriage.

Gabriel instinctively went to his fallen brother's side; I used the instant to pick up the Torah shield, still half trapped in its casing of wadding and broken ceramic, and push it up into the back of the wagon.

Immediately, I felt an iron grip seize my legs before I could crawl back onto the wagon: Gabriel had coldly chosen his priority. I struggled, but he pulled me facedown into the street, into the dust where he had taken down the old Jew and Antonio.

I lifted my head and screamed at Máriam. "Go! Go!!!"

Before Gabriel pinned me fast, I glimpsed dark figures looming at the intersection, making their way toward us: Armed guards on foot.

"Go!" I screamed at Máriam again. She whipped the horse, and remarkably the wagon finished its arc around the cul-de-sac before heading directly at the coming guards at high speed.

Compelled, I watched as the guards scattered to give way, and Máriam and the golden treasure careened into the intersection, then onto the half-filled street of San Pablo.

And I was left alone in the hands of the Inquisitor.

Twenty

Gabriel had no qualms about leaving his brother out in the street to lie in a pool of bloody vomit; if anything, he seemed to be relieved to be rid of him and ordered the armed guards to deal with him. I did not see what ultimately became of the so recently jubilant Fray Hojeda, except to know that none of the soldiers would go near him but stood around him in a leery half circle as he cried out weakly for help.

With the help of one of his guards, Gabriel dragged me into his house, into the dining hall where he had once swept all the dishes from the table in a burst of passion. I was made to sit in a chair while the guard tied my hands behind my back. Gabriel, far from being concerned about his brother's grave illness, seemed pleased and revitalized by the prospect of questioning me.

He stood over me, a pale-haired, hawk-nosed giant, his pallid face pushed near mine, his breath warm on my face.

"You are a crypto-Jew. The evidence is clear. That was some sort of Jewish ritual object."

"I am a crypto-Jew," I admitted softly. There was no point in denying the obvious, and speaking the truth aloud brought relief.

He grinned. The disturbing light in his eyes was the same one I had seen the day he had beaten Antonio and the Jew, the same as when he had swept all the dishes from the table, the same as the instant he had realized that I had no choice but to submit sexually to him. All his shyness, his timidity, had been an act in order to placate his brother, but Gabriel had been no less ambitious—only more patient.

"Tell me the truth," he demanded. "You and Antonio are working together as spies for don Francisco."

"I know nothing of either man," I said.

He struck me across the face with his open hand. The pain caused a flash of blue to shoot across the gray landscape of my closed eyelids.

I opened my eyes, and Gabriel said, "You are a whore who has lain with Antonio Vargas."

"No," I said, and he struck me again, this time causing me to bite my tongue. I spat blood on the stone floor but made no other sound.

"You have spoken with don Francisco. The proof is the golden ritual object. You got it from him and were hiding it inside the statue of a saint. How many other statues have you used to smuggle Jewish gold out of Seville?"

"I have never spoken alone with don Francisco," I lied. "The treasure was given me by my mother. I have never used a statue to smuggle anything out of Seville."

He struck me again, harder this time, and with his fist; too hard for his purposes, because after a sickening spiral of darkness that pulled me down with it, I fell unconscious.

. . .

When I woke, I didn't have to ask where I was: I already knew the stench of the Dominican prison. Somehow, I had never noticed the high stone walls in the cell where they had tortured my father, but surely they had been there, their whitewash long worn away, leaving behind a patchy, uneven gray, culminating in a dark beamed ceiling thick with spiderwebs.

I was lying down on my back, my feet slightly elevated above my head. I could not see the shackles binding my ankles and wrists fast to the tilted board on which I rested, but I could feel them. I tried to turn my head to see my captors—I could sense a presence in the room, perhaps more than one—but my arms were stretched so painfully tight above my head that I could not turn it far enough to see them. It was cold in the room, and I was shivering. I thought I was wearing my chemise, but I could not look down at myself to be sure I was not naked.

"Marisol García." It was Gabriel's voice. I sensed something tall and dark hovering in the periphery of my vision, but I could not see him. He sounded self-conscious, as if someone else in the room was watching him.

"You have been charged with conspiring to smuggle Jewish gold out of Seville, against the express decree of Her Majesty Queen Isabel. You are also charged with the heresy of crypto-Judaism. How to you plead?"

Gabriel, I said to myself. I was still stunned by my father's gruesome death, by Máriam's narrow escape, by Gabriel's hard fist. I could feel the extreme physical discomfort of being shackled to the board, but my mind and emotions were too numbed to grasp all of these as actual facts. "Am I on the rack?"

I could hear exasperation in his pause.

His tone hardened. "How do you plead, Marisol?"

"I don't know," I said, dazed. I wanted to ask where Antonio was, but I did not dare implicate him. If he had been captured, surely Gabriel would mention it to use it against me.

"You must plead guilty or innocent."

"I plead innocent," I answered.

"You've already confessed to me that you were guilty. Repeat that now for the scribe's records."

I had admitted the truth to Gabriel in private, but I had no intention of making the interrogation easy for him.

"I'm innocent," I said.

Someone stepped forward so that I could see him. It was the auburn-haired executioner, the young one who had lit the kindling around my kneeling father. He grinned impudently at me and pushed another figure into my line of sight.

Antonio staggered forward, visible from the waist up. He was shirtless, his body covered with sweat despite the chill in the room. The wound in his upper arm, near the shoulder, was bleeding so heavily that the stiches were invisible; most likely they had come undone. His bare chest was almost completely hairless; one nipple was blackened and inverted, the skin around it red and blistered.

The smell of scorched flesh was sickening. Antonio's expression was stern; he looked at me as though he did not recognize me, as if I weren't present at all—just as my father had.

"One more time, Marisol," Gabriel's voice said. "Admit your guilt."

I remained silent.

As I did, the grinning executioner produced a large black kerchief. He unfurled it over my face, blotting out the sight of Antonio, of the walls and ceiling.

"Now repeat the question," a third voice said softly—to Gabriel, not me. Fray Morillo was in the room, watching.

Gabriel spoke again. "Are you certain of your plea?"

"As certain as I am of the fact that my father agreed to denounce himself if you would protect me," I said clearly.

I heard Morillo draw in a breath of surprise; I imagined Gabriel flushing brightly at the accusation.

"Is this true?" Morillo asked softly.

"A filthy lie," Gabriel answered. "Just like everything else she is saying." He addressed me. "You and your cohort will pay for this, Marisol."

Morillo said nothing more.

There was a long hesitation. I waited to feel my bones being pulled from their sockets, to hear the grind of the turning wheel, the clanking of chains, but instead heard water sloshing from a bucket.

Suddenly, the black cloth covering my face was soaked, and there was water pouring down my nose. I opened my mouth to scream, and the water rushed in, reducing my shrieks to a strangled, gurgling noise. Antonio's shouts were distant, muffled.

The water kept coming until my throat and chest were burning, until I knew I was drowning. And then it abruptly stopped. I drew a gasping breath, sucking in the drenched cloth. My ears were full of liquid; I tried to shake my head to clear them, to hear what Antonio was yelling, but I could not move and water from the cloth slowly trickled into them. The cloth plastered my eyes shut.

I drew another wheezing breath.

This time, I was uncertain whether the voice was Gabriel's or Fray Morillo's.

"Will you confess to the crimes of smuggling and heresy?"

"No," I gasped.

"Will you confess to conspiring with don Francisco Sánchez and Antonio Vargas?"

"No," I said.

They allowed me a full breath, then another.

The flood came again. The rushing water caught me in mid-breath, and I choked, inhaling some of it into my lungs, swallowing the rest—and still it would not stop coming. I was gagging, spewing, mindless with desperation.

The water stopped.

"Will you confess?"

I thought of don Francisco and Máriam, and wondered whether they and the treasure were safe. Antonio's breath was ragged; I felt guilt that he was forced to watch, knowing that the sight of someone else's suffering was more painful to him than his own.

"No," I answered Gabriel.

This time when the water came, I tried to swallow it. Impossible; it streamed down my throat, filling my mouth and nose until I was forced to breathe it in and gag. My body spasmed uncontrollably. Somewhere in the violent struggle, my mind grew separate and calm. In a dreamlike vision, my mother appeared in the Guadalquivir, and the moon shone, its light silver on the rippling waters.

The flood stopped. My body took one long, hitching gasp of air, then two.

"Will you confess?"

My mother sank into the river, the water lifting her blue-green skirts with the hoops of the *verdugado* around her waist, then her shoulders. She opened her mouth and chanted, her voice low and sweet, and I chanted with her.

"Shema Yisrael," I gasped, *"Adonai Eloheinu."*

"You admit to being a crypto-Jew, then, in front of these witnesses!"

"Adonai Echad," I finished.

I never uttered another word. The water streamed down my throat and nose. I fought to hold my breath, but it was useless: The water flooded into my gut, my lungs, and my body responded reflexively by retching. Once again, my mind detached: Beautiful Magdalena was standing in the river, praying in the light of the moon.

The water came again and again and again. I vomited it up and fainted, but the auburn-haired man forced me awake again to choke on water and my own bile, my lungs burning. On the dark gray inside of my closed eyelids, my mother and Antonio were smiling and waving from the Triana shore on the opposite side of the river.

Abruptly, I was yanked up into a sitting position, resting against Gabriel's sturdy arm; I could not see his face, but I recognized his smell. Unseen hands pulled the black cloth from my face. Antonio now sat shackled to a chair, wearing only his leggings. From behind me came the smoky scent of a lit hearth, the sound of scraping. Soon the auburn-haired executioner emerged into my field of vision bearing what looked at first like a poker, but they were pincers, glowing white-hot at the tips.

I wanted to close my eyes, yet as with my father, I felt compelled to watch. The red-haired man waved the pincers teasingly in front of Antonio's chest. Antonio paid no attention to either the pincers or the torturer but stared defiantly at a point just beyond me—at Gabriel's eyes.

Gabriel spoke into my ear. "Marisol, do you confess to conspiring with don Francisco?"

"Why don't you ask me?" Antonio demanded. "You were always a coward, Gabriel. Always picking on someone smaller than yourself."

Against my back, Gabriel's arm tensed. He repeated, with barely controlled fury: "Marisol, do you confess to conspiring with don Francisco?"

"No," I said.

I felt rather than saw Gabriel nod to the auburn-haired man.

The torturer opened the pincers, applied them to Antonio's unharmed nipple, and twisted savagely. Flesh sizzled, giving off the smell of roasting pork. Despite Antonio's bucking, the torturer held the pincers fast until the skin began to blacken, then pulled away a bit of charred meat.

Antonio screamed but focused his pain on attacking Gabriel. "Fucking coward! Great big fucking coward!" He gritted his teeth and lowered his head as the auburn-haired man displayed the smoking, bubbling bit of skin in the air like a trophy.

I retched, but nothing came up.

The torturer grinned with delight.

Gabriel asked me the same question about don Francisco, while the red-haired man went to reheat the pincers in the hearth. I refused to answer.

The torturer once again went over to Antonio, who strained against his shackles painfully; the former, still smiling, waved the pincers menacingly over the bare skin of Antonio's torso and looked to Gabriel.

I felt Gabriel's gaze on me; I closed my eyes and drew my lips tightly shut. I heard another sizzle and opened my eyes.

The torturer had seized another piece of flesh, this one from Antonio's rib cage, where a blackened, still smoking wound the size of a coin had appeared; the skin around it was red and blistering. Antonio bowed, gasping with the pain. "Fucking idiot!" he screamed at Gabriel. "Fucking great brute of an idiot!"

Behind me, the muscles in Gabriel's arm grew increasingly rigid. "Pull his leggings down," he coldly ordered.

I looked away, to spare Antonio's dignity. The leggings couldn't come all the way off, of course, since his ankles were shackled to the chair. But when the torturer returned this time from reheating his weapon, I couldn't keep from watching where the pincers were headed next.

Between Antonio's legs.

"*Don't*—" I began, my voice high-pitched with fear. I forced myself to break off.

A pause ensued while I wrestled with myself.

"What is that?" Gabriel asked behind me, his voice rising with glee.

"Don't," I repeated, my tone flat, disappointed. I looked at Antonio and he looked back at me sharply, questioningly.

"Do you confess?" Gabriel asked, as the pincers loomed perilously close to Antonio's unprotected genitalia. The heat was singeing the hair on his naked thighs.

Antonio held my gaze solemnly, intensely; his eyes held the haunted look of a man surrendering. "The river docks, Marisol," he said.

If trouble befalls you, don Francisco had said, *go to the river docks near San Pablo Street . . . Let Antonio tell you when the time draws nearer. . . .*

"Don't tell them anything," I said, regretting my weakness. But Antonio would not remain silent anymore; he looked away from me as if ashamed.

"The river docks," he said. "The Guadalquivir, near San Pablo Street. Take us there, and they will come for us."

If trouble befalls you, go to the river.

The late afternoon had turned cold, and the sinking sun stirred a breeze, causing the last coral rays to glitter like fire off the rippling waters. The larger ships—the great trading vessels from foreign lands—were beginning to weigh anchor and furl their sails, leaving their masts bared like spines at the docks near the brick armory. Its sulfur stink carried on the wind, along with that of fish, mixed with the sweeter fragrance of cedar from the lumberyard. Smaller ships were still afloat: skiffs and fishing boats and scows.

Antonio and I stood upon the dock nearest my house, I shivering in my soaked chemise, he shuddering with pain at the feel of a rough burlap tunic against his burns. My left hand was shackled to his right, but the manacle was small so that those watching from a distance would not see it.

We were not far from a trading vessel anchored at a dock perpendicular to ours, or from the patch of golden sand where my mother Magdalena had entered the water. Near the spot where

Gabriel had held me back from diving into the river after her, a single guard in pedestrian clothing stood watching. Gabriel and Fray Morillo were not far off, accompanied by more guards, hidden out of sight behind the trading vessel. A pair of young boys fishing off the far end of the pier had each been paid a silver coin to intervene if anyone came onto the dock to rescue us. To make certain no one could, another guard, posing as a fisherman, was posted where the dock met the shore.

We were bait; while the Inquisitors believed nothing else we told them, they were willing to gamble that some *converso* would come to rescue us. This despite the fact that I was half naked and clearly the worse for wear, my hair damp and bedraggled.

I gazed out at the maritime scenery. Gulls flew overhead, their cries shrill and raucous; the occasional rat skittered across the dock and entered the water with a light splash.

The waters beneath me were clouded gray-green, as opaque as Fray Hojeda's eyes. I contemplated the water; I could not believe I would be saved, any more than my mother was on the night of her death. Antonio had pretended to confess while in the prison, revealing a secret escape plan, and showed great shame while I feigned anger at him. Once we were out on the dock, he became silent, his gaze calm. He was looking down at the river with a fatalistic expression, and I thought I understood: It would be impossible, exposed as we were, with so many guards watching, for any of don Francisco's men to rescue us. Perhaps don Francisco's advice was the course my mother had taken: to dive into the waters, to take her own life before she yielded to the Inquisition.

If Antonio and I had to die, at least we would do so on our own terms, together, without enduring further torture. I far preferred water to fire.

If the danger is extreme . . .

The danger was extreme. But there was a score I had to settle before dying.

I turned and faced the place where Gabriel hid with Fray Morillo, on the dock behind one of the anchored vessels.

I started to shout, but my voice was raw and rasping. I cleared my throat and called out again, using all the strength left in my lungs to be sure my voice could be heard above the gulls and the lapping water.

"Gabriel Hojeda is a crypto-Jew," I shouted, to the surprise of a dazed boy fishing with a net on the nearby shore. I hoped Fray Morillo was listening carefully. "Go to his house; you'll find a mezuzah hidden in his apartments."

No sound issued from behind the trading vessel. The boys on the dock stared at me as they would at a madwoman.

I turned to Antonio. "I love you," I said.

He looked back at me, his eyes bright and loving. "I love you, Marisol," he said. "Take a deep breath."

Together we jumped.

The cold and the impact drove the air from my lungs as I hit the water. For an instant the manacle shackling me by my left hand to Antonio's right pulled us down, but with great effort, Antonio thrashed and brought us bobbing to the surface.

I fought him. "Why?" I shrieked, though I could barely hear myself over the splashing. "Let me go. . . ."

"Marisol, trust me!" he shouted back. "Swim!"

The guard on the shore was shouting, too. He called out to the boys on the pier, to the fishermen nearby on the river. I did not wait to hear whether they answered him. My will took over where my body failed. Somehow I moved my aching arms through the water, struggling to work in tandem with Antonio.

The opposite shore of Triana seemed so very far away. Did Antonio think we could outswim the guards and reach it?

"Now," Antonio shouted in my ear. Our legs grew tangled, kicking at each other; he held his still for a minute, sinking into the water until it was up to his ears, until only his face showed. "Now we dive under. Take a deep breath and *swim*."

I managed only half a breath before going under. The heavy water drowned out the shouts of the guards and Inquisitors; the wake of Antonio's strong strokes surrounded me with bubbles. His pale arms and dark legs cut through the water as he swam in the direction of a large sailing vessel to the south of the pontoon bridge.

We'll be rescued by a sea captain, I thought, remembering that my mother had no such refuge to swim to. But when we arrived at the barnacled hull and bobbed to the surface, Antonio gasped and waited until the guards caught sight of us and called out to the Inquisitors.

"There they are! At the ship!"

At that instant, Antonio tugged at me, drew a loud breath, and I did likewise. We went under the water again, and Antonio kicked his legs to propel himself downward, deep beneath the surface. I followed suit, our hands joined together, as we swam *away* from the vessel, back toward the pontoon bridge.

Somehow, we found the strength to keep the manacle from dragging us down. I swam until my arms and lungs shrieked from the effort, until my feet and hands went numb from the cold. I swam until I began to gulp water, and still I swam.

The water was gray-green and murky; I couldn't make out Antonio's face, only his thrashing arms. I realized that if I didn't get air soon, I would drown, and my weight would drag him to his doom. Yet when I opened my mouth to cry out to him, I only swallowed more water.

I grew light-headed and soon unable to hold up my aching left arm, the one shackled to Antonio. Amazingly, he managed to pull me along, to keep going although I was of little help. I retched in the water, and became even more light-headed—then I could no longer paddle at all but felt my limbs grow weak and still. I closed my eyes to the deep and stopped struggling, and imagined I saw my mother waving to me from the shore.

Marisol, someone called from a great distance away. *Marisol!*

His hands clutching either side of my face, Antonio pulled me up where there was air; my head struck something wooden. I opened my eyes to gray twilight and the pervasive lapping of water. My left arm ached terribly; it was pulled over my head, and I was hanging from it, and Antonio was hanging beside me, both of us in water up to our shoulders. The dank, fishy smell told me we were still in the Guadalquivir.

I coughed, my teeth chattering from the cold. "Where are we?"

"Underneath the pontoon bridge. There are jutting beams under here." He jangled the manacle binding us, and thumped wood. "Hurry, it's only a matter of time before they start looking under the bridge." He paused and his tone grew concerned. "You've got to be strong, Marisol. You've got to find the strength to pull yourself out of the water."

Utterly confused, I watched as he braced his legs against the wooden pontoon. With a grunt, he swung himself up out of the water, his right arm still attached to mine. I yelped as he nearly pulled my left arm out of its socket; I was hanging from my left arm in the water, while he looked down at me from a wooden platform hidden inside the pontoon, its ceiling so low he could not even crouch but was forced to lie on his stomach.

"Give me your other hand," he hissed.

I gritted my teeth as I raised my right arm overhead, joining my left; both ached from being bound tightly in the torture chamber, but my pain was nothing to what Antonio must have felt from his wounds.

"Crawl up, Marisol! Hurry! It's only a matter of time before they realize we're not on the ship and start searching the river."

"Did they see us?" I asked.

"We sank like stones."

"But won't they look for us here?"

"Don Francisco had this platform secretly constructed. They don't know it exists." He paused. "I'm sorry I had to pull you under so deep. Now push with your feet against the pontoon. *Push!*"

I found the wooden scaffolding of the pontoon and pushed with all my might; my bare feet slipped against the slime. On the third try, both Antonio and I roared through gritted teeth as I wriggled upward and he pulled with impossible strength. My ribs hit the edge of the platform with bruising force, but I used my elbows to wriggle forward while Antonio kept pulling. Soon my waist was out of the water, and I was able to pull my trembling legs up.

Antonio and I lay beside each other on an algae-covered platform hidden at the top of the pontoon's scaffolding. Slats of wood surrounding us kept us invisible from the outside—as well as kept the outside invisible to us. Only small cracks in the wood revealed light: They were using lanterns to look for us. Shouts echoed from the bridge, from the waters.

"My poor Marisol, I thought I'd lost you," Antonio whispered. He put a hand to my face; I couldn't tell which was colder, my skin or his.

"I saw my mother," I told him, shivering. "On Triana's shore."

I heard the smile in his voice. "She's not in Triana, Marisol. She should already be in Portugal by now."

"Don't be cruel," I hissed, but broke off as footsteps crossed overhead; our pontoon swayed like a boat.

We remained silent as another set of footsteps joined them; the light coming through the cracks in the wood grew brighter. Antonio and I held our breath as the steps grew farther away. Even then, I dared not make a sound; swimmers were thrashing nearby in the water.

I lay motionless, trying to keep my teeth from chattering too loudly. Eventually, the swimmers headed away. We waited for what seemed like hours, until twilight became night, until the sweep of lanterns faded and eventually disappeared.

Silence came, and with it, greater cold. My body shook uncontrollably next to Antonio's; I would have clung to him for warmth, but the platform we lay on was too low and narrow to allow it.

"How long?" I asked him. "Do we stay here forever?"

I could feel him shake his head in the darkness. "We have to wait. Only be patient."

"My mother," I said. "You were lying about her, weren't you? You were only being cruel so that I would be angry, so that I would keep going . . . ?"

"I would never lie to you, Marisol. Your mother knew about this place beneath the bridge."

Tears came to my eyes. "Do you think she made it here? Do you think she actually escaped?"

Antonio let go a teeth-chattering sigh. "I don't know. But she's a strong woman, like you. I'm sure she tried."

As time passed, Antonio and I jiggled our limbs to keep from freezing, and tried to stay alert by telling each other stories. Antonio spoke of Portugal and Lisbon, about the great Tejo River, about my great-uncle Isaac Abravanel and his charities. I told him the story of Máriam's rescue of little Raquelita. But exhaustion overtook both of us, and we eventually grew silent. The cold was painful, and I knew we were in danger of freezing to death, but I could no longer keep moving; I let my eyes close and dozed.

And I saw my mother, veiled, her profile translucent in the light of Shabbat candles. She made a sweeping gesture.

Behind her in the distance lay Sepharad, golden and gleaming. Moor and Jew and Christian, the black eyed and the pale, at peace, tilling the rich rolling earth, marked by endless rows of orchards, fragrant and heavy with blossom. The waters reflected the blue of the sky and sparkled in the sun like a thousand jewels. And the sun kissed the spires of mosques and churches, the stones of synagogues, sweet as dates and honey, beautiful as heaven, peaceful as the sleep deep beneath the waters.

The river grew heavily silent, yet in my mind I heard the sound of lyres and my mother singing.

There was suddenly light—"Three blinks, it's them," Antonio said—and then the light grew glaring. There was movement. I was pushed and pulled and cradled, too frozen to move my limbs, vaguely aware of the lapping of water and the rocking of a boat. I was wrapped in something soft, and as my body warmed, the stabbing pain in my limbs made me groan.

"Marisol, can you hear me?" someone asked, but I was still too cold and too exhausted to speak. I shuddered against the growing warmth and let the rocking lull me back to sleep. Somewhere in my dreams, I heard the song of the plague driver, calling for the dead.

When I finally woke, the rattle of wheels caused my whole body to vibrate, my teeth to chatter. I was still cold, though warm enough to move, and I grew frightened at the realization that my eyes were covered by a stiff gray cloth: Was I back in the Dominican prison? Would the water come again?

No, I was in motion, lying between a pair of silent bodies, radiant with heat, and I was looking up at the tarp covering us.

Above me, the unseen man steering the wagon let go the chant of the plague driver: "Bring out your bodies," he sang.

Had I been taken for dead and thrown in with those who perished from plague? I started to draw in a breath to scream, but a hand clamped over my mouth—one bearing a manacle connected to my own hand. "Marisol," a familiar voice hissed, and I fell silent. The wagon rolled over cobblestones, the horses' hooves clattering until they grew muted, echoing off a partially enclosed structure. A city wall.

"The bodies of the dead," our driver sang again cheerfully, and the guard at the city gate replied in a far grimmer voice.

"Pass. And don't tarry!"

The wagon rattled again; the echo of cobblestone faded, replaced by the duller, thumping sound of hooves against the unpaved earth outside the city. For several moments, we continued at a steady pace, and then the wagon moved faster and faster, as the driver gave the horses their heads.

The body next to mine reached for my hand and squeezed it; I squeezed back, in my weakness, reduced to tears.

In the distance came the approaching thunder of men on horseback, and I grew once again terrified. As they came alongside our wagon, those beside me did not cry out or scream; instead, they sat up, throwing off the tarp that covered us.

I was sitting beside Antonio—wan and smiling, exhausted from his wounds. Máriam sat beside him—and to my surprise, don Francisco's granddaughter Luz was lying next to her, a newborn infant in her arms.

Flanking our wagon were men-at-arms on horseback. I remained uneasy until the captain smiled at us. "We'll be escorting you to don Francisco today. You'll join him and his family before you start your journey."

"The Torah shield?" I asked Máriam.

"Safe," she said, and I threw my free arm around her.

She grinned. "We are going to Portugal, Marisol. Where we will see doña Magdalena again." From her belt she produced a letter; I recognized the handwriting.

I stared at her huge smile and remembered.

She is a hero, Luz had said of my mother. *Is,* not *was. You're not alone. You've never been alone.*

Because I love your mother, don Francisco had said. Not *loved.*

I thought of one of the last things my mother had said to me: *Antonio loves you and will come for you. Only wait.*

She had known. As Antonio had said, she had known about the beams under the pontoon bridge in the river. And she was a strong woman. She had survived, just as I had.

I began to sob, as much from joy over my mother and Antonio as from sorrow over my father. I wept so loudly that the infant at Luz's breast stirred and wakened and emitted a high-pitched wail.

Luz began to sing a lullaby.

"Durme, durme, querido hijico . . ."

The captain gave a signal, and the wagon lurched into motion again, this time flanked by the guards on horseback, headed into the countryside.

"Durme sin ansia y dolor," Luz sang to her child.

"Cerra tus chicos ojicos," I sang with her, high and sweet, and never wanted to stop singing again.

AFTERWORD

The characters of Marisol García, Gabriel Hojeda, and Antonio
Vargas are fictional; however, Fray Hojeda, Queen Isabel, Fray
Torquemada, and Fray Morillo were real historical personages.
I have set my fictional characters against the actual events in
Seville of the winter of 1480–1481.

Three days after his exuberant sermon at the first auto-de-fé
(the term *auto-da-fé* did not come into use until the eighteenth century, well after the Inquisition spread to Portugal), Fray Alonso
Hojeda died of the plague.

Reading
Group
Gold

THE INQUISITOR'S WIFE

Jeanne Kalogridis

About the Author
- A Conversation with Jeanne Kalogridis

Behind the Novel
- Historical Perspective

Keep on Reading
- Recommended Reading
- Reading Group Questions

A
Reading
Group Gold
Selection

For more reading group suggestions,
visit www.readinggroupgold.com.

 ST. MARTIN'S GRIFFIN

"I work obsessively to re-create eras and personas as carefully as possible."

What was the inspiration for *The Inquisitor's Wife* and its titular heroine?

I'd researched the Inquisition in 1300s France for my novel *The Burning Times*, and I'd always wanted to know more about the famous Spanish Inquisition (beyond the Monty Python sketch, "No one expects..."). So when I was casting about for an idea for a new novel, I decided to look at the origins of the Spanish Inquisition. I *thought* I already knew the basic facts, but the more I researched the topic, the more I realized that, like everyone else, I had major misconceptions about the Inquisition. I quickly became fascinated by the underlying politics, and by Queen Isabella's real reasons for engineering the Inquisition. She was not the frail, pious saint of legend. And her husband Fernando was king in name only; Isabella was the real power behind the throne, although in writing she always deferred to her husband, claiming that she was simply going along with the king's wishes. Although the two unquestionably loved each other, they regularly had knock-down, drag-out fights with much shouting and tears. And they all ended with Isabella getting her way. Interestingly enough, King Fernando had a Jewish ancestor, something that Isabella wasn't above pointing out during their squabbles.

Did you take any "artistic liberties" in telling this story? Could you share an example of how you altered a fact (or two!) for dramatic or thematic effect?

My heroine is fictional, although her father is based on a real person; her mother is representative of the Inquisition's targets. Everything else—detailed descriptions of Isabella and Torquemada, dates, places, names, historical characters—is as accurate as careful research allows. I did, however, take liberties: Queen Isabella probably never visited Seville during the period my novel takes place, so I had her make a "secret" visit because it made the story far

more exciting and allowed us a glimpse of Isabella as she really was. Many older biographies give us the inaccurate picture of her as small, quiet, pious, and dark-haired. I relied on an excellent recent biography by Peggy Liss, and learned that Isabella was auburn-haired, big-boned, taller than most men (including Fernando), and fond of bawdy jokes. Politically, she was incredibly shrewd and ruthless. The image of her as intensely pious and resorting to the Inquisition as a result of that piety is inaccurate—an example of Isabella's brilliance at creating a consistent public image. She was a master at public relations.

My rule for writing a historical novel is this: I never contradict an established fact but will allow myself to create "situations that *might* have been." Beyond that, I work obsessively to re-create eras and personas as carefully as possible. For example, I have a character hide a mezuzah inside a statue of a Madonna—a technique that had actually been used in Inquisitional Spain and Latin America. I fear I suffer from the phenomenon known as "research rapture"—details so delight me that I always do far too much research, never too little. Most of the heroines in my other novels, however, are based on actual historical figures. I departed from that with *The Inquisitor's Wife*.

Can you tell us a bit more about your research? What was the most surprising—or shocking—thing you learned about this time period?
I managed to get my hands on some great resources. There's a marvelous 1,500-page history by B. Netanyahu (father of, yes, *that* Netanyahu) regarding the origins of the Inquisition. It's incredibly detailed, with documents and letters from the period.

The single most surprising thing I learned (outside of Isabella's real appearance and personality) was that the

Spanish Inquisition *did not persecute Jews*. Church law actually forbade the persecution of Jews and protected them; the Church had no legal jurisdiction over them (although civil authorities did). Therefore, the Inquisition focused on *Christians*, specifically those "new" Christians who were *conversos*—i.e., converts from Judaism. My story takes place in 1481, when the Inquisition first appeared in Spain; but back in the 1390s, prompted in part by hysteria over the plague, Spanish Christians slaughtered thousands of Jews. Those that survived the slaughter were forced to convert to Christianity at knifepoint.

The great majority of these *conversos* became sincere practitioners of their new faith. A few, however, continued to practice the rituals of Judaism in secret. This went on for generations. By Isabella's time, many Old Christians still looked on *conversos* with suspicion. A very few *conversos* in Seville were blatant about their loyalty to their old religion, and this caused hostility and occasional violence.

Since the *conversos* were Christian, the Church had full authority to persecute them as heretics if there was any evidence that they were still practicing Judaism. Some of the *conversos* who were arrested and subsequently burned at the stake were in fact heretics by the Church's definition, but many were falsely accused and completely innocent. Many fled Seville and settled south in Morocco, or east in Portugal (where the Inquisition took hold a century later).

I believe, as does Netanyahu and other historians, that Isabella shrewdly played on this antagonism between Old Christian and New in order to start the Inquisition. Before I did my research, I didn't realize that the Spanish Crown seized the lion's portion of any arrested *converso's* wealth and property. Both the Church and the Crown made an obscene fortune off the Inquisition—at a time when Isabella was actively seeking money to fuel wars.

"Those seeking power (today) still use racial, sexual, and ethnic divisions to their political advantage."

The most frightening thing about the Spanish Inquisition
was that Isabella and Fernando insisted that the pope give
them complete control over the Inquisition. That had never
been done before; monarchs were always answerable to
the Church. As a result, there was no third party oversight,
and no legal rights for the accused. For the first time in any
Inquisition, the accused had no right to confront his accuser or even know who he was, and one could denounce
one's neighbor while remaining completely anonymous.
Many innocents were denounced by enemies.

**What parallels, if any, do you find between the politics
of identity then and now?**

Nothing has changed. Those seeking power still use racial,
sexual, and ethnic divisions to their political advantage.
They ruthlessly foment hatred for political purposes,
dividing the world into "us" and "other." Look at how
unscrupulous politicians today are fanning the fires of
hatred over issues like marriage rights and immigration
reform.

**Do you personally know anyone who had to hide his or
her Jewish identity during World War II, for example?**
Not personally, but I read Anne Frank's *The Diary of a
Young Girl* when I was very young, and being a young girl
who loved to write, I identified with her. It touched me
deeply; it was hard for me to imagine that someone wanted
her dead because of her DNA. I also grew up in the Deep
South and witnessed the civil rights struggles firsthand; the
Ku Klux Klan was very active in our little town, and even
paraded in the streets. I remember the day that blacks were
first admitted to our school—how truly terrified those
children were, how very cruelly other children treated
them. It was sickening and heartrending to watch.

Are you currently working on another book? And if so, what—or who—is your subject?

I'm having a blast writing my current (untitled for the moment) book, which has a much lighter, fun feel and greased-lightning pace. It's about a young woman who grew up in Florence, in the Ospedale degli Innocenti, Italy's landmark orphanage. In those days, a fifteen-year-old girl in the orphanage was considered an adult, and had to leave. She was given two choices: Marry (usually an undesirable older man looking more for a servant than a real wife) or join a nunnery. Well, my heroine, Giulia, is too headstrong and independent to countenance either. She escapes to the street. Rather than become a prostitute, like most unmarried, uncloistered orphaned girls, she becomes a highly skilled pickpocket, giving most of her earnings to her fellow orphans.

The period is 1479-80, during Florence's war with the King of Naples and the Pope of Rome. And Florence was losing big-time. Lorenzo de' Medici, the first citizen of Florence, risked his neck by paying a secret visit to the King of Naples himself, and launched a one-man diplomatic campaign to save Florence using nothing but his wit and personal charm. It was an amazing, difficult time, and one of the most fascinating events of the Italian Renaissance.

My heroine Giulia will find herself entangled in the intrigue and espionage surrounding Lorenzo's famous visit to Naples, at which point her life changes forever. Lorenzo is a pivotal character. The story starts two years after Giulia's departure from the orphanage. We find her on page one with her hand in the pocket of a victim, just as an extremely attractive young policeman catches and arrests her....

Historical Perspective

Do You Know?

• The Spanish Inquisition did not persecute Jews. Instead, it targeted those Christians of Jewish ancestry who were suspected of practicing Jewish rituals. While there were, in fact, *conversos* who secretly practiced Judaism, they were few in number.

• The Jews in Spain had been living there for a thousand years when the first Visigoths (who ultimately became Spain's rulers) arrived to conquer them. When the Moors subsequently arrived to throw out the Visigoths, the Jews welcomed them. With the exception of a few individual rulers, the Moors tolerated the Jews well, allowing them more status and freedom than Christian rulers eventually would.

• Jews in Spain were not persecuted during the Inquisition, but they were expelled en masse from the country by Queen Isabella's decree in 1492, as she prepared to seize the last Moorish stronghold in Spain, Granada. Some think that Isabella expelled the Jews because she needed their wealth to fund her war against Granada.

• The famous Grand Inquisitor, Tomás de Torquemada, who was known for his vitriolic hatred of Jews and *conversos*, had Jewish blood on his grandmother's side.

• The Dominican order of monks ran the Inquisition and became the symbol of intolerance and racial hatred; however, many Dominicans were against the persecution of Jews and *conversos*. Torquemada's uncle, the respected scholar Cardinal Juan de Torquemada, also a Dominican, didn't hide his Jewish ancestry, and argued strenuously for tolerance for *conversos* and Jews.

• Just for fun: Certain varieties of orange trees in Seville hold ripe fruit at the same time they're blooming. (The same thing happens here in southern California, where the climate is very similar to Seville's.)

- Three days after preaching a sermon of gratitude at the very first auto-de-fé (the term *auto-da-fé* would not come into use for another hundred years), the Jew and *converso* hater, Fray Alonso Hojeda—the man who single-handedly convinced Queen Isabella of the need for an Inquisition—dropped dead of the plague. (Maybe it's not a shocking fact, but I particularly like it.)

- Unlike their sumptuously dressed counterparts in Italy and France, married women in Renaissance Spain dressed in plain high-necked gowns, usually black; men wore tunics that fell to their knees while the rest of men in Europe were starting to ditch tunics in favor of farsettos and codpieces. Dress in Spain was so austere that Spanish visitors to other European countries were scandalized.

- Queen Isabella never wore jewelry (except for a small crucifix) in public, in keeping with her pious image. However, in private, she wore pounds of gold and dozens of precious jewels (including a ring on each finger), pushing the limits of good taste even for a wealthy monarch. At the same time, she didn't pamper herself where duty was concerned, and thought nothing of riding off pregnant to join her husband in battle.

- The Spanish Inquisition also took virulent hold in the New World, where many *conversos* had settled. Part of Columbus's crew on his 1492 voyage were *conversos*. Today in Latin America, there are Christian families who identify themselves as *conversos* and celebrate certain Jewish practices.

- I tried not to make Torquemada a cartoonish, one-dimensional villain, I really did. But I had an obligation to present the character accurately. He apparently really was as cold, heartless, power-hungry, sadistic, and one-dimensional as our culture has come to portray him. And astoundingly ugly, to boot. He was very secretive, with the result that court members and chroniclers of the period knew virtually nothing about him.

Recommended Reading

Reading Group Gold

Keep on Reading

Isabel the Queen: Life and Times by Peggy K. Liss
An in-depth, exhaustively researched, and sometimes startling biography of Isabella. Approachable, fascinating reading. There are several biographies of Isabella, but this is the most scholarly and well-researched, relying on original source materials instead of other biographies. It became one of my main sources.

The Spanish Inquisition by Joseph Pérez
An overview of the Inquisition from its inception to its demise. It gives a brief background of the politics of the era, plus explicit explanations of the Inquisition's policies, procedures, and personae.

The Origins of the Inquisition in Fifteenth-Century Spain by B. Netanyahu
A massive, exquisite collection of research, containing many translations of letters, legal documents, public speeches, and essays from 1400s Spain. (A "research rapture" sufferer's dream.) Netanyahu put many misconceptions about the Inquisition to rest in this volume, supporting his opinions with a wealth of documents from the period. I relied on it heavily, and based my heroine's father on a real individual cited in one of the excerpts from a fifteenth-century historian. Not a casual read, but a masterpiece.

Seville & Andalusia: A DK Eyewitness Travel Guide
An in-depth guide to the area, containing hundreds of photographs, maps, and cultural and historical tidbits. One of the better travel guides. I always draw and refer to a map of whatever city I'm writing about (and of course, have to be sure I have a proper fifteenth-century map). I need to know whether my character's turning right or left, north or south, after all.

The Spanish Inquisition: A Historical Revision
by **Henry Kamen**
A defense of the Inquisition, from a churchman's point of view. Not very well-researched, but an interesting polemic from "the other side."

The Queen's Vow by **C. W. Gortner**
A fascinating novel about Isabella's early years, including her perilous ascent to the throne and her determination to marry Fernando of Aragon despite all opposition.

The Burning Times by **Jeanne Kalogridis**
My novel about one of the first appearances of the Inquisition in Europe: in Carcassonne, France, in the mid-1300s. The story of a midwife arrested for witchcraft.

Reading Group Questions

1. What did you know about the Spanish Inquisition—either from your own studies, or as portrayed in popular film/television adaptations—before reading *The Inquisitor's Wife*? How, if at all, did this book teach you about, or change your impression of, this important chapter in Spanish history?

2. How were Marisol and her family different from other Spaniards in fifteenth-century Seville? Do you think Marisol's attitudes were "ahead of her time"? What do you see as Marisol's most and least admirable qualities? Take a moment to talk about Marisol's evolution from a woman who hates her Jewish background to one who embraces it.

3. What parallels do you see between today's political events and those of fifteenth-century Spain? Is the "Inquisition" (i.e., persecutory institutions and attitudes) alive and well in the twenty-first century?

4. To what extent do you think Jeanne Kalogridis took artistic liberties with this work? What does it take for a novelist to bring a "real" historical period to life?

5. Discuss the nature of fact versus fiction in *The Inquisitor's Wife*. You may wish to take this opportunity to compare it with other historical novels you've read (as a group or on your own).

6. Why *do* modern readers enjoy novels about the past? How and when can a powerful piece of fiction be a history lesson in itself?

7. We are taught, as young readers, that every story has a "moral." Is there a moral to *The Inquisitor's Wife*? What can we learn about our world—and ourselves—from Marisol's story?

From the pen of critically acclaimed author

JEANNE KALOGRIDIS—

more irresistible historical novels filled with danger and passion...

Download reading group guides at www.ReadingGroupGold.com.

St. Martin's Griffin